Everyman, I will go with thee,
and be thy guide

D. H. Lawrence

SHORT STORIES

Edited by
Stephen Gill
Lincoln College, Oxford

EVERYMAN
J. M. DENT · LONDON

Introduction and selection
© David Campbell Publishers Ltd 1981
Chronology © J. M. Dent 1994

First published by Everyman Paperbacks in 1981
Reprinted, with revisions, 1986
Reissued with revisions, 1992
Reprinted, with revisions, 1996

J. M. Dent
Orion Publishing Group
Orion House
5 Upper St Martin's Lane,
London WC2H 9EA

Printed in Great Britain by
The Guernsey Press Co. Ltd, Guernsey, C.I.

British Library Cataloguing-in-Publication Data is
available upon request.

ISBN 0 460 87127 7

CONTENTS

NOTE ON THE AUTHOR AND EDITOR

DAVID HERBERT LAWRENCE was born into a working-class mining family in Eastwood, Nottinghamshire in 1885. He began writing poems and stories when he was nineteen, and, after training as a teacher at University College, Nottingham and working in a school in Croydon, he fully dedicated himself to writing when his first novel, *The White Peacock*, was published in 1911. In 1912 Lawrence met Frieda Weekley, the German wife of his tutor, and the two fell in love. They ran off together to Germany and then Italy. After Frieda's difficult divorce from Weekley, which separated her from her children, she and Lawrence married in London in 1914. *Sons and Lovers* and what was to become *The Lost Girl* were written during this early period abroad with Frieda, and in 1913 Lawrence began work on *The Sisters*. That work grew so voluminous that it was eventually split into two novels, *The Rainbow* and *Women in Love*. The Lawrences were in Britain when the First World War broke out in 1914, and, prevented from travelling to America as they had hoped, they lived unhappily in Cornwall (which they were ordered to leave on suspicion of spying) and Berkshire until the war ended. In 1915 *The Rainbow* was published in London by Methuen and immediately suppressed on obscenity grounds, but Lawrence continued to work and rework *Women in Love* even though publication difficulties with *The Rainbow* meant that it did not appear until 1920. During this period he forged important friendships with members of what came to be known as 'the Other Bloomsbury', particularly with John Middleton Murry, Katherine Mansfield, the poet H. D., Lady Ottoline Morrell, Richard Aldington and Lady Cynthia Asquith. In 1919 Lawrence and Frieda finally left England, moving first to Italy, then to Ceylon, Australia and, in 1922, to New Mexico. This was an extremely productive period which saw the completion of *The Lost Girl* and *Aaron's Rod*, as well as the writing of *Sea and Sardinia, Fantasia of the Unconscious, Kangaroo* and *Studies in Classic American Literature.* In 1923 and 1924 Lawrence travelled to Mexico, writing *The Plumed Serpent* and *Mornings in Mexico,* before returning to Italy in 1925. In 1926, after his last trip to England, he began *The First Lady Chatterley,* the first version of the novel which would be privately published as *Lady Chatterley's Lover* in 1928, and only published unexpurgated in Britain in 1960, after the trial of Penguin Books. Lawrence's paintings were also seized from the gallery which was exhibiting them in 1929 on obscenity grounds. In March 1930, after a lifetime of ill-health, Lawrence died of consumption in Vence, France, at the age of forty-four.

STEPHEN GILL is a Reader in English Literature at Oxford University and a Fellow of Lincoln College, Oxford. He has written on a variety of nineteenth and twentieth century authors and is the General Editor of the Oxford University Press World's Classics D. H. Lawrence series.

CHRONOLOGY OF LAWRENCE'S LIFE

Year	Age	Life
1885		David Herbert Lawrence born, 11 September in Eastwood, Nottinghamshire into working-class mining family
1898–1901	13–16	Scholarship to Nottingham High School
1901	16	Leaves school, and around this time develops a growing friendship with Jessie Chambers (Miriam in *Sons and Lovers*)
1901–2	16–17	Works at Haywood's surgical appliances factory in Nottingham as a clerk
1902–6	17–21	Works as pupil-teacher in Eastwood
1905	20	Writes his first poems, 'To Guelder Roses' and 'To Campions'
1906	21	Begins first novel, *The White Peacock* (then called *Laetitia*) as well as stories and poems, and starts teacher training studies at Nottingham University College
1907	22	Short story 'A Prelude' wins *Nottinghamshire Guardian* competition

CHRONOLOGY OF HIS TIMES

Year	Artistic Events	Historical Events
1885		General Gordon dies at Khartoum
1887		Golden Jubilee of Queen Victoria
1890		Parnell resigns as Irish National leader
1898		Gladstone dies
1899	James, *The Awkward Age*	Boer War begins
1900	Conrad, *Lord Jim* Freud, *The Interpretation of Dreams*	British Labour Party founded. Commonwealth of Australia founded
1901	Kipling, *Kim*	Queen Victoria dies and Edward VII accedes to the throne
1902	Conrad, *Heart of Darkness* Yeats, *Cathleen ni Houlihan*	Boer War ends. Secondary schools established by Education Act in England and Wales
1903	James, *The Ambassadors*	Emmeline Pankhurst founds Women's Social and Political Union. Wright brothers' first flight
1904	Bradley, *Shakespearean Tragedy* James, *The Golden Bowl*	Entente Cordiale between Britain and France
1905	Wilde, *De Profundis* Shaw, *Major Barbara*	Unrest in Russia
1906	Yeats, *Poetical Works*	
1907	Conrad, *The Secret Agent, Nostromo* Synge, *Playboy of the Western World*	

Year	Age	Life
1908	23	Begins teaching at Davidson Road School in Croydon
1909	24	Jessie Chambers sends selection of Lawrence's poems to the *English Review* in June and the poems are published in November
1910	25	Lawrence's mother dies of cancer; Lawrence begins *Sons and Lovers*, partly in tribute to her
1911	26	*The White Peacock* is published in January, and later in the year Lawrence contracts severe pneumonia
1912	27	Resigns from post in Croydon after convalescence in Bournemouth. In March Lawrence meets and elopes with Frieda Weekley; he travels abroad to Germany and Italy for the first time
1913	28	Publishes *Love Poems and Others* and *Sons and Lovers*, and begins *The Sisters* (which eventually becomes both *The Rainbow* and *Women in Love*)
1914	29	Frieda's divorce from Weekley comes through, and Lawrence and Frieda are married in Kensington in July. World War I breaks out and Lawrence and Frieda settle in Berkshire, Sussex and Cornwall, which they are eventually ordered to leave on suspicion of spying. Publishes *The Prussian Officer*
1915	30	Finishes *The Rainbow* in March; it is published in September and suppressed in November. Sets up *The Signature* magazine with John Middleton Murry and Katherine Mansfield in the autumn
1916	31	Completes version of *Women in Love* but because of controversy over *The Rainbow* fails to find a publisher. Publishes *Twilight in Italy*
1917	32	Lawrence is called up and rejected from military service on grounds of ill health. Publishes *Look! We Have Come Through!*

Year	Artistic Events	Historical Events
1908	Forster, *A Room with a View*	
1909	Marinetti, *Manifeste du Futurisme*	Pensions introduced in England for those over 70
1910	Forster, *Howard's End* Post-Impressionism Exhibition in London	Death of Edward VII; accession of George V. Life of Parliament reduced from seven to five years
1911	Brooke, *Poems* Conrad, *Under Western Eyes*	Passage of the Copyright Act: British Museum and other copyright libraries take copies of all British publications. National Insurance Bill introduced by Lloyd George. Suffragette riots in London
1912	Robert Bridges, *Poetical Works*. First of the *Georgian Poetry* anthologies	Commons reject Women's Franchise Bill
1913	Hardy, *1912–1913 Poems*	Commons pass Irish Home Rule Bill which is rejected by the Lords; 'Cat and Mouse' Act
1914	Joyce, *Dubliners*. First Imagist anthology edited by Ezra Pound appears, *Des Imagistes*	Germany declares war on Russia; Britain declares war on Germany; World War I begins
1915	John Buchan, *The Thirty-Nine Steps*. Woolf, *The Voyage Out*. Ford, *The Good Soldier*. Richardson, *Pilgrimage*	Battle of Ypres; English and French forces land at Gallipoli
1916	Joyce, *Portrait of the Artist as a Young Man*	Battle of Verdun. Lloyd George becomes Prime Minister of Britain
1917	Eliot, *Prufrock and Other Observations*. Yeats, 'Wild Swans at Coole'. Pound, first sections of *The Cantos* published	Abdication of Czar Nicholas II; October Revolution in Russia; Lenin leads Bolsheviks against Kerensky. United States declares war on Germany

Year	Age	Life
1918	33	Publishes *New Poems*
1919	34	Lawrence is seriously ill with influenza. He and Frieda gain passports and live in Capri and Sicily. Finishes *The Lost Girl, Mr Noon, Fantasia of the Unconscious* and *Aaron's Rod*
1920	35	*Women in Love* finally published in New York 'for subscribers only'
1921	36	*The Lost Girl* is published, winning the 1921 James Tait Black prize
1922	37	Travels to Ceylon en route to Australia, where he writes *Kangaroo*. Moves on to Taos in New Mexico, where he finishes *Studies in Classic American Literature*
1923	38	After a trip to Mexico, begins *The Plumed Serpent*
1924	39	After a short return visit to England, Frieda buys a ranch in New Mexico where Lawrence writes *The Women Who Rode Away, St Mawr* and *The Princess*
1925	40	Lawrence seriously ill with malaria in Mexico, and his tuberculosis is diagnosed. The Lawrences return to Italy late in the year. *Reflections on the Death of a Porcupine* published
1926	41	*The Plumed Serpent* is published. Lawrence visits England for the last time, and begins *Lady Chatterley's Lover*
1927–8	42–43	The Lawrences live in Italy, and then move to Switzerland. *Lady Chatterley's Lover* published privately in 1928

Year	Artistic Events	Historical Events
1918	Brooke, *Collected Poems*. Hopkins, *Poems*. Mansfield, 'Prelude'	Second Battle of the Somme; Second Battle of the Marne; World War I ends. Execution of Nicholas II. Women over 30 given the vote in England
1919	Eliot, *Poems*. Hardy, *Collected Poems*	Treaty of Versailles; adoption of Covenant of the League of Nations
1920	Pound, *Hugh Selwyn Mauberley*. Mansfield, 'Bliss'. Eliot, *The Sacred Wood*. Freud, *Beyond the Pleasure Principle*	League of Nations formed. Government of Ireland Act passed, providing for Northern and Southern Ireland to have their own parliaments
1922	Eliot, *The Waste Land*. Galsworthy, *The Forsyte Saga*. Joyce, *Ulysses*	Proclamation of Irish Free State. Mussolini joins Fascist government in Italy
1923		Establishment of USSR. British Matrimonial Causes Act gives equality to women in divorce proceedings
1924	Forster, *A Passage to India*. Mary Webb, *Precious Bane*	Ramsay MacDonald forms first Labour Government
1925	I. A. Richards, *Principles of Literary Criticism*. Woolf, *Mrs Dalloway*	British Unemployment Insurance Act
1926	Seigfried Sassoon, *Satirical Poems*	General Strike in Britain. Germany joins League of Nations
1927	Graves, *Poems*. Woolf, *To the Lighthouse*. Rosamund Lehmann, *Dusty Answer*	German financial and economic crisis. Rise of Stalin in USSR; expulsion of Trotsky
1928	Waugh, *Decline and Fall*. Woolf, *Orlando*. Radcliffe Hall, *The Well of Loneliness*	Minimum voting age for women in England reduced to 21 from 30 years

Year	Age	Life
1929	44	Lawrence's paintings, exhibited in London, are seized by the police
1930	44	March, dies of consumption at Vence in the south of France

Year	Artistic Events	Historical Events
1929	Woolf, *A Room of One's Own*. Robert Graves, *Goodbye to All That*. I. A. Richards, *Practical Criticism*	General Election victory for Labour Party. Wall Street Crash; collapse of US Stock Exchange
1930	Auden, *Poems*. Henry Green, *Party-Going*. William Empson, *Seven Types of Ambiguity*	The New Party formed by Oswald Mosley; National Government formed by Ramsey MacDonald. Invergordon naval mutiny

INTRODUCTION

_____

'Never trust the artist. Trust the tale.'

I

D.H. Lawrence : Novelist – that is the title of F.R. Leavis's famous study and its emphasis is surely right.[1] Lawrence's reputation must rest on *Sons and Lovers, The Rainbow, Women in Love* and, largely for non-aesthetic reasons, on *Lady Chatterley's Lover*. But to concentrate only on the novels is to gain a false sense of the nature of Lawrence's creativity. He was fecund in so many ways and achieved so much in different genres that one wonders how he managed to live so intensely and so variously in the tragically few years of maturity illness allowed him, as well as write so much. The answer, of course, is that for Lawrence living and writing were inextricable – though emphatically not synonymous. Travels to Europe, the Mediterranean and New Mexico turned into travel books and sketches. Absorption in literature led to some of the most combative and stimulating criticism of this century in the *Study of Thomas Hardy* and *Studies in Classic American Literature,* while his quarrel with contemporary aesthetic orthodoxies spilled out in reviews and articles whose tone is caught by the title of one of them, 'Surgery for the Novel, or a Bomb?' Lawrence's quarrel was with more than aesthetic orthodoxies, of course, and was carried on in articles and more sustained essays on twentieth-century civilisation and its discontents which contain many of his best insights. He wrote plays, some of which have recently been revived with real success on the stage and on television. His collected poems fill two substantial volumes. He was a painter whose achievement has yet to be fully understood, partly because of the dispersal of his paintings about the world. There are the letters, amongst the most attractive in our language. And there are the tales, which span the whole of Lawrence's writing life, an integral part of this great creative flow.

Leavis's emphasis is, nonetheless, just, for it is as a writer of fiction that Lawrence really matters and within that fiction it is the novels which most clearly indicate the originality of his achievement. Like Joyce, Lawrence was one of the great forces that made early twentieth-century fiction fit heir to the dynasty established by the nineteenth-century giants, but unlike him Lawrence did not refine his work and publish only masterpieces. Lawrence's novels are very uneven, from the magnificent – *The Rainbow* and *Women in Love* – to the second-rate – *The Lost Girl* – to the downright awful – *The Plumed Serpent* – but good and bad have qualities in common. They are all restless novels, each one containing much totally assured art together which much that seems uncertain, still to be fully realised. Each asks questions which demand other novels for the answer. They all emerge from an artist who was impatient with the static, the completed, the formal solidity rather than flow, and who characteristically spoke of his own creative process as a journey of discovery, a labour of exploration. In letters of 24 February 1913, 26 April 1913, 6 October 1913 and 29 January 1914[2] Lawrence dramatises himself as an artist struggling with recalcitrant material but excited by shapes emerging unforeseen. And as the last letter makes clear, each resting place in the exploration is only provisional, a stage in a process.

With his novels Lawrence was always going through a transition stage, as if, like Ursula at the end of *The Rainbow*, he continually 'grasped and groped to find the creation of the living God, instead of the old, hard barren form of bygone living'. And the result is a pattern of novels which continually surprises, which never rests. From *The Rainbow* to the three times written *Lady Chatterley's Lover* Lawrence wrestled to realise his truest insights in truest art, compelled to move on from assured methods and established positions, willing to risk total failure rather than repeat the known and safe, faithful only to his conviction that the importance of the novel, 'properly handled', is that it 'can inform and lead into new places the flow of our sympathetic consciousness, and it can lead our sympathy away in recoil from things gone dead' (*Lady Chatterley's Lover*).

With some exceptions discussed in section II below, Lawrence's short stories are not at the centre of his creative travail and so cannot claim the importance of the novels. But to say that is not to downgrade them significantly, for, as Graham Hough has said in his excellent study, *The Dark Sun*, 'In sustained realisation, in formal completeness, there is certainly nothing to better the best of his shorter tales . . .' No, the contrast with the novels only serves to bring out the nature, not the quality of the shorter fiction. Clearly related to the concerns of the major novels as they are, the short stories seem like particles which have broken clear of the energy mass which constitutes the larger works. There is nothing predictable about them, none of that formulaic quality that so often constricts stories written for magazines and which makes, say, Maugham's stories so wearisome overall, but they do have a completeness, a sense of total artistic realisation, which cannot be claimed for the novels. They were, of course, written for publication – and it is important to register this. Lawrence is so often portrayed as a prophet who sojourned in the wilderness while creating what his generation would not heed, a prophet without honour, whose books were banned or expurgated and whose paintings were suppressed. There is much truth in this, but a glance at the headnotes to each story reveals a different Lawrence, the professional writer being published in the *English Review, Metropolitan, Forum, Dial, Smart Set*, and a man who did not scorn (could not afford to scorn) to shape his experiences, observations, insights into a flourishing literary mode.

This selection of the best and most representative stories could easily be three times as bulky and in this selectivity there is much to regret. Many good stories are not included, such as 'The Thorn in the Flesh', 'England, My England', 'Samson and Delilah', 'The Border Line', but in a way this does not matter, as those which are here fully represent the nature and quality of those which have had to be omitted. More sad is the omission of the novellas, *The Captain's Doll, The Ladybird, St Mawr, The Princess, The Virgin and the Gypsy*. The decision to omit them was inevitable, as these long tales alone would have taken up three-quarters of the volume, but it is made reluctantly, for readers of this book will have little idea how resourcefully Lawrence handles this most difficult form. *The Fox*, which has been retained, inconsistently it might seem, has to exemplify an aspect of Lawrence's work which any admirer of the short fiction will want to explore further. The absence of *St Mawr* and *The Princess* is to be regretted, too, because it means that Lawrence's transforming experience of New Mexico is under-represented. Only 'The Woman Who Rode Away' remains from the geographical encounter which affected him more strangely than any other.

While the aim is to represent Lawrence at his best, the selection is also intended to suggest the nature of the short stories throughout his career. The word 'development' will not do here, for it implies growth from immature beginnings through to some generally recognised mature period, a pattern which the tales, unlike the

novels, simply will not fit. The early stories are every bit
as impressive as the later ones, but they are different, and
the difference is what the organisation of this selection
hopes to convey. The stories are ordered chronologically,
on date of composition, but this principle is not entirely
satisfactory and readers must be aware of its short-
comings. The first is that it violates to some degree,
Lawrence's own practice. Normally he published stories
in magazines and then gathered them for presentation as
a collection: *The Prussian Officer* (1914); *England, My
England* (1922); *The Ladybird* (1923); *St Mawr* (1925); *The
Woman Who Rode Away* (1928); *The Lovely Lady*,
posthumous (1933). Within each volume, however, little
attempt was made to suggest chronology of composition.
Much more important is the fact that with many of the
stories no single date of composition can be given, for
Lawrence regularly revised his work, sometimes
radically altering his earlier conception. 'The White
Stocking', for example, originated in a story of 1907, but
revision in 1913 and 1914 was so substantial that perhaps
it ought to be presented as the work of those years. In its
origin, however, the story belongs to Lawrence's earliest
years and the chronological ordering, crude though it is,
serves to bring this out. As long as the reader realises that
no statement about Lawrence's development, in any
sense, can be made safely *on the evidence of this ordering alone*,
there is little danger and some real advantage in present-
ing the tales in this way.

II

This fussiness about dating, far from being mere
pedantry, is a key to understanding one of the most
interesting aspects of *The Prussian Officer* collection. The

earliest story originates from 1907, the latest from 1913. The whole volume can be said to belong to none of these years, and yet in a sense to all of them, so intertwined are the stories with Lawrence's growth as man and artist during this, the most important period of his life. In 1909 Lawrence submitted work to the *English Review*. Ford Madox Ford's recollection of reading the first paragraph of 'Odour of Chrysanthemums' is well known:

> I was reading in the twilight in the long eighteenth-century room that was at once the office of the *English Review* and my drawing-room. My eyes were tired; I had been reading all day so I did not go any further with the story. It was called 'Odour of Chrysanthemums'. I laid it in the basket for accepted manuscripts. My secretary looked up and said: 'You've got another genius?' I answered: 'It's a big one this time', and went upstairs to dress.[3]

The story was published in June 1911 and attracted the attention of Martin Secker who offered to publish a volume of short stories by this promising new man. The scheme fell through, but not before Lawrence had been stirred to revise his work to date. Further extensive revision took place in the summer of 1913 as he attempted to publish all of his shorter fiction and again in 1914, revision which in many respects is more a recasting of all of the most important work that Lawrence had yet written. The complexities of this period have been unravelled by Keith Cushman, whose *D. H. Lawrence at Work: The Emergence of the Prussian Officer Stories* is indispensable. Cushman concludes that, 'The 1914 revisions transformed the best of *The Prussian Officer* stories into products of Lawrence's mature imagination.' Why? Why was this continual process of revision necessary, even after stories had been published, and why is 1913–14 the most important period of all?

For answers one has to look at the significance of 1907 – 14 to Lawrence as man and as artist. When he began writing Lawrence was a student, shortly to be a teacher, a provincial young man beginning the slow and confusing journey away from his origins. His early world was rich in ways that are almost inconceivable in our homogenised society, in benefits beautifully described in Jessie Chambers's *D. H. Lawrence: A Personal Record.* But Jessie Chambers's account of her life with Lawrence also demonstrates, in ways she was not aware of, how trammelling, intense and demanding that world was too, and it is no surprise that the volume of letters from the early years through to 1913 should reveal the young Lawrence rather desperately thrashing about, searching for release. He went to Croydon to teach, broke with Jessie (the Miriam of *Sons and Lovers*), became engaged to another friend and broke with her, suffered under the death of his mother, started writing seriously, resigned his teaching post and finally, after very brief acquaintance, left for Europe with Frieda Weekley, the wife of a professor at Nottingham University and mother of three children.

It is difficult to overemphasise the effect of this move, the first of many flights into the unknown, of Lawrence's first confrontation with foreign culture, people and landscapes, exiled with a strong and passionate woman he hardly knew. His past life and relationships took on a new colour, and emerged, tempered by Frieda's merciless analysis, as *Sons and Lovers,* which he recognised, in a letter of 19 May 1913, was the end of his early phase. His present life, poverty and exile notwithstanding, amazed and strengthened him. From the letters of this period one might think Lawrence believed himself the first man to discover that life is transformed by close, loving relationship, so often does he return to this theme. The reader should look up the letters of the period, especially those of [11? November 1912], 17 January, [2? May] 1913 and 2 June 1914, which all reflect what Lawrence spelled out in a letter of 7 July 1914, that loving another person, the basis of all inner harmony, is an agonising process demanding imagination, self-appraisal and humility. In one of the letters listed above Lawrence declared that the strength of his feeling about the importance of the male – female relation determined the subject matter of his art. With his own experience of that relation so transformed it was inevitable that Lawrence should look back on old work and recast its incompleteness in the mould of his own new self.

In the case of *Sons and Lovers*, coming to grips with an earlier self meant shaping his own experiences into as honest a form as he could manage and then casting them off. With the stories the situation is rather different, for while the revisions do to some extent reflect on Lawrence's changing awareness of his formative experiences, their main interest is what they indicate about the development of Lawrence's art after *Sons and Lovers* and the part they play in the artist's discovery of his new direction.

On 30 December 1913 Lawrence confided to Edward Garnett that he knew he had abandoned the style of *Sons and Lovers* for ever. What the new style would be, however, was less clear to him. The letters of 1913 and 1914 show Lawrence struggling to define the meaning of the writing he was doing towards the novel that eventually became *The Rainbow*. The new style is clearly linked to developing ideas about human character, outlined in a letter of 17 January 1913 and, most importantly, in the very difficult manifesto of 5 June 1914, in which Lawrence struggles to pin-point for the uncomprehending Garnett just how the new conception of character portrayal differs from that found in the nineteenth-century masters. The new style, as the letters of this period show, has to serve Lawrence's determination to get beyond the changing manifestations of the surface of life to its unchanging, impersonal essence.

These letters are worth dwelling on not only because they suggest how inextricable is Lawrence's developing conception of character from his emerging style but also because they are available to the general reader (and must be consulted and mulled over by any serious reader of this selection). What is not accessible is all of the evidence in the manuscripts of just how arduous the formation of *The Rainbow* was. In a magnificent essay Mark Kinkead-Weekes has traced the development from *The Sisters* to *The Rainbow* and emphasised the crucial part played by the *Study of Thomas Hardy* in Lawrence's exploration of his insights into human character and the nature and significance of sexual relationships. Keith Cushman's achievement has been to show that even before the Hardy study Lawrence was working towards the distinctive style and themes of *The Rainbow* through revision of his short stories. The ending to 'Odour of Chrysanthemums' in which Elizabeth Bates is forced to ask: 'Who am I?', the sexually charged dance sequences in 'The White Stocking', the awakening of Louisa and Durant to a sense of the unknown through recognition of sexual need in 'Daughters of the Vicar', the exploration of violence and sexuality in 'The Prussian Officer' – all these emerge in the revision of 1913 and 1914 and offer a foretaste of the mature fiction which was to so appal the guardians of public morality when *The Rainbow* was published a year later.

III

Especial interest attaches to work which marks the formative struggle of a great writer, but *The Prussian Officer* collection needs no special pleading from the scholars to establish its claims. This is not apprentice stuff, to be gilded by the lustre of what follows: it is the assured art of a writer who has found his true voice. And that voice carries conviction. In his recollection of first reading Lawrence, Ford Madox Ford goes on, after the passage quoted above, to analyse the opening of 'Odour of Chrysanthemums' to explain why he felt so confident that he had discovered a real writer. He dwells on the

skill with which Lawrence dramatises what the reader
needs to know at the outset of the story, on his powers of
observation and description, and concludes: 'This man
knows what he wants. He sees the scene of his story
exactly. He has an authoritative mind.'

Ford has seized on just that quality which impresses
one immediately about all of these stories: their sense of
command. Characters and situations are presented with
powerful economy, each paragraph packed with detail
that one soon realises means something in the structure
of the whole. Take the opening of one of the best stories
in the collection, 'The White Stocking':

> 'I'm getting up, Teddilinks,' said Mrs Whiston,
> and she sprang out of bed briskly.
>   'What the Hanover's got you?' asked Whiston.
>   'Nothing. Can't I get up?' she replied animatedly.
>   It was about seven o'clock, scarcely light yet in
> the cold bedroom. Whiston lay still and looked at
> his wife. She was a pretty little thing, with her
> fleecy, short black hair all tousled. He watched her
> as she dressed quickly, flicking her small, delightful
> limbs, throwing her clothes about her. Her
> slovenliness and untidiness did not trouble him.
> When she picked up the edge of her petticoat,
> ripped off a torn string of white lace, and flung it on
> the dressing-table, her careless abandon made his
> spirits glow. She stood before the mirror and
> roughly scrambled together her profuse little mane
> of hair. He watched the quickness and softness of
> her young shoulders, calmly, like a husband, and
> appreciatively.
>   'Rise up,' she cried, turning to him with a quick
> wave of her arm–'and shine forth.'
>   They had been married two years. But still, when
> she had gone out of the room, he felt as if all his light
> and warmth were taken away, he became aware of
> the raw, cold morning. So he rose himself, wonder-
> ing casually what had roused her so early. Usually
> she lay in bed as late as she could.

Details unobtrusively set the scene. It must be winter, since it is barely light at seven o'clock in the morning, and we are clearly not in the middle classes, as the bedroom is cold and small. Mrs Whiston dresses in the same room, there being no question of a dressing room adjoining, as a better house might boast. The characters are young – Mrs Whiston springs out of bed, talks animatedly, flicks her limbs – and not long married, as the affectionate name 'Teddilinks' suggests. There is a sexual glow here which warms both people, the husband watching his wife's body, the woman careless of her clothes but confident in the attractiveness of 'her profuse little mane of hair'. But there is uncertainty too. Why is she behaving so out of character, what has made her so eager to get up? And as the story unfolds all that has been suggested deftly comes into play. This is not just any winter's day, but St Valentine's Day and Mrs Whiston is expecting a token from an admirer, a token which is later to pain her husband deeply and unleash in him violence which will startle both of them to a fuller appreciation of what this sexual glow amounts to.

Or consider the opening of 'The Prussian Officer'. This is a very different story from 'The White Stocking'. Violence forms its climax, too, but whereas Whiston's blow to his wife has its origin in easily understandable sexual jealousy and wounded pride, the violence here is provoked by forces which neither man can understand and which the officer desperately refuses even to acknowledge. Mrs Whiston taunts her husband in animated language: officer and orderly barely communicate in words. So it is right that the story should begin with the anonymity of the group of soldiers and should introduce us to the only characters as the 'Captain' and the 'orderly'; right, also, that the opening paragraph should dwell on pain, pain that has to be endured because of military discipline. But all of the soldiers suffer from the march in the heat, only the orderly is 'determined not to limp', concentrating on ignoring 'deep bruises on the backs of his thighs'. We know no more than that, but the fourth paragraph begins, 'The Captain's hand had trembled at taking his coffee at dawn', and we are prepared for the flashback that follows and the setting up of the action of the story which is going to explain how and why an unimportant soldier has bruised thighs.

The authority of Lawrence as narrator is not conveyed only by the opening of the stories, of course, though it is most obviously felt there. It could be exemplified by analysis of the structure of 'Daughters of the Vicar', where Lawrence attempts to establish with equal weight very different worlds – the vicarage and the Durants' cottage, the marriages of the vicar and his wife, their daughter Mary and her genteely vicious husband, and the awakening love of Louisa and Alfred the collier – through short sections of dialogue, action and analysis, deployed essentially on the principle of contrast. One could point to the dramatic skill with which the scene of the baby bathing is organised to convey simultaneously the ludicrousness of the whole business and the suppressed anger coursing through all the participants, or to the splendid way Lawrence uses coarse language at the climax of 'The Shadow in the Rose Garden' to reveal the collier husband's incredulity that his more decorous wife has had a lover before their marriage. Nothing is wasted, no effect is missed, so that one feels, against all the evidence about revisions, that each story must always have had this form, that it could not be in any other way.

This total assurance, this sense that, 'This man knows what he wants', is vital to *The Prussian Officer* volume because the stories lead into strange places, where readers might be reluctant to follow. In June 1914, at the intensest pitch of his travail over *The Rainbow*, Lawrence had declared that men and women must find the courage to draw near to one another and allow themselves to be changed by a knowledge that would bring suffering and joy. This, essentially, is the theme of the volume, but the emphasis rests much more on suffering than on joy. It is true that 'Daughters of the Vicar' celebrates the triumph of love and sexual union over money and class. Mary, daughter of the vicar of Aldecross, escapes the impoverishment of genteel penury by consciously marrying a clergyman who is summed up in the exclamation, 'What a little abortion!' She pays for her independence by sacrificing her bodily self: 'Mary, in marrying him, tried to become a pure reason such as he was, without feeling or impulse. She shut herself up, she shut herself rigid against the agonies of shame and the terror of violation which came at first. She *would* not feel . . .' Louisa, by contrast, chooses the way of life. Through ministering to a dying parishioner, she comes close to Alfred Durant, a collier, and claims him for a mate. Such an outline might make the story sound very schematic, but it does not seem so in the least, because of the delicacy with which Lawrence describes her washing the miner's back and sensing the man, and the wholly convincing mixture of tenderness and comedy in the climax as the miner, still blackened with his pit-dirt, takes the woman in his arms. This marriage, at least, founded on the need of two people, irrespective of their class and expectations, will survive.

Such joyousness, however, is hardly the staple of the other stories. In one of the poems from the collection, *'Look! We Have Come Through!'* Lawrence caught the confusion of feeling within marriage:

> You are the call and I am the answer.
> You are the wish, and I the fulfilment,
> You are the night, and I the day,
>> What else? it is perfect enough.
>> It is perfectly complete,
>> You and I,
>> What more–?

Strange, how we suffer in spite of this![4]

This is really the keynote. Lawrence is marvellously

perceptive about the violent swings of emotion which shape any relationship, about the sense of isolation and apartness which can come over two people living together in apparent intimacy, about the mixture of violence and tenderness which constitutes sexual arousal, about the inhibitions and stunting inherent in sexual possession. Louisa's triumph is the climax of 'Daughters of the Vicar', but it has to be balanced against the more 'normal' marriages of the vicar and his psycho-somatically invalid wife and Mary and her death-in-life husband. In 'Odour of Chrysanthemums' Elizabeth Bates lays out her husband's corpse and sums up a short life of poverty, squalor and neglect in the questions, 'Who am I? What have I been doing?' Guilt at her denial of her husband's identity, terror at the sense of the distance between them, blankness at the recognition that one period of her life is now over, all crowd in on this woman to exclude the normal emotions of grief. In 'The Shadow in the Rose Garden' a young husband learns that his wife has loved before and has even arranged their holiday so that she can revisit old haunts. The story ends:

> He stood and looked at her. At last he had learned the width of the breach between them. She still squatted on the bed. He could not go near her. It would be violation to each of them to be brought into contact with the other. The thing must work itself out. They were both shocked so much, they were impersonal, and no longer hated each other. After some minutes he left her and went out.

Most impressively of all, 'The White Stocking' also dwells on this theme. As the story opens Elsie Whiston receives a love-token from her former employer and admirer. A flashback then narrates the earlier events when Elsie has succumbed to the sensuality of Adams in the socially acceptable embrace of the dance. The scene – which anticipates the sexually charged dances of *The*

Rainbow – marvellously captures the real call to one another of the two dancers and the impotence of the accepted lover. In the final section we return to the present and the climax as, goaded by the evidence that his wife has been receiving presents from Adams, and taunted by her unrepentant independence, Whiston smashes Elsie against the wall, with a 'lust to see her bleed, to break her and destroy her . . .' The conclusion is optimistic in that both realise the depth of their feelings and acknowledge their need of one another, but they have moved a long way from the careless innocence of the opening paragraphs. Mrs Whiston is not likely to call her husband 'Teddilinks' any more.

Like the fine tale, 'The Thorn in the Flesh' (not included here), 'The Prussian Officer' makes a dramatic contrast with the other stories in this first collection. In May 1912 Lawrence and Frieda left England for Europe. To the difficulties inherent in the situation – Lawrence was not allowed near Frieda's family – was added his instinctive dislike of German militancy much in evidence in Metz, and German notions of honour and decorum. A brush with the police, who took him for a spy, only hastened Lawrence's flight onwards to Trier. But the experience of alien culture stimulated Lawrence: to revision of his work, to poems and sketches and, most important, to what he felt was his best work so far.

Just before publication of the collection, much to Lawrence's dismay, Edward Garnett decided that this story should be called 'The Prussian Officer'. Garnett's instincts may have been commercially sound, but the change is regrettable, for it suggests that Lawrence was virtually contributing to the war effort and enabled the reviewer in *Outlook*, for example, to make amusing play with the difference between Lawrence's Prussian and 'the Hunnish individual to whom the war has given his chance of exhibiting himself in his true light'.[5] But this tone is quite inappropriate. Lawrence's title was 'Honour and Arms', an ironic introduction to an episode which could as easily have an English setting as a Prussian one, for Lawrence's stated analysis of militarism makes no national distinctions. Violence and atrocity, he declares in a letter of [11? November 1912] are fermented by sexual lust and repression channelled in perverted ways.

Leaving aside the obvious difference of setting – Germany, not England – and characters – men only not men-women – the contrast with the other stories strikes one in two ways. The first is that a pitch of intensity is maintained throughout. In 'The White Stocking', for example, gaiety modulates into gravity, which is then distilled until violent action unleashes feelings before which the characters are powerless. In 'The Prussian Officer' the intensity is felt from the very start. The story begins with the young orderly concentrating with all his energy on his pain. His battle is with himself, for he is determined to maintain his identity and not give in. But this introverted struggle cannot be fought alone, although none of his companions know of it, for the orderly's identity has been violated by the captain who has beaten him and who, almost unwillingly, will strike again. So this is an elemental conflict – no one and nothing exists but it. Lawrence tells us nothing about military hierarchy, or about the other soldiers, or the orderly's girl friend, for he is not interested in providing any determinist framework for his story, as George Eliot would have been, or in creating a dense setting to give human credibility to his actors, as Chekhov might have done. These are just two men, and we do not even learn their names.

In its language the tale shares the intensity of the moments in *The Rainbow* where Ursula and Anton fight for mastery. There is little dialogue, and even the action itself – the kicking and the eventual murder – is secondary to the feelings of both men which Lawrence largely conveys through passages of analysis which envelop both officer and orderly in the language of their

creator. This passage is typical, taken from the moment
when the officer has kicked and humiliated his servant:

> The officer, left alone, held himself rigid, to prevent
> himself from thinking. His instinct warned him that
> he must not think. Deep inside him was the intense
> gratification of his passion, still working powerfully.
> Then there was a counter-action, a horrible break-
> ing down of something inside him, a whole agony of
> reaction. He stood there for an hour motionless, a
> chaos of sensations, but rigid with a will to keep
> blank his consciousness, to prevent his mind grasp-
> ing. And he held himself so until the worst of the
> stress had passed, when he began to drink, drank
> himself to an intoxication, till he slept obliterated.
> When he woke in the morning he was shaken to the
> base of his nature. But he had fought off the realiza-
> tion of what he had done. He had prevented his
> mind from taking it in, had suppressed it along with
> his instincts, and the conscious man had nothing to
> do with it. He felt only as after a bout of intoxica-
> tion, weak, but the affair itself all dim and not to be
> recovered. Of the drunkenness of his passion he
> successfully refused remembrance. And when his
> orderly appeared with coffee, the officer assumed
> the same self he had had the morning before. He
> refused the event of the past night – denied it had
> ever been – and was successful in his denial. He had
> not done any such thing – not he himself. Whatever
> there might be lay at the door of a stupid,
> insubordinate servant.

This is a crucial moment. The officer is determined to
refuse to recognise what is happening and on his success
will depend his survival as an independent being. But
this struggle cannot be dramatised, nor conveyed in
dialogue, and so great weight rests on Lawrence's powers
of exposition. One notices characteristic Lawrencean
diction – 'intense gratification', 'horrible', 'agony',
'chaos', 'obliterated', and the characteristically insistent

sentence and paragraph structure rising to the repetitions of ideas of denial at the end. Perhaps, too, the reader is already uneasy at the amount of work Lawrence is forcing this kind of language to do, anticipating one's anxieties in *The Rainbow* and *Women in Love* that he is, to quote Denis Donoghue, 'bullying the [words] . . . to give up secrets we cannot really believe they possess'.[6]

The passage directs us, also, to the second contrast between this and the other tales. In 'Odour of Chrysanthemums' and 'The White Stocking' characters are shocked into recognition of forces in their lives whose presence they have not needed to confront before. But the forces themselves are explicable in terms of 'normal' human psychology. Elizabeth Bates is alone, suddenly bereft, and her most self-accusatory questionings arise naturally from the life she has had to lead. Whiston's momentary hatred of his wife, his discovery that, 'He had a long score against her', is not a surprising result of his wife's heedless arousal of his jealousy and anger. In 'The Prussian Officer', however, the two protagonists confront darker, less explicable forces in themselves; after the captain's first expression of anger against his servant 'an undiscovered feeling had held between the two men'. It is the feeling which each fights against, the captain becoming 'madly irritable' in the process, unable 'to rest when the soldier was away', and the orderly growing in hate 'responsive to the officer's passion'. Each gains 'intense gratification of his passion', the officer by bringing blood to his servant's mouth and by kicking him again and again on the buttocks, the orderly by taking his master's chin in his hands and, 'exquisite with relief', breaking his neck.

What is so unexpected is that this violent act of release is also the servant's undoing. He now disintegrates – and the last section is marvellously done – unable to face human contact or return to the real world. This adventurer has 'gone out from everyday life into the unknown', but unlike other adventurers in Lawrence, the strain of release into the realm of the unknown is too great. Like Gerald at the end of *Women in Love*, the soldier becomes immune to death, overwhelmed by powers he would not have been able to name. With this story Lawrence announces the greatest, the most original and most challenging period of his work.

IV

With the publication of *The Prussian Officer* on 26 November 1914 a prosperous phase in Lawrence's life ought to have begun. He was twenty-nine, married, a respected author, confident that in *The Rainbow* he had brought to conclusion his most ambitious novel yet. In fact he was about to enter what Paul Delany has recently called *D.H. Lawrence's Nightmare*. On 30 September 1915 *The Rainbow* was published. Some discerned its power, but many took their cue from James Douglas in *Star*: 'The wind of war is sweeping over our life, and it is demolishing many of the noisome pestilences of peace. A thing like *The Rainbow* has no right to exist in the wind of war. It is a greater menace to our public health than any of the epidemic diseases which we pay our medical officers to fight inch by inch wheresoever they appear. In November Methuens offered no defence at Bow Street Police Court and agreed to the destruction of the novel. After his most sustained artistic struggle Lawrence found himself branded as a writer of dirty books. What followed, as the war fever raged, was penury, homelessness, police harassment, conflict with friends, and a growing sense of isolation and impotence in an artist who at all times valued his Englishness. Never physically strong, Lawrence fell seriously ill during the influenza epidemic of 1919 and after convalescence decided to leave England for what proved to be prolonged exile.

Given the horror of these years and the difficulties of

mere survival, it is amazing that Lawrence's work should be as substantial and as assured as it is. *Women in Love*, in which he said 'the bitterness of the war may be taken for granted in the characters', is a more ambitious novel still than *The Rainbow*, whose formal order and coherence reveal none of the hysteria and anguish shrieking from Lawrence's letters of the period. The tales gathered in *England, My England* (1922) likewise consolidate the achievement of *The Prussian Officer* volume, without revealing in any loss of artistic control the inferno through which their creator had passed.

This assurance of art, however, stands in contrast to a marked tentativeness in the concerns of the stories, whose keynote is often the unexpected and the unresolved. Take, for example, perhaps the finest of the four selected, 'The Blind Man'. Formally it is a masterpiece of economical presentation. The opening depicts Isabel Pervin listening for two sounds – her husband's footsteps and the arrival of her oldest and dearest friend. At the end Isabel stands looking at the two men, registering the change that has come over both. In between, all that has happened has been a brief meal and two journeys: Isabel's to the barn to find her blind husband and Bertie's similar errand. Apart from a telling moment of contrast as Isabel looks into the crowded farm kitchen, no other people intrude into this sequence or into the atmosphere of tight intimacy. And yet, in the space of this one evening, the lives of all three are changed.

This account of the story's structure, however, suggests a definiteness of movement, a conclusiveness which simply eludes one if one tries to pin the story down. Isabel and Maurice are living in the warmth of an 'unspeakable intimacy' which has come over their marriage since Maurice's blinding in the war. It is rich, satisfying, indefinable, and yet . . . It cannot hold Isabel subject forever. Often she longs to escape, even if death is the release. And Maurice, who generally does not regret loss of sight, so marvellous is his sense of touch, 'this sheer immediacy of blood-contact with the substantial world', at times collapses into chaos that tortures him. The reader can sympathise with both people, so well does Lawrence convey both their loving closeness and the claustrophobia of this relationship, and expects that the coming of the third person will somehow release a new current of feeling. In a sense it does. Bertie, a man who lives in the mind and on the surface only, who fears close human contact, has to endure ordeal by touch as the blind man first feels his head and face in a slow and deliberate exploration and then insists that he touch his eye-sockets as a seal of their new friendship. But the transformation announced by Maurice in triumph is visible only to his inner eye, for Isabel, who it has been stressed fears the darkness of the barn in which her husband moves so surely, can *see* what Maurice cannot, that Bertie is shattered. His eyes are 'as if glazed with misery'. He is 'like a mollusc whose shell is broken'. So what next?

The same question forces itself on the reader in 'The Horse Dealer's Daughter' and 'You Touched Me'. In both stories simple human contact transforms lives that had gone dead, wedding mate to mate after the experience of touch has broken through the rind of daily living. But what odd experiences they are. In 'The Horse Dealer's Daughter' Mabel Pervin, a silent, powerful woman in her late twenties, is left homeless and aimless after the collapse of the family business. She decides to follow her mother to the grave and after tending the actual grave wades into a pool. She is rescued by a local doctor, who takes her home, undresses her and wraps her in blankets. When the woman recovers consciousness she looks at the young man 'with flaring, humble eyes of transfiguration, triumphant in first possession' and declares: 'You love me. I know you love me, I know.' Although the doctor has thought of this woman with 'no single personal thought of her', he is overwhelmed and recognises an answer to her passion in himself. They kiss, 'with the one kiss that is an eternal pledge' and agree to marry. But the story ends thus:

> But she only sobbed terribly, and cried:
>   'I feel awful. I feel awful. I feel I'm horrible to you.'
>   'No, I want you, I want you,' was all he answered blindly, with that terrible intonation which frightened her almost more than her horror lest he should *not* want her.

In 'You Touched Me' the uncertainty about the sexual contact-contract is even more disturbing. Matilda touches the young man who is to claim her for his mate by mistake, thinking she was caressing her dying father. But Hadrian declares this touch is meaningful: 'I know it was a mistake – but I shan't forget it. If you wake a man up, he can't go to sleep again because he's told to.' In the end Matilda acquiesces in his will and to the threats of her father and agrees to marry him, even though she looks down on her husband 'both literally and figuratively'. The last words of the story are: ' "That's right! That's right!" murmured the dying man.' Hadrian may have been awakened to new life, but the close insists that we recognise how implicated he is in the last exercise of a dying man's will over his dependent daughters. These epiphanies, where the normal flow of life is changed by touch, contact, claim, are a very long way from the unequivocal triumph of Browning's exclamation in 'By the Fireside':

> Oh, the little more, and how much it is!
> And the little less, and what worlds away!

V

After *England, My England* (1922), Lawrence did not

publish a collection of short stories until *The Woman Who Rode Away* (1928). Not to represent the work between these dates, however, would be unfortunate and misleading, for at least two reasons. One is that the shorter fictions Lawrence did write are undoubtedly his major achievement during these years. After *Women in Love* (1920) Lawrence's full-length novels suffer from a marked lessening in formal control and completeness. In *Aaron's Rod, Kangaroo, The Plumed Serpent,* the exploratory art of *The Rainbow* and *Women in Love* loses vigour, and what is exciting openness and freedom in the earlier works comes to seem like carelessness and irresolution in the later. But the same charges cannot be levelled at the novellas – *The Ladybird, The Fox, The Captain's Doll, The Princess, St Mawr* – which are as controlled and powerful as anything Lawrence ever wrote. The second reason is that these stories are unlike what has preceded them and most of what follows. They are strange, disturbing, in many respects unappealing, but undeniably challenging, and they represent a period in Lawrence's career which anyone who cares to know him whole must encounter. For these reasons, therefore, *The Fox* has been included in this selection in the hope that it will stimulate the reader to discover the others.

The Fox is a particularly interesting story, because evidence survives which reveals (as with some of *The Prussian Officer* stories) an emerging Lawrence imposing new ideas and a new style of treatment on to earlier ones. In its first form, published in H.T. Moore's *A D.H. Lawrence Miscellany,* the story is quite straightforward. Two women, Banford and March, are trying unsuccessfully to run a smallholding. The cows are recalcitrant, the hens won't lay and a fox carries them off one by one anyway. One day March comes face to face with the fox but is powerless to shoot him, and, in fact, the animal so enters her consciousness that she dreams of him biting her and drawing blood on her mouth with his brush. A young soldier who used to live on their holding arrives. He makes himself useful, stays, and eventually decides to marry March. Banford is angry, March timorous, but in the end he gets his way because, like the fox, he has captured March with the sure instinct of the hunter. The story is economically and realistically presented, the narrative tone is subdued, and the theme clearly related to the other tales in which a human being, man or woman, chooses to mate.

In its expanded version, published here, *The Fox* is a very different and altogether more disturbing work. Although the naturalistic setting of the story is retained, the depressing November darkness being particularly well evoked, the story line has been changed and the conflicts of the characters heightened in a way that moves further beyond the naturalistic than even the most charged moments of the major novels. As the story opens much greater emphasis is laid than in the earlier version on March's confrontation with the fox. He knows her, he absorbs her, and he enters her life with overwhelming force when Henry, the young soldier, appears and *is* the fox: 'But to March he was the fox. Whether it was the thrusting forward of his head, or the glisten of fine whitish hairs on the ruddy cheek-bones, or the bright, keen eyes, that can never be said: but the boy was to her the fox, and she could not see him otherwise.' True to his nature Henry stalks March and, as in the earlier version, persuades her to marry him. But here the two versions diverge dramatically. The first change is that Henry kills the fox. The second is that he kills Banford. And the two kills are linked.

Before Henry shoots the fox a lengthy passage has discussed the nature of hunting. 'It is a subtle, profound battle of wills which takes place in the invisible . . . It is your own *will* which carries the bullet into the heart of your quarry . . . It happens like a supreme wish, a supreme act of volition . . .' Banford is Henry's real quarry. Whereas in the earlier version she is little more than hurt and angry that her relationship with March is being broken, in the later she works with all of her will to prevent the marriage taking place and so far succeeds that March does renounce her engagement. But Henry's will is the stronger. By cunning and considered manipulation he fells a tree so that it falls, as if by accident, on the hated obstacle, and Banford, like the fox, twitches in death. The climax reads: 'The body was quivering with little convulsions. But she was dead really. He knew it, that it was so. He knew it in his soul and his blood. The inner necessity of his life was fulfilling itself, it was he who was to live. The thorn was drawn out of his bowels. So he put her down gently. She was dead.'

This passage and what follows as the story ends, is disturbing in many ways. One is that references to Henry's 'soul', 'blood' and the 'inner necessity of his life' unequivocally justify his act. This has been a struggle between the forces of life and the forces of death, and 'it was he who was to live'. Now this dualism has underpinned all of Lawrence's work, from the earliest *The White Peacock* onwards. It shapes Ursula Brangwen's struggles against Skrebensky and Birkin's against Hermione. It is the meaning of 'The Daughters of the Vicar' and 'The Horse Dealer's Daughter'. But never before has Lawrence so starkly dramatised the conflict or insisted so ruthlessly that in the struggle nothing, not even another human life, must be allowed to thwart the claims of 'life'. In *The Deed of Life*, Julian Moynahan declares: 'Henry's act is not a murder. It is an inspired and creative deed,' and he is surely right. But he goes on to flinch from his perception when he claims: 'It is an indication of Lawrence's firm artistic control that the reader can accept without reservation this nominally horrifying incident as an image of the triumph of life over death; for it means that a vision of reality has conquered the banality of the nominally and conventionally real.'[8] But Henry's act is not a nominally horrifying incident, it *is* a horrifying incident, taking place in a real world, however intensified, and Moynahan's attempt to remove it to the safe context of 'myth' weakens the impact of Lawrence's assault on our hold on the meanings of the words 'life' and 'death'.

A second reason for finding the conclusion disturbing is that Henry's triumph is presented as a *male* triumph. After the death scene Lawrence interpolates into the narrative a lengthy discourse on love and the pursuit of happiness, which condescends to women, discussed in the general, and comes to rest with Henry and this paragraph:

> And then he would have her, and he would have his own life at last. He chafed, feeling he hadn't got his own life. He would never have it till she yielded and slept in him. Then he would have all his own life as a young man and a male, and she would have all her own life as a woman and a female. There would be no more of this awful straining. She would not be a man any more, an independent woman with a man's responsibility. Nay, even the responsibility for her own soul she would have to commit to him. He knew it was so, and obstinately held out against her, waiting for the surrender.

So far Henry has always got what he willed and, unresolved though the end of the story is, nothing in it suggests he is about to fail. Again and again in this period the Lawrence who has so remarkably depicted male-female inter-relation and joint-discovery celebrates male dominance and female submission. It is a celebration of 'life' that denies life and it leads him only to the dead end of *The Plumed Serpent*.

VI

Between 1920 and 1926 Lawrence wandered: from Italy, to Sicily, to Germany, to Ceylon, to Australia, to New Mexico, to England, back to America, to London, back to Italy – and this is just the outline of his itinerary. The lure of fresh experience of the unknown in a new world is constantly countered by a sense of unfinished business in the old. The exotic setting of *The Plumed Serpent* softens into the English landscape of *Lady Chatterley's Lover* as Lawrence's quest for a religious experience gives way to his desire to make contact once again with his own country, sterile and dying though he feared it was. The object of the search remains unchanged, to find full and harmonious relationship between oneself and other human beings and oneself and the world (see letter of 11 October 1926), but its expression in art is more varied than before and the reader who wants to know this Lawrence well must read *Etruscan Places* as well as *Lady Chatterley's Lover,* 'Return to Bestwood' (available in *Phoenix II*) as well as *The Plumed Serpent*.

The later short stories collected in *The Woman Who Rode Away* (1928) and the posthumous *The Lovely Lady* (1933) reflect this duality of setting and style. Many will seem familiar. They are English stories, with familiar characters and contexts. But there is a new insouciance of tone, an underlying wryness, which suggests that Lawrence is so completely at ease with his material that he is even able to regard it with some detachment. 'Jimmy and the Desperate Woman', for example, depicts a man claiming his mate across the division of class, which recalls 'Daughters of the Vicar', but the seriousness of the earlier story is missing. This is no triumph of love, but a shot in the dark by a man who is a fool. Looking for a woman who will make him feel like a king, Jimmy meets his mirror-image in the miner who wants *his* woman to serve him likewise, and is mastered by the coarser consciousness of the working man and by the decisiveness of the desperate woman, his wife. Jimmy deserves, one feels, all that he is certain to get.

It is impossible to become involved with the characters in 'Jimmy and the Desperate Woman' – Lawrence's tone prevents it – and the same is true of 'In

Love'. What a dismal depiction of 'Modern Love' this story offers. In one of his most penetrating essays on the nature of sexuality, 'A Propos of *Lady Chatterley's Lover*', (available in *Phoenix II*), Lawrence writes with great insight about false emotions and declares, 'Sex lashes out against counterfeit emotion, and is ruthless, devastating against false love. The peculiar hatred of people who have not loved one another, but who have pretended to, even perhaps imagined they really did love, is one of the phenomena of our time.' This statement might be the text for this depressing little story, in which two 'lovers' act out their roles untouched by sexual feelings at all. After a horrifying outburst in which each claims to 'loathe' the other, Hester and Joe are shocked into a fresh awareness of their relationship, but their coming together is mere words:

> 'I'm sorry, Hester,' said he.
> 'You know, Joe,' she said, 'I don't mind what you do, if you love me *really*.'

Compared with the end of 'The White Stocking', this is perfunctory, and such a contrast to the faith embodied in the fable of *Lady Chatterley's Lover* and Lawrence's last completed work of fiction, the fine story 'The Blue Mocassins', that people could, even now, actually change their relationship to the great physical truths of life.

Lawrence's greatest gift, according to Jessie Chambers, was 'his power to transmute the common experiences into significance . . . He did not distinguish between small and great happenings; the common round was full of mystery, awaiting interpretation.'[9] All of the stories discussed so far demonstrate this power, the power of the realist. Lawrence certainly is not like Maupassant or Arnold Bennett, but he does remain close to the observable world, and presents it with such power 'that we feel it is more exciting, more moving, in some ways fuller of life than one had thought real life could be . . .'[10] He never offers merely a 'slice of life', but

always an insight into what life is, beneath the layer
upon layer of social convention and form, or a vision of
what it might be. The characters in their relationships
ask to be assessed in terms of our own experience of
people in this world. The two stories 'The Woman Who
Rode Away' and 'The Escaped Cock', however, move
beyond realism. They, too, project a vision of life, but
they work through fable and come near to the lyrical
power of poetry. To some readers they will seem silly,
but to those familiar with all of Lawrence's later writings
'The Escaped Cock', at least, will seem the summation of
his work.

The vision of 'The Woman Who Rode Away' is not
an attractive one. The thirty-three-year-old woman –
whose name we do not learn – stupefied in marriage to
an older business man in Mexico, rides out alone to the
hills to find a fabled Indian tribe. They take her and,
hearing that she has come to honour their gods, believe
that she has been delivered to them to regain their
ancient power over the sun. On the shortest day of the
year she is anointed, prepared and ritually sacrificed.
With its motif of female submission and the obliteration
of 'the fallen individual independence of woman', the
story has clear links with *The Captain's Doll, The Ladybird*
and *The Princess,* but whereas these stories raise ugly
questions about the male-female relationships in them
because they are set in the real world, amongst recognis-
able people, 'The Woman Who Rode Away' does not.
To experience the narrative to the full is simply to be
drugged into the same powerless state as the woman, to
share her fear as she realises the doom prepared for her, a
second death, and to share the exultation of the Indians
who await the flash when 'the red sun should send his
ray through the column of ice' and signal that the
moment of sacrifice has come.

Throughout the tale Lawrence attempts to convey
something of the 'passional cosmic consciousness', the
'heavily religious natures' of the Indians, which had hit

him 'with shattering force' as he says in his essay 'New Mexico' (available in *Phoenix*). In 'The Escaped Cock' he returns to the religion of Europe and rewrites the story of the resurrection of Christ. At the height of the war Lawrence had declared in 'The Crown' (*Phoenix II*) that 'immortality is not a question of time, of everlasting life. It is a question of consummate being.' This very late story is a hymn to that continuing belief. Lawrence celebrates 'The Risen Lord', but not, as he explains in an essay of that name (in *Phoenix II*) the Christ Crucified preached by the churches, about to ascend to the Father out of this world, but the risen Lord to whom belongs 'all the full-flowering spring, all summer, and then the autumn of wheat and fruit . . .' This Jesus, still alive after the crucifixion, wakes up pained and weary after his great agony. At first he is aware only that he has died out of 'the natural world, thronging with greenness', but slowly he awakens to the wonder of the phenomenal world and is able to announce to Mary Magdalen, 'My triumph . . . is that I am not dead.' In the second part of the story he meets a priestess of Isis, loves her and fathers a child, delighting 'in being in touch, delighting to hear the sea, and the rain on the earth, and to see one white-and-gold narcissus bowing wet, and still wet'. Like the woman in Wallace Stevens's poem on the same theme, 'Sunday Morning', Jesus is

> content when wakened birds,
> Before they fly, test the reality
> Of misty fields, by their sweet questionings.

'The Escaped Cock' is the climax of Lawrence's life-long consideration of the meaning of the Christian myth and his most beautiful embodiment of his belief that, 'We must have a new conception of what it means to live.'

VII

The epigraph to this introduction, 'Never trust the artist. Trust the tale', taken from Lawrence's *Studies in Classic American Literature,* directs us to one of his passionately held beliefs about reading fiction. For such a didactic writer, one who drew so largely upon his own experiences, Lawrence was surprisingly insistent that we must attend to the art not the artist, to the life in the created work itself. In an essay, 'The Novel and the Feelings' he declares that fiction can help us 'educate ourselves in the feelings' if we will but listen, but, 'Not listen to the didactic statements of the author, but to the low, calling cries of the characters, as they wander in the dark woods of their destiny.' This caution should be borne in mind when reading these stories. They do not need and are resistant to the biographical speculation which has so harmed appreciation of the novels. Was Lawrence fair to Jessie Chambers when he created Miriam in *Sons and Lovers*? Is Hermione in *Women in Love* an ungrateful kick against Lady Ottoline Morrell? This kind of questioning need never enter our assessment of these tales. They do not require knowledge of Lawrence's biography, nor demand adherence to his 'philosophy'. They just ask for attentive reading. What the *New York Times Book Review* said of *England, My England* is true for them all:

> They are not tales for those who wish merely to be amused, to read and enjoy without using their own brains, these tales of Mr Lawrence's. He is one of those writers who demand more than a little co-

operation from their readers. But to those able and willing to give that co-operation [they] will prove a fruitful and long-enduring source of pleasure.[11]

Stephen Gill

1. To avoid cumbersome footnotes wherever possible, bibliographical information on works mentioned in the introduction is placed in the section *Suggestions for Further Reading*.

2. Lawrence's letters are being collected in seven volumes, under the general editorship of James T. Boulton. For copyright reasons I am not able to quote from these letters. Readers should in all cases read for themselves the letters referred to in this introduction.

3. Quoted from *The Bodley Head Ford Madox Ford,* ed. Graham Greene, I, (London, 1962), p.320.

4. 'Bei Hennef' in *The Complete Poems of D. H. Lawrence,* 2 vols. (London, 1928).

5. R. P. Draper, ed., *D. H. Lawrence: The Critical Heritage* (London, 1970), p.81.

6. Denis Donoghue, *Thieves of Fire* (London, 1973), p.129.

7. *D. H. Lawrence: The Critical Heritage,* op. cit., p.94.

8. Julian Moynahan, *The Deed of Life: The Novels and Tales of D. H. Lawrence* (Princeton and London, 1963), p.199.

9. 'E.T.' (Jessie Chambers), *D. H. Lawrence: A Personal Record* (London, 1935); 2nd ed. J. D. Chambers (London, 1965), p.198.

10. Virginia Woolf, 'Notes on D. H. Lawrence', *Collected Essays,* 4 vols. (London, 1966-7), I, p.353.

11. *D. H. Lawrence: The Critical Heritage,* op. cit., p.190.

NOTE ON THE TEXT

As the headnotes to the stories make clear, Lawrence usually published his shorter pieces in a magazine before gathering them together, often in a revised form, in a single volume. The text of the stories in this selection is taken from the following publications issued in Lawrence's lifetime: *The Prussian Officer and Other Stories* (London, 1914); *England, My England and Other Stories* (New York, 1922; London, 1924); *The Ladybird, The Fox, The Captain's Doll* (London, 1923); *The Woman Who Rode Away and Other Stories* (London, 1928); *The Escaped Cock* (Paris, 1929).

John Worthen presents an authoritative text of the stories, with very valuable notes, in his edition of *The Prussian Officer* for the Cambridge Edition of the Works of D. H. Lawrence (Cambridge: Cambridge U.P., 1983). I am very grateful to Dr Worthen for assistance given for this second edition both in private correspondence and through his published scholarship.

SUGGESTIONS FOR FURTHER READING

This is not a bibliography either of D. H. Lawrence's works or of works about him. Such will be found in Warren Roberts's *A Bibliography of D. H. Lawrence* (1963; 2nd ed. 1982) and supplement in Sagar's *Calendar* below. Much bibliographical information will also be found in Sagar's *Handbook* below; in the reviews of scholarship published annually in the *D. H. Lawrence Review*, and in the invaluable James C. Cowan, *D. H. Lawrence: An Annotated Bibliography of Writings about Him* (1982, 1985).

There have been many biographies of Lawrence. The fullest and best promises to be the three-volume life published by Cambridge University Press, judged by the first volume, John Worthen, *D. H. Lawrence: The Early Years 1885-1912* (1991). Also readily available and recommended are John Worthen, *D. H. Lawrence: A Literary Life* (1989); Jeffrey Meyers, *D. H. Lawrence: A Biography* (1990), K. M. Sagar's illustrated *Life of D. H. Lawrence* (1980) and his *Life into Art: A Critical Biography of D. H. Lawrence* (1985). The same author's *D. H. Lawrence: A Calendar of His Works* (1979) and *A D. H. Lawrence Handbook* (1982) contain much biographical information. Paul Delany has studied in depth *D. H. Lawrence's Nightmare: The Writer and His Circle in the Years of the Great War* (1979).

Lawrences's entire corpus is being presented in the Cambridge Edition of the Works of D. H. Lawrence, under the General Editorship of James T. Boulton. Each text is established afresh from all available materials and accompanied by valuable notes. This is the essential edition for all students of Lawrence at whatever level. The best alternative texts for general use at the time of writing are the annotated editions in the Penguin English Library. Until the completion of the

Cambridge edition, two collections of Lawrence's essays, reviews, etc. are still essential for the study of his work, *Phoenix: The Posthumous Papers of D. H. Lawrence*, ed. Edward D. McDonald (1936) and *Phoenix II: Uncollected, Unpublished and Other Prose Works by D. H. Lawrence*, ed. Warren Roberts and Harry T. Moore (1968).

Harry T. Moore's *The Collected Letters of D. H. Lawrence* (1962) has served as the standard edition for many years, but it is currently being entirely superseded by the seven volume *The Letters of D. H. Lawrence*, General Editor James T. Boulton (1979-).

A very large number of critical studies of Lawrence's work has been published. The following are most likely to assist new readers. It must be remembered, however, that information in the older books about dates of composition etc. will be subject to revision in the light of the information being made available in the Cambridge edition of the complete works. From the period in which critics were mainly concerned to make a case for Lawrence's stature, the following can be recommended: Mark Spilka, *The Love Ethic of D. H. Lawrence* (1955), F. R. Leavis, *D. H. Lawrence: Novelist* (1955), Graham Hough, *The Dark Sun* (1956), Julian Moynahan, *The Deed of Life: The Novels and Tales of D. H. Lawrence* (1963), H. M. Daleski, *The Forked Flame* (1965), K. M. Sagar, *The Art of D. H. Lawrence* (1966), John Worthen, *D. H. Lawrence and the Idea of the Novel* (1979). More recently, after a period in which Lawrence's canonical status was largely accepted, critics have begun to re-assess his work in the light of the challenge presented by contemporary debate about language, ideology, gender, class, and history. Recommended studies are Sheila MacLeod, *Lawrence's Men and Women* (1985), Hilary Simpson, *D. H. Lawrence and Feminism* (1982), *The Challenge of D. H. Lawrence*, ed. Michael Squires and Keith Cushman (1990), *D. H.*

Lawrence in the Modern World, ed. Peter Preston and Peter Hoare (1989), Tony Pinkney, *D. H. Lawrence* (1990), James C. Cowan, *D. H. Lawrence and the Trembling Balance* (1990) and Allan Ingram, *The Language of D. H. Lawrence* (1990).

John Worthen sets the standard for scholarly study of the short stories in his Cambridge edition of *The Prussian Officer* (1983). Also recommended is Keith Cushman, *D. H. Lawrence at Work: The Emergence of the Prussian Officer Stories* (1978). There has been little criticism of the short stories, however, outside the pages of learned journals. H. E. Bates places Lawrence in context in *The Modern Short Story* (1941), as do Walter Allen in *The Short Story in English* (1981) and Valerie Shaw in *The Short Story: A Critical Introduction* (1982). More sustained treatment will be found in Kingsley Widmer, *The Art of Perversity: D. H. Lawrence's Shorter Fictions* (1962), Janice Hubbard, *The Short Fiction of D. H. Lawrence* (1984), and Michael Black, *D. H. Lawrence: The Early Fiction* (1986).

Information about the composition and publication of each story given in the headnotes has been drawn from the various scholarly works by Roberts, Sagar, Cushman, and Worthen, mentioned above.

SHORT STORIES

The White Stocking

Written March–April 1911 from short story submitted to Christmas Short Story Competition of the *Nottinghamshire Guardian* in 1907. Revised again August 1913, text published in *Smart Set*, October 1914. Before this publication Lawrence again substantially revised in July and October 1914 for the text published in *The Prussian Officer* collection.

I

'I'm getting up, Teddilinks,' said Mrs Whiston, and she sprang out of bed briskly.

'What the Hanover's got you?' asked Whiston.

'Nothing. Can't I get up?' she replied animatedly.

It was about seven o'clock, scarcely light yet in the cold bedroom. Whiston lay still and looked at his wife. She was a pretty little thing, with her fleecy, short black hair all tousled. He watched her as she dressed quickly, flicking her small, delightful limbs, throwing her clothes about her. Her slovenliness and untidiness did not trouble him. When she picked up the edge of her petticoat, ripped off a torn string of white lace, and flung it on the dressing-table, her careless abandon made his spirit glow. She stood before the mirror and roughly scrambled together her profuse little mane of hair. He watched the quickness and softness of her young shoulders, calmly, like a husband, and appreciatively.

'Rise up,' she cried, turning to him with a quick wave of her arm– 'and shine forth.'

They had been married two years. But still when she had gone out of the room, he felt as if all his light and warmth were taken away, he became aware of the raw,

1

cold morning. So he rose himself, wondering casually what had roused her so early. Usually she lay in bed as late as she could.

Whiston fastened a belt round his loins and went downstairs in shirt and trousers. He heard her singing in her snatchy fashion. The stairs creaked under his weight. He passed down the narrow little passage, which she called a hall, of the seven and sixpenny house which was his first home.

He was a shapely young fellow of about twenty-eight, sleepy now and easy with well-being. He heard the water drumming into the kettle, and she began to whistle. He loved the quick way she dodged the supper cups under the tap to wash them for breakfast. She looked an untidy minx, but she was quick and handy enough.

'Teddilinks,' she cried.

'What?'

'Light a fire, quick.'

She wore an old, sack-like dressing-jacket of black silk pinned across her breast. But one of the sleeves, coming unfastened, showed some delightful pink upper-arm.

'Why don't you sew your sleeve up?' he said, suffering from the sight of the exposed soft flesh.

'Where?' she cried, peering round. 'Nuisance,' she said, seeing the gap, then with light fingers went on drying the cups.

The kitchen was of fair size, but gloomy. Whiston poked out the dead ashes.

Suddenly a thud was heard at the door down the passage.

'I'll go,' cried Mrs Whiston, and she was gone down the hall.

The postman was a ruddy-faced man who had been a soldier. He smiled broadly, handing her some packages.

'They've not forgot you,' he said impudently.

'No—lucky for them,' she said, with a toss of the head. But she was interested only in her envelopes this morning. The postman waited inquisitively, smiling in an ingratiating fashion. She slowly, abstractedly, as if she did not know anyone was there, closed the door in his face, continuing to look at the addresses on her letters.

She tore open the thin envelope. There was a long, hideous, cartoon valentine. She smiled briefly and dropped it on the floor. Struggling with the string of a packet, she opened a white cardboard box, and there lay a white silk handkerchief packed neatly under the paper lace of the box, and her initial, worked in heliotrope, fully displayed. She smiled pleasantly, and gently put the box aside. The third envelope contained another white packet—apparently a cotton handkerchief neatly folded. She shook it out. It was a long white stocking, but there was a little weight in the toe. Quickly, she thrust down her arm, wriggling her fingers into the little, cold toe of the stocking, and brought out a small box. She peeped inside the box, then hastily opened a door on her left hand, and went into the little, cold sitting-room. She had her lower lip caught earnestly between her teeth.

With a little flash of triumph, she lifted a pair of pearl ear-rings from the small box, and she went to the mirror. There, earnestly, she began to hook them through her ears, looking at herself sideways in the glass. Curiously concentrated and intent she seemed as she fingered the lobes of her ears, her head bent on one side.

Then the pearl ear-rings dangled under her rosy, small ears. She shook her head sharply, to see the swing of the drops. They went chill against her neck, in little, sharp touches. Then she stood still to look at herself, bridling her head in the dignified fashion. Then she simpered at herself. Catching her own eye, she could not help winking at herself and laughing.

She turned to look at the box. There was a scrap of paper with this posy:

'Pearls may be fair, but thou art fairer.
Wear these for me, and I'll love the wearer.'

She made a grimace and a grin. But she was drawn to the mirror again, to look at her ear-rings.

Whiston had made the fire burn, so he came to look for her. When she heard him, she started round quickly, guiltily. She was watching him with intent blue eyes when he appeared.

He did not see much, in his morning-drowsy warmth. He gave her, as ever, a feeling of warmth and slowness. His eyes were very blue, very kind, his manner simple.

'What ha' you got?' he asked.

'Valentines,' she said briskly, ostentatiously turning to show him the silk handkerchief. She thrust it under his nose. 'Smell how good,' she said.

'Who's that from?' he replied, without smelling.

'It's a valentine,' she cried. 'How do I know who it's from?'

'I'll bet you know,' he said.

'Ted!—I don't?' she cried, beginning to shake her head, then stopping because of the ear-rings.

He stood still a moment, displeased.

'They've no right to send you valentines, now,' he said.

'Ted?—Why not? You're not jealous, are you? I haven't the least idea who it's from. Look—there's my initial'—she pointed with an emphatic finger at the heliotrope embroidery—

'E for Elsie,
Nice little gelsie,'

she sang.

'Get out,' he said. 'You know who it's from.'

'Truth, I don't,' she cried.

He looked round, and saw the white stocking lying on a chair.

'Is this another?' he said.

'No, that's a sample,' she said. 'There's only a comic.' And she fetched in the long cartoon.

He stretched it out and looked at it solemnly.

'Fools!' he said, and went out of the room.

She flew upstairs and took off the ear-rings. When she returned, he was crouched before the fire, blowing the coals. The skin of his face was flushed, and slightly pitted, as if he had had small-pox. But his neck was white and smooth and goodly. She hung her arms round his neck as he crouched there, and clung to him. He balanced on his toes.

'This fire's a slow-coach,' he said.

'And who else is a slow-coach?' she said.

'One of us two, I know,' he said, and he rose carefully. She remained clinging round his neck, so that she was lifted off her feet.

'Ha!—swing me,' she cried.

He lowered his head, and she hung in the air, swinging from his neck, laughing. Then she slipped off.

'The kettle is singing,' she sang, flying for the teapot. He bent down again to blow the fire. The veins in his neck stood out, his shirt collar seemed too tight.

> 'Doctor Wyer,
> Blow the fire,
> Puff! puff! puff!'

she sang, laughing.

He smiled at her.

She was so glad because of her pearl ear-rings.

Over the breakfast she grew serious. He did not notice. She became portentous in her gravity. Almost it penetrated through his steady good humour to irritate him.

'Teddy!' she said at last.

'What?' he asked.

'I told you a lie,' she said, humbly tragic.

His soul stirred uneasily.

'Oh aye?' he said casually.

She was not satisfied. He ought to be more moved.

'Yes,' she said.

He cut a piece of bread.

'Was it a good one?' he asked.

She was piqued. Then she considered–*was* it a good one? Then she laughed.

'No,' she said, 'it wasn't up to much.'

'Ah!' he said easily, but with a steady strength of fondness for her in his tone. 'Get it out then.'

It became a little more difficult.

'You know that white stocking,' she said earnestly. 'I told you a lie. It wasn't a sample. It was a valentine.'

A little frown came on his brow.

Then what did you invent it as a sample for?' he said. But he knew this weakness of hers. The touch of anger in his voice frightened her.

'I was afraid you'd be cross,' she said pathetically.

'I'll bet you were vastly afraid,' he said.

'I *was,* Teddy.'

There was a pause. He was resolving one or two things in his mind.

'And who sent it?' he asked.

'I can guess,' she said, 'though there wasn't a word with it– except—'

She ran to the sitting-room and returned with a slip of paper.

'Pearls may be fair, but thou art fairer
Wear these for me, and I'll love the wearer.'

He read it twice, then a dull red flush came on his face.

'And *who* do you guess it is?' he asked, with a ringing of anger in his voice.

'I suspect it's Sam Adams,' she said, with a little virtuous indignation.

Whiston was silent for a moment.

'Fool!' he said. 'An' what's it got to do with

pearls?–and how can he say "wear these for me" when there's only one? He hasn't got the brain to invent a proper verse.'

He screwed the slip of paper into a ball and flung it into the fire.

'I suppose he thinks it'll make a pair with the one last year,' she said.

'Why, did he send one then?'

'Yes. I thought you'd be wild if you knew.'

His jaw set rather sullenly.

Presently he rose, and went to wash himself, rolling back his sleeves and pulling open his shirt at the breast. It was as if his fine, clear-cut temples and steady eyes were degraded by the lower, rather brutal part of his face. But she loved it. As she whisked about, clearing the table, she loved the way in which he stood washing himself. He was such a man. She liked to see his neck glistening with water as he swilled it. It amused her and pleased her and thrilled her. He was so sure, so permanent, he had her so utterly in his power. It gave her a delightful mischievous sense of liberty. Within his grasp, she could dart about excitingly.

He turned round to her, his face red from the cold water, his eyes fresh and very blue.

'You haven't been seeing anything of him, have you?' he asked roughly.

'Yes,' she answered, after a moment, as if caught guilty. 'He got into the tram with me, and he asked me to drink a coffee and a Benedictine in the Royal.'

'You've got it off fine and glib,' he said sullenly. 'And did you?'

'Yes,' she replied, with the air of a traitor before the rack.

The blood came up into his neck and face, he stood motionless, dangerous.

'It was cold, and it was such fun to go into the Royal,' she said.

'You'd go off with a nigger for a packet of chocolate,'

he said, in anger and contempt, and some bitterness. Queer how he drew away from her, cut her off from him.

'Ted—how beastly!' She caught her lip, flushed, and the tears came to her eyes.

He turned away, to put on his necktie. She went about her work, making a queer pathetic little mouth, down which occasionally dripped a tear.

He was ready to go. With his hat jammed down on his head, and his overcoat buttoned up to his chin, he came to kiss her. He would be miserable all the day if he went without. She allowed herself to be kissed. Her cheek was wet under his lips, and his heart burned. She hurt him so deeply. And she felt aggrieved, and did not quite forgive him.

In a moment she went upstairs to her ear-rings. Sweet they looked nestling in the little drawer—sweet! She examined them with voluptuous pleasure, she threaded them in her ears, she looked at herself, she posed and postured and smiled, and looked sad and tragic and winning and appealing, all in turn before the mirror. And she was happy, and very pretty.

She wore her ear-rings all morning, in the house. She was self-conscious, and quite brilliantly winsome, when the baker came, wondering if he would notice. All the tradesmen left her door with a glow in them, feeling elated, and unconsciously favouring the delightful little creature, though there had been nothing to notice in her behaviour.

She was stimulated all the day. She did not think about her husband. He was the permanent basis from which she took these giddy little flights into nowhere. At night, like chickens and curses, she would come home to him, to roost.

Meanwhile Whiston, a traveller and confidential support of a small firm, hastened about his work, his heart all the while anxious for her, yearning for surety, and kept tense by not getting it.

II

She had been a warehouse girl in Adams's lace factory before she was married. Sam Adams was her employer. He was a bachelor of forty, growing stout, a man well dressed and florid, with a large brown moustache and thin hair. From the rest of his well-groomed, showy appearance, it was evident his baldness was a chagrin to him. He had a good presence, and some Irish blood in his veins.

His fondness for the girls, or the fondness of the girls for him, was notorious. And Elsie, quick, pretty, almost witty little thing—she *seemed* witty, although, when her sayings were repeated, they were entirely trivial—she had a great attraction for him. He would come into the warehouse dressed in a rather sporting reefer coat, of fawn colour, and trousers of fine black-and-white check, a cap with a big peak and a scarlet carnation in his button-hole, to impress her. She was only half impressed. He was too loud for her good taste. Instinctively perceiving this, he sobered down to navy blue. Then a well-built man, florid, with large brown whiskers, smart navy blue suit, fashionable boots, and manly hat, he was the irreproachable. Elsie was impressed.

But meanwhile Whiston was courting her, and she made splendid little gestures, before her bedroom mirror, of the constant-and-true sort.

'True, true till death—'

That was her song. Whiston was made that way, so there was no need to take thought for him.

Every Christmas Sam Adams gave a party at his house, to which he invited his superior work-people—not factory hands and labourers, but those above. He was a generous man in his way, with a real warm feeling for giving pleasure.

Two years ago Elsie had attended this Christmas-party for the last time. Whiston had accompanied her. At that time he worked for Sam Adams.

She had been very proud of herself, in her close-fitting, full-skirted dress of blue silk. Whiston called for her. Then she tripped beside him, holding her large cashmere shawl across her breast. He strode with long strides, his trousers handsomely strapped under his boots, and her silk shoes bulging the pockets of his full-skirted overcoat.

They passed through the park gates, and her spirits rose. Above them the Castle Rock loomed grandly in the night, the naked trees stood still and dark in the frost, along the boulevard.

They were rather late. Agitated with anticipation, in the cloak-room she gave up her shawl, donned her silk shoes, and looked at herself in the mirror. The loose bunches of curls on either side her face danced prettily, her mouth smiled.

She hung a moment in the door of the brilliantly lighted room. Many people were moving within the blaze of lamps, under the crystal chandeliers, the full skirts of the women balancing and floating, the side-whiskers and white cravats of the men bowing above. Then she entered the light.

In an instant Sam Adams was coming forward, lifting both his arms in boisterous welcome. There was a constant red laugh on his face.

'Come late, would you,' he shouted, 'like royalty.'

He seized her hands and led her forward. He opened his mouth wide when he spoke, and the effect of the warm, dark opening behind the brown whiskers was disturbing. But she was floating into the throng on his arm. He was very gallant.

'Now then,' he said, taking her card to write down the dances, 'I've got carte blanche, haven't I?'

'Mr Whiston doesn't dance,' she said.

'I am a lucky man!' he said, scribbling his initials. 'I was born with an *amourette* in my mouth.'

He wrote on, quietly. She blushed and laughed, not

knowing what it meant.

'Why, what is that?' she said.

'It's you, even littler than you are, dressed in little wings,' he said.

'I should have to be pretty small to get in your mouth,' she said.

'You think you're too big, do you!' he said easily.

He handed her her card, with a bow.

'Now I'm set up, my darling, for this evening,' he said.

Then, quick, always at his ease, he looked over the room. She waited in front of him. He was ready. Catching the eye of the band, he nodded. In a moment, the music began. He seemed to relax, giving himself up.

'Now then, Elsie,' he said, with a curious caress in his voice that seemed to lap the outside of her body in a warm glow, delicious. She gave herself to it. She liked it.

He was an excellent dancer. He seemed to draw her close in to him by some male warmth of attraction, so that she became all soft and pliant to him, flowing to his form, whilst he united her with him and they lapsed along in one movement. She was just carried in a kind of strong, warm flood, her feet moved of themselves, and only the music threw her away from him, threw her back to him, to his clasp, in his strong form moving against her, rhythmically, deliciously.

When it was over, he was pleased and his eyes had a curious gleam which thrilled her and yet had nothing to do with her. Yet it held her. He did not speak to her. He only looked straight into her eyes with a curious, gleaming look that disturbed her fearfully and deliciously. But also there was in his look some of the automatic irony of the *roué*. It left her partly cold. She was not carried away.

She went, driven by an opposite, heavier impulse, to Whiston. He stood looking gloomy, trying to admit that she had a perfect right to enjoy herself apart from him. He received her with rather grudging kindliness.

'Aren't you going to play whist?' she asked.

'Aye,' he said. 'Directly.'

'I do wish you could dance.'

'Well I can't,' he said. 'So you enjoy yourself.'

'But I should enjoy it better if I could dance with you.'

'Nay, you're all right,' he said. 'I'm not made that way.'

'Then you ought to be!' she cried.

'Well, it's my fault, not yours. You enjoy yourself,' he bade her. Which she proceeded to do, a little bit irked.

She went with anticipation to the arms of Sam Adams, when the time came to dance with him. It *was* so gratifying, irrespective of the man. And she felt a little grudge against Whiston, soon forgotten when her host was holding her near to him, in a delicious embrace. And she watched his eyes, to meet the gleam in them, which gratified her.

She was getting warmed right through, the glow was penetrating into her, driving away everything else. Only in her heart was a little tightness, like conscience.

When she got a chance, she escaped from the dancing-room to the card-room. There, in a cloud of smoke, she found Whiston playing cribbage. Radiant, roused, animated, she came up to him and greeted him. She was too strong, too vibrant a note in the quiet room. He lifted his head, and a frown knitted his gloomy forehead.

'Are you playing cribbage? Is it exciting? How are you getting on?' she chattered.

He looked at her. None of these questions needed answering, and he did not feel in touch with her. She turned to the cribbage-board.

'Are you white or red?' she asked.

'He's red,' replied the partner.

'Then you're losing,' she said, still to Whiston. And she lifted the red peg from the board. 'One–two–three–four–five–six–seven–eight—Right up there you ought to jump—'

'Now put it back in its right place,' said Whiston.

'Where was it?' she asked gaily, knowing her transgression. He took the little red peg away from her and stuck it in its hole.

The cards were shuffled.

'What a shame you're losing!' said Elsie.

'You'd better cut for him,' said the partner.

She did so, hastily. The cards were dealt. She put her hand on his shoulder, looking at his cards.

'It's good,' she cried, 'isn't it?'

He did not answer, but threw down two cards. It moved him more strongly than was comfortable, to have her hand on his shoulder, her curls dangling and touching his ears, whilst she was roused to another man. It made the blood flame over him.

At that moment Sam Adams appeared, florid and boisterous, intoxicated more with himself, with the dancing, than with wine. In his eye the curious, impersonal light gleamed.

'I thought I should find you here, Elsie,' he cried boisterously, a disturbing, high note in his voice.

'What made you think so?' she replied, the mischief rousing in her.

The florid, well-built man narrowed his eyes to a smile.

'I should never look for you among the ladies,' he said, with a kind of intimate, animal call to her. He laughed, bowed, and offered her his arm.

'Madam, the music waits.'

She went almost helplessly, carried along with him, unwilling, yet delighted.

That dance was an intoxication to her. After the first few steps, she felt herself slipping away from herself. She almost knew she was going, she did not even want to go. Yet she must have chosen to go. She lay in the arm of the steady, close man with whom she was dancing, and she seemed to swim away out of contact with the room, into him. She had passed into another, denser element of him, an essential privacy. The room was all vague around her, like an atmosphere, like under sea, with a flow of ghostly, dumb movements. But she herself was held real against her partner, and it seemed she was connected with him, as if the movements of his body and limbs were her own movements, yet not her own movements–and oh, delicious! He also was given up, oblivious, concentrated, into the dance. His eye was unseeing. Only his large, voluptuous body gave off a subtle activity. His fingers seemed to search into her flesh. Every moment, and every moment, she felt she would give way utterly, and sink molten: the fusion point was coming when she would fuse down into perfect unconsciousness at his feet and knees. But he bore her round the room in the dance, and he seemed to sustain all her body with his limbs, his body, and his warmth seemed to come closer into her, nearer, till it would fuse right through her, and she would be a liquid to him, as an intoxication only.

It was exquisite. When it was over, she was dazed, and was scarcely breathing. She stood with him in the middle of the room as if she were alone in a remote place. He bent over her. She expected his lips on her bare shoulder, and waited. Yet they were not alone, they were not alone. It was cruel.

' 'Twas good, wasn't it, my darling?' he said to her, low and delighted. There was a strange impersonality about his low, exultant call that appealed to her irresistibly. Yet why was she aware of some part shut off in her? She pressed his arm, and he led her towards the door.

She was not aware of what she was doing, only a little grain of resistant trouble was in her. The man, possessed, yet with a superficial presence of mind, made way to the dining-room, as if to give her refreshment, cunningly working to his own escape with her. He was molten hot, filmed over with presence of mind, and bottomed with cold disbelief.

In the dining-room was Whiston, carrying coffee to

the plain, neglected ladies. Elsie saw him, but felt as if he could not see her. She was beyond his reach and ken. A sort of fusion existed between her and the large man at her side. She ate her custard, but an incomplete fusion all the while sustained and contained within the being of her employer.

But she was growing cooler. Whiston came up. She looked at him, and saw him with different eyes. She saw his slim, young man's figure real and enduring before her. That was he. But she was in the spell with the other man, fused with him, and she could not be taken away.

'Have you finished your cribbage?' she asked, with hasty evasion of him.

'Yes,' he replied. 'Aren't you getting tired of dancing?'

'Not a bit,' she said.

'Not she,' said Adams heartily. 'No girl with any spirit gets tired of dancing.–Have something else, Elsie. Come–sherry. Have a glass of sherry with us, Whiston.'

Whilst they sipped the wine, Adams watched Whiston almost cunningly, to find his advantage.

'We'd better be getting back–there's the music,' he said. 'See the women get something to eat, Whiston, will you, there's a good chap.'

And he began to draw away. Elsie was drifting helplessly with him. But Whiston put himself beside them, and went along with them. In silence they passed through to the dancing-room. There Adams hesitated, and looked round the room. It was as if he could not see.

A man came hurrying forward, claiming Elsie, and Adams went to his other partner. Whiston stood watching during the dance. She was conscious of him standing there observant of her, like a ghost, or a judgment, or a guardian angel. She was also conscious, much more intimately and impersonally, of the body of the other man moving somewhere in the room. She still belonged to him, but a feeling of distraction possessed her, and helplessness. Adams danced on, adhering to

Elsie, waiting his time, with the persistence of cynicism.

The dance was over. Adams was detained. Elsie found herself beside Whiston. There was something shapely about him as he sat, about his knees and his distinct figure, that she clung to. It was as if he had enduring form. She put her hand on his knee.

'Are you enjoying yourself?' he asked.

'*Ever* so,' she replied, with a fervent, yet detached tone.

'It's going on for one o'clock,' he said.

'Is it?' she answered. It meant nothing to her.

'Should we be going?' he said.

She was silent. For the first time for an hour or more an inkling of her normal consciousness returned. She resented it.

'What for?' she said.

'I thought you might have had enough,' he said.

A slight soberness came over her, an irritation at being frustrated of her illusion.

'Why?' she said.

'We've been here since nine,' he said.

That was no answer, no reason. It conveyed nothing to her. She sat detached from him. Across the room Sam Adams glanced at her. She sat there exposed for him.

'You don't want to be too free with Sam Adams,' said Whiston cautiously, suffering. 'You know what he is.'

'How, free?' she asked.

'Why—you don't want to have too much to do with him.'

She sat silent. He was forcing her into consciousness of her position. But he could not get hold of her feelings, to change them. She had a curious, perverse desire that he should not.

'I like him,' she said.

'What do you find to like in him?' he said, with a hot heart.

'I don't know—but I like him,' she said.

She was immutable. He sat feeling heavy and dulled with rage. He was not clear as to what he felt. He sat there unliving whilst she danced. And she, distracted, lost to herself between the opposing forces of the two men, drifted. Between the dances, Whiston kept near to her. She was scarcely conscious. She glanced repeatedly at her card, to see when she would dance again with Adams, half in desire, half in dread. Sometimes she met his steady, glaucous eye as she passed him in the dance. Sometimes she saw the steadiness of his flank as he danced. And it was always as if she rested on his arm, were borne along, upborne by him, away from herself. And always there was present the other's antagonism. She was divided.

The time came for her to dance with Adams. Oh, the delicious closing of contact with him, of his limbs touching her limbs, his arm supporting her. She seemed to resolve. Whiston had not made himself real to her. He was only a heavy place in her consciousness.

But she breathed heavily, beginning to suffer from the closeness of strain. She was nervous. Adams also was constrained. A tightness, a tension was coming over them all. And he was exasperated, feeling something counteracting physical magnetism, feeling a will stronger with her than his own, intervening in what was becoming a vital necessity to him.

Elsie was almost lost to her own control. As she went forward with him to take her place at the dance, she stooped for her pocket-handkerchief. The music sounded for quadrilles. Everybody was ready. Adams stood with his body near her, exerting his attraction over her. He was tense and fighting. She stooped for her pocket-handkerchief, and shook it as she rose. It shook out and fell from her hand. With agony, she saw she had taken a white stocking instead of a handkerchief. For a second it lay on the floor, a twist of white stocking. Then, in an instant, Adams picked it up, with a little, surprised laugh of triumph.

'That'll do for me,' he whispered—seeming to take possession of her. And he stuffed the stocking in his trousers pocket, and quickly offered her his handkerchief.

The dance began. She felt weak and faint, as if her will were turned to water. A heavy sense of loss came over her. She could not help herself any more. But it was peace.

When the dance was over, Adams yielded her up. Whiston came to her.

'What was it as you dropped?' Whiston asked.

'I thought it was my handkerchief—I'd taken a stocking by mistake,' she said, detached and muted.

'And he's got it?'

'Yes.'

'What does he mean by that?'

She lifted her shoulders.

'Are you going to let him keep it?' he asked.

'I don't let him.'

There was a long pause.

'Am I to go and have it out with him?' he asked, his face flushed, his blue eyes going hard with opposition.

'No,' she said, pale.

'Why?'

'No—I don't want you to say anything about it.'

He sat exasperated and nonplussed.

'You'll let him keep it, then?' he asked.

She sat silent and made no form of answer.

'What do you mean by it?' he said, dark with fury. And he started up.

'No!' she cried. 'Ted!' And she caught hold of him, sharply detaining him.

It made him black with rage.

'Why?' he said.

Then something about her mouth was pitiful to him. He did not understand, but he felt she must have her reasons.

'Then I'm not stopping here,' he said. 'Are you coming with me?'

She rose mutely, and they went out of the room. Adams had not noticed.

In a few moments they were in the street.

'What the hell do you mean?' he said, in a black fury.

She went at his side, in silence, neutral.

'That great hog, an' all,' he added.

Then they went a long time in silence through the frozen, deserted darkness of the town. She felt she could not go indoors. They were drawing near her house.

'I don't want to go home,' she suddenly cried in distress and anguish. 'I don't want to go home.'

He looked at her.

'Why don't you?' he said.

'I don't want to go home,' was all she could sob.

He heard somebody coming.

'Well, we can walk a bit further,' he said.

She was silent again. They passed out of the town into the fields. He held her by the arm—they could not speak.

'What's a-matter?' he asked at length, puzzled.

She began to cry again.

At last he took her in his arms, to soothe her. She sobbed by herself, almost unaware of him.

'Tell me what's a-matter, Elsie,' he said. 'Tell me what's a-matter—my dear—tell me, then—'

He kissed her wet face, and caressed her. She made no response. He was puzzled and tender and miserable.

At length she became quiet. Then he kissed her, and she put her arms round him, and clung to him very tight, as if for fear and anguish. He held her in his arms, wondering.

'Ted!' she whispered, frantic. 'Ted!'

'What, my love?' he answered, becoming also afraid.

'Be good to me,' she cried. 'Don't be cruel to me.'

'No my pet,' he said, amazed and grieved. 'Why?'

'Oh, be good to me,' she sobbed.

And he held her very safe, and his heart was white-hot with love for her. His mind was amazed. He could only hold her against his chest that was white-hot with love and belief in her. So she was restored at last.

III

She refused to go to her work at Adams's any more. Her father had to submit and she sent in her notice–she was not well. Sam Adams was ironical. But he had a curious patience. He did not fight.

In a few weeks, she and Whiston were married. She loved him with passion and worship, a fierce little abandon of love that moved him to the depths of his being, and gave him a permanent surety and sense of realness in himself. He did not trouble about himself any more: he felt he was fulfilled and now he had only the many things in the world to busy himself about. Whatever troubled him, at the bottom was surety. He had found himself in this love.

They spoke once or twice of the white stocking.

'Ah!' Whiston exclaimed. 'What does it matter?'

He was impatient and angry, and could not bear to consider the matter. So it was left unresolved.

She was quite happy at first, carried away by her adoration of her husband. Then gradually she got used to him. He always was the ground of her happiness, but she got used to him, as to the air she breathed. He never got used to her in the same way.

Inside of marriage she found her liberty. She was rid of the responsibility of herself. Her husband must look after that. She was free to get what she could out of her time.

So that, when, after some months, she met Sam Adams, she was not quite as unkind to him as she might have been. With a young wife's new and exciting knowledge of men, she perceived he was in love with her, she knew he had always kept an unsatisfied desire for her. And, sportive, she could not help playing a little with this, though she cared not one jot for the man himself.

When Valentine's day came, which was near the first anniversary of her wedding day, there arrived a white stocking with a little amethyst brooch. Luckily Whiston did not see it, so she said nothing of it to him. She had not the faintest intention of having anything to do with Sam Adams, but once a little brooch was in her possession, it was hers, and she did not trouble her head for a moment how she had come by it. She kept it.

Now she had the pearl ear-rings. They were a more valuable and a more conspicuous present. She would have to ask her mother to give them to her, to explain their presence. She made a little plan in her head. And she was extraordinarily pleased. As for Sam Adams, even if he saw her wearing them, he would not give her away. What fun, if he saw her wearing his ear-rings! She would pretend she had inherited them from her grandmother, her mother's mother. She laughed to herself as she went down town in the afternoon, the pretty drops dangling in front of her curls. But she saw no one of importance.

Whiston came home tired and depressed. All day the male in him had been uneasy, and this had fatigued him. She was curiously against him, inclined, as she sometimes was nowadays, to make mock of him and jeer at him and cut him off. He did not understand this, and it angered him deeply. She was uneasy before him.

She knew he was in a state of suppressed irritation. The veins stood out on the backs of his hands, his brow was drawn stiffly. Yet she could not help goading him.

'What did you do wi' that white stocking?' he asked, out of a gloomy silence, his voice strong and brutal.

'I put it in a drawer—why?' she replied flippantly.

'Why didn't you put it on the fire back?' he said harshly. 'What are you hoarding it up for?'

'I'm not hoarding it up,' she said. 'I've got a pair.'

He relapsed into gloomy silence. She, unable to move him, ran away upstairs, leaving him smoking by the fire. Again she tried on the ear-rings. Then another little inspiration came to her. She drew on the white stockings, both of them.

Presently she came down in them. Her husband still sat immovable and glowering by the fire.

'Look!' she said. 'They'll do beautifully.'

And she picked up her skirts to her knees, and twisted round, looking at her pretty legs in the neat stockings.

He filled with unreasonable rage, and took the pipe from his mouth.

'Don't they look nice?' she said. 'One from last year and one from this, they just do. Save you buying a pair.'

And she looked over her shoulders at her pretty calves, and at the dangling frills of her knickers.

'Put your skirts down and don't make a fool of yourself,' he said.

'Why a fool of myself?' she asked.

And she began to dance slowly round the room, kicking up her feet half reckless, half jeering, in a ballet-dancer's fashion. Almost fearfully, yet in defiance, she kicked up her legs at him, singing as she did so. She resented him.

'You little fool, ha' done with it,' he said.

'And you'll backfire them stockings, I'm telling you.' He was angry. His face flushed dark, he kept his head bent. She ceased to dance.

'I shan't,' she said. 'They'll come in very useful.'

He lifted his head and watched her, with lighted, dangerous eyes.

'You'll put 'em on the fire back, I tell you,' he said.

It was a war now. She bent forward, in a ballet-dancer's fashion, and put her tongue between her teeth.

'I shan't backfire them stockings,' she sang, repeating his words, 'I shan't, I shan't, I shan't.'

And she danced round the room doing a high kick to the tune of her words. There was a real biting indifference in her behaviour.

'We'll see whether you will or not,' he said, 'trollops! You'd like Sam Adams to know you was wearing 'em, wouldn't you? That's what would please you.'

'Yes, I'd like him to see how nicely they fit me, he might give me some more then.'

And she looked down at her pretty legs.

He knew somehow that she *would* like Sam Adams to see how pretty her legs looked in the white stockings. It made his anger go deep, almost to hatred.

'Yer nasty trolley,' he cried. 'Put yer petticoats down, and stop being so foul-minded.'

'I'm not foul-minded,' she said. 'My legs are my own. And why shouldn't Sam Adams think they're nice?'

There was a pause. He watched her with eyes glittering to a point.

'Have you been havin' owt to do with him?' he asked.

'I've just spoken to him when I've seen him,' she said. 'He's not as bad as you would make out.'

'Isn't he?' he cried, a certain wakefulness in his voice. 'Them who has anything to do wi' him is too bad for me, I tell you.'

'Why, what are you frightened of him for?' she mocked.

She was rousing all his uncontrollable anger. He sat glowering. Every one of her sentences stirred him up like a red-hot iron. Soon it would be too much. And she was afraid herself; but she was neither conquered nor convinced.

A curious little grin of hate came on his face. He had a long score against her.

'What am I frightened of him for?' he repeated automatically. 'What am I frightened of him for? Why, for you, you stray-running little bitch.'

She flushed. The insult went deep into her, right home.

'Well, if you're so dull—' she said, lowering her eyelids, and speaking coldly, haughtily.

'If I'm so dull I'll break your neck the first word you speak to him,' he said, tense.

'Pf!' she sneered. 'Do you think I'm frightened of you?' She spoke coldly, detached.

She was frightened, for all that, white round the mouth.

His heart was getting hotter.

'You *will* be frightened of me, the next time you have anything to do with him,' he said.

'Do you think *you'd* ever be told–ha!'

Her jeering scorn made him go white-hot, molten. He knew he was incoherent, scarcely responsible for what he might do. Slowly, unseeing, he rose and went out of doors, stifled, moved to kill her.

He stood leaning against the garden fence, unable either to see or hear. Below him, far off, fumed the lights of the town. He stood still, unconscious with a black storm of rage, his face lifted to the night.

Presently, still unconscious of what he was doing, he went indoors again. She stood, a small, stubborn figure with tight-pressed lips and big, sullen, childish eyes, watching him, white with fear. He went heavily across the floor and dropped into his chair.

There was a silence.

'*You're* not going to tell me everything I shall do, and everything I shan't,' she broke out at last.

He lifted his head.

'I tell you *this,*' he said, low and intense. 'Have anything to do with Sam Adams, and I'll break your neck.'

She laughed, shrill and false.

'How I hate your word "break your neck",' she said, with a grimace of the mouth. 'It sounds so common and beastly. Can't you say something else—'

There was a dead silence.

'And besides,' she said, with a queer chirrup of mocking laughter, 'what do you know about anything? He sent me an amethyst brooch and a pair of pearl ear-rings.'

'He what?' said Whiston, in a suddenly normal voice. His eyes were fixed on her.

'Sent me a pair of pearl ear-rings, and an amethyst brooch,' she repeated, mechanically, pale to the lips.

And her big, black, childish eyes watched him, fascinated, held in her spell.

He seemed to thrust his face and his eyes forward at her, as he rose slowly and came to her. She watched transfixed in terror. Her throat made a small sound, as she tried to scream.

Then, quick as lightning, the back of his hand struck her with a crash across the mouth, and she was flung back blinded against the wall. The shock shook a queer sound out of her. And then she saw him still coming on, his eyes holding her, his fist drawn back, advancing slowly. At any instant the blow might crash into her.

Mad with terror, she raised her hands with a queer clawing movement to cover her eyes and her temples, opening her mouth in a dumb shriek. There was no sound. But the sight of her slowly arrested him. He hung before her, looking at her fixedly, as she stood crouched against the wall with open, bleeding mouth, and wide-staring eyes, and two hands clawing over her temples. And his lust to see her bleed, to break her and destroy her, rose from an old source against her. It carried him. He wanted satisfaction.

But he had seen her standing there, a piteous, horrified thing, and he turned his face aside in shame and nausea. He went and sat heavily in his chair, and a curious ease, almost like sleep, came over his brain.

She walked away from the wall towards the fire, dizzy, white to the lips, mechanically wiping her small, bleeding mouth. He sat motionless. Then, gradually, her breath began to hiss, she shook, and was sobbing silently, in grief for herself. Without looking, he saw. It made his mad desire to destroy her come back.

At length he lifted his head. His eyes were glowing again, fixed on her.

'And what did he give them you for?' he asked, in a steady, unyielding voice.

Her crying dried up in a second. She also was tense.

'They came as valentines,' she replied, still not subjugated, even if beaten.

'When, to-day?'

'The pearl ear-rings to-day—the amethyst brooch last year.'

'You've had it a year?'

'Yes.'

She felt that now nothing would prevent him if he rose to kill her. She could not prevent him any more. She was yielded up to him. They both trembled in the balance, unconscious.

'What have you had to do with him?' he asked, in a barren voice.

'I've not had anything to do with him,' she quavered.

'You just kept 'em because they were jewellery?' he said.

A weariness came over him. What was the worth of speaking any more of it? He did not care any more. He was dreary and sick.

She began to cry again, but he took no notice. She kept wiping her mouth on her handkerchief. He could see it, the blood-mark. It made him only more sick and tired of the responsibility of it, the violence, the shame.

When she began to move about again, he raised his head once more from his dead, motionless position.

'Where are the things?' he said.

'They are upstairs,' she quavered. She knew the passion had gone down in him.

'Bring them down,' he said.

'I won't,' she wept, with rage. 'You're not going to bully me and hit me like that on the mouth.'

And she sobbed again. He looked at her in contempt and compassion and in rising anger.

'Where are they?' he said.

'They're in the little drawer under the looking-glass,' she sobbed.

He went slowly upstairs, struck a match, and found the trinkets. He brought them downstairs in his hand.

'These?' he said, looking at them as they lay in his palm.

She looked at them without answering. She was not interested in them any more.

He looked at the little jewels. They were pretty.

'It's none of their fault,' he said to himself.

And he searched round slowly, persistently, for a box. He tied the things up and addressed them to Sam Adams. Then he went out in his slippers to post the little package.

When he came back she was still sitting crying.

'You'd better go to bed,' he said.

She paid no attention. He sat by the fire. She still cried.

'I'm sleeping down here,' he said. 'Go you to bed.'

In a few moments she lifted her tear-stained, swollen face and looked at him with eyes all forlorn and pathetic. A great flash of anguish went over his body. He went over, slowly, and very gently took her in his hands. She let herself be taken. Then as she lay against his shoulder, she sobbed aloud:

'I never meant—'

'My love—my little love—' he cried, in anguish of spirit, holding her in his arms.

The Shadow in the Rose Garden

Written Autumn 1907 as 'The Vicar's Garden'.
Revised in 1911 and June–August 1913. Published
in the *Smart Set*, March 1914. Extensive revision July
and October for inclusion in *The Prussian Officer*
collection.

A rather small young man sat by the window of a pretty
seaside cottage trying to persuade himself that he was
reading the newspaper. It was about half-past eight in
the morning. Outside, the glory roses hung in the
morning sunshine, like little bowls of fire tipped up. The
young man looked at the table, then at the clock, then at
his own big silver watch. An expression of stiff endurance
came on to his face. Then he rose and reflected on the oil-
paintings that hung on the walls of the room, giving
careful but hostile attention to 'The Stag at Bay'. He
tried the lid of the piano, and found it locked. He caught
sight of his own face in a little mirror, pulled his brown
moustache, and an alert interest sprang into his eyes. He
was not ill-favoured. He twisted his moustache. His
figure was rather small, but alert and vigorous. As he
turned from the mirror a look of self-commiseration
mingled with his appreciation of his own physiognomy.

In a state of self-suppression, he went through into
the garden. His jacket, however, did not look dejected. It
was new, and had a smart and self-confident air, sitting
upon a confident body. He contemplated the Tree of
Heaven that flourished by the lawn, then sauntered on to
the next plant. There was more promise in a crooked
apple tree covered with brown-red fruit. Glancing round,

he broke off an apple and, with his back to the house, took a clean, sharp bite. To his surprise the fruit was sweet. He took another. Then again he turned to survey the bedroom windows overlooking the garden. He started, seeing a woman's figure; but it was only his wife. She was gazing across to the sea, apparently ignorant of him.

For a moment or two he looked at her, watching her. She was a good-looking woman, who seemed older than he, rather pale, but healthy, her face yearning. Her rich auburn hair was heaped in folds on her forehead. She looked apart from him and his world, gazing away to the sea. It irked her husband that she should continue abstracted and in ignorance of him; he pulled poppy fruits and threw them at the window. She started, glanced at him with a wild smile, and looked away again. Then almost immediately she left the window. He went indoors to meet her. She had a fine carriage, very proud, and wore a dress of soft white muslin.

'I've been waiting long enough,' he said.

'For me or for breakfast?' she said lightly. 'You know we said nine o'clock. I should have thought you could have slept after the journey.'

"You know I'm always up at five, and I couldn't stop in bed after six. You might as well be in pit as in bed, on a morning like this.'

'I shouldn't have thought the pit would occur to you, here.'

She moved about examining the room, looking at the ornaments under glass covers. He, planted on the hearthrug, watched her rather uneasily, and grudgingly indulgent. She shrugged her shoulders at the apartment.

'Come,' she said, taking his arm, 'let us go into the garden till Mrs Coates brings the tray.'

'I hope she'll be quick,' he said, pulling his moustache. She gave a short laugh, and leaned on his arm as they went. He had lighted a pipe.

Mrs Coates entered the room as they went down the

steps. The delightful, erect old lady hastened to the window for a good view of her visitors. Her china-blue eyes were bright as she watched the young couple go down the path, he walking in an easy, confident fashion. with his wife on his arm. The landlady began talking to herself in a soft, Yorkshire accent.

'Just of a height they are. She wouldn't ha' married a man less than herself in stature, I think, though he's not her equal otherwise.' Here her granddaughter came in, setting a tray on the table. The girl went to the old woman's side.

'He's been eating the apples, gran',' she said.

'Has he, my pet? Well, if he's happy, why not?'

Outside, the young, well-favoured man listened with impatience to the chink of the teacups. At last, with a sigh of relief, the couple came in to breakfast. After he had eaten for some time, he rested a moment and said:

'Do you think it's any better place than Bridlington?'

'I do,' she said, 'infinitely! Besides, I am at home here—it's not like a strange seaside place to me.'

'How long were you here?'

'Two years.'

He ate reflectively.

'I should ha' thought you'd rather go to a fresh place,' he said at length.

She sat very silent, and then, delicately, put out a feeler.

'Why?' she said. 'Do you think I shan't enjoy myself?'

He laughed comfortably, putting the marmalade thick on his bread.

'I hope so,' he said.

She again took no notice of him.

'But don't say anything about it in the village, Frank,' she said casually. 'Don't say who I am, or that I used to live here. There's nobody I want to meet, particularly, and we should never feel free if they knew me again.'

'Why did you come then?'

' "Why?" Can't you understand why?'

'Not if you don't want to know anybody.'

'I came to see the place, not the people.'

He did not say any more.

'Women,' she said, 'are different from men. I don't know why I wanted to come—but I did.'

She helped him to another cup of coffee, solicitously.

'Only,' she resumed, 'don't talk about me in the village.' She laughed shakily. 'I don't want my past brought up against me, you know.' And she moved the crumbs on the cloth with her finger-tip.

He looked at her as he drank his coffee; he sucked his moustache, and putting down his cup, said phlegmatically:

'I'll bet you've had a lot of past.'

She looked with a little guiltiness, that flattered him, down at the tablecloth.

'Well,' she said, caressive, 'you won't give me away, who I am, will you?'

'No,' he said, comforting, laughing, 'I won't give you away.'

He was pleased.

She remained silent. After a moment or two she lifted her head, saying:

'I've got to arrange with Mrs Coates, and do various things. So you'd better go out by yourself this morning—and we'll be in to dinner at one.'

'But you can't be arranging with Mrs Coates all morning,' he said.

'Oh, well—then I've some letters to write, and I must get that mark out of my skirt. I've got plenty of little things to do this morning. You'd better go out by yourself.'

He perceived that she wanted to be rid of him, so that when she went upstairs, he took his hat and lounged out on to the cliffs, suppressedly angry.

Presently she too came out. She wore a hat with roses, and a long lace scarf hung over her white dress. Rather nervously, she put up her sunshade, and her face was half-hidden in its coloured shadow. She went along the narrow track of flag-stones that were worn hollow by the feet of the fishermen. She seemed to be avoiding her surroundings, as if she remained safe in the little obscurity of her parasol.

She passed the church, and went down the lane till she came to a high wall by the wayside. Under this she went slowly, stopping at length by an open doorway, which shone like a picture of light in the dark wall. There in the magic beyond the doorway, patterns of shadow lay on the sunny court, on the blue and white sea-pebbles of its paving, while a green lawn glowed beyond, where a bay tree glittered at the edges. She tiptoed nervously into the courtyard, glancing at the house that stood in shadow. The uncurtained windows looked black and soulless, the kitchen door stood open. Irresolutely she took a stop forward, and again forward, leaning, yearning, towards the garden beyond.

She had almost gained the corner of the house when a heavy step came crunching through the trees. A gardener appeared before her. He held a wicker tray on which were rolling great, dark red gooseberries, over-ripe. He moved slowly.

'The garden isn't open today,' he said quietly to the attractive woman, who was poised for retreat.

For a moment she was silent with surprise. How should it be public at all?

'When is it open?' she asked, quick-witted.

'The rector lets visitors in on Fridays and Tuesdays.'

She stood still, reflecting. How strange to think of the rector opening his garden to the public!

'But everybody will be at church,' she said coaxingly to the man. 'There'll be nobody here, will there?'

He moved, and the big gooseberries rolled.

'The rector lives at the new rectory,' he said.

The two stood still. He did not like to ask her to go. At last she turned to him with a winning smile.

'Might I have *one* peep at the roses?' she coaxed, with pretty wilfulness.

'I don't suppose it would matter,' he said, moving aside; 'you won't stop long—'

She went forward, forgetting the gardener in a moment. Her face became strained, her movements eager. Glancing round, she saw all the windows giving on to the lawn were curtainless and dark. The house had a sterile appearance, as if it were still used, but not inhabited. A shadow seemed to go over her. She went across the lawn towards the garden, through an arch of crimson ramblers, a gate of colour. There beyond lay the soft blue sea within the bay, misty with morning, and the furthest headland of black rock jutting dimly out between blue and blue of the sky and water. Her face began to shine, transfigured with pain and joy. At her feet the garden fell steeply, all a confusion of flowers, and away below was the darkness of tree-tops covering the beck.

She turned to the garden that shone with sunny flowers around her. She knew the little corner where was the seat beneath the yew tree. Then there was the terrace where a great host of flowers shone, and from this, two paths went down, one at each side of the garden. She closed her sunshade and walked slowly among the many flowers. All round were rose bushes, big banks of roses, then roses hanging and tumbling from pillars, or roses balanced on the standard bushes. By the open earth were many other flowers. If she lifted her head, the sea was upraised beyond, and the Cape.

Slowly she went down one path, lingering, like one who has gone back into the past. Suddenly she was touching some heavy crimson roses that were soft as velvet, touching them thoughtfully, without knowing, as a mother sometimes fondles the hand of her child. She leaned slightly forward to catch the scent. Then she wandered on in abstraction. Sometimes a flame-coloured, scentless rose would hold her arrested. She stood gazing at it as if she could not understand it. Again the same softness of intimacy came over her, as she stood before a tumbling heap of pink petals. Then she wondered over the white rose, that was greenish, like ice, in the centre. So, slowly, like a white, pathetic butterfly, she drifted down the path, coming at last to a tiny terrace all full of roses. They seemed to fill the place, a sunny, gay throng. She was shy of them, they were so many and so bright. They seemed to be conversing and laughing. She felt herself in a strange crowd. It exhilarated her, carried her out of herself. She flushed with excitement. The air was pure scent.

Hastily, she went to a little seat among the white roses, and sat down. Her scarlet sunshade made a hard blot of colour. She sat quite still, feeling her own existence lapse. She was no more than a rose, a rose that could not quite come into blossom, but remained tense. A little fly dropped on her knee, on her white dress. She watched it, as if it had fallen on a rose. She was not herself.

Then she started cruelly as a shadow crossed her and a figure moved into her sight. It was a man who had come in slippers, unheard. He wore a linen coat. The morning was shattered, the spell vanished away. She was only afraid of being questioned. He came forward. She rose. Then, seeing him, the strength went from her and she sank on the seat again.

He was a young man, military in appearance, growing slightly stout. His black hair was brushed smooth and bright, his moustache was waxed. But there was something rambling in his gait. She looked up, blanched to the lips, and saw his eyes. They were black, and stared without seeing. They were not a man's eyes. He was coming towards her.

He stared at her fixedly, made an unconscious

salute, and sat down beside her on the seat. He moved on the bench, shifted his feet, saying, in a gentlemanly, military voice:

'I don't disturb you—do I?'

She was mute and helpless. He was scrupulously dressed in dark clothes and a linen coat. She could not move. Seeing his hands, with the ring she knew so well upon the little finger, she felt as if she were going dazed. The whole world was deranged. She sat unavailing. For his hands, her symbols of passionate love, filled her with horror as they rested now on his strong thighs.

'May I smoke?' he asked intimately, almost secretly, his hand going to his pocket.

She could not answer, but it did not matter, he was in another world. She wondered, craving, if he recognized her—if he could recognize her. She sat pale with anguish. But she had to go through it.

'I haven't got any tobacco,' he said thoughtfully.

But she paid no heed to his words, only she attended to him. Could he recognize her, or was it all gone? She sat still in a frozen kind of suspense.

'I smoke John Cotton,' he said, 'and I must economise with it, it is expensive. You know, I'm not very well off while these law suits are going on.'

'No,' she said, and her heart was cold, her soul kept rigid.

He moved, made a loose salute, rose, and went away. She sat motionless. She could see his shape, the shape she had loved with all her passion: his compact, soldier's head, his fine figure now slackened. And it was not he. It only filled her with horror too difficult to know.

Suddenly he came again, his hand in his jacket pocket.

'Do you mind if I smoke?' he said. 'Perhaps I shall be able to see things more clearly.'

He sat down beside her again, filling a pipe. She watched his hands with the fine strong fingers. They had always inclined to tremble slightly. It had surprised her, long ago, in such a healthy man. Now they moved inaccurately, and the tobacco hung raggedly out of the pipe.

'I have legal business to attend to. Legal affairs are always so uncertain. I tell my solicitor exactly, precisely what I want, but I can never get it done.'

She sat and heard him talking. But it was not he. Yet those were the hands she had kissed, there were the glistening, strange black eyes that she had loved. Yet it was not he. She sat motionless with horror and silence. He dropped his tobacco pouch, and groped for it on the ground. Yet she must wait to see if he would recognize her. Why could she not go!–In a moment he rose.

'I must go at once,' he said. 'The owl is coming.' Then he added confidentially: 'His name isn't really the owl, but I call him that. I must go and see if he has come.'

She rose too. He stood before her, uncertain. He was a handsome, soldierly fellow, and a lunatic. Her eyes searched him, and searched him, to see if he would recognize her, if she could discover him.

'You don't know me?' she asked, from the terror of her soul, standing alone.

He looked back at her quizzically. She had to bear his eyes. They gleamed on her, but with no intelligence. He was drawing nearer to her.

'Yes, I do know you,' he said, fixed, intent, but mad, drawing his face nearer hers. Her horror was too great. The powerful lunatic was coming too near to her.

A man approached, hastening.

'The garden isn't open this morning,' he said.

The deranged man stopped and looked at him. The keeper went to the seat and picked up the tobacco pouch left lying there.

'Don't leave your tobacco, sir,' he said, taking it to the gentleman in the linen coat.

'I was just asking this lady to stay to lunch,' the latter said politely. 'She is a friend of mine.'

The woman turned and walked swiftly, blindly, between the sunny roses, out from the garden, past the house with the blank, dark windows, through the sea-pebbled courtyard to the street. Hastening and blind, she went forward without hesitating, not knowing whither. Directly she came to the house she went upstairs, took off her hat, and sat down on the bed. It was as if some membrane had been torn in two in her, so that she was not an entity that could think and feel. She sat staring across at the window, where an ivy spray waved slowly up and down in the sea wind. There was some of the uncanny luminousness of the sunlit sea in the air. She sat perfectly still, without any being. She only felt she might be sick, and it might be blood that was loose in her torn entrails. She sat perfectly still and passive.

After a time she heard the hard tread of her husband on the floor below, and, without herself changing, she registered his movement. She heard his rather disconsolate footsteps go out again, then his voice speaking, answering, growing cheery, and his solid tread drawing near.

He entered, ruddy, rather pleased, an air of complacency about his alert, sturdy figure. She moved stiffly. He faltered in his approach.

'What's the matter?' he asked, a tinge of impatience in his voice. 'Aren't you feeling well?'

This was torture to her.

'Quite,' she replied.

His brown eyes became puzzled and angry.

'What is the matter?' he said.

'Nothing.'

He took a few strides, and stood obstinately, looking out of the window.

'Have you run up against anybody?' he asked.

'Nobody who knows me,' she said.

His hands began to twitch. It exasperated him, that she was no more sensible of him than if he did not exist. Turning on her at length, driven, he asked:

'Something has upset you, hasn't it?'

'No, why?' she said, neutral. He did not exist for
her, except as an irritant.

His anger rose, filling the veins in his throat.

'It seems like it,' he said, making an effort not to
show his anger, because there seemed no reason for it.
He went away downstairs. She sat still on the bed, and
with the residue of feeling left to her, she disliked him
because he tormented her. The time went by. She could
smell the dinner being served, the smoke of her
husband's pipe from the garden. But she could not move.
She had no being. There was a tinkle of the bell. She
heard him come indoors. And then he mounted the stairs
again. At every step her heart grew tight in her. He
opened the door.

'Dinner is on the table,' he said.

It was difficult for her to endure his presence, for he
would interfere with her. She could not recover her life.
She rose stiffly and went down. She could neither eat nor
talk during the meal. She sat absent, torn, without any
being of her own. He tried to go on as if nothing were the
matter. But at last he became silent with fury. As soon as
it was possible, she went upstairs again, and locked the
bedroom door. She must be alone. He went with his pipe
into the garden. All his suppressed anger against her who
held herself superior to him filled and blackened his
heart. Though he had not known it, yet he had never
really won her, she had never loved him. She had taken
him on sufferance. This had foiled him. He was only a
labouring electrician in the mine, she was superior to
him. He had always given way to her. But all the while,
the injury and ignominy had been working in his soul
because she did not hold him seriously. And now all his
rage came up against her.

He turned and went indoors. The third time, she
heard him mounting the stairs. Her heart stood still. He
turned the catch and pushed the door–it was locked. He
tried it again, harder. Her heart was standing still.

'Have you fastened the door?' he asked quietly, because of the landlady.

'Yes. Wait a minute.'

She rose and turned the lock, afraid he would burst it. She felt hatred towards him, because he did not leave her free. He entered, his pipe between his teeth, and she returned to her old position on the bed. He closed the door and stood with his back to it.

'What's the matter?' he asked determinedly.

She was sick with him. She could not look at him.

'Can't you leave me alone?' she replied, averting her face from him.

He looked at her quickly, fully, wincing with ignominy. Then he seemed to consider for a moment.

'There's something up with you, isn't there?' he asked definitely.

'Yes,' she said, 'but that's no reason why you should torment me.'

'I don't torment you. What's the matter?'

'Why should you know?' she cried, in hate and desperation.

Something snapped. He started and caught his pipe as it fell from his mouth. Then he pushed forward the bitten-off mouth-piece with his tongue, took it from off his lips, and looked at it. Then he put out his pipe, and brushed the ash from his waistcoat. After which he raised his head.

'I want to know,' he said. His face was greyish pale, and set uglily.

Neither looked at the other. She knew he was fired now. His heart was pounding heavily. She hated him, but she could not withstand him. Suddenly she lifted her head and turned on him.

'What right have you to know?' she asked.

He looked at her. She felt a pang of surprise for his tortured eyes and his fixed face. But her heart hardened swiftly. She had never loved him. She did not love him now.

But suddenly she lifted her head again swiftly, like a thing that tries to get free. She wanted to be free of it. It was not him so much, but it, something she had put on herself, that bound her so horribly. And having put the bond on herself, it was hardest to take it off. But now she hated everything and felt destructive. He stood with his back to the door, fixed, as if he would oppose her eternally, till she was extinguished. She looked at him. Her eyes were cold and hostile. His workman's hands spread on the panels of the door behind him.

'You know I used to live here?' she began, in a hard voice, as if wilfully to wound him. He braced himself against her, and nodded.

'Well, I was companion to Miss Birch of Torril Hall—she and the rector were friends, and Archie was the rector's son.' There was a pause. He listened without knowing what was happening. He stared at his wife. She was squatted in her white dress on the bed, carefully folding and refolding the hem of her skirt. Her voice was full of hostility.

'He was an officer — a sub-lieutenant — then he quarrelled with his colonel and came out of the army. At any rate' —she plucked at her skirt hem, her husband stood motionless, watching her movements which filled his veins with madness— 'he was awfully fond of me, and I was of him—awfully.'

'How old was he?' asked the husband.

'When?—when I first knew him? or when he went away?—'

'When you first knew him.'

'When I first knew him, he was twenty-six — now — he's thirty-one — nearly thirty-two — because I'm twenty-nine, and he is nearly three years older—'

She lifted her head and looked at the opposite wall.

'And what then?' said her husband.

She hardened herself, and said callously:

'We were as good as engaged for nearly a year, though nobody knew — at least — they talked — but — it wasn't open. Then he went away—'

'He chucked you?' said the husband brutally, wanting to hurt her into contact with himself. Her heart rose wildly with rage. Then 'Yes', she said, to anger him. He shifted from one foot to the other, giving a 'Ph!' of rage. There was silence for a time.

'Then,' she resumed, her pain giving a mocking note to her words, 'he suddenly went out to fight in Africa, and almost the very day I first met you, I heard from Miss Birch he'd got sunstroke—and two months after, that he was dead—'

'That was before you took on with me?' said the husband.

There was no answer. Neither spoke for a time. He had not understood. His eyes were contracted uglily.

'So you've been looking at your old courting places!' he said. 'That was what you wanted to go out by yourself for this morning.'

Still she did not answer him anything. He went away from the door to the window. He stood with his hands behind him, his back to her. She looked at him. His hands seemed gross to her, the back of his head paltry.

At length, almost against his will, he turned round, asking:

'How long were you carrying on with him?'

'What do you mean?' she replied coldly.

'I mean how long were you carrying on with him?'

She lifted her head, averting her face from him. She refused to answer. Then she said:

'I don't know what you mean, by carrying on. I loved him from the first days I met him—two months after I went to stay with Miss Birch.'

'And do you reckon he loved you?' he jeered.

'I know he did.'

'How do you know, if he'd have no more to do with you?'

There was a long silence of hate and suffering.

'And how far did it go between you?' he asked at length, in a frightened, stiff voice.

'I hate your not-straightforward questions,' she cried, beside herself with his baiting. 'We loved each other, and we *were* lovers—we were. I don't care what *you* think: what have you got to do with it? We were lovers before ever I knew you—'

'Lovers—lovers,' he said, white with fury. 'You mean you had your fling with an army man, and then came to me to marry you when you'd done—'

She sat swallowing her bitterness. There was a long pause.

'Do you mean to say you used to go—the whole hogger?' he asked, still incredulous.

'Why, what else do you think I mean?' she cried brutally.

He shrank, and became white, impersonal. There was a long, paralysed silence. He seemed to have gone small.

'You never thought to tell me all this before I married you,' he said, with bitter irony, at last.

'You never asked me,' she replied.

'I never thought there was any need.'

'Well, then, you *should* think.'

He stood with expressionless, almost childlike set face, revolving many thoughts, whilst his heart was mad with anguish.

Suddenly she added:

'And I saw him to-day,' she said. 'He is not dead, he's mad.'

Her husband looked at her, startled.

'Mad!' he said involuntarily.

'A lunatic,' she said. It almost cost her her reason to utter the word. There was a pause.

'Did he know you?' asked the husband, in a small voice.

'No,' she said.

He stood and looked at her. At last he had learned

the width of the breach between them. She still squatted on the bed. He could not go near her. It would be violation to each of them to be brought into contact with the other. The thing must work itself out. They were both shocked so much, they were impersonal, and no longer hated each other. After some minutes he left her and went out.

Odour of Chrysanthemums

Written late Autumn 1909. Revised repeatedly for publication in *English Review*, June 1911, and again in July and October 1914 for *The Prussian Officer* collection.

I

The small locomotive engine, Number 4, came clanking, stumbling down from Selston with seven full waggons. It appeared round the corner with loud threats of speed, but the colt that it startled from among the gorse, which still flickered indistinctly in the raw afternoon, out-distanced it at a canter. A woman, walking up the railway line to Underwood, drew back into the hedge, held her basket aside, and watched the footplate of the engine advancing. The trucks thumped heavily past, one by one, with slow inevitable movement, as she stood insignificantly trapped between the jolting black waggons and the hedge; then they curved away towards the coppice where the withered oak leaves dropped noiselessly, while the birds, pulling at the scarlet hips beside the track, made off into the dusk that had already crept into the spinney. In the open, the smoke from the engine sank and cleaved to the rough grass. The fields were dreary and forsaken, and in the marshy strip that led to the whimsey, a reedy pit-pond, the fowls had already abandoned their run among the alders, to roost in the tarred fowl-house. The pit-bank loomed up beyond the pond, flames like red sores licking its ashy sides, in the afternoon's stagnant light. Just beyond rose the tapering chimneys and the clumsy black headstocks of Brinsley Colliery. The two wheels were spinning fast up against the sky, and the winding-engine rapped out its little spasms. The miners were being turned up.

The engine whistled as it came into the wide bay of railway lines beside the colliery, where rows of trucks stood in harbour.

Miners, single, trailing and in groups, passed like shadows diverging home. At the edge of the ribbed level of sidings squat a low cottage, three steps down from the cinder track. A large bony vine clutched at the house, as if to claw down the tiled roof. Round the bricked yard grew a few wintry primroses. Beyond, the long garden sloped down to a bush-covered brook course. There were some twiggy apple trees, winter-crack trees, and ragged cabbages. Beside the path hung dishevelled pink chrysanthemums, like pink cloths hung on bushes. A woman came stooping out of the felt-covered fowl-house, half-way down the garden. She closed and padlocked the door, then drew herself erect, having brushed some bits from her white apron.

She was a tall woman of imperious mien, handsome, with definite black eyebrows. Her smooth black hair was parted exactly. For a few moments she stood steadily watching the miners as they passed along the railway: then she turned towards the brook course. Her face was calm and set, her mouth was closed with disillusionment. After a moment she called:

'John!' There was no answer. She waited, and then said distinctly:

'Where are you?'

'Here!' replied a child's sulky voice from among the bushes. The woman looked piercingly through the dusk.

'Are you at that brook?' she asked sternly.

For answer the child showed himself before the raspberry-canes that rose like whips. He was a small, sturdy boy of five. He stood quite still, defiantly.

'Oh!' said the mother, conciliated. 'I thought you were down at that wet brook–and you remember what I told you—'

The boy did not move or answer.

'Come, come on in,' she said more gently, 'it's getting dark. There's your grandfather's engine coming down the line!'

The lad advanced slowly, with resentful, taciturn movement. He was dressed in trousers and waistcoat of cloth that was too thick and hard for the size of the garments. They were evidently cut down from a man's clothes.

As they went slowly towards the house he tore at the ragged wisps of chrysanthemums and dropped the petals in handfuls along the path.

'Don't do that–it does look nasty,' said his mother. He refrained, and she, suddenly pitiful, broke off a twig with three or four wan flowers and held them against her face. When mother and son reached the yard her hand hesitated, and instead of laying the flower aside, she pushed it in her apron-band. The mother and son stood at the foot of the three steps looking across the bay of lines at the passing home of the miners. The trundle of the small train was imminent. Suddenly the engine loomed past the house and came to a stop opposite the gate.

The engine-driver, a short man with round grey beard, leaned out of the cab high above the woman.

'Have you got a cup of tea?' he said in a cheery, hearty fashion.

It was her father. She went in, saying she would mash. Directly, she returned.

'I didn't come to see you on Sunday,' began the little grey-bearded man.

'I didn't expect you,' said his daughter.

The engine-driver winced; then, reassuming his cheery, airy manner, he said:

'Oh, have you heard then? Well, and what do you

think—?'

'I think it is soon enough,' she replied.

At her brief censure the little man made an impatient gesture, and said coaxingly, yet with dangerous coldness:

'Well, what's a man to do... It's no sort of life for a man of my years, to sit at my own hearth like a stranger. And if I'm going to marry again it may as well be soon as late—what does it matter to anybody?'

The woman did not reply, but turned and went into the house. The man in the engine-cab stood assertive, till she returned with a cup of tea and a piece of bread and butter on a plate. She went up the steps and stood near the footplate of the hissing engine.

'You needn't 'a' brought me bread an' butter,' said her father. 'But a cup of tea'—he sipped appreciatively—'it's very nice.' He sipped for a moment or two, then: 'I hear as Walter's got another bout on,' he said.

'When hasn't he?' said the woman bitterly.

'I heered tell of him in the "Lord Nelson" braggin' as he was going to spend that b— afore he went: half a sovereign that was.'

'When?' asked the woman.

'A' Sat'day night—I know that's true.'

'Very likely,' she laughed bitterly. 'He gives me twenty-three shillings.'

'Aye, it's a nice thing, when a man can do nothing with his money but make a beast of himself!' said the grey-whiskered man. The woman turned her head away. Her father swallowed the last of his tea and handed her the cup.

'Aye,' he sighed, wiping his mouth. 'It's a settler, it is—'

He put his hand on the lever. The little engine strained and groaned, and the train rumbled towards the crossing. The woman again looked across the metals. Darkness was settling over the spaces of the railway and trucks: the miners, in grey sombre groups, were still passing home. The winding-engine pulsed hurriedly, with brief pauses. Elizabeth Bates looked at the dreary flow of men, then she went indoors. Her husband did not come.

The kitchen was small and full of firelight; red coals piled glowing up the chimney mouth. All the life of the room seemed in the white, warm hearth and the steel fender reflecting the red fire. The cloth was laid for tea; cups glinted in the shadows. At the back, where the lowest stairs protruded into the room, the boy sat struggling with a knife and a piece of whitewood. He was almost hidden in the shadow. It was half-past four. They had but to await the father's coming to begin tea. As the mother watched her son's sullen little struggle with the wood, she saw herself in his silence and pertinacity; she saw the father in her child's indifference to all but himself. She seemed to be occupied by her husband. He had probably gone past his home, slunk past his own door, to drink before he came in, while his dinner spoiled and wasted in waiting. She glanced at the clock, then took the potatoes to strain them in the yard. The garden and fields beyond the brook were closed in uncertain darkness. When she rose with the saucepan, leaving the drain steaming into the night behind her, she saw the yellow lamps were lit along the high road that went up the hill away beyond the space of the railway lines and the field.

Then again she watched the men trooping home, fewer now and fewer.

Indoors the fire was sinking and the room was dark red. The woman put her saucepan on the hob, and set a batter pudding near the mouth of the oven. Then she stood unmoving. Directly, gratefully, came quick young steps to the door. Someone hung on the latch a moment, then a little girl entered and began pulling off her outdoor things, dragging a mass of curls, just ripening from gold to brown, over her eyes with her hat.

Her mother chid her for coming late from school,

and said she would have to keep her at home the dark winter days.

'Why, mother, it's hardly a bit dark yet. The lamp's not lighted, and my father's not home.'

'No, he isn't. But it's a quarter to five! Did you see anything of him?'

The child became serious. She looked at her mother with large, wistful blue eyes.

'No, mother, I've never seen him. Why? Has he come up an' gone past, to Old Brinsley? He hasn't, mother, 'cos I never saw him.'

'He'd watch that,' said the mother bitterly, 'he'd take care as you didn't see him. But you may depend upon it, he's seated in the "Prince o' Wales". He wouldn't be this late.'

The girl looked at her mother piteously.

'Let's have our teas, mother, should we?' said she.

The mother called John to table. She opened the door once more and looked out across the darkness of the lines. All was deserted: she could not hear the winding-engines.

'Perhaps', she said to herself, 'he's stopped to get some ripping done.'

They sat down to tea. John, at the end of the table near the door, was almost lost in the darkness. Their faces were hidden from each other. The girl crouched against the fender slowly moving a thick piece of bread before the fire. The lad, his face a dusky mark on the shadow, sat watching her who was transfigured in the red glow.

'I do think it's beautiful to look in the fire,' said the child.

'Do you?' said her mother. 'Why?'

'It's so red, and full of little caves—and it feels so nice, and you can fair smell it.'

'It'll want mending directly,' replied her mother, 'and then if your father comes he'll carry on and say there never is a fire when a man comes home sweating from the pit.–A public-house is always warm enough.'

There was silence till the boy said complainingly: 'Make haste, our Annie.'

'Well, I am doing! I can't make the fire do it no faster, can I?'

'She keeps wafflin' it about so's to make 'er slow,' grumbled the boy.

'Don't have such an evil imagination, child,' replied the mother.

Soon the room was busy in the darkness with the crisp sound of crunching. The mother ate very little. She drank her tea determinedly, and sat thinking. When she rose her anger was evident in the stern unbending of her head. She looked at the pudding in the fender, and broke out:

'It is a scandalous thing as a man can't even come home to his dinner! If it's crozzled up to a cinder I don't see why I should care. Past his very door he goes to get to a public-house, and here I sit with his dinner waiting for him—'

She went out. As she dropped piece after piece of coal on the red fire, the shadows fell on the walls, till the room was almost in total darkness.

'I canna see,' grumbled the invisible John. In spite of herself, the mother laughed.

'You know the way to your mouth,' she said. She set the dustpan outside the door. When she came again like a shadow on the hearth, the lad repeated, complaining sulkily:

'I canna see.'

'Good gracious!' cried the mother irritably, 'you're as bad as your father if it's a bit dusk!'

Nevertheless she took a paper spill from a sheaf on the mantelpiece and proceeded to light the lamp that hung from the ceiling in the middle of the room. As she reached up, her figure displayed itself just rounding with maternity.

'Oh, mother—!' exlaimed the girl.

'What?' said the woman, suspended in the act of putting the lamp glass over the flame. The copper reflector shone handsomely on her, as she stood with uplifted arm, turning to face her daughter.

'You've got a flower in your apron!' said the child, in a little rapture at this unusual event.

'Goodness me!' exclaimed the woman, relieved. 'One would think the house was afire.' She replaced the glass and waited a moment before turning up the wick. A pale shadow was seen floating vaguely on the floor.

'Let me smell!' said the child, still rapturously, coming forward and putting her face to her mother's waist.

'Go along, silly!' said the mother, turning up the lamp. The light revealed their suspense so that the woman felt it almost unbearable. Annie was still bending at her waist. Irritably, the mother took the flowers out from her apron-band.

'Oh, mother—don't take them out!' Annie cried, catching her hand and trying to replace the sprig.

'Such nonsense!' said the mother, turning away. The child put the pale chrysanthemums to her lips, murmuring:

'Don't they smell beautiful!'

Her mother gave a short laugh.

'No,' she said, 'not to me. It was chrysanthemums when I married him, and chrysanthemums when you were born, and the first time they ever brought him home drunk, he'd got brown chrysanthemums in his buttonhole.'

She looked at the children. Their eyes and their parted lips were wondering. The mother sat rocking in silence for some time. Then she looked at the clock.

'Twenty minutes to six!' In a tone of fine bitter carelessness she continued: 'Eh, he'll not come now till they bring him. There he'll stick! But he needn't come rolling in here in his pit-dirt, for *I* won't wash him. He can lie on the floor—Eh, what a fool I've been, what a fool! And this is what I came here for, to this dirty hole, rats and all, for him to slink past his very door. Twice last week—he's begun now—'

She silenced herself, and rose to clear the table.

While for an hour or more the children played, subduedly intent, fertile of imagination, united in fear of the mother's wrath, and in dread of their father's homecoming, Mrs Bates sat in her rocking-chair making a 'singlet' of thick cream-coloured flannel, which gave a dull wounded sound as she tore off the grey edge. She worked at her sewing with energy, listening to the children, and her anger wearied itself, lay down to rest, opening its eyes from time to time and steadily watching, its ears raised to listen. Sometimes even her anger quailed and shrank, and the mother suspended her sewing, tracing the footsteps that thudded along the sleepers outside; she would lift her head sharply to bid the children 'hush', but she recovered herself in time, and the footsteps went past the gate, and the children were not flung out of their play-world.

But at last Annie sighed, and gave in. She glanced at her waggon of slippers, and loathed the game. She turned plaintively to her mother.

'Mother!'—but she was inarticulate.

John crept out like a frog from under the sofa. His mother glanced up.

'Yes,' she said, 'just look at those shirt-sleeves!'

The boy held them out to survey them, saying nothing. Then somebody called in a hoarse voice away down the line, and suspense bristled in the room, till two people had gone by outside, talking.

'It is time for bed,' said the mother.

'My father hasn't come,' wailed Annie plaintively. But her mother was primed with courage.

'Never mind. They'll bring him when he does come—like a log.' She meant there would be no scene. 'And he may sleep on the floor till he wakes himself. I know he'll not go to work tomorrow after this!'

The children had their hands and faces wiped with a flannel. They were very quiet. When they had put on their nightdresses, they said their prayers, the boy mumbling. The mother looked down at them, at the brown silken bush of intertwining curls in the nape of the girl's neck, at the little black head of the lad, and her heart burst with anger at their father who caused all three such distress. The children hid their faces in her skirts for comfort.

When Mrs Bates came down, the room was strangely empty, with a tension of expectancy. She took up her sewing and stitched for some time without raising her head. Meantime her anger was tinged with fear.

II

The clock struck eight and she rose suddenly, dropping her sewing on her chair. She went to the stairfoot door, opened it, listening. Then she went out, locking the door behind her.

Something scuffled in the yard, and she started, though she knew it was only the rats with which the place was overrun. The night was very dark. In the great bay of railway lines, bulked with trucks, there was no trace of light, only away back she could see a few yellow lamps at the pit-top, and the red smear of the burning pit-bank on the night. She hurried along the edge of the track, then, crossing the converging lines, came to the stile by the white gates, whence she emerged on the road. Then the fear which had led her shrank. People were walking up to New Brinsley; she saw the lights in the houses; twenty yards further on were the broad windows of the 'Prince of Wales', very warm and bright, and the loud voices of men could be heard distinctly. What a fool she had been to imagine that anything had happened to him! He was merely drinking over there at the 'Prince of Wales'. She faltered. She had never yet been to fetch him, and she never would go. So she continued her walk towards the long straggling line of houses, standing blank on the highway. She entered a passage between the dwellings.

'Mr Rigley?–Yes! Did you want him? No, he's not in at this minute.'

The raw-boned woman leaned forward from her dark scullery and peered at the other, upon whom fell a dim light through the blind of the kitchen window.

'Is it Mrs Bates?' she asked in a tone tinged with respect.

'Yes. I wondered if your Master was at home. Mine hasn't come yet.'

' 'Asn't 'e! Oh, Jack's been 'ome and 'ad 'is dinner an' gone out. E's just gone for 'alf an hour afore bedtime. Did you call at the "Prince of Wales"?'

'No—'

'No, you didn't like—! It's not very nice.' The other woman was indulgent. There was an awkward pause. 'Jack never said nothink about–about your Mester,' she said.

'No!–I expect he's stuck in there!'

Elizabeth Bates said this bitterly, and with recklessness. She knew that the woman across the yard was standing at her door listening, but she did not care. As she turned:

'Stop a minute! I'll just go an' ask Jack if e' knows anythink,' said Mrs Rigley.

'Oh, no–I wouldn't like to put—!'

'Yes, I will, if you'll just step inside an' see as th' childer doesn't come downstairs and set theirselves afire.'

Elizabeth Bates, murmuring a remonstrance, stepped inside. The other woman apologised for the state of the room.

The kitchen needed apology. There were little frocks and trousers and childish undergarments on the squab and on the floor, and a litter of play-things everywhere. On the black American cloth of the table were pieces of bread and cake, crusts, slops, and a teapot with cold tea.

'Eh, ours is just as bad,' said Elizabeth Bates, looking at the woman, not at the house. Mrs Rigley put a shawl over her head and hurried out, saying:

'I shanna be a minute.'

The other sat, noting with faint disapproval the general untidiness of the room. Then she fell to counting the shoes of various sizes scattered over the floor. There were twelve. She sighed and said to herself, 'No wonder!'–glancing at the litter. There came the scratching of two pairs of feet on the yard, and the Rigleys entered. Elizabeth Bates rose. Rigley was a big man, with very large bones. His head looked particularly bony. Across his temple was a blue scar, caused by a wound got in the pit, a wound in which the coal-dust remained blue like tattooing.

' 'Asna 'e come whoam yit?' asked the man, without any form of greeting, but with deference and sympathy. 'I couldna say wheer he is–'e's non ower theer!'–he jerked his head to signify the 'Prince of Wales'.

' 'E's 'appen gone up to th' "Yew",' said Mrs Rigley.

There was another pause. Rigley had evidently something to get off his mind:

'Ah left 'im finishin' a stint,' he began. 'Loose–all 'ad bin gone about ten minutes when we com'n away, an' I shouted, "Are ter comin', Walt?" an' 'e said, "Go on. Ah shanna be but a 'ef a minnit," so we com'n ter th' bottom, me an' Bowers, thinkin' as 'e wor just behint, an' 'ud come up i' th' next bantle—'

He stood perplexed, as if answering a charge of deserting his mate. Elizabeth Bates, now again certain of disaster, hastened to reassure him:

'I expect 'e's gone up to th' "Yew Tree", as you say. It's not the first time. I've fretted myself into a fever before now. He'll come home when they carry him.'

'Ay, isn't it too bad!' deplored the other woman.

'I'll just step up to Dick's an' see if 'e *is* theer,' offered the man, afraid of appearing alarmed, afraid of taking liberties.

'Oh, I wouldn't think of bothering you that far,' said Elizabeth Bates, with emphasis, but he knew she was glad of his offer.

As they stumbled up the entry, Elizabeth Bates heard Rigley's wife run across the yard and open her neighbour's door. At this, suddenly all the blood in her body seemed to switch away from her heart.

'Mind!' warned Rigley. 'Ah've said many a time as Ah'd fill up them ruts in this entry, sumb'dy 'll be breakin' their legs yit.'

She recovered herself and walked quickly along with the miner.

'I don't like leaving the children in bed, and nobody in the house,' she said.

'No, you dunna!' he replied courteously. They were soon at the gate of the cottage.

'Well, I shanna be many minnits. Dunna you be frettin' now, 'e'll be all right,' said the butty.

'Thank you very much, Mr Rigley,' she replied.

'You're welcome!' he stammered, moving away. 'I shanna be many minnits.'

The house was quiet. Elizabeth Bates took off her hat and shawl, and rolled back the rug. When she had finished, she sat down. It was a few minutes past nine. She was startled by the rapid chuff of the winding-engine at the pit, and the sharp whirr of the brakes on the rope as it descended. Again she felt the painful sweep of her blood, and she put her hand to her side, saying aloud, 'Good gracious!—it's only the nine o'clock deputy going down,' rebuking herself.

She sat still, listening. Half an hour of this, and she was wearied out.

'What am I working myself up like this for?' she said pitiably to herself, 'I s'll only be doing myself some damage.'

She took out her sewing again.

At a quarter to ten there were footsteps. One

person! She watched for the door to open. It was an elderly woman, in a black bonnet and a black woollen shawl–his mother. She was about sixty years old, pale, with blue eyes, and her face all wrinkled and lamentable. She shut the door and turned to her daughter-in-law peevishly.

'Eh, Lizzie, whatever shall we do, whatever shall we do!' she cried.

Elizabeth drew back a little, sharply.

'What is it, mother?' she said.

The elder woman seated herself on the sofa.

'I don't know, child, I can't tell you!'–she shook her head slowly. Elizabeth sat watching her, anxious and vexed.

'I don't know,' replied the grandmother, sighing very deeply. 'There's no end to my troubles, there isn't. The things I've gone through, I'm sure it's enough—!' She wept without wiping her eyes, the tears running.

'But, mother,' interrupted Elizabeth, 'what do you mean? What is it?'

The grandmother slowly wiped her eyes. The fountains of her tears were stopped by Elizabeth's directness. She wiped her eyes slowly.

'Poor child! Eh, you poor thing!' she moaned. 'I don't know what we're going to do, I don't–and you as you are–it's a thing, it is indeed!'

Elizabeth waited.

'Is he dead?' she asked, and at the words her heart swung violently, though she felt a slight flush of shame at the ultimate extravagance of the question. Her words sufficiently frightened the old lady, almost brought her to herself.

'Don't say so, Elizabeth! We'll hope it's not as bad as that; no, may the Lord spare us that, Elizabeth. Jack Rigley came just as I was sittin' down to a glass afore going to bed, an' 'e said, " 'Appen you'll go down th' line, Mrs Bates. Walt's had an accident. 'Appen you'll go an' sit wi' 'er till we can get him home." I hadn't time to

ask him a word afore he was gone. An' I put my bonnet
on an' come straight down, Lizzie. I thought to myself,
"Eh, that poor blessed child, if anybody should come an'
tell her of a sudden, there's no knowin' what'll 'appen to
'er." You mustn't let it upset you, Lizzie–or you know
what to expect. How long is it, six months–or is it five,
Lizzie? Ay!'–the old woman shook her head–'time slips
on, it slips on! Ay!'

Elizabeth's thoughts were busy elsewhere. If he was
killed–would she be able to manage on the little pension
and what she could earn?–she counted up rapidly. If he
was hurt–they wouldn't take him to the hospital–how
tiresome he would be to nurse!–but perhaps she'd be
able to get him away from the drink and his hateful ways.
She would–while he was ill. The tears offered to come to
her eyes at the picture. But what sentimental luxury was
this she was beginning?–She turned to consider the
children. At any rate she was absolutely necessary for
them. They were her business.

'Ay!' repeated the old woman, 'it seems but a week
or two since he brought me his first wages. Ay–he was a
good lad, Elizabeth, he was, in his way. I don't know
why he got to be such a trouble, I don't. He was a happy
lad at home, only full of spirits. But there's no mistake
he's been a handful of trouble, he has! I hope the Lord'll
spare him to mend his ways. I hope so, I hope so. You've
had a sight o' trouble with him, Elizabeth, you have
indeed. But he was a jolly enough lad wi' me, he was, I
can assure you. I don't know how it is . . .'

The old woman continued to muse aloud, a
monotonous irritating sound, while Elizabeth thought
concentratedly, startled once, when she heard the
winding-engine chuff quickly, and the brakes skirr with a
shriek. Then she heard the engine more slowly, and the
brakes made no sound. The old woman did not notice.
Elizabeth waited in suspense. The mother-in-law talked,
with lapses into silence.

'But he wasn't your son, Lizzie, an' it makes a

difference. Whatever he was, I remember him when he was little, an' I learned to understand him and to make allowances. You've got to make allowances for them—'

It was half-past ten, and the old woman was saying: 'But it's trouble from beginning to end; you're never too old for trouble, never too old for that—' when the gate banged back, and there were heavy feet on the steps.

'I'll go, Lizzie, let me go,' cried the old woman, rising. But Elizabeth was at the door. It was a man in pit-clothes.

'They're bringin' 'im, Missis,' he said. Elizabeth's heart halted a moment. Then it surged on again, almost suffocating her.

'Is he—is it bad?' she asked.

The man turned away, looking at the darkness:

'The doctor says 'e'd been dead hours. 'E saw 'im i' th' lamp-cabin.'

The old woman, who stood just behind Elizabeth, dropped into a chair, and folded her hands, crying: 'Oh, my boy, my boy!'

'Hush!' said Elizabeth, with a sharp twitch of a frown. 'Be still, mother, don't waken th' children: I wouldn't have them down for anything!'

The old woman moaned softly, rocking herself. The man was drawing away. Elizabeth took a step forward.

'How was it?' she asked.

'Well, I couldn't say for sure,' the man replied, very ill at ease. ''E wor finishin' a stint an' th' butties 'ad gone, an' a lot o' stuff come down atop 'n 'im.'

'And crushed him?' cried the widow, with a shudder.

'No,' said the man, 'it fell at th' back of 'im. 'E wor under th' face, an' it niver touched 'im. It shut 'im in. It seems 'e wor smothered.'

Elizabeth shrank back. She heard the old woman behind her cry:

'What?—what did 'e say it was?'

The man replied, more loudly: ' 'E wor smothered!'

Then the old woman wailed aloud, and this relieved Elizabeth.

'Oh, mother,' she said, putting her hand on the old woman, 'don't waken th' children, don't waken th' children.'

She wept a little, unknowing, while the old mother rocked herself and moaned. Elizabeth remembered that they were bringing him home, and she must be ready. 'They'll lay him in the parlour,' she said to herself, standing a moment pale and perplexed.

Then she lighted a candle and went into the tiny room. The air was cold and damp, but she could not make a fire, there was no fireplace. She set down the candle and looked round. The candle-light glittered on the lustre-glasses, on the two vases that held some of the pink chrysanthemums, and on the dark mahogany. There was a cold, deathly smell of chrysanthemums in the room. Elizabeth stood looking at the flowers. She turned away, and calculated whether there would be room to lay him on the floor, between the couch and the chiffonier. She pushed the chairs aside. There would be room to lay him down and to step round him. Then she fetched the old red tablecloth, and another old cloth, spreading them down to save her bit of carpet. She shivered on leaving the parlour; so, from the dresser-drawer she took a clean shirt and put it at the fire to air. All the time her mother-in-law was rocking herself in the chair and moaning.

'You'll have to move from there, mother,' said Elizabeth. 'They'll be bringing him in. Come in the rocker.'

The old mother rose mechanically, and seated herself by the fire, continuing to lament. Elizabeth went into the pantry for another candle, and there, in the little penthouse under the naked tiles, she heard them coming. She stood still in the pantry doorway, listening. She heard them pass the end of the house, and come awkwardly down the three steps, a jumble of shuffling footsteps and muttering voices. The old woman was silent. The men were in the yard.

Then Elizabeth heard Matthews, the manager of the pit, say: 'You go in first, Jim. Mind!'

The door came open, and the two women saw a collier backing into the room, holding one end of a stretcher, on which they could see the nailed pit-boots of the dead man. The two carriers halted, the man at the head stooping to the lintel of the door.

'Wheer will you have him?' asked the manager, a short, white-bearded man.

Elizabeth roused herself and came from the pantry carrying the unlighted candle.

'In the parlour,' she said.

'In there, Jim!' pointed the manager, and the carriers backed round into the tiny room. The coat with which they had covered the body fell off as they awkwardly turned through the two doorways, and the women saw their man, naked to the waist, lying stripped for work. The old woman began to moan in a low voice of horror.

'Lay th' stretcher at th' side,' snapped the manager, 'an' put 'im on th' cloths. Mind now, mind! Look you now—!'

One of the men had knocked off a vase of chrysanthemums. He stared awkwardly, then they set down the stretcher. Elizabeth did not look at her husband. As soon as she could get in the room, she went and picked up the broken vase and the flowers.

'Wait a minute!' she said.

The three men waited in silence while she mopped up the water with a duster.

'Eh, what a job, what a job, to be sure!' the manager was saying, rubbing his brow with trouble and perplexity. 'Never knew such a thing in my life, never! He'd no business to ha' been left. I never knew such a thing in my life! Fell over him clean as a whistle, an' shut him in. Not four foot of space, there wasn't—yet it scarce bruised him.'

He looked down at the dead man, lying prone, half naked, all grimed with coal-dust.

' " 'Sphyxiated", the doctor said. It *is* the most terrible job I've ever known. Seems as if it was done o' purpose. Clean over him, an' shut 'im in, like a mouse-trap'—he made a sharp, descending gesture with his hand.

The colliers standing by jerked aside their heads in hopeless comment.

The horror of the thing bristled upon them all.

Then they heard the girl's voice upstairs calling shrilly: 'Mother, mother—who is it? Mother, who is it?'

Elizabeth hurried to the foot of the stairs and opened the door:

'Go to sleep!' she commanded sharply. 'What are you shouting about? Go to sleep at once—there's nothing—'

Then she began to mount the stairs. They could hear her on the boards, and on the plaster floor of the little bedroom. They could hear her distinctly:

'What's the matter now?—what's the matter with you, silly thing?'—her voice was much agitated, with an unreal gentleness.

'I thought it was some men come,' said the plaintive voice of the child. 'Has he come?'

'Yes, they've brought him. There's nothing to make a fuss about. Go to sleep now, like a good child.'

They could hear her voice in the bedroom, they waited whilst she covered the children under the bedclothes.

'Is he drunk?' asked the girl, timidly, faintly.

'No! No—he's not! He—he's asleep.'

'Is he asleep downstairs?'

'Yes—and don't make a noise.'

There was silence for a moment, then the men heard the frightened child again:

'What's that noise?'

'It's nothing, I tell you, what are you bothering for?'

The noise was the grandmother moaning. She was oblivious of everything, sitting on her chair rocking and moaning. The manager put his hand on her arm and bade her 'Sh–sh!!'

The old woman opened her eyes and looked at him. She was shocked by this interruption, and seemed to wonder.

'What time is it?'–the plaintive thin voice of the child, sinking back unhappily into sleep, asked this last question.

'Ten o'clock,' answered the mother more softly. Then she must have bent down and kissed the children.

Matthews beckoned to the men to come away. They put on their caps and took up the stretcher. Stepping over the body, they tiptoed out of the house. None of them spoke till they were far from the wakeful children.

When Elizabeth came down she found her mother alone on the parlour floor, leaning over the dead man, the tears dropping on him.

'We must lay him out,' the wife said. She put on the kettle, then returning knelt at the feet, and began to unfasten the knotted leather laces. The room was clammy and dim with only one candle, so that she had to bend her face almost to the floor. At last she got off the heavy boots and put them away.

'You must help me now,' she whispered to the old woman. Together they stripped the man.

When they arose, saw him lying in the naïve dignity of death, the women stood arrested in fear and respect. For a few moments they remained still, looking down, the old mother whimpering. Elizabeth felt counter-manded. She saw him, how utterly inviolable he lay in himself. She had nothing to do with him. She could not accept it. Stooping, she laid her hand on him, in claim. He was still warm, for the mine was hot where he had died. His mother had his face between her hands, and was murmuring incoherently. The old tears fell in succession as drops from wet leaves; the mother was not weeping, merely her tears flowed. Elizabeth embraced the body of her husband, with cheek and lips. She seemed to be listening, inquiring, trying to get some connection. But she could not. She was driven away. He was impregnable.

She rose, went into the kitchen, where she poured warm water into a bowl, brought soap and flannel and a soft towel.

'I must wash him,' she said.

Then the old mother rose stiffly, and watched Elizabeth as she carefully washed his face, carefully brushing the big blonde moustache from his mouth with the flannel. She was afraid with a bottomless fear, so she ministered to him. The old woman, jealous, said:

'Let me wipe him!'–and she kneeled on the other side drying slowly as Elizabeth washed, her big black bonnet sometimes brushing the dark head of her daughter. They worked thus in silence for a long time. They never forgot it was death, and the touch of the man's dead body gave them strange emotions, different in each of the women; a great dread possessed them both, the mother felt the lie was given to her womb, she was denied; the wife felt the utter isolation of the human soul, the child within her was a weight apart from her.

At last it was finished. He was a man of handsome body, and his face showed no traces of drink. He was blonde, full-fleshed, with fine limbs. But he was dead.

'Bless him,' whispered his mother, looking always at his face, and speaking out of sheer terror. 'Dear lad–bless him!' She spoke in a faint, sibilant ecstasy of fear and mother love.

Elizabeth sank down again to the floor, and put her face against his neck, and trembled and shuddered. But she had to draw away again. He was dead, and her living flesh had no place against his. A great dread and weariness held her: she was so unavailing. Her life was gone like this.

'White as milk he is, clear as a twelve-month baby, bless him, the darling!' the old mother murmured to herself. 'Not a mark on him, clear and clean and white, beautiful as ever a child was made,' she murmured with pride. Elizabeth kept her face hidden.

'He went peaceful, Lizzie–peaceful as sleep. Isn't he beautiful, the lamb? Ay–he must ha' made his peace, Lizzie. 'Appen he made it all right, Lizzie, shut in there. He'd have time. He wouldn't look like this if he hadn't made his peace. The lamb, the dear lamb. Eh, but he had a hearty laugh. I loved to hear it. He had the heartiest laugh, Lizzie, as a lad—'

Elizabeth looked up. The man's mouth was fallen back, slightly open under the cover of the moustache. The eyes, half shut, did not show glazed in the obscurity. Life with its smoky burning gone from him, had left him apart and utterly alien to her. And she knew what a stranger he was to her. In her womb was ice of fear, because of this separate stranger with whom she had been living as one flesh. Was this what it all meant–utter, intact separateness, obscured by heat of living? In dread she turned her face away. The fact was too deadly. There had been nothing between them, and yet they had come together, exchanging their nakedness repeatedly. Each time he had taken her, they had been two isolated beings, far apart as now. He was no more responsible than she. The child was like ice in her womb. For as she looked at the dead man, her mind, cold and detached, said clearly: 'Who am I? What have I been doing? I have been fighting a husband who did not exist. *He* existed all the time. What wrong have I done? What was that I have been living with? There lies the reality, this man.'–And her soul died in her for fear: she knew she had never seen him, he had never seen her, they had met in the dark and had fought in the dark, not knowing whom they met nor whom they fought. And now she saw, and turned silent in seeing. For she had been wrong. She had said he was something he was not: she had felt familiar with him.

Whereas he was apart all the while, living as she never lived, feeling as she never felt.

In fear and shame she looked at his naked body, that she had known falsely. And he was the father of her children. Her soul was torn from her body and stood apart. She looked at his naked body and was ashamed, as if she had denied it. After all, it was itself. It seemed awful to her. She looked at his face, and she turned her own face to the wall. For his look was other than hers, his way was not her way. She had denied him what he was—she saw it now. She had refused him as himself.—And this had been her life, and his life.—She was grateful to death, which restored the truth. And she knew she was not dead.

And all the while her heart was bursting with grief and pity for him. What had he suffered? What stretch of horror for this helpless man! She was rigid with agony. She had not been able to help him. He had been cruelly injured, this naked man, this other being, and she could make no reparation. There were the children—but the children belonged to life. This dead man had nothing to do with them. He and she were only channels through which life had flowed to issue in the children. She was a mother—but how awful she knew it now to have been a wife. And he, dead now, how awful he must have felt it to be a husband. She felt that in the next world he would be a stranger to her. If they met there, in the beyond, they would only be ashamed of what had been before. The children had come, for some mysterious reason, out of both of them. But the children did not unite them. Now he was dead, she knew how eternally he was apart from her, how eternally he had nothing more to do with her. She saw this episode of her life closed. They had denied each other in life. Now he had withdrawn. An anguish came over her. It was finished then: it had become hopeless between them long before he died. Yet he had been her husband. But how little!

'Have you got his shirt, 'Lizabeth?'

Elizabeth turned without answering, though she strove to weep and behave as her mother-in-law expected. But she could not, she was silenced. She went into the kitchen and returned with the garment.

'It is aired,' she said, grasping the cotton shirt here and there to try. She was almost ashamed to handle him: what right had she or anyone to lay hands on him; but her touch was humble on his body. It was hard work to clothe him. He was so heavy and inert. A terrible dread gripped her all the while: that he could be so heavy and utterly inert, unresponsive, apart. The horror of the distance between them was almost too much for her—it was so infinite a gap she must look across.

At last it was finished. They covered him with a sheet and left him lying, with his face bound. And she fastened the door of the little parlour, lest the children should see what was lying there. Then, with peace sunk heavy on her heart, she went about making tidy the kitchen. She knew she submitted to life, which was her immediate master. But from death, her ultimate master, she winced with fear and shame.

Daughters of the Vicar

Early version called 'Two Marriages' dates from
July–October 1911. Revised in July 1913 to create
'Daughters of the Vicar'. Further revision in July
and October 1914 for *The Prussian Officer* collection.

I

Mr Lindley was first vicar of Aldecross. The cottages
of this tiny hamlet had nestled in peace since their beginning, and the country folk had crossed the lanes and
farm-lands, two or three miles, to the parish church at
Greymeed, on the bright Sunday mornings.

But when the pits were sunk, blank rows of dwellings started up beside the high roads, and a new population, skimmed from the floating scum of workmen, was
filled in, the cottages and the country people almost
obliterated.

To suit the convenience of these new collier-
inhabitants, a church must be built at Aldecross. There
was not too much money. And so the little building
crouched like a humped stone-and-mortar mouse, with
two little turrets at the west corners for ears, in the fields
near the cottages and the apple trees, as far as possible
from the dwellings down the high road. It had an
uncertain, timid look about it. And so they planted big-
leaved ivy, to hide its shrinking newness. So that now the
little church stands buried in its greenery, stranded and
sleeping among the fields, while the brick houses elbow

nearer and nearer, threatening to crush it down. It is already obsolete.

The Reverend Ernest Lindley, aged twenty-seven, and newly married, came from his curacy in Suffolk to take charge of his church. He was just an ordinary young man, who had been to Cambridge and taken orders. His wife was a self-assured young woman, daughter of a Cambridgeshire rector. Her father had spent the whole of his thousand a year, so that Mrs Lindley had nothing of her own. Thus the young married people came to Aldecross to live on a stipend of about a hundred and twenty pounds, and to keep up a superior position.

They were not very well received by the new, raw, disaffected population of colliers. Being accustomed to farm labourers, Mr Lindley had considered himself as belonging indisputably to the upper or ordering classes. He had to be humble to the county families, but still, he was of their kind, whilst the common people were something different. He had no doubts of himself.

He found, however, that the collier population refused to accept this arrangement. They had no use for him in their lives, and they told him so, callously. The women merely said, 'they were throng,' or else, 'Oh, it's no good you coming here we're Chapel'. The men were quite good-humoured so long as he did not touch them too nigh, they were cheerfully contemptuous of him, with a preconceived contempt he was powerless against.

At last, passing from indignation to silent resentment, even, if he dared have acknowledged it, to conscious hatred of the majority of his flock, and unconscious hatred of himself, he confined his activities to a narrow round of cottages, and he had to submit. He had no particular character, having always depended on his position in society to give him position among men. Now he was so poor, he had no social standing even among the common vulgar tradespeople of the district, and he had not the nature nor the wish to make his society agreeable to them, nor the strength to impose himself where he would have liked to be recognised. He dragged on, pale and miserable and neutral.

At first his wife raged with mortification. She took on airs and used a high hand. But her income was too small, the wrestling with tradesmen's bills was too pitiful, she only met with general, callous ridicule when she tried to be impressive.

Wounded to the quick of her pride, she found herself isolated in an indifferent, callous population. She raged indoors and out. But soon she learned that she must pay too heavily for her outdoor rages, and then she only raged within the walls of the rectory. There her feeling was so strong, that she frightened herself. She saw herself hating her husband, and she knew that, unless she were careful she would smash her form of life and bring catastrophe upon him and upon herself. So in very fear, she went quiet. She hid, bitter and beaten by fear, behind the only shelter she had in the world, her gloomy, poor parsonage.

Children were born one every year; almost mechanically, she continued to perform her maternal duty, which was forced upon her. Gradually, broken by the suppressing of her violent anger and misery and disgust, she became an invalid and took to her couch.

The children grew up healthily, but unwarmed and rather rigid. Their father and mother educated them at home, made them very proud and very genteel, put them definitely and cruelly in the upper classes, apart from the vulgar around them. So they lived quite isolated. They were good-looking, and had that curiously clean, semi-transparent look of the genteel, isolated poor.

Gradually Mr and Mrs Lindley lost all hold on life, and spent their hours, weeks and years merely haggling to make ends meet, and bitterly repressing and pruning their children into gentility, urging them to ambition, weighting them with duty. On Sunday morning the whole family, except the mother, went down the lane to church, the long-legged girls in skimpy frocks, the boys in black coats and long, grey, unfitting trousers. They passed by their father's parishioners with mute, clear faces, childish mouths closed in pride that was like a doom to them, and childish eyes already unseeing. Miss Mary, the eldest, was the leader. She was a long, slim thing with a fine profile and a proud, pure look of submission to a high fate. Miss Louisa, the second, was short and plump and obstinate-looking. She had more enemies than ideals. She looked after the lesser children, Miss Mary after the elder. The collier children watched this pale, distinguished procession of the vicar's family pass mutely by, and they were impressed by the air of gentility and distance, they made mock of the trousers of the small sons, they felt inferior in themselves, and hate stirred their hearts.

In her time, Miss Mary received as governess a few little daughters of tradesmen; Miss Louisa managed the house and went among her father's church-goers, giving lessons on the piano to the colliers' daughters at thirteen shillings for twenty-six lessons.

II

One winter morning, when his daughter Mary was about twenty years old, Mr Lindley, a thin, unobtrusive figure in his black overcoat and his wideawake, went down into Aldecross with a packet of white papers under his arm. He was delivering the parish almanacs.

A rather pale, neutral man of middle age, he waited while the train thumped over the level-crossing, going up to the pit which rattled busily just along the line. A wooden-legged man hobbled to open the gate, Mr Lindley passed on. Just at his left hand, below the road and the railway, was the red roof of a cottage, showing through the bare twigs of apple trees. Mr Lindley passed round the low wall, and descended the worn steps that led from the highway down to the cottage which crouched darkly and quietly away below the rumble of passing trains and the clank of coal-carts, in a quiet little under-world of its own. Snowdrops with tight-shut buds were hanging very still under the bare currant bushes.

The clergyman was just going to knock when he heard a clinking noise, and turning saw through the open door of a black shed just behind him an elderly woman in a black lace cap stooping among reddish big cans, pouring a very bright liquid into a tundish. There was a smell of paraffin. The woman put down her can, took the tundish and laid it on a shelf, then rose with a tin bottle. Her eyes met those of the clergyman.

'Oh, is it you, Mr Lin'ley!' she said, in a complaining tone. 'Go in.'

The minister entered the house. In the hot kitchen sat a big, elderly man with a great grey beard, taking snuff. He grunted in a deep, muttering voice, telling the minister to sit down, and then took no more notice of him, but stared vacantly into the fire. Mr Lindley waited.

The woman came in, the ribbons of her black lace cap, or bonnet, hanging on her shawl. She was of medium stature, everything about her was tidy. She went up a step out of the kitchen, carrying the paraffin tin. Feet were heard entering the room up the step. It was a little haberdashery shop, with parcels on the shelves of the walls, a big, old-fashioned sewing machine with tailor's work lying round it, in the open space. The woman went behind the counter, gave the child who had entered the paraffin bottle, and took from her a jug.

'My mother says shall yer put it down,' said the child, and she was gone. The woman wrote in a book, then came into the kitchen with her jug. The husband, a very large man, rose and brought more coal to the already hot fire. He moved slowly and sluggishly. Already he was going dead; being a tailor, his large form had become an encumbrance to him. In his youth he had been a great dancer and boxer. Now he was taciturn, and inert. The minister had nothing to say, so he sought for his phrases. But John Durant took no notice, existing silent and dull.

Mrs Durant spread the cloth. Her husband poured himself beer into a mug, and began to smoke and drink.

'Shall you have some?' he growled through his beard at the clergyman, looking slowly from the man to the jug, capable of this one idea.

'No, thank you,' replied Mr Lindley, though he would have liked some beer. He must set the example in a drinking parish.

'We need a drop to keep us going,' said Mrs Durant.

She had rather a complaining manner. The clergyman sat on uncomfortably while she laid the table for the half-past ten lunch. Her husband drew up to eat. She remained in her little round arm-chair by the fire.

She was a woman who would have liked to be easy in her life, but to whose lot had fallen a rough and turbulent family, and a slothful husband who did not care what became of himself or anybody. So, her rather good-looking square face was peevish, she had that air of having been compelled all her life to serve unwillingly, and to control where she did not want to control. There was about her, too, that masterful *aplomb* of a woman who has brought up and ruled her sons: but even them she had ruled unwillingly. She had enjoyed managing her little haberdashery shop, riding in the carrier's cart to Nottingham, going through the big warehouses to buy her goods. But the fret of managing her sons she did not like. Only she loved her youngest boy, because he was her last, and she saw herself free.

This was one of the houses the clergyman visited occasionally. Mrs Durant, as part of her regulation, had brought up all her sons in the Church. Not that she had any religion. Only, it was what she was used to. Mr Durant was without religion. He read the fervently evangelical 'Life of John Wesley' with a curious pleasure, getting from it a satisfaction as from the warmth of the fire, or a glass of brandy. But he cared no more about John Wesley, in fact, than about John Milton, of whom he had never heard.

Mrs Durant took her chair to the table.

'I don't feel like eating,' she sighed.

'Why—aren't you well?' asked the clergyman, patronizing.

'It isn't that,' she sighed. She sat with shut, straight mouth. 'I don't know what's going to become of us.'

But the clergyman had ground himself down so long, that he could not easily sympathize.

'Have you any trouble?' he asked.

'Ay, have I any trouble!' cried the elderly woman. 'I shall end my days in the workhouse.'

The minister waited unmoved. What could she know of poverty, in her little house of plenty!

'I hope not,' he said.

'And the one lad as I wanted to keep by me—' she lamented.

The minister listened without sympathy, quite neutral.

'And the lad as would have been a support to my old age! What is going to become of us?' she said.

The clergyman, justly, did not believe in the cry of poverty, but wondered what had become of the son.

'Has anything happened to Alfred?' he asked.

'We've got word he's gone for a Queen's sailor,' she said sharply.

'He has joined the Navy!' exclaimed Mr Lindley. 'I think he could scarcely have done better—to serve his Queen and country on the sea. . . .'

'He is wanted to serve *me*,' she cried. 'And I wanted my lad at home.'

Alfred was her baby, her last, whom she had allowed herself the luxury of spoiling.

'You will miss him,' said Mr Lindley, 'that is certain. But this is no regrettable step for him to have taken—on the contrary.'

'That's easy for you to say, Mr Lindley,' she replied tartly. 'Do you think I want my lad climbing ropes at another man's bidding, like a monkey—?'

'There is no *dishonour*, surely, in serving in the Navy?'

'Dishonour this dishonour that,' cried the angry old woman. 'He goes and makes a slave of himself, and he'll rue it.'

Her angry, scornful impatience nettled the clergyman, and silenced him for some moments.

'I do not see', he retorted at last, white at the gills and inadequate, 'that the Queen's service is any more to be called slavery than working in a mine.'

'At home he was at home, and his own master. *I* know he'll find a difference.'

'It may be the making of him,' said the clergyman. 'It will take him away from bad companionship and drink.'

Some of the Durants' sons were notorious drinkers, and Alfred was not quite steady.

'And why indeed shouldn't he have his glass?' cried the mother. 'He picks no man's pocket to pay for it!'

The clergyman stiffened at what he thought was an allusion to his own profession, and his unpaid bills.

'With all due consideration, I am glad to hear he has joined the Navy,' he said.

'Me with my old age coming on, and his father working very little! I'd thank you to be glad about something else besides that, Mr Lindley.'

The woman began to cry. Her husband, quite impassive, finished his lunch of meat-pie, and drank some beer. Then he turned to the fire, as if there were no one in the room but himself.

'I shall respect all men who serve God and their country on the sea, Mrs Durant,' said the clergyman stubbornly.

'That is very well, when they're not your sons who are doing the dirty work.—It makes a difference,' she replied tartly.

'I should be proud if one of my sons were to enter

the Navy.'

'Ay–well–we're not all of us made alike—.'

The minister rose. He put down a large folded paper.

'I've brought the almanac,' he said.

Mrs Durant unfolded it.

'I do like a bit of colour in things,' she said, petulantly.

The clergyman did not reply.

'There's that envelope for the organist's fund–' said the old woman, and rising, she took the thing from the mantelpiece, went into the shop, and returned sealing it up.

'Which is all I can afford,' she said.

Mr Lindley took his departure, in his pocket the envelope containing Mrs Durant's offering for Miss Louisa's services. He went from door to door delivering the almanacs, a dull routine. Jaded with the monotony of the business, and with the repeated effort of greeting half-known people, he felt barren and rather irritable. At last he returned home.

In the dining-room was a small fire. Mrs Lindley, growing very stout, lay on her couch. The vicar carved the cold mutton; Miss Louisa, short and plump and rather flushed, came in from the kitchen; Miss Mary, dark, with a beautiful white brow and grey eyes, served the vegetables; the children chattered a little, but not exuberantly. The very air seemed starved.

'I went to the Durants,' said the vicar, as he served out small portions of mutton; 'it appears Alfred has run away to join the Navy.'

'Do him good,' came the rough voice of the invalid.

Miss Louisa, attending to the youngest child, looked up in protest.

'Why has he done that?' asked Mary's low, musical voice.

'He wanted some excitement, I suppose,' said the vicar. 'Shall we say grace?'

The children were arranged, all bent their heads, grace was pronounced, at the last word every face was being raised to go on with the interesting subject.

'He's just done the right thing, for once,' came the rather deep voice of the mother; 'save him from becoming a drunken sot, like the rest of them.'

'They're not *all* drunken, mama,' said Miss Louisa, stubbornly.

'It's no fault of their upbringing if they're not. Walter Durant is a standing disgrace.'

'As I told Mrs Durant,' said the vicar, eating hungrily, 'it is the best thing he could have done. It will take him away from temptation during the most dangerous years of his life–how old is he–nineteen?'

'Twenty,' said Miss Louisa.

'Twenty!' repeated the vicar. 'It will give him wholesome discipline and set before him some sort of standard of duty and honour–nothing could have been better for him. But—'

'We shall miss him from the choir,' said Miss Louisa, as if taking opposite sides to her parents.

'That is as it may be,' said the vicar. 'I prefer to know he is safe in the Navy, than running the risk of getting into bad ways here.'

'Was he getting into bad ways?' asked the stubborn Miss Louisa.

'You know, Louisa, he wasn't quite what he used to be,' said Miss Mary gently and steadily. Miss Louisa shut her rather heavy jaw sulkily. She wanted to deny it, but she knew it was true.

For her he had been a laughing, warm lad, with something kindly and something rich about him. He had made her feel warm. It seemed the days would be colder since he had gone.

'Quite the best thing he could do,' said the mother with emphasis.

'I think so,' said the vicar. 'But his mother was almost abusive because I suggested it.'

He spoke in an injured tone.

'What does she care for her children's welfare?' said the invalid. 'Their wages is all her concern.'

'I suppose she wanted him at home with her,' said Miss Louisa.

'Yes, she did—at the expense of his learning to be a drunkard like the rest of them,' retorted her mother.

'George Durant doesn't drink,' defended her daughter.

'Because he got burned so badly when he was nineteen—in the pit—and that frightened him. The Navy is a better remedy than that, at least.'

'Certainly,' said the vicar. 'Certainly.'

And to this Miss Louisa agreed. Yet she could not but feel angry that he had gone away for so many years. She herself was only nineteen.

III

It happened when Miss Mary was twenty-three years old, that Mr Lindley was very ill. The family was exceedingly poor at the time, such a lot of money was needed, so little was forthcoming. Neither Miss Mary nor Miss Louisa had suitors. What chance had they? They met no eligible young men in Aldecross. And what they earned was a mere drop in a void. The girls' hearts were chilled and hardened with fear of this perpetual, cold penury, this narrow struggle, this horrible nothingness of their lives.

A clergyman had to be found for the church work. It so happened the son of an old friend of Mr Lindley's was waiting three months before taking up his duties. He would come and officiate, for nothing. The young clergyman was keenly expected. He was not more than twenty-seven, a Master of Arts of Oxford, had written his thesis on Roman Law. He came of an old Cambridgeshire family, had some private means, was going to take a church in Northamptonshire with a good stipend, and was not married. Mrs Lindley incurred new debts, and scarcely regretted her husband's illness.

But when Mr Massy came, there was a shock of disappointment in the house. They had expected a young man with a pipe and a deep voice, but with better manners than Sidney, the eldest of the Lindleys. There arrived instead a small, chétif man, scarcely larger than a boy of twelve, spectacled, timid in the extreme, without a word to utter at first; yet with a certain inhuman self-sureness.

'What a little abortion!' was Mrs Lindley's exclamation to herself on first seeing him, in his buttoned-up clerical coat. And for the first time for many days, she was profoundly thankful to God, that all her children were decent specimens.

He had not normal powers of perception. They soon saw that he lacked the full range of human feelings, but had rather a strong, philosophical mind, from which he lived. His body was almost unthinkable, in intellect he was something definite. The conversation at once took a balanced, abstract tone when he participated. There was no spontaneous exclamation, no violent assertion or expression of personal conviction, but all cold, reasonable assertion. This was very hard on Mrs Lindley. The little man would look at her, after one of her pronouncements, and then give, in his thin voice, his own calculated version, so that she felt as if she were tumbling into thin air through a hole in the flimsy floor on which their conversation stood. It was she who felt a fool. Soon she was reduced to a hardy silence.

Still, at the back of her mind, she remembered that he was an unattached gentleman, who would shortly have an income altogether of six or seven hundred a year. What did the man matter, if there were pecuniary ease! The man was a trifle thrown in. After twenty-two years her sentimentality was ground away, and only the millstone of poverty mattered to her. So she supported the little man as a representative of a decent income.

His most irritating habit was that of a sneering little
giggle, all on his own, which came when he perceived or
related some illogical absurdity on the part of another
person. It was the only form of humour he had. Stupidity
in thinking seemed to him exquisitely funny. But any
novel was unintelligibly meaningless and dull, and to an
Irish sort of humour he listened curiously, examining it
like mathematics, or else simply not hearing. In normal
human relationship he was not there. Quite unable to
take part in simple everyday talk, he padded silently
round the house, or sat in the dining-room looking
nervously from side to side, always apart in a cold,
rarefied little world of his own. Sometimes he made an
ironic remark, that did not seem humanly relevant, or he
gave his little laugh, like a sneer. He had to defend
himself and his own insufficiency. And he answered
questions grudgingly, with a yes or no, because he did
not see their import and was nervous. It seemed to Miss
Louisa he scarcely distinguished one person from
another, but that he liked to be near to her, or to Miss
Mary, for some sort of contact which stimulated him
unknown.

Apart from all this, he was the most admirable
workman. He was unremittingly shy, but perfect in his
sense of duty: as far as he could conceive Christianity, he
was a perfect Christian. Nothing that he realized he
could do for anyone did he leave undone, although he
was so incapable of coming into contact with another
being, that he could not proffer help. Now he attended
assiduously to the sick man, investigated all the affairs of
the parish or the church which Mr Lindley had in
control, straightened out accounts, made lists of the sick
and needy, padded round with help and to see what he
could do. He heard of Mrs Lindley's anxiety about her
sons, and began to investigate means of sending them to
Cambridge. His kindness almost frightened Miss Mary.
She honoured it so, and yet she shrank from it. For, in it
all Mr Massy seemed to have no sense of any person, any

human being whom he was helping: he only realized a kind of mathematical working out, solving of given situations, a calculated well-doing. And it was as if he had accepted the Christian tenets as axioms. His religion consisted in what his scrupulous, abstract mind approved of.

Seeing his acts, Miss Mary must respect and honour him. In consequence she must serve him. To this she had to force herself, shuddering and yet desirous, but he did not perceive it. She accompanied him on his visiting in the parish, and whilst she was cold with admiration for him, often she was touched with pity for the little padding figure with bent shoulders, buttoned up to the chin in his overcoat. She was a handsome, calm girl, tall, with a beautiful repose. Her clothes were poor, and she wore a black silk scarf, having no furs. But she was a lady. As the people saw her walking down Aldecross beside Mr Massy, they said:

'My word, Miss Mary's got a catch. Did ever you see such a sickly little shrimp!'

She knew they were talking so, and it made her heart grow hot against them, and she drew herself as it were protectively towards the little man beside her. At any rate, she could see and give honour to his genuine goodness.

He could not walk fast, or far.

'You have not been well?' she asked, in her dignified way.

'I have an internal trouble.'

He was not aware of her slight shudder. There was silence, whilst she bowed to recover her composure, to resume her gentle manner towards him.

He was fond of Miss Mary. She had made it a rule of hospitality that he should always be escorted by herself or by her sister on his visits in the parish, which were not many. But some mornings she was engaged. Then Miss Louisa took her place. It was no good Miss Louisa's trying to adopt to Mr Massy an attitude of queenly service. She was unable to regard him save with aversion. When she saw him from behind, thin and bent-shouldered, looking like a sickly lad of thirteen, she disliked him exceedingly, and felt a desire to put him out of existence. And yet a deeper justice in Mary made Louisa humble before her sister.

They were going to see Mr Durant, who was paralysed and not expected to live. Miss Louisa was crudely ashamed at being admitted to the cottage in company with the little clergyman.

Mrs Durant was, however, much quieter in the face of her real trouble.

'How is Mr Durant?' asked Louisa.

'He is no different—and we don't expect him to be,' was the reply. The little clergyman stood looking on.

They went upstairs. The three stood for some time looking at the bed, at the grey head of the old man on the pillow, the grey beard over the sheet. Miss Louisa was shocked and afraid.

'It is so dreadful,' she said, with a shudder.

'It is how I always thought it would be,' replied Mrs Durant.

Then Miss Louisa was afraid of her. The two women were uneasy, waiting for Mr Massy to say something. He stood, small and bent, too nervous to speak.

'Has he any understanding?' he asked at length.

'Maybe,' said Mrs Durant. 'Can you hear, John?' she asked loudly. The dull blue eye of the inert man looked at her feebly.

'Yes, he understands,' said Mrs Durant to Mr Massy. Except for the dull look in his eyes, the sick man lay as if dead. The three stood in silence. Miss Louisa was obstinate but heavy-hearted under the load of unlivingness. It was Mr Massy who kept her there in discipline. His non-human will dominated them all.

Then they heard a sound below, a man's footsteps, and a man's voice called subduedly:

'Are you upstairs, mother?'

Mrs Durant started and moved to the door. But already a quick, firm step was running up the stairs.

'I'm a bit early, mother,' a troubled voice said, and on the landing they saw the form of the sailor. His mother came and clung to him. She was suddenly aware that she needed something to hold on to. He put his arms around her, and bent over her, kissing her.

'He's not gone, mother?' he asked anxiously, struggling to control his voice.

Miss Louisa looked away from the mother and son who stood together in the gloom on the landing. She could not bear it that she and Mr Massy should be there. The latter stood nervously, as if ill at ease before the emotion that was running. He was a witness, nervous, unwilling, but dispassionate. To Miss Louisa's hot heart it seemed all, all wrong that they should be there.

Mrs Durant entered the bedroom, her face wet.

'There's Miss Louisa and the vicar,' she said, out of voice and quavering.

Her son, red-faced and slender, drew himself up to salute. But Miss Louisa held out her hand. Then she saw his hazel eyes recognize her for a moment, and his small white teeth showed in a glimpse of the greeting she used to love. She was covered with confusion. He went round to the bed; his boots clicked on the plaster floor, he bowed his head with dignity.

'How are you, dad?' he said, laying his hand on the sheet, faltering. But the old man stared fixedly and unseeing. The son stood perfectly still for a few minutes, then slowly recoiled. Miss Louisa saw the fine outline of his breast, under the sailor's blue blouse, as his chest began to heave.

'He doesn't know me,' he said, turning to his mother. He gradually went white.

'No, my boy!' cried the mother, pitiful, lifting her face. And suddenly she put her face against his shoulder, he was stooping down to her, holding her against him, and she cried aloud for a moment or two. Miss Louisa saw his sides heaving, and heard the sharp hiss of his breath. She turned away, tears streaming down her face. The father lay inert upon the white bed, Mr Massy looked queer and obliterated, so little now that the sailor with his sunburned skin was in the room. He stood waiting. Miss Louisa wanted to die, she wanted to have done. She dared not turn round again to look.

'Shall I offer a prayer?' came the frail voice of the clergyman, and all kneeled down.

Miss Louisa was frightened of the inert man upon the bed. Then she felt a flash of fear of Mr Massy, hearing his thin, detached voice. And then, calmed, she looked up. On the far side of the bed were the heads of the mother and son, the one in the black lace cap, with the small white nape of the neck beneath, the other, with brown, sun-scorched hair too close and wiry to allow of a parting, and neck tanned firm, bowed as if unwillingly. The great grey beard of the old man did not move, the prayer continued. Mr Massy prayed with a pure lucidity, that they all might conform to the higher Will. He was like something that dominated the bowed heads, something dispassionate that governed them inexorably. Miss Louisa was afraid of him. And she was bound, during the course of the prayer, to have a little reverence for him. It was like a foretaste of inexorable, cold death, a taste of pure justice.

That evening she talked to Mary of the visit. Her heart, her veins were possessed by the thought of Alfred Durant as he held his mother in his arms; then the break in his voice, as she remembered it again and again, was like a flame through her; and she wanted to see his face more distinctly in her mind, ruddy with the sun, and his golden-brown eyes, kind and careless, strained now with a natural fear, the fine nose tanned hard by the sun, the mouth that could not help smiling at her. And it went through her with pride, to think of his figure, a straight, fine jet of life.

'He is a handsome lad,' said she to Miss Mary, as if

he had not been a year older than herself. Underneath
was the deeper dread, almost hatred, of the inhuman
being of Mr Massy. She felt she must protect herself and
Alfred from him.

'When I felt Mr Massy there,' she said, 'I almost
hated him. What right had he to be there!'

'Surely he has all right,' said Miss Mary after a
pause. 'He is *really* a Christian.'

'He seems to me nearly an imbecile,' said Miss
Louisa.

Miss Mary, quiet and beautiful, was silent for a
moment:

'Oh no,' she said, 'Not *imbecile*—'

'Well then–he reminds me of a six months' child–or
a five months' child–as if he didn't have time to get
developed enough before he was born.'

'Yes,' said Miss Mary, slowly. 'There is something
lacking. But there is something wonderful in him: and he
is really *good*—'

'Yes,' said Miss Louisa, 'it doesn't seem right that
he should be. What right has *that* to be called goodness!'

'But it *is* goodness,' persisted Mary. Then she
added, with a laugh: 'And come, you wouldn't deny
that as well.'

There was a doggedness in her voice. She went
about very quietly. In her soul, she knew what was going
to happen. She knew that Mr Massy was stronger than
she, and that she must submit to what he was. Her
physical self was prouder, stronger than he, her physical
self disliked and despised him. But she was in the grip of
his moral, mental being. And she felt the days allotted
out to her. And her family watched.

IV

A few days after, old Mr Durant died. Miss Louisa saw
Alfred once more, but he was stiff before her now, treating her not like a person, but as if she were some sort of

will in command and he a separate, distinct will waiting
in front of her. She had never felt such utter steel-plate
separation from anyone. It puzzled her and frightened
her. What had become of him? And she hated the
military discipline—she was antagonistic to it. Now he
was not himself. He was the will which obeys set over
against the will which commands. She hesitated over
accepting this. He had put himself out of her range. He
had ranked himself inferior, subordinate to her. And that
was how he would get away from her, that was how he
would avoid all connection with her: by fronting her
impersonally from the opposite camp, by taking up the
abstract position of an inferior.

She went brooding steadily and sullenly over this,
brooding and brooding. Her fierce, obstinate heart could
not give way. It clung to its own rights. Sometimes she
dismissed him. Why should he, her inferior, trouble her?

Then she relapsed to him, and almost hated him. It
was his way of getting out of it. She felt the cowardice of
it, his calmly placing her in a superior class, and placing
himself inaccessibly apart, in an inferior, as if she, the
sentient woman who was fond of him, did not count. But
she was not going to submit. Dogged in her heart she
held on to him.

V

In six months' time Miss Mary had married Mr Massy.
There had been no love-making, nobody had made any
remark. But everybody was tense and callous with
expectation. When one day Mr Massy asked for Mary's
hand, Mr Lindley started and trembled from the thin,
abstract voice of the little man. Mr Massy was very
nervous, but so curiously absolute.

'I shall be very glad,' said the vicar, 'but of course
the decision lies with Mary herself.' And his still feeble
hand shook as he moved a Bible on his desk.

The small man, keeping fixedly to his idea, padded

out of the room to find Miss Mary. He sat a long time by her, while she made some conversation, before he had readiness to speak. She was afraid of what was coming, and sat stiff in apprehension. She felt as if her body would rise and fling him aside. But her spirit quivered and waited. Almost in expectation she waited, almost wanting him. And then she knew he would speak.

'I have already asked Mr Lindley,' said the clergyman, while suddenly she looked with aversion at his little knees, 'if he would consent to my proposal.' He was aware of his own disadvantage, but his will was set.

She went cold as she sat, and impervious, almost as if she had become stone. He waited a moment nervously. He would not persuade her. He himself never even heard persuasion, but pursued his own course. He looked at her, sure of himself, unsure of her, and said:

'Will you become my wife, Mary?'

Still her heart was hard and cold. She sat proudly.

'I should like to speak to mama first,' she said.

'Very well,' replied Mr Massy. And in a moment he padded away.

Mary went to her mother. She was cold and reserved.

'Mr Massy has asked me to marry him, mama,' she said. Mrs Lindley went on staring at her book. She was cramped in her feeling.

'Well, and what did you say?'

They were both keeping calm and cold.

'I said I would speak to you before answering him.'

This was equivalent to a question. Mrs Lindley did not want to reply to it. She shifted her heavy form irritably on the couch. Miss Mary sat calm and straight, with closed mouth.

'Your father thinks it would not be a bad match,' said the mother, as if casually.

Nothing more was said. Everybody remained cold and shut-off. Miss Mary did not speak to Miss Louisa, the Reverend Ernest Lindley kept out of sight.

At evening Miss Mary accepted Mr Massy.

'Yes, I will marry you,' she said, with even a little movement of tenderness towards him. He was embarrassed, but satisfied. She could see him making some movement towards her, could feel the male in him, something cold and triumphant, asserting itself. She sat rigid, and waited.

When Miss Louisa knew, she was silent with bitter anger against everybody, even against Mary. She felt her faith wounded. Did the real things to her not matter after all? She wanted to get away. She thought of Mr Massy. He had some curious power, some unanswerable right. He was a will that they could not controvert. Suddenly a flush started in her. If he had come to her she would have flipped him out of the room. He was never going to touch *her*. And she was glad. She was glad that her blood would rise and exterminate the little man, if he came too near to her, no matter how her judgment was paralysed by him, no matter how he moved in abstract goodness. She thought she was perverse to be glad, but glad she was. 'I would just flip him out of the room,' she said, and she derived great satisfaction from the open statement. Nevertheless, perhaps she ought still to feel that Mary, on her plane, was a higher being than herself. But then Mary was Mary, and she was Louisa, and that also was inalterable.

Mary, in marrying him, tried to become a pure reason such as he was, without feeling or impulse. She shut herself up, she shut herself rigid against the agonies of shame and the terror of violation which came at first. She *would* not feel, and she *would* not feel. She was a pure will acquiescing to him. She elected a certain kind of fate. She would be good and purely just, she would live in a higher freedom than she had ever known, she would be free of mundane care, she was a pure will towards right. She had sold herself, but she had a new freedom. She had got rid of her body. She had sold a lower thing, her body, for a higher thing, her freedom from material things. She considered that she paid for all she got from her husband. So, in a kind of independence, she moved proud and free. She had paid with her body: that was henceforward out of consideration. She was glad to be rid of it. She had bought her position in the world–that henceforth was taken for granted. There remained only the direction of her activity towards charity and high-minded living.

She could scarcely bear other people to be present with her and her husband. Her private life was her shame. But then, she could keep it hidden. She lived almost isolated in the rectory of the tiny village miles from the railway. She suffered as if it were an insult to her own flesh, seeing the repulsion which some people felt for her husband, or the special manner they had of treating him, as if he were a 'case'. But most people were uneasy before him, which restored her pride.

If she had let herself, she would have hated him, hated his padding round the house, his thin voice devoid of human understanding, his bent little shoulders and rather incomplete face that reminded her of an abortion. But rigorously she kept to her position. She took care of him and was just to him. There was also a deep, craven fear of him, something slave-like.

There was not much fault to be found with his behaviour. He was scrupulously just and kind according to his lights. But the male in him was cold and self-complete, and utterly domineering. Weak, insufficient little thing as he was, she had not expected this of him. It was something in the bargain she had not understood. It made her hold her head, to keep still. She knew, vaguely, that she was murdering herself. After all, her body was not quite so easy to get rid of. And this manner of dispos-ing of it–ah, sometimes she felt she must rise and bring about death, lift her hand for utter denial of everything, by a general destruction.

He was almost unaware of the conditions about him. He did not fuss in the domestic way, she did as she liked in the house. Indeed, she was a great deal free of him. He would sit obliterated for hours. He was kind, and almost anxiously considerate. But when he considered he was right, his will was just blindly male, like a cold machine. And on most points he was logically right, or he had with him the right of the creed they both accepted. It was so. There was nothing for her to go against.

Then she found herself with child, and felt for the first time horror, afraid before God and man. This also she had to go through—it was the right. When the child arrived, it was a bonny, healthy lad. Her heart hurt in her body, as she took the baby between her hands. The flesh that was trampled and silent in her must speak again in the boy. After all, she had to live—it was not so simple after all. Nothing was finished completely. She looked and looked at the baby, and almost hated it, and suffered an anguish of love for it. She hated it because it made her live again in the flesh, when she *could* not live in the flesh, she could not. She wanted to trample her flesh down, down, extinct, to live in the mind. And now there was this child. It was too cruel, too racking. For she must love the child. Her purpose was broken in two again. She had to become amorphous, purposeless, without real being. As a mother, she was a fragmentary, ignoble thing.

Mr Massy, blind to everything else in the way of human feeling, became obsessed by the idea of his child. When it arrived, suddenly it filled the whole world of feeling for him. It was his obsession, his terror was for its safety and well-being. It was something new, as if he himself had been born a naked infant, conscious of his own exposure, and full of apprehension. He who had never been aware of anyone else, all his life, now was aware of nothing but the child. Not that he ever played with it, or kissed it, or tended it. He did nothing for it. But it dominated him, it filled, and at the same time emptied his mind. The world was all baby for him.

This his wife must also bear, his question: 'What is the reason that he cries?'–his reminder, at the first sound: 'Mary, that is the child,'–his restlessness if the feeding-time were five minutes past. She had bargained for this–now she must stand by her bargain.

VI

Miss Louisa, at home in the dingy vicarage, had suffered a great deal over her sister's wedding. Having once begun to cry out against it, during the engagement, she had been silenced by Mary's quiet: 'I don't agree with you about him, Louisa, I *want* to marry him.' Then Miss Louisa had been angry deep in her heart, and therefore silent. This dangerous state started the change in her. Her own revulsion made her recoil from the hitherto undoubted Mary.

'I'd beg the streets barefoot first,' said Miss Louisa, thinking of Mr Massy.

But evidently Mary could perform a different heroism. So she, Louisa the practical, suddenly felt that Mary, her ideal, was questionable after all. How could she be pure–one cannot be dirty in act and spiritual in being. Louisa distrusted Mary's high spirituality. It was no longer genuine for her. And if Mary were spiritual and misguided, why did not her father protect her? Because of the money. He disliked the whole affair, but he backed away, because of the money. And the mother frankly did not care: her daughters could do as they liked. Her mother's pronouncement:

'Whatever happens to *him*, Mary is safe for life,'–so evidently and shallowly a calculation, incensed Louisa.

'I'd rather be safe in the workhouse,' she cried.

'Your father will see to that,' replied her mother brutally. This speech, in its indirectness, so injured Miss Louisa that she hated her mother deep, deep in her heart, and almost hated herself. It was a long time resolving itself out, this hate. But it worked and worked, and at last the young woman said:

'They are wrong—they are all wrong. They have
ground out their souls for what isn't worth anything, and
there isn't a grain of love in them anywhere. And I *will*
have love. They want us to deny it. They've never found
it, so they want to say it doesn't exist. But I *will* have it. I
will love—it is my birthright. I will love the man I
marry—that is all I care about.'

So Miss Louisa stood isolated from everybody. She
and Mary had parted over Mr Massy. In Louisa's eyes,
Mary was degraded, married to Mr Massy. She could
not bear to think of her lofty, spiritual sister degraded in
the body like this. Mary was wrong, wrong, wrong: she
was not superior, she was flawed, incomplete. The two
sisters stood apart. They still loved each other, they
would love each other as long as they lived. But they had
parted ways. A new solitariness came over the obstinate
Louisa, and her heavy jaw set stubbornly. She was going
on her own way. But which way? She was quite alone,
with a blank world before her. How could she be said to
have any way? Yet she had her fixed will to love, to have
the man she loved.

VII

When her boy was three years old, Mary had another
baby, a girl. The three years had gone by monotonously.
They might have been an eternity, they might have been
brief as a sleep. She did not know. Only, there was
always a weight on top of her, something that pressed
down her life. The only thing that had happened was
that Mr Massy had had an operation. He was always
exceedingly fragile. His wife had soon learned to attend
to him mechanically, as part of her duty.

But this third year, after the baby girl had been
born, Mary felt oppressed and depressed. Christmas
drew near: the gloomy, unleavened Christmas of the
rectory, where all the days were of the same dark fabric.
And Mary was afraid. It was as if the darkness were

coming upon her.

'Edward, I should like to go home for Christmas,' she said, and a certain terror filled her as she spoke.

'But you can't leave baby,' said her husband, blinking.

'We can all go.'

He thought, and stared in his collective fashion.

'Why do you wish to go?' he asked.

'Because I need a change. A change would do me good, and it would be good for the milk.'

He heard the will in his wife's voice, and was at a loss. Her language was unintelligible to him. But somehow he felt that Mary was set upon it. And while she was breeding, either about to have a child, or nursing, he regarded her as a special sort of being.

'Wouldn't it hurt baby to take her by the train?' he said.

'No,' replied the mother, 'why should it?'

They went. When they were in the train, it began to snow. From the window of his first-class carriage the little clergyman watched the big flakes sweep by, like a blind drawn across the country. He was obsessed by thought of the baby, and afraid of the draughts of the carriage.

'Sit right in the corner,' he said to his wife, 'and hold baby close back.'

She moved at his bidding, and stared out of the window. His eternal presence was like an iron weight on her brain. But she was going partially to escape for a few days.

'Sit on the other side, Jack,' said the father. 'It is less draughty. Come to this window.'

He watched the boy in anxiety. But his children were the only beings in the world who took not the slightest notice of him.

'Look, mother, look!' cried the boy. 'They fly right in my face'—he meant the snowflakes.

'Come into this corner,' repeated his father, out of

another world.

'He's jumped on this one's back, mother, an' they're riding to the bottom!' cried the boy, jumping with glee.

'Tell him to come on this side,' the little man bade his wife.

'Jack, kneel on this cushion,' said the mother, putting her white hand on the place.

The boy slid over in silence to the place she indicated, waited still for a moment, then almost deliberately, stridently cried:

'Look at all those in the corner, mother, making a heap,' and he pointed to the cluster of snowflakes with finger pressed dramatically on the pane, and he turned to his mother a bit ostentatiously.

'All in a heap!' she said.

He had seen her face, and had her response, and he was somewhat assured. Vaguely uneasy, he was reassured if he could win her attention.

They arrived at the vicarage at half-past two, not having had lunch.

'How are you, Edward?' said Mr Lindley, trying on his side to be fatherly. But he was always in a false position with his son-in-law, frustrated before him, therefore, as much as possible, he shut his eyes and ears to him. The vicar was looking thin and pale and ill-nourished. He had gone quite grey. He was, however, still haughty; but, since the growing-up of his children, it was a brittle haughtiness, that might break at any moment and leave the vicar only an impoverished, pitiable figure. Mrs Lindley took all the notice of her daughter, and of the children. She ignored her son-in-law. Miss Louisa was clucking and laughing and rejoicing over the baby. Mr Massy stood aside, a bent, persistent little figure.

'Oh a pretty!—a little pretty! oh a cold little pretty come in a railway-train!' Miss Louisa was cooing to the infant, crouching on the hearthrug opening the white woollen wraps and exposing the child to the fireglow.

'Mary,' said the little clergyman, 'I think it would

be better to give baby a warm bath; she may take a cold.'

'I think it is not necessary,' said the mother, coming and closing her hand judiciously over the rosy feet and hands of the mite. 'She is not chilly.'

'Not a bit,' cried Miss Louisa. 'She's not caught cold.'

'I'll go and bring her flannels,' said Mr Massy, with one idea.

'I can bath her in the kitchen then,' said Mary, in an altered, cold tone.

'You can't, the girl is scrubbing there,' said Miss Louisa. 'Besides, she doesn't want a bath at this time of day.'

'She'd better have one,' said Mary, quietly, out of submission. Miss Louisa's gorge rose, and she was silent. When the little man padded down with the flannels on his arm, Mrs Lindley asked:

'Hadn't *you* better take a hot bath, Edward?'

But the sarcasm was lost on the little clergyman. He was absorbed in the preparations round the baby.

The room was dull and threadbare, and the snow outside seemed fairy-like by comparison, so white on the lawn and tufted on the bushes. Indoors the heavy pictures hung obscurely on the walls, everything was dingy with gloom.

Except in the fireglow, where they had laid the bath on the hearth. Mrs Massy, her black hair always smoothly coiled and queenly, kneeled by the bath, wearing a rubber apron, and holding the kicking child. Her husband stood holding the towels and the flannels to warm. Louisa, too cross to share in the joy of the baby's bath, was laying the table. The boy was hanging on the door-knob, wrestling with it to get out. His father looked round.

'Come away from the door, Jack,' he said, ineffectually. Jack tugged harder at the knob as if he did not hear. Mr Massy blinked at him.

'He must come away from the door, Mary,' he said.

'There will be a draught if it is opened.'

'Jack, come away from the door, dear,' said the mother, dexterously turning the shiny wet baby on to her towelled knee, then glancing round: 'Go and tell Auntie Louisa about the train.'

Louisa, also afraid to open the door, was watching the scene on the hearth. Mr Massy stood holding the baby's flannel, as if assisting at some ceremonial. If everybody had not been subduedly angry, it would have been ridiculous.

'I want to see out of the window,' Jack said. His father turned hastily.

'Do *you* mind lifting him on to a chair, Louisa,' said Mary hastily. The father was too delicate.

When the baby was flannelled, Mr Massy went upstairs and returned with four pillows, which he set in the fender to warm. Then he stood watching the mother feed her child, obsessed by the idea of his infant.

Louisa went on with her preparations for the meal. She could not have told why she was so sullenly angry. Mrs Lindley, as usual, lay silently watching.

Mary carried her child upstairs, followed by her husband with the pillows. After a while he came down again.

'What is Mary doing? Why doesn't she come down to eat?' asked Mrs Lindley.

'She is staying with baby. The room is rather cold. I will ask the girl to put in a fire.' He was going absorbedly to the door.

'But Mary has had nothing to eat. It is *she* who will catch cold,' said the mother, exasperated.

Mr Massy seemed as if he did not hear. Yet he looked at his mother-in-law, and answered:

'I will take her something.'

He went out. Mrs Lindley shifted on her couch with anger. Miss Louisa glowered. But no one said anything, because of the money that came to the vicarage from Mr Massy.

Louisa went upstairs. Her sister was sitting by the bed, reading a scrap of paper.

'Won't you come down and eat?' the younger asked.

'In a moment or two,' Mary replied, in a quiet, reserved voice, that forbade anyone to approach her.

It was this that made Miss Louisa most furious. She went downstairs, and announced to her mother:

'I am going out. I may not be home to tea.'

VIII

No one remarked on her exit. She put on her fur hat, that the village people knew so well, and the old Norfolk jacket. Louisa was short and plump and plain. She had her mother's heavy jaw, her father's proud brow, and her own grey, brooding eyes that were very beautiful when she smiled. It was true, as the people said, that she looked sulky. Her chief attraction was her glistening, heavy, deep-blond hair, which shone and gleamed with a richness that was not entirely foreign to her.

'Where am I going?' she said to herself, when she got outside in the snow. She did not hesitate, however, but by mechanical walking found herself descending the hill towards Old Aldecross. In the valley that was black with trees, the colliery breathed in stertorous pants, sending out high conical columns of steam that remained upright, whiter than the snow on the hills, yet shadowy, in the dead air. Louisa would not acknowledge to herself whither she was making her way, till she came to the railway crossing. Then the bunches of snow in the twigs of the apple tree that leaned towards the fence told her she must go and see Mrs Durant. The tree was in Mrs Durant's garden.

Alfred was now at home again, living with his mother in the cottage below the road. From the highway hedge, by the railway crossing, the snowy garden sheered down steeply, like the side of a hole, then dropped straight in a wall. In this depth the house was snug, its chimney just level with the road. Miss Louisa descended the stone stairs, and stood below in the little backyard, in the dimness and semi-secrecy. A big tree leaned overhead, above the paraffin hut. Louisa felt secure from all the world down there. She knocked at the open door, then looked round. The tongue of garden narrowing in from the quarry bed was white with snow: she thought of the thick fringes of snowdrops it would show beneath the currant bushes in a month's time. The ragged fringe of pinks hanging over the garden brim behind her was whitened now with snowflakes, that in summer held white blossom to Louisa's face. It was pleasant, she thought, to gather flowers that stooped to one's face from above.

She knocked again. Peeping in, she saw the scarlet glow of the kitchen, red firelight falling on the brick floor and on the bright chintz cushions. It was alive and bright as a peep-show. She crossed the scullery, where still an almanac hung. There was no one about. 'Mrs Durant,' called Louisa softly, 'Mrs Durant.'

She went up the brick step into the front room, that still had its little shop counter and its bundles of goods, and she called from the stair-foot. Then she knew Mrs Durant was out.

She went into the yard, to follow the old woman's footsteps up the garden path.

She emerged from the bushes and raspberry canes. There was the whole quarry bed, a wide garden white and dimmed, brindled with dark bushes, lying half submerged. On the left, overhead, the little colliery train rumbled by. Right away at the back was a mass of trees.

Louisa followed the open path, looking from right to left, and then she gave a cry of concern. The old woman was sitting rocking slightly among the ragged snowy cabbages. Louisa ran to her, found her whimpering with little, involuntary cries.

'Whatever have you done?' cried Louisa, kneeling in the snow.

'I've–I've–I was pulling a brussel-sprout stalk–and–oh-h!–something tore inside me. I've had a pain,' the old woman wept from shock and suffering, gasping between her whimpers,–'I've had a pain there–a long time–and now–oh–oh!' She panted, pressed her hand on her side, leaned as if she would faint, looking yellow against the snow. Louisa supported her.

'Do you think you could walk now?' she asked.

'Yes,' gasped the old woman.

Louisa helped her to her feet.

'Get the cabbage–I want it for Alfred's dinner,' panted Mrs Durant. Louisa picked up the stalk of brussel-sprouts, and with difficulty got the old woman indoors. She gave her brandy, laid her on the couch, saying:

'I'm going to send for a doctor–wait just a minute.'

The young woman ran up the steps to the public-house a few yards away. The landlady was astonished to see Miss Louisa.

'Will you send for a doctor at once to Mrs Durant,' she said, with some of her father in her commanding tone.

'Is something the matter?' fluttered the landlady in concern.

Louisa, glancing out up the road, saw the grocer's cart driving to Eastwood. She ran and stopped the man, and told him.

Mrs Durant lay on the sofa, her face turned away, when the young woman came back.

'Let me put you to bed,' Louisa said. Mrs Durant did not resist.

Louisa knew the ways of the working people. In the bottom drawer of the dresser she found dusters and flannels. With the old pit-flannel she snatched out the oven shelves, wrapped them up, and put them in the bed. From the son's bed she took a blanket, and, running down, set it before the fire. Having undressed the little old woman, Louisa carried her upstairs.

'You'll drop me, you'll drop me!' cried Mrs Durant.

Louisa did not answer, but bore her burden quickly. She could not light a fire, because there was no fire-place in the bedroom. And the floor was plaster. So she fetched the lamp, and stood it lighted in one corner.

'It will air the room,' she said.

'Yes,' moaned the old woman.

Louisa ran with more hot flannels, replacing those from the oven shelves. Then she made a bran-bag and laid it on the woman's side. There was a big lump on the side of the abdomen.

'I've felt it coming a long time,' moaned the old lady, when the pain was easier, 'but I've not said anything; I didn't want to upset our Alfred.'

Louisa did not see why 'our Alfred' should be spared.

'What time is it?' came the plaintive voice.

'A quarter to four.'

'Oh!' wailed the old lady, 'he'll be here in half an hour, and no dinner ready for him.'

'Let me do it?' said Louisa, gently.

'There's that cabbage–and you'll find the meat in the pantry–and there's an apple pie you can hot up. But *don't you* do it–!'

'Who will, then?' asked Louisa.

'I don't know,' moaned the sick woman, unable to consider.

Louisa did it. The doctor came and gave serious examination. He looked very grave.

'What is it, doctor?' asked the old lady, looking up at him with old, pathetic eyes in which already hope was dead.

'I think you've torn the skin in which a tumour hangs,' he replied.

'Ay!' she murmured, and she turned away.

'You see, she may die any minute–and it *may* be swaled away,' said the old doctor to Louisa.

The young woman went upstairs again.

'He says the lump may be swaled away, and you may get quite well again,' she said.

'Ay!' murmured the old lady. It did not deceive her. Presently she asked:

'Is there a good fire?'

'I think so,' answered Louisa.

'He'll want a good fire,' the mother said. Louisa attended to it.

Since the death of Durant, the widow had come to church occasionally, and Louisa had been friendly to her. In the girl's heart the purpose was fixed. No man had affected her as Alfred Durant had done, and to that she kept. In her heart, she adhered to him. A natural sympathy existed between her and his rather hard, materialistic mother.

Alfred was the most lovable of the old woman's sons. He had grown up like the rest, however, headstrong and blind to everything but his own will. Like the other boys, he had insisted on going into the pit as soon as he left school, because that was the only way speedily to become a man, level with all the other men. This was a great chagrin to his mother, who would have liked to have this last of her sons a gentleman.

But still he remained constant to her. His feeling for her was deep and unexpressed. He noticed when she was tired, or when she had a new cap. And he bought little things for her occasionally. She was not wise enough to see how much he lived by her.

At the bottom he did not satisfy her, he did not seem manly enough. He liked to read books occasionally, and better still he liked to play the piccolo. It amused her to see his head nod over the instrument as he made an effort to get the right note. It made her fond of him, with tenderness, almost pity, but not with respect. She wanted a man to be fixed, going his own way without knowledge of women. Whereas she knew Alfred depended on her. He sang in the choir because he liked singing. In the summer he worked in the garden, attended to the fowls and pigs. He kept pigeons. He played on Saturday in the cricket or football team. But to her he did not seem the man, the independent man her other boys had been. He was her baby—and whilst she loved him for it, she was a little bit contemptuous of him.

There grew up a little hostility between them. Then he began to drink, as the others had done; but not in their blind, oblivious way. He was a little self-conscious over it. She saw this, and she pitied it in him. She loved him most, but she was not satisfied with him because he was not free of her. He could not quite go his own way.

Then at twenty he ran away and served his time in the Navy. This had made a man of him. He had hated it bitterly, the service, the subordination. For years he fought with himself under the military discipline, for his own self-respect, struggling through blind anger and shame and a cramping sense of inferiority. Out of humiliation and self-hatred, he rose into a sort of inner freedom. And his love for his mother, whom he idealised, remained the fact of hope and of belief.

He came home again, nearly thirty years old, but naïve and inexperienced as a boy, only with a silence about him that was new: a sort of dumb humility before life, a fear of living. He was almost quite chaste. A strong sensitiveness had kept him from women. Sexual talk was all very well among men, but somehow it had no application to living women. There were two things for him, the *idea* of women, with which he sometimes debauched himself, and real women, before whom he felt a deep uneasiness, and a need to draw away. He shrank and defended himself from the approach of any woman. And then he felt ashamed. In his innermost soul he felt he was not a man, he was less than the normal man. In Genoa he went with an under officer to a drinking house where the cheaper sort of girl came in to look for lovers. He sat there with his glass, the girls looked at him, but they never came to him. He knew that if they did come he could only pay for food and drink for them, because he felt a pity for them, and was anxious lest they lacked good necessities. He could not have gone with one of them: he knew it, and was ashamed, looking with curious envy at the swaggering, easy-passionate Italian whose body went to a woman by instinctive impersonal attraction. They were men, he was not a man. He sat feeling short, feeling like a leper. And he went away imagining sexual scenes between himself and a woman, walking wrapt in this indulgence. But when the ready woman presented herself, the very fact that she was a palpable woman made it impossible for him to touch her. And this incapacity was like a core of rottenness in him.

So several times he went, drunk, with his companions, to the licensed prostitute houses abroad. But the sordid insignificance of the experience appalled him. It had not been anything really: it meant nothing. He felt as if he were, not physically, but spiritually impotent: not actually impotent, but intrinsically so.

He came home with this secret, never changing burden of his unknown, unbestowed self torturing him. His navy training left him in perfect physical condition. He was sensible of, and proud of his body. He bathed and used dumb-bells, and kept himself fit. He played cricket and football. He read books and began to hold fixed ideas which he got from the Fabians. He played his piccolo, and was considered an expert. But at the bottom of his soul was always this canker of shame and incompleteness: he was miserable beneath all his healthy cheerfulness, he was uneasy and felt despicable among all his confidence and superiority of ideas. He would have changed with any mere brute, just to be free of himself, to be free of this shame of self-consciousness. He saw some collier lurching straight forward without misgiving, pursuing his own satisfactions, and he envied him. Anything, he would have given anything for this spontaneity and this blind stupidity which went to its own satisfaction direct.

IX

He was not unhappy in the pit. He was admired by the men, and well enough liked. It was only he himself who felt the difference between himself and the others. He seemed to hide his own stigma. But he was never sure that the others did not really despise him for a ninny, as being less a man than they were. Only he pretended to be more manly, and was surprised by the ease with which they were deceived. And, being naturally cheerful, he was happy at work. He was sure of himself there. Naked to the waist, hot and grimy with labour, they squatted on their heels for a few minutes and talked, seeing each other dimly by the light of the safety lamps, while the black coal rose jutting round them, and the props of wood stood like little pillars in the low, black, very dark temple. Then the pony came and the gang-lad with a message from Number 7, or with a bottle of water from the horse-trough or some news of the world above. The day passed pleasantly enough. There was an ease, a go-as-you-please about the day underground, a delightful camaraderie of men shut off alone from the rest of the world, in a dangerous place, and a variety of labour, holing, loading, timbering, and a glamour of mystery and adventure in the atmosphere, that made the pit not unattractive to him when he had again got over his anguish of desire for the open air and the sea.

This day there was much to do and Durant was not in humour to talk. He went on working in silence through the afternoon.

'Loose-all' came, and they tramped to the bottom. The whitewashed underground office shone brightly. Men were putting out their lamps. They sat in dozens round the bottom of the shaft, down which black, heavy drops of water fell continuously into the sumph. The electric lights shone away down the main underground road.

'Is it raining?' asked Durant.

'Snowing,' said an old man, and the younger was pleased. He liked to go up when it was snowing.

'It'll just come right for Christmas?' said the old man.

'Ay,' replied Durant.

'A green Christmas, a fat churchyard,' said the other sententiously.

Durant laughed, showing his small, rather pointed teeth.

The cage came down, a dozen men lined on. Durant noticed tufts of snow on the perforated, arched roof of the chain, and he was pleased. He wondered how it liked its excursion underground. But already it was getting soppy with black water.

He liked things about him. There was a little smile on his face. But underlying it was the curious consciousness he felt in himself.

The upper world came almost with a flash, because of the glimmer of snow. Hurrying along the bank, giving up his lamp at the office, he smiled to feel the open about him again, all glimmering round him with snow. The hills on either hand were pale blue in the dusk, and the hedges looked savage and dark. The snow was trampled between the railway lines. But far ahead, beyond the black figures of miners moving home, it became smooth again, spreading right up to the dark wall of the coppice.

To the west there was a pinkness, and a big star hovered half revealed. Below, the lights of the pit came out crisp and yellow among the darkness of the buildings, and the lights of Old Aldecross twinkled in rows down the bluish twilight.

Durant walked glad with life among the miners, who were all talking animatedly because of the snow. He liked their company, he liked the white dusky world. It gave him a little thrill to stop at the garden gate and see the light of home down below, shining on the silent blue snow.

X

By the big gate of the railway, in the fence, was a little gate, that he kept locked. As he unfastened it, he watched the kitchen light that shone on to the bushes and the snow outside. It was a candle burning till night set in, he thought to himself. He slid down the steep path to the level below. He liked making the first marks in the smooth snow. Then he came through the bushes to the house. The two women heard his heavy boots ring outside on the scraper, and his voice as he opened the door:

'How much worth of oil do you reckon to save by that candle, mother?' He liked a good light from the lamp.

He had just put down his bottle and snap-bag and was hanging his coat behind the scullery door, when Miss Louisa came upon him. He was startled, but he smiled.

His eyes began to laugh—then his face went suddenly straight, and he was afraid.

'Your mother's had an accident,' she said.

'How?' he exclaimed.

'In the garden,' she answered. He hesitated with his coat in his hands. Then he hung it up and turned to the kitchen.

'Is she in bed?' he asked.

'Yes,' said Miss Louisa, who found it hard to deceive him. He was silent. He went into the kitchen, sat down heavily in his father's old chair, and began to pull off his boots. His head was small, rather finely shapen. His brown hair, close and crisp, would look jolly whatever happened. He wore heavy, moleskin trousers that gave off the stale, exhausted scent of the pit. Having put on his slippers, he carried his boots into the scullery.

'What is it?' he asked, afraid.

'Something internal,' she replied.

He went upstairs. His mother kept herself calm for

his coming. Louisa felt his tread shake the plaster floor of the bedroom above.

'What have you done?' he asked.

'It's nothing, my lad,' said the old woman, rather hard. 'It's nothing. You needn't fret, my boy, it's nothing more the matter with me than I had yesterday, or last week. The doctor said I'd done nothing serious.'

'What were you doing?' asked her son.

'I was pulling up a cabbage, and I suppose I pulled too hard; for, oh–there was such a pain—'

Her son looked at her quickly. She hardened herself.

'But who doesn't have a sudden pain sometimes, my boy. We all do.'

'And what's it done?'

'I don't know,' she said, 'but I don't suppose it's anything.'

The big lamp in the corner was screened with a dark green screen, so that he could scarcely see her face. He was strung tight with apprehension and many emotions. Then his brow knitted.

'What did you go pulling your inside out at cabbages for,' he asked, 'and the ground frozen? You'd go on dragging and dragging, if you killed yourself.'

'Somebody's got to get them,' she said.

'You needn't do yourself harm.'

But they had reached futility.

Miss Louisa could hear plainly downstairs. Her heart sank. It seemed so hopeless between them.

'Are you sure it's nothing much, mother?' he asked, appealing, after a little silence.

'Ay, it's nothing,' said the old woman, rather bitter.

'I don't want you to–to–to be badly–you know.'

'Go an' get your dinner,' she said. She knew she was going to die: moreover, the pain was torture just then. 'They're only cosseting me up a bit because I'm an old woman. Miss Louisa's *very* good–and she'll have got your dinner ready, so you'd better go and eat it.'

He felt stupid and ashamed. His mother put him off.

He had to turn away. The pain burned in his bowels. He went downstairs. The mother was glad he was gone, so that she could moan with pain.

He had resumed the old habit of eating before he washed himself. Miss Louisa served his dinner. It was strange and exciting to her. She was strung up tense, trying to understand him and his mother. She watched him as he sat. He was turned away from his food, looking in the fire. Her soul watched, trying to see what he was. His black face and arms were uncouth, he was foreign. His face was masked black with coal-dust. She could not see him, she could not know him. The brown eyebrows, the steady eyes, the coarse, small moustache above the closed mouth–these were the only familiar indications. What was he, as he sat there in his pit-dirt? She could not see him, and it hurt her.

She ran upstairs, presently coming down with the flannels and the bran-bag, to heat them, because the pain was on again.

He was half-way through his dinner. He put down the fork, suddenly nauseated.

'They will soothe the wrench,' she said. He watched, useless and left out.

'Is she bad?' he asked.

'I think she is,' she answered.

It was useless for him to stir or comment. Louisa was busy. She went upstairs. The poor old woman was in a white, cold sweat of pain. Louisa's face was sullen with suffering as she went about to relieve her. Then she sat and waited. The pain passed gradually, the old woman sank into a state of coma. Louisa still sat silent by the bed. She heard the sound of water downstairs. Then came the voice of the old mother, faint but unrelaxing:

'Alfred's washing himself–he'll want his back washing—'

Louisa listened anxiously, wondering what the sick woman wanted.

'He can't bear if his back isn't washed—' the old

woman persisted, in a cruel attention to his needs. Louisa rose and wiped the sweat from the yellowish brow.

'I will go down,' she said soothingly.

'If you would,' murmured the sick woman.

Louisa waited a moment. Mrs Durant closed her eyes, having discharged her duty. The young woman went downstairs. Herself, or the man, what did they matter? Only the suffering woman must be considered.

Alfred was kneeling on the hearthrug, stripped to the waist, washing himself in a large panchion of earthenware. He did so every evening, when he had eaten his dinner; his brothers had done so before him. But Miss Louisa was strange in the house.

He was mechanically rubbing the white lather on his head, with a repeated, unconscious movement, his hand every now and then passing over his neck. Louisa watched. She had to brace herself to this also. He bent his head into the water, washed it free of soap, and pressed the water out of his eyes.

'Your mother said you would want your back washing,' she said.

Curious how it hurt her to take part in their fixed routine of life! Louisa felt the almost repulsive intimacy being forced upon her. It was all so common, so like herding. She lost her own distinctness.

He ducked his face round, looking up at her in what was a very comical way. She had to harden herself.

'How funny he looks with his face upside down,' she thought. After all, there was a difference between her and the common people. The water in which his arms were plunged was quite black, the soap-froth was darkish. She could scarcely conceive him as human. Mechanically, under the influence of habit, he groped in the black water, fished out soap and flannel, and handed them backward to Louisa. Then he remained rigid and sub-missive, his two arms thrust straight in the panchion, supporting the weight of his shoulders. His skin was beautifully white and unblemished, of an opaque, solid whiteness. Gradually Louisa saw it: this also was what he was. It fascinated her. Her feeling of separateness passed away: she ceased to draw back from contact with him and his mother. There was this living centre. Her heart ran hot. She had reached some goal in this beautiful, clear, male body. She loved him in a white, impersonal heat. But the sun-burnt, reddish neck and ears: they were more personal, more curious. A tenderness rose in her, she loved even his queer ears. A person—an intimate being he was to her. She put down the towel and went upstairs again, troubled in her heart. She had only seen one human being in her life—and that was Mary. All the rest were strangers. Now her soul was going to open, she was going to see another. She felt strange and pregnant.

'He'll be more comfortable,' murmured the sick woman abstractedly, as Louisa entered the room. The latter did not answer. Her own heart was heavy with its own responsibility. Mrs Durant lay silent awhile, then she murmured plaintively:

'You mustn't mind, Miss Louisa.'

'Why should I?' replied Louisa, deeply moved.

'It's what we're used to,' said the old woman.

And Louisa felt herself excluded again from their life. She sat in pain, with tears of disappointment distilling in her heart. Was that all?

Alfred came upstairs. He was clean, and in his shirt-sleeves. He looked a workman now. Louisa felt that she and he were foreigners, moving in different lives. It dulled her again. Oh, if she could only find some fixed relations, something sure and abiding.

'How do you feel?' he said to his mother.

'It's a bit better,' she replied, wearily, impersonally. This strange putting herself aside, this abstracting herself and answering him only what she thought good for him to hear, made the relations between mother and son poignant and cramping to Miss Louisa. It made the man so ineffectual, so nothing. Louisa groped as if she had lost him. The mother was real and positive–he was not very actual. It puzzled and chilled the young woman.

'I'd better fetch Mrs Harrison?' he said, waiting for his mother to decide.

'I suppose we shall have to have somebody,' she replied.

Miss Louisa stood by, afraid to interfere in their business. They did not include her in their lives, they felt she had nothing to do with them, except as a help from outside. She was quite external to them. She felt hurt and powerless against this unconscious difference. But something patient and unyielding in her made her say:

'I will stay and do the nursing: you can't be left.'

The other two were shy, and at a loss for an answer.

'We'll manage to get somebody,' said the old woman wearily. She did not care very much what happened, now.

'I will stay until to-morrow, in any case,' said Louisa. 'Then we can see.'

'I'm sure you've no right to trouble yourself,' moaned the old woman. But she must leave herself in any hands.

Miss Louisa felt glad that she was admitted, even in an official capacity. She wanted to share their lives. At home they would need her, now Mary had come. But they must manage without her.

'I must write a note to the vicarage,' she said.

Alfred Durant looked at her inquiringly, for her service. He had always that intelligent readiness to serve, since he had been in the Navy. But there was a simple independence in his willingness, which she loved. She felt nevertheless it was hard to get at him. He was so deferential, quick to take the slightest suggestion of an order from her, implicitly, that she could not get at the man in him.

He looked at her very keenly. She noticed his eyes were golden brown, with a very small pupil, the kind of

eyes that can see a long way off. He stood alert, at
military attention. His face was still rather weather-
reddened.

'Do you want pen and paper?' he asked, with
deferential suggestion to a superior, which was more
difficult for her than reserve.

'Yes, please,' she said.

He turned and went downstairs. He seemed to her
so self-contained, so utterly sure in his movement. How
was she to approach him? For he would take not one step
towards her. He would only put himself entirely and
impersonally at her service, glad to serve her, but keeping
himself quite removed from her. She could see he felt real
joy in doing anything for her, but any recognition would
confuse him and hurt him. Strange it was to her, to have
a man going about the house in his shirt-sleeves, his
waistcoat unbuttoned, his throat bare, waiting on her.
He moved well, as if he had plenty of life to spare. She
was attracted by his completeness. And yet, when all was
ready, and there was nothing more for him to do, she
quivered, meeting his questioning look.

As she sat writing, he placed another candle near to
her. The rather dense light fell in two places on the over-
foldings of her hair till it glistened heavy and bright, like
a dense golden plumage folded up. Then the nape of her
neck was very white, with fine down and pointed wisps of
gold. He watched it as it were a vision, losing himself.
She was all that was beyond him, of revelation and
exquisiteness. All that was ideal and beyond him, she
was that—and he was lost to himself in looking at her. She
had no connection with him. He did not approach her.
She was there like a wonderful distance. But it was a
treat, having her in the house. Even with this anguish for
his mother tightening about him, he was sensible of the
wonder of living this evening. The candles glistened on
her hair, and seemed to fascinate him. He felt a little awe
of her, and a sense of uplifting, that he and she and his
mother should be together for a time, in the strange,

unknown atmosphere. And, when he got out of the house, he was afraid. He saw the stars above ringing with fine brightness, the snow beneath just visible, and a new night was gathering round him. He was afraid almost with obliteration. What was this new night ringing about him, and what was he? He could not recognize himself nor any of his surroundings. He was afraid to think of his mother. And yet his chest was conscious of her, and of what was happening to her. He could not escape from her, she carried him with her into an unformed, unknown chaos.

XI

He went up the road in an agony, not knowing what it was all about, but feeling as if a red-hot iron were gripped round his chest. Without thinking, he shook two or three tears on to the snow. Yet in his mind he did not believe his mother would die. He was in the grip of some greater consciousness. As he sat in the hall of the vicarage, waiting whilst Mary put things for Louisa into a bag, he wondered why he had been so upset. He felt abashed and humbled by the big house, he felt again as if he were one of the rank and file. When Miss Mary spoke to him, he almost saluted.

'An honest man,' thought Mary. And the patronage was applied as salve to her own sickness. She had station, so she could patronize: it was almost all that was left to her. But she could not have lived without having a certain position. She could never have trusted herself outside a definite place, nor respected herself except as a woman of superior class.

As Alfred came to the latch-gate, he felt the grief at his heart again, and saw the new heavens. He stood a moment looking northward to the Plough climbing up the night, and at the far glimmer of snow in distant fields. Then his grief came on like physical pain. He held tight to the gate, biting his mouth, whispering 'Mother!' It

was a fierce, cutting, physical pain of grief, that came on
in bouts, as his mother's pain came on in bouts, and was
so acute he could scarcely keep erect. He did not know
where it came from, the pain, nor why. It had nothing to
do with his thoughts. Almost it had nothing to do with
him. Only it gripped him and he must submit. The
whole tide of his soul, gathering in its unknown towards
this expansion into death, carried him with it helplessly,
all the fritter of his thought and consciousness caught up
as nothing, the heave passing on towards its breaking,
taking him further than he had ever been. When the
young man had regained himself, he went indoors, and
there he was almost gay. It seemed to excite him. He felt
in high spirits: he made whimsical fun of things. He sat
on one side of his mother's bed, Louisa on the other, and
a certain gaiety seized them all. But the night and the
dread was coming on.

Alfred kissed his mother and went to bed. When he
was half undressed the knowledge of his mother came
upon him, and the suffering seized him in its grip like two
hands, in agony. He lay on the bed screwed up tight. It
lasted so long, and exhausted him so much, that he fell
asleep, without having the energy to get up and finish
undressing. He awoke after midnight to find himself
stone cold. He undressed and got into bed, and was soon
asleep again.

At a quarter to six he woke, and instantly remembered. Having pulled on his trousers and lighted a
candle, he went into his mother's room. He put his hand
before the candle flame so that no light fell on the bed.

'Mother!' he whispered.

'Yes,' was the reply.

There was a hesitation.

'Should I go to work?'

He waited, his heart was beating heavily.

'I think I'd go, my lad.'

His heart went down in a kind of despair.

'You want me to?'

He let his hand down from the candle flame. The light fell on the bed. There he saw Louisa lying looking up at him. Her eyes were upon him. She quickly shut her eyes and half buried her face in the pillow, her back turned to him. He saw the rough hair like bright vapour about her round head, and the two plaits flung coiled among the bedclothes. It gave him a shock. He stood almost himself, determined. Louisa cowered down. He looked, and met his mother's eyes. Then he gave way again, and ceased to be sure, ceased to be himself.

'Yes, go to work, my boy,' said the mother.

'All right,' replied he, kissing her. His heart was down at despair, and bitter. He went away.

'Alfred!' cried his mother faintly.

He came back with beating heart.

'What, mother?'

'You'll always do what's right, Alfred?' the mother asked, beside herself in terror now he was leaving her. He was too terrified and bewildered to know what she meant.

'Yes,' he said.

She turned her cheek to him. He kissed her, then went away, in bitter despair. He went to work.

XII

By midday his mother was dead. The word met him at the pit-mouth. As he had known, inwardly, it was not a shock to him, and yet he trembled. He went home quite calmly, feeling only heavy in his breathing.

Miss Louisa was still at the house. She had seen to everything possible. Very succinctly, she informed him of what he needed to know. But there was one point of anxiety for her.

'You *did* half expect it—it's not come as a blow to you?' she asked, looking up at him. Her eyes were dark and calm and searching. She too felt lost. He was so dark and inchoate.

'I suppose–yes,' he said stupidly. He looked aside, unable to endure her eyes on him.

'I could not bear to think you might not have guessed,' she said.

He did not answer.

He felt it a great strain to have her near him at this time. He wanted to be alone. As soon as the relatives began to arrive, Louisa departed and came no more. While everything was arranging, and a crowd was in the house, whilst he had business to settle, he went well enough, with only those uncontrollable paroxysms of grief. For the rest, he was superficial. By himself, he endured the fierce, almost insane bursts of grief which passed again and left him calm, almost clear, just wondering. He had not known before that everything could break down, that he himself could break down, and all be a great chaos, very vast and wonderful. It seemed as if life in him had burst its bounds, and he was lost in a great, bewildering flood, immense and unpeopled. He himself was broken and spilled out amid it all. He could only breathe panting in silence. Then the anguish came on again.

When all the people had gone from the Quarry Cottage, leaving the young man alone with an elderly housekeeper, then the long trial began. The snow had thawed and frozen, a fresh fall had whitened the grey, this then began to thaw. The world was a place of loose grey slosh. Alfred had nothing to do in the evenings. He was a man whose life had been filled up with small activities. Without knowing it, he had been centralised, polarised in his mother. It was she who had kept him. Even now, when the old housekeeper had left him, he might still have gone on in his old way. But the force and balance of his life was lacking. He sat pretending to read, all the time holding his fists clenched, and holding himself in, enduring he did not know what. He walked the black and sodden miles of field-paths, till he was tired out: but all this was only running away from whence he must return. At work he was all right. If it had been summer he might have escaped by working in the garden till bedtime. But now, there was no escape, no relief, no help. He, perhaps, was made for action rather than for understanding; for doing than for being. He was shocked out of his activities, like a swimmer who forgets to swim.

For a week, he had the force to endure this suffocation and struggle, then he began to get exhausted, and knew it must come out. The instinct of self-preservation became strongest. But there was the question: Where was he to go? The public-house really meant nothing to him, it was no good going there. He began to think of emigration. In another country he would be all right. He wrote to the emigration offices.

On the Sunday after the funeral, when all the Durant people had attended church, Alfred had seen Miss Louisa, impassive and reserved, sitting with Miss Mary, who was proud and very distant, and with the other Lindleys, who were people removed. Alfred saw them as people remote. He did not think about it. They had nothing to do with his life. After service Louisa had come to him and shaken hands.

'My sister would like you to come to supper one evening, if you would be so good.'

He looked at Miss Mary, who bowed. Out of kindness, Mary had proposed this to Louisa, disapproving of herself even as she did so. But she did not examine herself closely.

'Yes,' said Durant awkwardly, 'I'll come if you want me.' But he vaguely felt that it was misplaced.

'You'll come to-morrow evening, then, about half-past six.'

He went. Miss Louisa was very kind to him. There could be no music, because of the babies. He sat with his fists clenched on his thighs, very quiet and unmoved, lapsing, among all those people, into a kind of muse or daze. There was nothing between him and them. They knew it as well as he. But he remained very steady in

himself, and the evening passed slowly. Mrs Lindley
called him 'young man'.

'Will you sit here, young man?'

He sat there. One name was as good as another.
What had they to do with him?

Mr Lindley kept a special tone for him, kind,
indulgent, but patronising. Durant took it all without
criticism or offence, just submitting. But he did not want
to eat—that troubled him, to have to eat in their presence.
He knew he was out of place. But it was his duty to stay
yet awhile. He answered precisely, in monosyllables.

When he left he winced with confusion. He was glad
it was finished. He got away as quickly as possible. And
he wanted still more intensely to go right away, to
Canada.

Miss Louisa suffered in her soul, indignant with all
of them, with him too, but quite unable to say why she
was indignant.

XIII

Two evenings after, Louisa tapped at the door of the
Quarry Cottage, at half-past six. He had finished dinner,the woman had washed up and gone away, but still
he sat in his pit dirt. He was going later to the New Inn.
He had begun to go there because he must go somewhere. The mere contact with other men was necessary
to him, the noise, the warmth, the forgetful flight of the
hours. But still he did not move. He sat alone in the
empty house till it began to grow on him like something
unnatural.

He was in his pit dirt when he opened the door.

'I have been wanting to call—I thought I would,' she
said, and she went to the sofa. He wondered why she
wouldn't use his mother's round arm-chair. Yet something stirred in him, like anger, when the housekeeper
placed herself in it.

'I ought to have been washed by now,' he said,

glancing at the clock, which was adorned with butterflies and cherries, and the name of 'T. Brooks, Mansfield'. He laid his black hands along his mottled dirty arms. Louisa looked at him. There was the reserve, and the simple neutrality towards her, which she dreaded in him. It made it impossible for her to approach him.

'I am afraid,' she said, 'that I wasn't kind in asking you to supper.'

'I'm not used to it,' he said, smiling with his mouth, showing the interspaced white teeth. His eyes, however, were steady and unseeing.

'It's not *that*,' she said hastily. Her repose was exquisite and her dark grey eyes rich with understanding. He felt afraid of her as she sat there, as he began to grow conscious of her.

'How do you get on alone?' she asked.

He glanced away to the fire.

'Oh—' he answered, shifting uneasily, not finishing his answer.

Her face settled heavily.

'How close it is in this room. You have such immense fires. I will take off my coat,' she said.

He watched her take off her hat and coat. She wore a cream cashmir blouse embroidered with gold silk. It seemed to him a very fine garment, fitting her throat and wrists close. It gave him a feeling of pleasure and cleanness and relief from himself.

'What were you thinking about, that you didn't get washed?' she asked, half intimately. He laughed, turning aside his head. The whites of his eyes showed very distinct in his black face.

'Oh,' he said, 'I couldn't tell you.'

There was a pause.

'Are you going to keep this house on?' she asked.

He stirred in his chair, under the question.

'I hardly know,' he said, 'I'm very likely going to Canada.'

Her spirit became very quiet and attentive.

'What for?' she asked.

Again he shifted restlessly on his seat.

'Well'–he said slowly–'to try the life.'

'But which life?'

'There's various things–farming or lumbering or mining. I don't mind much what it is.'

'And is that what you want?'

He did not think in these times, so he could not answer.

'I don't know,' he said, 'till I've tried.'

She saw him drawing away from her for ever.

'Aren't you sorry to leave this house and garden?' she asked.

'I don't know,' he answered reluctantly. 'I suppose our Fred would come in–that's what he's wanting.'

'You don't want to settle down?' she asked.

He was leaning forward on the arms of his chair. He turned to her. Her face was pale and set. It looked heavy and impassive, her hair shone richer as she grew white. She was to him something steady and immovable and eternal presented to him. His heart was hot in an anguish of suspense. Sharp twitches of fear and pain were in his limbs. He turned his whole body away from her. The silence was unendurable. He could not bear her to sit there any more. It made his heart go hot and stifled in his breast.

'Were you going out to-night?' she asked.

'Only to the New Inn,' he said.

Again there was silence.

She reached for her hat. Nothing else was suggested to her. She *had* to go. He sat waiting for her to be gone, for relief. And she knew that if she went out of that house as she was, she went out a failure. Yet she continued to pin on her hat; in a moment she would have to go. Something was carrying her.

Then suddenly a sharp pang, like lightning, seared her from head to foot, and she was beyond herself.

'Do you want me to go?' she asked, controlled, yet

speaking out of a fiery anguish, as if the words were spoken from her without her intervention.

He went white under his dirt.

'Why?' he asked, turning to her in fear, compelled.

'Do you want me to go?' she repeated.

'Why?' he asked again.

'Because I wanted to stay with you,' she said, suffocated, with her lungs full of fire.

His face worked, he hung forward a little, suspended, staring straight into her eyes, in torment, in an agony of chaos, unable to collect himself. And as if turned to stone, she looked back into his eyes. Their souls were exposed bare for a few moments. It was agony. They could not bear it. He dropped his head, whilst his body jerked with little sharp twitchings.

She turned away for her coat. Her soul had gone dead in her. Her hands trembled, but she could not feel any more. She drew on her coat. There was a cruel suspense in the room. The moment had come for her to go. He lifted his head. His eyes were like agate, expressionless, save for the black points of torture. They held her, she had no will, no life any more. She felt broken.

'Don't you want me?' she said helplessly.

A spasm of torture crossed his eyes, which held her fixed.

'I–I—' he began, but he could not speak. Something drew him from his chair to her. She stood motionless, spellbound, like a creature given up as prey. He put his hand tentatively, uncertainly, on her arm. The expression of his face was strange and inhuman. She stood utterly motionless. Then clumsily he put his arms round her, and took her, cruelly, blindly, straining her till she nearly lost consciousness, till he himself had almost fallen.

Then, gradually, as he held her gripped, and his brain reeled round, and he felt himself falling, falling from himself, and whilst she, yielded up, swooned to a kind of death of herself, a moment of utter darkness came over him, and they began to wake up again as if from a long sleep. He was himself.

After a while his arms slackened, she loosened herself a little, and put her arms round him, as he held her. So they held each other close, and hid each against the other for assurance, helpless in speech. And it was ever her hands that trembled more closely upon him, drawing him nearer into her, with love.

And at last she drew back her face and looked up at him, her eyes wet, and shining with light. His heart, which saw, was silent with fear. He was with her. She saw his face all sombre and inscrutable, and he seemed eternal to her. And all the echo of pain came back into the rarity of bliss, and all her tears came up.

'I love you,' she said, her lips drawn to sobbing. He put down his head against her, unable to hear her, unable to bear the sudden coming of the peace and passion that almost broke his heart. They stood together in silence whilst the thing moved away a little.

At last she wanted to see him. She looked up. His eyes were strange and glowing, with a tiny black pupil. Strange, they were, and powerful over her. And his mouth came to hers, and slowly her eyelids closed, as his mouth sought hers closer and closer, and took possession of her.

They were silent for a long time, too much mixed up with passion and grief and death to do anything but hold each other in pain and kiss with long, hurting kisses wherein fear was transfused into desire. At last she disengaged herself. He felt as if his heart were hurt, but glad, and he scarcely dared look at her.

'I'm glad,' she said also.

He held her hands in passionate gratitude and desire. He had not yet the presence of mind to say anything. He was dazed with relief.

'I ought to go,' she said.

He looked at her. He could not grasp the thought of

her going, he knew he could never be separated from her any more. Yet he dared not assert himself. He held her hands tight.

'Your face is black,' she said.

He laughed.

'Yours is a bit smudged,' he said.

They were afraid of each other, afraid to talk. He could only keep her near to him. After a while she wanted to wash her face. He brought her some warm water, standing by and watching her. There was something he wanted to say, that he dared not. He watched her wiping her face, and making tidy her hair.

'They'll see your blouse is dirty,' he said.

She looked at her sleeves and laughed for joy.

He was sharp with pride.

'What shall you do?' he asked.

'How?' she said.

He was awkward at a reply.

'About me,' he said.

'What do you want me to do?' she laughed.

He put his hand out slowly to her. What did it matter!

'But make yourself clean,' she said.

XIV

As they went up the hill, the night seemed dense with the unknown. They kept close together, feeling as if the darkness were alive and full of knowledge, all around them. In silence they walked up the hill. At first the street lamps went their way. Several people passed them. He was more shy than she, and would have let her go had she loosened in the least. But she held firm.

Then they came into the true darkness, between the fields. They did not want to speak, feeling closer together in silence. So they arrived at the Vicarage gate. They stood under the naked horse-chestnut tree.

'I wish you didn't have to go,' he said.

She laughed a quick little laugh.

'Come to-morrow,' she said, in a low tone, 'and ask father.'

She felt his hand close on hers.

She gave the same sorrowful little laugh of sympathy. Then she kissed him, sending him home.

At home, the old grief came on in another paroxysm, obliterating Louisa, obliterating even his mother for whom the stress was raging like a burst of fever in a wound. But something was sound in his heart.

XV

The next evening he dressed to go to the vicarage, feeling it was to be done, not imagining what it would be like. He would not take this seriously. He was sure of Louisa, and this marriage was like fate to him. It filled him also with a blessed feeling of fatality. He was not responsible, neither had her people anything really to do with it.

They ushered him into the little study, which was fireless. By and by the vicar came in. His voice was cold and hostile as he said:

'What can I do for you, young man?'

He knew already, without asking.

Durant looked up at him, again like a sailor before a superior. He had the subordinate manner. Yet his spirit was clear.

'I wanted, Mr Lindley—' he began respectfully, then all the colour suddenly left his face. It seemed now a violation to say what he had to say. What was he doing there? But he stood on, because it had to be done. He held firmly to his own independence and self-respect. He must not be indecisive. He must put himself aside: the matter was bigger than just his personal self. He must not feel. This was his highest duty.

'You wanted—' said the vicar.

Durant's mouth was dry, but he answered with steadiness:

'Miss Louisa–Louisa–promised to marry me—'

'You asked Miss Louisa if she would marry you–yes—' corrected the vicar. Durant reflected he had not asked her this:

'If she would marry me, sir. I hope you–don't mind.'

He smiled. He was a good-looking man, and the vicar could not help seeing it.

'And my daughter was willing to marry you?' said Mr Lindley.

'Yes,' said Durant seriously. It was pain to him, nevertheless. He felt the natural hostility between himself and the elder man.

'Will you come this way?' said the vicar. He led into the dining-room, where were Mary, Louisa, and Mrs Lindley. Mr Massy sat in a corner with a lamp.

'This young man has come on your account, Louisa?' said Mr Lindley.

'Yes,' said Louisa, her eyes on Durant, who stood erect, in discipline. He dared not look at her, but he was aware of her.

'You don't want to marry a collier, you little fool,' cried Mrs Lindley harshly. She lay obese and helpless upon the couch, swathed in a loose, dove-grey gown.

'Oh, hush, mother,' cried Mary, with quiet intensity and pride.

'What means have you to support a wife?' demanded the vicar's wife roughly.

'I!' Durant replied, starting. 'I think I can earn enough.'

'Well, and how much?' came the rough voice.

'Seven and six a day,' replied the young man.

'And will it get to be any more?'

'I hope so.'

'And are you going to live in that poky little house?'

'I think so,' said Durant, 'if it's all right.'

He took small offence, only was upset, because they would not think him good enough. He knew that, in their sense, he was not.

'Then she's a fool, I tell you, if she marries you,' cried the mother roughly, casting her decision.

'After all, mama, it is Louisa's affair,' said Mary distinctly, 'and we must remember—'

'As she makes her bed, she must lie–but she'll repent it,' interrupted Mrs Lindley.

'And after all,' said Mr Lindley, 'Louisa cannot quite hold herself free to act entirely without consideration for her family.'

'What do you want, papa?' asked Louisa sharply.

'I mean that if you marry this man, it will make my position very difficult for me, particularly if you stay in this parish. If you were moving quite away, it would be simpler. But living here in a collier's cottage, under my nose, as it were–it would be almost unseemly. I have my position to maintain, and a position which may not be taken lightly.'

'Come over here, young man,' cried the mother, in her rough voice, 'and let us look at you.'

Durant, flushing, went over and stood–not quite at attention, so that he did not know what to do with his hands. Miss Louisa was angry to see him standing there, obedient and acquiescent. He ought to show himself a man.

'Can't you take her away and live out of sight?' said the mother. 'You'd both of you be better off.'

'Yes, we can go away,' he said.

'Do you want to?' asked Miss Mary clearly.

He faced round. Mary looked very stately and impressive. He flushed.

'I do if it's going to be a trouble to anybody,' he said.

'For yourself, you would rather stay?' said Mary.

'It's my home,' he said, 'and that's the house I was born in.'

'Then'–Mary turned clearly to her parents, 'I really don't see how you can make the conditions, papa. He has his own rights, and if Louisa wants to marry him—'

'Louisa, Louisa,' cried the father impatiently. 'I

cannot understand why Louisa should not behave in the normal way. I cannot see why she should only think of herself, and leave her family out of count. The thing is enough in itself, and she ought to try to ameliorate it as much as possible. And if—'

'But I love the man, papa,' said Louisa.

'And I hope you love your parents, and I hope you want to spare them as much of the—the loss of prestige, as possible.'

'We *can* go away to live,' said Louisa, her face breaking to tears. At last she was really hurt.

'Oh, yes, easily,' Durant replied hastily, pale, distressed.

There was dead silence in the room.

'I think it would really be better,' murmured the vicar, mollified.

'Very likely it would,' said the rough-voiced invalid.

'Though I think we ought to apologize for asking such a thing,' said Mary haughtily.

'No,' said Durant. 'It will be best all round.' He was glad there was no more bother.

'And shall we put up the banns here or go to the registrar?' he asked clearly, like a challenge.

'We will go to the registrar,' replied Louisa decidedly.

Again there was a dead silence in the room.

'Well, if you will have your own way, you must go your own way,' said the mother emphatically.

All the time Mr Massy had sat obscure and unnoticed in a corner of the room. At this juncture he got up, saying:

'There is baby, Mary.'

Mary rose and went out of the room, stately; her little husband padded after her. Durant watched the fragile, small man go, wondering.

'And where,' asked the vicar, almost genial, 'do you think you will go when you are married?'

Durant started.

'I was thinking of emigrating,' he said.

'To Canada? or where?'

'I think to Canada.'

'Yes, that would be very good.'

Again there was a pause.

'We shan't see much of you then, as a son-in-law,' said the mother, roughly but amicably.

'Not much,' he said.

Then he took his leave. Louisa went with him to the gate. She stood before him in distress.

'You won't mind them, will you?' she said humbly.

'I don't mind them, if they don't mind me!' he said. Then he stooped and kissed her.

'Let us be married soon,' she murmured, in tears.

'All right,' he said. 'I'll go to-morrow to Barford.'

The Prussian Officer

Written as 'Honour and Arms' in June 1913.
Revised in July 1913 and again in July and October
1914. For printing in *English Review*, August 1914,
unauthorised cuts were made. Title change made by
Edward Garnett, against Lawrence's wishes.

I

They had marched more than thirty kilometres since
dawn, along the white, hot road where occasional
thickets of trees threw a moment of shade, then out into
the glare again. On either hand, the valley, wide and
shallow, glittered with heat; dark green patches of rye,
pale young corn, fallow and meadow and black pine
woods spread in a dull, hot diagram under a glistening
sky. But right in front the mountains ranged across, pale
blue and very still, snow gleaming gently out of the deep
atmosphere. And towards the mountains, on and on, the
regiment marched between the rye fields and the
meadows, between the scraggy fruit trees set regularly on
either side the high road. The burnished, dark green rye
threw off a suffocating heat, the mountains drew
gradually nearer and more distinct. While the feet of the
soldiers grew hotter, sweat ran through their hair under
their helmets, and their knapsacks could burn no more in
contact with their shoulders, but seemed instead to give
off a cold, prickly sensation.

He walked on and on in silence, staring at the
mountains ahead, that rose sheer out of the land, and
stood fold behind fold, half earth, half heaven, the

heaven, the barrier with slits of soft snow, in the pale, bluish peaks.

He could now walk almost without pain. At the start, he had determined not to limp. It had made him sick to take the first steps, and during the first mile or so, he had compressed his breath, and the cold drops of sweat had stood on his forehead. But he had walked it off. What where they after all but bruises! He had looked at them, as he was getting up: deep bruises on the backs of his thighs. And since he had made his first step in the morning, he had been conscious of them, till now he had a tight, hot place in his chest, with suppressing the pain, and holding himself in. There seemed no air when he breathed. But he walked almost lightly.

The Captain's hand had trembled at taking his coffee at dawn: his orderly saw it again. And he saw the fine figure of the Captain wheeling on horse-back at the farm-house ahead, a handsome figure in pale blue uniform with facings of scarlet, and the metal gleaming on the black helmet and the sword-scabbard, and dark streaks of sweat coming on the silky bay horse. The orderly felt he was connected with that figure moving so suddenly on horseback: he followed it like a shadow, mute and inevitable and damned by it. And the officer was always aware of the tramp of the company behind, the march of his orderly among the men.

The Captain was a tall man of about forty, grey at the temples. He had a handsome, finely knit figure, and was one of the best horsemen in the West. His orderly, having to rub him down, admired the amazing riding-muscles of his loins.

For the rest, the orderly scarcely noticed the officer any more than he noticed himself. It was rarely he saw his master's face: he did not look at it. The Captain had reddish-brown, stiff hair, that he wore short upon his skull. His moustache was also cut short and bristly over a full, brutal mouth. His face was rather rugged, the cheeks thin. Perhaps the man was the more handsome for the deep lines in his face, the irritable tension of his brow, which gave him the look of a man who fights with life. His fair eyebrows stood bushy over light blue eyes that were always flashing with cold fire.

He was a Prussian aristocrat, haughty and over-bearing. But his mother had been a Polish Countess. Having made too many gambling debts when he was young, he had ruined his prospects in the Army, and remained an infantry captain. He had never married: his position did not allow of it, and no woman had ever moved him to it. His time he spent riding—occasionally he rode one of his own horses at the races—and at the officers' club. Now and then he took himself a mistress. But after such an event, he returned to duty with his brow still more tense, his eyes still more hostile and irrit-able. With the men, however, he was merely impersonal, though a devil when roused; so that, on the whole, they feared him, but had no great aversion from him. They accepted him as the inevitable.

To his orderly he was at first cold and just and indifferent: he did not fuss over trifles. So that his servant knew practically nothing about him, except just what orders he would give, and how he wanted them obeyed. That was quite simple. Then the change gradually came.

The orderly was a youth of about twenty-two, of medium height, and well built. He had strong, heavy limbs, was swarthy, with a soft, black, young moustache. There was something altogether warm and young about him. He had firmly marked eyebrows over dark, expressionless eyes, that seemed never to have thought, only to have received life direct through his senses, and acted straight from instinct.

Gradually the officer had become aware of his servant's young, vigorous, unconscious presence about him. He could not get away from the sense of the youth's person, while he was in attendance. It was like a warm flame upon the older man's tense, rigid body, that had become almost unliving, fixed. There was something so free and self-contained about him, and something in the young fellow's movement, that made the officer aware of him. And this irritated the Prussian. He did not choose to be touched into life by his servant. He might easily have changed his man, but he did not. He now very rarely looked direct at his orderly, but kept his face averted, as if to avoid seeing him. And yet as the young soldier moved unthinking about the apartment, the elder watched him, and would notice the movement of his strong young shoulders under the blue cloth, the bend of his neck. And it irritated him. To see the soldier's young, brown, shapely peasant's hand grasp the loaf or the wine-bottle sent a flash of hate or of anger through the elder man's blood. It was not that the youth was clumsy: it was rather the blind, instinctive sureness of movement of an unhampered young animal that irritated the officer to such a degree.

Once, when a bottle of wine had gone over, and the red gushed out on to the tablecloth, the officer had started up with an oath, and his eyes, bluey like fire, had held those of the confused youth for a moment. It was a shock for the young soldier. He felt something sink deeper, deeper into his soul, where nothing had ever gone before. It left him rather blank and wondering. Some of his natural completeness in himself was gone, a little uneasiness took its place. And from that time an undiscovered feeling had held between the two men.

Henceforward the orderly was afraid of really meeting his master. His subconsciousness remembered those steely blue eyes and the harsh brows, and did not intend to meet them again. So he always stared past his master, and avoided him. Also, in a little anxiety, he waited for the three months to have gone, when his time would be up. He began to feel a constraint in the Captain's presence, and the soldier even more than the officer wanted to be left alone, in his neutrality as servant.

He had served the Captain for more than a year, and knew his duty. This he performed easily, as if it were natural to him. The officer and his commands he took for granted, as he took the sun and the rain, and he served as a matter of course. It did not implicate him personally.

But now if he were going to be forced into a personal interchange with his master he would be like a wild thing caught, he felt he must get away.

But the influence of the young soldier's being had penetrated through the officer's stiffened discipline, and perturbed the man in him. He, however, was a gentleman, with long, fine hands and cultivated movements, and was not going to allow such a thing as the stirring of his innate self. He was a man of passionate temper, who had always kept himself suppressed. Occasionally there had been a duel, an outburst before the soldiers. He knew himself to be always on the point of breaking out. But he kept himself hard to the idea of the Service. Whereas the young soldier seemed to live out his warm, full nature, to give it off in his very movements, which had a certain zest, such as wild animals have in free movement. And this irritated the officer more and more.

In spite of himself, the Captain could not regain his neutrality of feeling towards his orderly. Nor could he leave the man alone. In spite of himself, he watched him, gave him sharp orders, tried to take up as much of his time as possible. Sometimes he flew into a rage with the young soldier, and bullied him. Then the orderly shut himself off, as it were out of earshot, and waited, with sullen, flushed face, for the end of the noise. The words never pierced to his intelligence, he made himself, protectively, impervious to the feelings of his master.

He had a scar on his left thumb, a deep seam going across the knuckle. The officer had long suffered from it, and wanted to do something to it. Still it was there, ugly and brutal on the young, brown hand. At last the Captain's reserve gave way. One day, as the orderly was smoothing out the tablecloth, the officer pinned down his thumb with a pencil, asking:

'How did you come by that?'

The young man winced and drew back at attention.

'A wood axe, Herr Hauptmann,' he answered.

The officer waited for further explanation. None came. The orderly went about his duties. The elder man was sullenly angry. His servant avoided him. And the next day he had to use all his will-power to avoid seeing the scarred thumb. He wanted to get hold of it and— A hot flame ran in his blood.

He knew his servant would soon be free, and would be glad. As yet, the soldier had held himself off from the elder man. The Captain grew madly irritable. He could not rest when the soldier was away, and when he was present, he glared at him with tormented eyes. He hated those fine, black brows over the unmeaning, dark eyes, he was infuriated by the free movement of the handsome limbs, which no military discipline could make stiff. And he became harsh and cruelly bullying, using contempt and satire. The young soldier only grew more mute and expressionless.

'What cattle were you bred by, that you can't keep straight eyes? Look me in the eyes when I speak to you.'

And the soldier turned his dark eyes to the other's face, but there was no sight in them: he stared with the slightest possible cast, holding back his sight, perceiving the blue of his master's eyes, but receiving no look from them. And the elder man went pale, and his reddish eyebrows twitched. He gave his order, barrenly.

Once he flung a heavy military glove into the young soldier's face. Then he had the satisfaction of seeing the black eyes flare up into his own, like a blaze when straw is thrown on a fire. And he had laughed with a little tremor and a sneer.

But there were only two months more. The youth instinctively tried to keep himself intact: he tried to serve the officer as if the latter were an abstract authority and not a man. All his instinct was to avoid personal contact, even definite hate. But in spite of himself the hate grew, responsive to the officer's passion. However, he put it in the background. When he had left the Army he could dare acknowledge it. By nature he was active, and had many friends. He thought what amazing good fellows they were. But, without knowing it, he was alone. Now this solitariness was intensified. It would carry him through his term. But the officer seemed to be going irritably insane, and the youth was deeply frightened.

The soldier had a sweetheart, a girl from the mountains, independent and primitive. The two walked together, rather silently. He went with her, not to talk, but to have his arm round her, and for the physical contact. This eased him, made it easier for him to ignore the Captain; for he could rest with her held fast against his chest. And she, in some unspoken fashion, was there for him. They loved each other.

The Captain perceived it, and was mad with irritation. He kept the young man engaged all the evenings long, and took pleasure in the dark look that came on his face. Occasionally, the eyes of the two men met, those of the younger sullen and dark, doggedly unalterable, those of the elder sneering with restless contempt.

The officer tried hard not to admit the passion that had got hold of him. He would not know that his feeling for his orderly was anything but that of a man incensed by his stupid, perverse servant. So, keeping quite justified and conventional in his consciousness, he let the other thing run on. His nerves, however, were suffering. At last he slung the end of a belt in his servant's face. When he saw the youth start back, the pain-tears in his eyes and the blood on his mouth, he had felt at once a thrill of deep pleasure and of shame.

But this, he acknowledged to himself, was a thing he had never done before. The fellow was too exasperating. His own nerves must be going to pieces. He went away for some days with a woman.

It was a mockery of pleasure. He simply did not want the woman. But he stayed on for his time. At the end of it, he came back in an agony of irritation, torment, and misery. He rode all the evening, then came straight in to supper. His orderly was out. The officer sat with his long, fine hands lying on the table, perfectly still, and all his blood seemed to be corroding.

At last his servant entered. He watched the strong, easy young figure, the fine eyebrows, the thick black hair. In a week's time the youth had got back his old well-being. The hands of the officer twitched and seemed to be full of mad flame. The young man stood at attention, unmoving, shut off.

The meal went in silence. But the orderly seemed eager. He made a clatter with the dishes.

'Are you in a hurry?' asked the officer, watching the intent, warm face of his servant. The other did not reply.

'Will you answer my question?' said the Captain.

'Yes, sir,' replied the orderly, standing with his pile of deep Army plates. The Captain waited, looked at him, then asked again:

'Are you in a hurry?'

'Yes, sir,' came the answer, that sent a flash through the listener.

'For what?'

'I was going out, sir.'

'I want you this evening.'

There was a moment's hesitation. The officer had a curious stiffness of countenance.

'Yes, sir,' replied the servant, in his throat.

'I want you to-morrow evening also—in fact, you may consider your evenings occupied, unless I give you leave.'

The mouth with the young moustache set close.

'Yes, sir,' answered the orderly, loosening his lips for a moment.

He again turned to the door.

'And why have you a piece of pencil in your ear?'

The orderly hesitated, then continued on his way without answering. He set the plates in a pile outside the door, took the stump of pencil from his ear, and put it in his pocket. He had been copying a verse for his sweetheart's birthday card. He returned to finish clearing the table. The officer's eyes were dancing, he had a little, eager smile.

'Why have you a piece of pencil in your ear?' he asked.

The orderly took his hands full of dishes. His master was standing near the great green stove, a little smile on his face, his chin thrust forward. When the young soldier saw him his heart suddenly ran hot. He felt blind. Instead of answering, he turned dazedly to the door. As he was crouching to set down the dishes, he was pitched forward by a kick from behind. The pots went in a stream down the stairs, he clung to the pillar of the banisters. And as he was rising he was kicked heavily again and again, so that he clung sickly to the post for some moments. His master had gone swiftly into the room and closed the door. The maid-servant downstairs looked up the staircase and made a mocking face at the crockery disaster.

The officer's heart was plunging. He poured himself a glass of wine, part of which he spilled on the floor, and gulped the remainder, leaning against the cool, green stove. He heard his man collecting the dishes from the stairs. Pale, as if intoxicated, he waited. The servant entered again. The Captain's heart gave a pang, as of pleasure, seeing the young fellow bewildered and uncertain on his feet, with pain.

'Schöner!' he said.

The soldier was a little slower in coming to attention.

'Yes, sir!'

The youth stood before him, with pathetic young moustache, and fine eyebrows very distinct on his forehead of dark marble.

'I asked you a question.'

'Yes, sir.'

The officer's tone bit like acid.

'Why had you a pencil in your ear?'

Again the servant's heart ran hot, and he could not breathe. With dark, strained eyes, he looked at the officer, as if fascinated. The withering smile came into the Captain's eyes, and he lifted his foot.

'I–I forgot it–sir,' panted the soldier, his dark eyes fixed on the other man's dancing blue ones.

'What was it doing there?'

He saw the young man's breast heaving as he made an effort for words.

'I had been writing.'

'Writing what?'

Again the soldier looked him up and down. The officer could hear him panting. The smile came into the blue eyes. The soldier worked his dry throat, but could not speak. Suddenly the smile lit like a flame on the officer's face, and a kick came heavily against the orderly's thigh. The youth moved a pace sideways. His face went dead, with two black, staring eyes.

'Well?' said the officer.

The orderly's mouth had gone dry, and his tongue rubbed in it as on dry brown-paper. He worked his throat. The officer raised his foot. The servant went stiff.

'Some poetry, sir,' came the crackling, unrecognizable sound of his voice.

'Poetry, what poetry?' asked the Captain, with a sickly smile.

Again there was the working in the throat. The Captain's heart had suddenly gone down heavily, and he stood sick and tired.

'For my girl, sir,' he heard the dry, inhuman sound.

'Oh!' he said, turning away. 'Clear the table.'

'Click!' went the soldier's throat; then again, 'click!' and then the half-articulate:

'Yes, sir.'

The young soldier was gone, looking old, and walking heavily.

The officer, left alone, held himself rigid, to prevent himself from thinking. His instinct warned him that he must not think. Deep inside him was the intense gratification of his passion, still working powerfully. Then there was a counter-action, a horrible breaking down of something inside him, a whole agony of reaction. He stood there for an hour motionless, a chaos of sensations, but rigid with a will to keep blank his consciousness, to prevent his mind grasping. And he held himself so until the worst of the stress had passed, when he began to drink, drank himself to an intoxication, till he slept obliterated. When he woke in the morning he was shaken to the base of his nature. But he had fought off the realisation of what he had done. He had prevented his mind from taking it in, had suppressed it along with his instincts, and the conscious man had nothing to do with it. He felt only as after a bout of intoxication, weak, but the affair itself all dim and not to be recovered. Of the drunkenness of his passion he successfully refused remembrance. And when his orderly appeared with coffee, the officer assumed the same self he had had the morning before. He refused the event of the past night–denied it had ever been–and was successful in his denial. He had not done any such thing–not he himself. Whatever there might be lay at the door of the stupid, insubordinate servant.

The orderly had gone about in a stupor all the evening. He drank some beer because he was parched, but not much, the alcohol made his feeling come back,and he could not bear it. He was dulled, as if nine-tenths of the ordinary man in him were inert. He crawled about disfigured. Still, when he thought of the kicks, he went sick, and when he thought of the threat of more kicking, in the room afterwards, his heart went hot and faint, and he panted remembering the one that had come. He had been forced to say, 'For my girl.' He was much too done even to want to cry. His mouth hung slightly open, like an idiot's. He felt vacant, and wasted.

So, he wandered at his work, painfully, and very slowly and clumsily, fumbling blindly with the brushes, and finding it difficult, when he sat down, to summon the energy to move again. His limbs, his jaw, were slack and nerveless. But he was very tired. He got to bed at last, and slept inert, relaxed, in a sleep that was rather stupor than slumber, a dead night of stupefaction shot through with gleams of anguish.

In the morning were the manoeuvres. But he woke even before the bugle sounded. The painful ache in his chest, the dryness of his throat, the awful steady feeling of misery made his eyes come awake and dreary at once. He knew, without thinking, what had happened. And he knew that the day had come again, when he must go on with his round. The last bit of darkness was being pushed out of the room. He would have to move his inert body and go on. He was so young, and had known so little trouble, that he was bewildered. He only wished it would stay night, so that he could lie still, covered up by the darkness. And yet nothing would prevent the day from coming, nothing would save him from having to get up and saddle the Captain's horse, and make the Captain's coffee. It was there, inevitable. And then, he thought, it was impossible. Yet they would not leave him free. He must go and take the coffee to the Captain. He was too stunned to understand it. He only knew it was inevitable–inevitable, however long he lay inert.

At last, after heaving at himself, for he seemed to be a mass of inertia, he got up. But he had to force every one of his movements from behind, with his will. He felt lost, and dazed, and helpless. Then he clutched hold of the bed, the pain was so keen. And looking at his thighs, he saw the darker bruises on his swarthy flesh and he knew that, if he pressed one of his fingers on one of the bruises, he should faint. But he did not want to faint–he did not want anybody to know. No one should ever know. It was between him and the Captain. There were only the two people in the world now–himself and the Captain.

Slowly, economically, he got dressed and forced himself to walk. Everything was obscure, except just what he had his hands on. But he managed to get through his work. The very pain revived his dull senses. The worst remained yet. He took the tray and went up to the Captain's room. The officer, pale and heavy, sat at the table. The orderly, as he saluted, felt himself put out of existence. He stood still for a moment submitting to his own nullification–then he gathered himself, seemed to regain himself, and then the Captain began to grow vague, unreal, and the younger soldier's heart beat up. He clung to this situation–that the Captain did not exist–so that he himself might live. But when he saw his officer's hand tremble as he took the coffee, he felt everything falling shattered. And he went away, feeling as if he himself were coming to pieces, disintegrated. And when the Captain was there on horseback, giving orders, while he himself stood, with rifle and knapsack, sick with pain, he felt as if he must shut his eyes–as if he must shut his eyes on everything. It was only the long agony of marching with a parched throat that filled him with one single, sleep-heavy intention: to save himself.

II

He was getting used even to his parched throat. That the snowy peaks were radiant among the sky, that the whity-green glacier-river twisted through its pale shoals, in the valley below, seemed almost supernatural. But he was going mad with fever and thirst. He plodded on uncomplaining. He did not want to speak, not to anybody. There were two gulls, like flakes of water and snow, over the river. The scent of green rye soaked in sunshine came like a sickness. And the march continued, monotonously, almost like a bad sleep.

At the next farm-house, which stood low and broad near the high road, tubs of water had been put out. The soldiers clustered round to drink. They took off their helmets, and the steam mounted from their wet hair. The Captain sat on horseback, watching. He needed to see his orderly. His helmet threw a dark shadow over his light, fierce eyes, but his moustache and mouth and chin were distinct in the sunshine. The orderly must move under the presence of the figure of the horseman. It was not that he was afraid, or cowed. It was as if he was disembowelled, made empty, like an empty shell. He felt himself as nothing, a shadow creeping under the sunshine. And, thirsty as he was, he could scarcely drink, feeling the Captain near him. He would not take off his helmet to wipe his wet hair. He wanted to stay in shadow, not to be forced into consciousness. Starting, he saw the light heel of the officer prick the belly of the horse; the Captain cantered away, and he himself could relapse into vacancy.

Nothing, however, could give him back his living place in the hot, bright morning. He felt like a gap among it all. Whereas the Captain was prouder, overriding. A hot flash went through the young servant's body. The Captain was firmer and prouder with life, he himself was empty as a shadow. Again the flash went through him, dazing him out. But his heart ran a little firmer.

The company turned up the hill, to make a loop for the return. Below, from among the trees, the farm-bell clanged. He saw the labourers, mowing barefoot at the thick grass, leave off their work and go downhill, their scythes hanging over their shoulders, like long, bright claws curving down behind them. They seemed like dream-people, as if they had no relation to himself. He felt as in a blackish dream: as if all the other things were there and had form, but he himself was only a consciousness, a gap that could think and perceive.

The soldiers were tramping silently up the glaring hillside. Gradually his head began to revolve, slowly, rhythmically. Sometimes it was dark before his eyes, as if he saw this world through a smoked glass, frail shadows and unreal. It gave him a pain in his head to walk.

The air was too scented, it gave no breath. All the lush green-stuff seemed to be issuing its sap, till the air was deathly, sickly with the smell of greenness. There was the perfume of clover, like pure honey and bees. Then there grew a faint acrid tang—they were near the beeches; and then a queer clattering noise, and a suffocating, hideous smell; they were passing a flock of sheep, a shepherd in a black smock, holding his crook. Why should the sheep huddle together under this fierce sun? He felt that the shepherd would not see him, though he could see the shepherd.

At last there was the halt. They stacked rifles in a conical stack, put down their kit in a scattered circle around it, and dispersed a little, sitting on a small knoll high on the hillside. The chatter began. The soldiers were steaming with heat, but were lively. He sat still, seeing the blue mountains rising upon the land, twenty kilometres away. There was a blue fold in the ranges, then out of that, at the foot, the broad, pale bed of the river, stretches of whity-green water between pinkish-grey shoals among the dark pine woods. There it was, spread out a long way off. And it seemed to come downhill, the river. There was a raft being steered, a mile away. It was a strange country. Nearer, a red-roofed, broad farm with white base and square dots of windows crouched beside the wall of beech foliage on the wood's edge. There were long strips of rye and clover and pale green corn. And just at his feet, below the knoll, was a darkish bog, where globe flowers stood breathless still on their slim stalks. And some of the pale gold bubbles were burst, and a broken fragment hung in the air. He thought he was going to sleep.

Suddenly something moved into this coloured mirage before his eyes. The Captain, a small, light-blue and scarlet figure, was trotting evenly between the strips of corn, along the level brow of the hill. And the man making flag-signals was coming on. Proud and sure moved the horseman's figure, the quick, bright thing, in which was concentrated all the light of this morning, which for the rest lay a fragile, shining shadow. Submissive, apathetic, the young soldier sat and stared. But as the horse slowed to a walk, coming up the last steep path, the great flash flared over the body and soul of the orderly. He sat waiting. The back of his head felt as if it were weighted with a heavy piece of fire. He did not want to eat. His hands trembled slightly as he moved them. Meanwhile the officer on horseback was approaching slowing and proudly. The tension grew in the orderly's soul. Then again, seeing the Captain ease himself on the saddle, the flash blazed through him.

The Captain looked at the patch of light blue and scarlet, and dark heads, scattered closely on the hillside. It pleased him. The command pleased him. And he was feeling proud. His orderly was among them in common subjection. The officer rose a little on his stirrups to look. The young soldier sat with averted, dumb face. The Captain relaxed on his seat. His slim-legged, beautiful horse, brown as a beech nut, walked proudly uphill. The Captain passed into the zone of the company's atmosphere: a hot smell of men, of sweat, of leather. He knew it very well. After a word with the lieutenant, he went a few paces higher, and sat there, a dominant figure, his sweat-marked horse swishing its tail, while he looked down on his men, on his orderly, a nonentity among the crowd.

The young soldier's heart was like fire in his chest, and he breathed with difficulty. The officer, looking downhill, saw three of the young soldiers, two pails of water between them, staggering across a sunny green field. A table had been set up under a tree, and there the slim lieutenant stood, importantly busy. Then the Captain summoned himself to an act of courage. He called his orderly.

The flame leapt into the young soldier's throat as he heard the command, and he rose blindly, stifled. He saluted, standing below the officer. He did not look up.

But there was the flicker in the Captain's voice.

'Go to the inn and fetch me . . .' the officer gave his commands. 'Quick!' he added.

At the last word, the heart of the servant leapt with a flash, and he felt the strength come over his body. But he turned in mechanical obedience, and set off at a heavy run downhill, looking almost like a bear, his trousers bagging over his military boots. And the officer watched this blind, plunging run all the way.

But it was only the outside of the orderly's body that was obeying so humbly and mechanically. Inside had gradually accumulated a core into which all the energy of that young life was compact and concentrated. He executed his commission, and plodded quickly back uphill. There was a pain in his head, as he walked, that made him twist his features unknowingly. But hard there in the centre of his chest was himself, himself firm, and not to be plucked to pieces.

The captain had gone up into the wood. The orderly plodded through the hot, powerfully smelling zone of the company's atmosphere. He had a curious mass of energy inside him now. The Captain was less real than himself. He approached the green entrance to the wood. There, in the half-shade, he saw the horse standing, the sunshine and the flickering shadow of leaves dancing over his brown body. There was a clearing where timber had lately been felled. Here, in the gold-green shade beside the brilliant cup of sunshine, stood two figures, blue and pink, the bits of pink showing out plainly. The Captain was talking to his lieutenant.

The orderly stood on the edge of the bright clearing, where great trunks of trees, stripped and glistening, lay stretched like naked, brown-skinned bodies. Chips of wood littered the trampled floor, like splashed light, and the bases of the felled trees stood here and there, with their raw, level tops. Beyond was the brilliant, sunlit green of a beech.

'Then I will ride forward,' the orderly heard his

Captain say. The lieutenant saluted and strode away. He himself went forward. A hot flash passed through his belly, as he tramped towards his officer.

The Captain watched the rather heavy figure of the young soldier stumble forward, and his veins, too, ran hot. This was to be man to man between them. He yielded before the solid, stumbling figure with bent head. The orderly stooped and put the food on a level-sawn tree-base. The Captain watched the glistening, sun-inflamed, naked hands. He wanted to speak to the young soldier, but could not. The servant propped a bottle against his thigh, pressed open the cork, and poured out the beer into the mug. He kept his head bent. The Captain accepted the mug.

'Hot!' he said, as if amiably.

The flame sprang out of the orderly's heart, nearly suffocating him.

'Yes, sir,' he replied, between shut teeth.

And he heard the sound of the Captain's drinking, and he clenched his fists, such a strong torment came into his wrists. Then came the faint clang of the closing of the pot-lid. He looked up. The Captain was watching him. He glanced swiftly away. Then he saw the officer stoop and take a piece of bread from the tree-base. Again the flash of flame went through the young soldier, seeing the stiff body stoop beneath him, and his hands jerked. He looked away. He could feel the officer was nervous. The bread fell as it was being broken. The officer ate the other piece. The two men stood tense and still, the master laboriously chewing his bread, the servant staring with averted face, his fist clenched.

Then the young soldier started. The officer had pressed open the lid of the mug again. The orderly watched the lid of the mug, and the white hand that clenched the handle, as if he were fascinated. It was raised. The youth followed it with his eyes. And then he saw the thin, strong throat of the elder man moving up and down as he drank, the strong jaw working. And the instinct which had been jerking at the young man's wrists suddenly jerked free. He jumped, feeling as if it were rent in two by a strong flame.

The spur of the officer caught in a tree-root, he went down backwards with a crash, the middle of his back thudding sickeningly against a sharp-edged tree-base, the pot flying away. And in a second the orderly, with serious, earnest young face, and underlip between his teeth, had got his knee in the officer's chest and was pressing the chin backward over the farther edge of the tree-stump, pressing, with all his heart behind in a passion of relief, the tension of his wrists exquisite with relief. And with the base of his palms he shoved at the chin, with all his might. And it was pleasant, too, to have that chin, that hard jaw already slightly rough with beard, in his hands. He did not relax one hair's breadth, but, all the force of all his blood exulting in his thrust, he shoved back the head of the other man, till there was a little 'cluck' and a crunching sensation. Then he felt as if his head went to vapour. Heavy convulsions shook the body of the officer, frightening and horrifying the young soldier. Yet it pleased him, too, to repress them. It pleased him to keep his hands pressing back the chin, to feel the chest of the other man yield in expiration to the weight of his strong, young knees, to feel the hard twitchings of the prostrate body jerking his own whole frame, which was pressed down on it.

But it went still. He could look into the nostrils of the other man, the eyes he could scarcely see. How curiously the mouth was pushed out, exaggerating the full lips, and the moustache bristling up from them. Then, with a start, he noticed the nostrils gradually filled with blood. The red brimmed, hesitated, ran over, and went in a thin trickle down the face to the eyes.

It shocked and distressed him. Slowly, he got up. The body twitched and sprawled there, inert. He stood and looked at it in silence. It was a pity *it* was broken. It represented more than the thing which had kicked and bullied him. He was afraid to look at the eyes. They were hideous now, only the whites showing, and the blood running to them. The face of the orderly was drawn with horror at the sight. Well, it was so. In his heart he was satisfied. He had hated the face of the Captain. It was extinguished now. There was a heavy relief in the orderly's soul. That was as it should be. But he could not bear to see the long, military body lying broken over the tree-base, the fine fingers crisped. He wanted to hide it away.

Quickly, busily, he gathered it up and pushed it under the felled tree-trunks, which rested their beautiful, smooth length either end on logs. The face was horrible with blood. He covered it with the helmet. Then he pushed the limbs straight and decent, and brushed the dead leaves off the fine cloth of the uniform. So, it lay quite still in the shadow under there. A little strip of sunshine ran along the breast, from a chink between the logs. The orderly sat by it for a few moments. Here his own life also ended.

Then, through his daze, he heard the lieutenant, in a loud voice, explaining to the men outside the wood, that they were to suppose the bridge on the river below was held by the enemy. Now they were to march to the attack in such and such a manner. The lieutenant had no gift of expression. The orderly, listening from habit, got muddled. And when the lieutenant began it all again he ceased to hear.

He knew he must go. He stood up. It surprised him that the leaves were glittering in the sun, and the chips of wood reflecting white from the ground. For him a change had come over the world. But for the rest it had not—all seemed the same. Only he had left it. And he could not go back. It was his duty to return with the beer-pot and the bottle. He could not. He had left all that. The lieutenant was still hoarsely explaining. He must go, or they would overtake him. And he could not bear contact with anyone now.

He drew his fingers over his eyes, trying to find out where he was. Then he turned away. He saw the horse standing in the path. He went up to it and mounted. It hurt him to sit in the saddle. The pain of keeping his seat occupied him as they cantered through the wood. He would not have minded anything, but he could not get away from the sense of being divided from the others. The path led out of the trees. On the edge of the wood he pulled up and stood watching. There in the spacious sunshine of the valley soldiers were moving in a little swarm. Every now and then, a man harrowing on a strip of fallow shouted to his oxen, at the turn. The village and the white-towered church was small in the sunshine. And he no longer belonged to it—he sat there, beyond, like a man outside in the dark. He had gone out from everyday life into the unknown, and he could not, he even did not want to go back.

Turning from the sun-blazing valley, he rode deep into the wood. Tree-trunks, like people standing grey and still, took no notice as he went. A doe, herself a moving bit of sunshine and shadow, went running through the flecked shade. There were bright green rents in the foliage. Then it was all pine wood, dark and cool. And he was sick with pain, he had an intolerable great pulse in his head, and he was sick. He had never been ill in his life. He felt lost, quite dazed with all this.

Trying to get down from the horse, he fell, astonished at the pain and his lack of balance. The horse shifted uneasily. He jerked its bridle and sent it cantering jerkily away. It was his last connection with the rest of things.

But he only wanted to lie down and not be disturbed. Stumbling through the trees, he came on a quiet place where beeches and pine trees grew on a slope. Immediately he had lain down and closed his eyes, his consciousness went racing on without him. A big pulse of sickness beat in him as if it throbbed through the whole earth. He was burning with dry heat. But he was too busy, too tearingly active in the incoherent race of delirium to observe.

III

He came to with a start. His mouth was dry and hard, his heart beat heavily, but he had not the energy to get up. His heart beat heavily. Where was he?–the barracks–at home? There was something knocking. And, making an effort, he looked round–trees, and litter of greenery, and reddish, bright, still pieces of sunshine on the floor. He did not believe he was himself, he did not believe what he saw. Something was knocking. He made a struggle towards consciousness, but relapsed. Then he struggled again. And gradually his surroundings fell into relationship with himself. He knew, and a great pang of fear went through his heart. Somebody was knocking. He could see the heavy, black rags of a fir tree overhead. Then everything went black. Yet he did not believe he had closed his eyes. He had not. Out of the blackness sight slowly emerged again. And someone was knocking. Quickly, he saw the blood-disfigured face of his Captain, which he hated. And he held himself still with horror. Yet, deep inside him, he knew that it was so, the Captain should be dead. But the physical delirium got hold of him. Someone was knocking. He lay perfectly still, as if dead, with fear. And he went unconscious.

When he opened his eyes again, he started, seeing something creeping swiftly up a tree-trunk. It was a little bird. And the bird was whistling overhead. Tap-tap-tap–it was the small, quick bird rapping the tree-trunk with its beak, as if its head were a little round hammer. He watched it curiously. It shifted sharply, in its creeping fashion. Then, like a mouse, it slid down the bare trunk. Its swift creeping sent a flash of revulsion through him. He raised his head. It felt a great weight. Then, the little bird ran out of the shadow across a still patch of sunshine, its little head bobbing swiftly, its white legs twinkling brightly for a moment. How neat it was in its build, so compact, with pieces of white on its wings. There were several of them. They were so pretty—but they crept like swift, erratic mice, running here and there among the beech-mast.

He lay down again exhausted, and his consciousness lapsed. He had a horror of the little creeping birds. All his blood seemed to be darting and creeping in his head. And yet he could not move.

He came to with a further ache of exhaustion. There was the pain in his head, and the horrible sickness, and his inability to move. He had never been ill in his life. He did not know where he was or what he was. Probably he had got sunstroke. Or what else?—he had silenced the Captain for ever—some time ago—oh, a long time ago. There had been blood on his face, and his eyes had turned upwards. It was all right, somehow. It was peace. But now he had got beyond himself. He had never been here before. Was it life, or not life? He was by himself. They were in a big, bright place, those others, and he was outside. The town, all the country, a big bright place of light: and he was outside, here, in the darkened open beyond, where each thing existed alone. But they would all have to come out there sometime, those others. Little, and left behind him, they all were. There had been father and mother and sweetheart. What did they all matter? This was the open land.

He sat up. Something scuffled. It was a little, brown squirrel running in lovely, undulating bounds over the floor, its red tail completing the undulation of its body—and then, as it sat up, furling and unfurling. He watched it, pleased. It ran on again, friskily, enjoying itself. It flew wildly at another squirrel, and they were chasing each other, and making little scolding, chattering noises. The soldier wanted to speak to them. But only a hoarse sound came out of his throat. The squirrels burst away—they flew up the trees. And then he saw the one peeping round at him, half-way up a tree-trunk. A start of fear went through him, though, in so far as he was conscious, he was amused. It still stayed, its little, keen face staring at him half-way up the tree-trunk, its little ears pricked up, its clawey little hands clinging to the bark, its white breast reared. He started from it in panic.

Struggling to his feet, he lurched away. He went on walking, walking, looking for something—for a drink. His brain felt hot and inflamed for want of water. He stumbled on. Then he did not know anything. He went unconscious as he walked. Yet he stumbled on, his mouth open.

When, to his dumb wonder, he opened his eyes on the world again, he no longer tried to remember what it was. There was thick, golden light behind golden-green glitterings, and tall, grey-purple shafts, and darknesses further off, surrounding him, growing deeper. He was conscious of a sense of arrival. He was amid the reality, on the real, dark bottom. But there was the thirst burning in his brain. He felt lighter, not so heavy. He supposed it was newness. The air was muttering with thunder. He thought he was walking wonderfully swiftly and was coming straight to relief—or was it to water?

Suddenly he stood still with fear. There was a tremendous flare of gold, immense—just a few dark trunks like bars between him and it. All the young level wheat was burnished gold glaring on its silky green. A woman, full-skirted, a black cloth on her head for head-dress, was passing like a block of shadow through the glistening, green corn, into the full glare. There was a farm, too, pale blue in shadow, and the timber black. And there was a church spire, nearly fused away in the gold. The woman moved on, away from him. He had no language with which to speak to her. She was the bright, solid unreality. She would make a noise of words that would confuse him, and her eyes would look at him without seeing him. She was crossing there to the other side. He stood against a tree.

When at last he turned, looking down the long, bare grove whose flat bed was already filling dark, he saw the mountains in a wonder-light, not far away, and radiant. Behind the soft, grey ridge of the nearest range the further mountains stood golden and pale grey, the snow all radiant like pure, soft gold. So still, gleaming in the sky, fashioned pure out of the ore of the sky, they shone in their silence. He stood and looked at them, his face illuminated. And like the golden, lustrous gleaming of the snow he felt his own thirst bright in him. He stood and gazed, leaning against a tree. And then everything slid away into space.

During the night the lightning fluttered perpetually, making the whole sky white. He must have walked again. The world hung livid round him for moments, fields a level sheen of grey-green light, trees in dark bulk, and the range of clouds black across the white sky. Then the darkness fell like a shutter, and the night was whole. A faint flutter of a half-revealed world, that could not quite leap out of the darkness!—Then there again stood a sweep of pallor for the land, dark shapes looming, a range of clouds hanging overhead. The world was a ghostly shadow, thrown for a moment upon the pure darkness, which returned ever whole and complete.

And the mere delirium of sickness and fever went on inside him—his brain opening and shutting like the night—then sometimes convulsions of terror from something with great eyes that stared round a tree—then the long agony of the march, and the sun decomposing his blood—then the pang of hate for the Captain, followed by a pang of tenderness and ease. But everything was distorted, born of an ache and resolving into an ache.

In the morning he came definitely awake. Then his brain flamed with the sole horror of thirstiness! The sun was on his face, the dew was steaming from his wet clothes. Like one possessed, he got up. There, straight in front of him, blue and cool and tender, the mountains ranged across the pale edge of the morning sky. He wanted them–he wanted them alone–he wanted to leave himself and be identified with them. They did not move, they were still and soft, with white, gentle markings of snow. He stood still, mad with suffering, his hands crisping and clutching. Then he was twisting in a paroxysm on the grass.

He lay still, in a kind of dream of anguish. His thirst seemed to have separated itself from him, and to stand apart, a single demand. Then the pain he felt was another single self. Then there was the clog of his body, another separate thing. He was divided among all kinds of separate beings. There was some strange, agonized connection between them, but they were drawing further apart. Then they would all split. The sun, drilling down on him, was drilling through the bond. Then they would all fall, fall through the everlasting lapse of space. Then again, his consciousness reasserted itself. He roused on to his elbow and stared at the gleaming mountains. There they ranked, all still and wonderful between earth and heaven. He stared till his eyes went black, and the mountains, as they stood in their beauty, so clean and cool, seemed to have it, that which was lost in him.

IV

When the soldiers found him, three hours later, he was lying with his face over his arm, his black hair giving off heat under the sun. But he was still alive. Seeing the open, black mouth the young soldiers dropped him in horror.

He died in the hospital at night, without having seen again.

The doctors saw the bruises on his legs, behind, and were silent.

The bodies of the two men lay together, side by side, in the mortuary, the one white and slender, but laid rigidly at rest, the other looking as if every moment it must rouse into life again, so young and unused, from a slumber.

The Horse Dealer's Daughter

Written January 1916 as 'The Miracle'. Revised
October 1921 for publication in *English Review*,
April 1922 and the collection *England, My England*.

'Well, Mabel, and what are you going to do with
yourself?' asked Joe, with foolish flippancy. He felt quite
safe himself. Without listening for an answer, he turned
aside, worked a grain of tobacco to the tip of his tongue,
and spat it out. He did not care about anything, since he
felt safe himself.

The three brothers and the sister sat round the
desolate breakfast table, attempting some sort of
desultory consultation. The morning's post had given the
final tap to the family fortunes, and all was over. The
dreary dining-room itself, with its heavy mahogany furniture, looked as if it were waiting to be done away with.

But the consultation amounted to nothing. There
was a strange air of ineffectuality about the three men, as
they sprawled at table, smoking and reflecting vaguely
on their own condition. The girl was alone, a rather
short, sullen-looking young woman of twenty-seven. She
did not share the same life as her brothers. She would
have been good-looking, save for the impassive fixity of
her face, 'bull-dog', as her brothers called it.

There was a confused tramping of horses' feet
outside. The three men all sprawled round in their chairs
to watch. Beyond the dark holly-bushes that separated
the strip of lawn from the highroad, they could see a

cavalcade of shire horses swinging out of their own yard, being taken for exercise. This was the last time. These were the last horses that would go through their hands. The young men watched with critical, callous look. They were all frightened at the collapse of their lives, and the sense of disaster in which they were involved left them no inner freedom.

Yet they were three fine, well-set fellows enough. Joe, the eldest, was a man of thirty-three, broad and handsome in a hot, flushed way. His face was red, he twisted his black moustache over a thick finger, his eyes were shallow and restless. He had a sensual way of uncovering his teeth when he laughed, and his bearing was stupid. Now he watched the horses with a glazed look of helplessness in his eyes, a certain stupor of downfall.

The great draught-horses swung past. They were tied head to tail, four of them, and they heaved along to where a lane branched off from the highroad, planting their great hoofs floutingly in the fine black mud, swinging their great rounded haunches sumptuously, and trotting a few sudden steps as they were led into the lane, round the corner. Every movement showed a massive, slumbrous strength, and a stupidity which held them in subjection. The groom at the head looked back, jerking the leading rope. And the cavalcade moved out of sight up the lane, the tail of the last horse, bobbed up tight and stiff, held out taut from the swinging great haunches as they rocked behind the hedges in a motion like sleep.

Joe watched with glazed hopeless eyes. The horses were almost like his own body to him. He felt he was done for now. Luckily he was engaged to a woman as old as himself, and therefore her father, who was steward of a neighbouring estate, would provide him with a job. He would marry and go into harness. His life was over, he would be a subject animal now.

He turned uneasily aside, the retreating steps of the horses echoing in his ears. Then, with foolish restlessness, he reached for the scraps of bacon-rind from the plates, and making a faint whistling sound, flung them to the terrier that lay against the fender. He watched the dog swallow them, and waited till the creature looked into his eyes. Then a faint grin came on his face, and in a high, foolish voice he said:

'You won't get much more bacon, shall you, you little b——?'

The dog faintly and dismally wagged its tail, then lowered its haunches, circled round, and lay down again.

There was another helpless silence at the table. Joe sprawled uneasily in his seat, not willing to go till the family conclave was dissolved. Fred Henry, the second brother, was erect, clean-limbed, alert. He had watched the passing of the horses with more *sang-froid*. If he was an animal, like Joe, he was an animal which controls, not one which is controlled. He was master of any horse, and he carried himself with a well-tempered air of mastery. But he was not master of the situations of life. He pushed his coarse brown moustache upwards, off his lip, and glanced irritably at his sister, who sat impassive and inscrutable.

'You'll go and stop with Lucy for a bit, shan't you?' he asked. The girl did not answer.

'I don't see what else you can do,' persisted Fred Henry.

'Go as a skivvy,' Joe interpolated laconically.

The girl did not move a muscle.

'If I was her, I should go in for training for a nurse,' said Malcolm, the youngest of them all. He was the baby of the family, a young man of twenty-two, with a fresh, jaunty *museau*.

But Mabel did not take any notice of him. They had talked at her and round her for so many years, that she hardly heard them at all.

The marble clock on the mantel-piece softly chimed the half-hour, the dog rose uneasily from the hearthrug and looked at the party at the breakfast table. But still they sat on in ineffectual conclave.

'Oh, all right,' said Joe suddenly, *à propos* of nothing.
'I'll get a move on.'

He pushed back his chair, straddled his knees with a
downward jerk, to get them free, in horsey fashion, and
went to the fire. Still he did not go out of the room; he
was curious to know what the others would do or say. He
began to charge his pipe, looking down at the dog and
saying, in a high, affected voice:

'Going wi' me? Going wi' me are ter? Tha'rt goin'
further than tha counts on just now, dost hear?'

The dog faintly wagged its tail, the man stuck out
his jaw and covered his pipe with his hands, and puffed
intently, losing himself in the tobacco, looking down all
the while at the dog, with an absent brown eye. The dog
looked up at him in mournful distrust. Joe stood with his
knees stuck out, in real horsey fashion.

'Have you had a letter from Lucy?' Fred Henry
asked of his sister.

'Last week,' came the neutral reply.

'And what does she say?'

There was no answer.

'Does she *ask* you to go and stop there?' persisted
Fred Henry.

'She says I can if I like.'

'Well, then, you'd better. Tell her you'll come on
Monday.'

This was received in silence.

'That's what you'll do then, is it?' said Fred Henry,
in some exasperation.

But she made no answer. There was a silence of
futility and irritation in the room. Malcolm grinned
fatuously.

'You'll have to make up your mind between now
and next Wednesday,' said Joe loudly, 'or else find
yourself lodgings on the kerbstone.'

The face of the young woman darkened, but she sat
on immutable.

'Here's Jack Fergusson!' exclaimed Malcolm, who was looking aimlessly out of the window.

'Where?' exclaimed Joe, loudly.

'Just gone past.'

'Coming in?'

Malcolm craned his neck to see the gate.

'Yes,' he said.

There was a silence. Mabel sat on like one condemned, at the head of the table. Then a whistle was heard from the kitchen. The dog got up and barked sharply. Joe opened the door and shouted:

'Come on.'

After a moment, a young man entered. He was muffled up in overcoat and a purple woollen scarf, and his tweed cap, which he did not remove, was pulled down on his head. He was of medium height, his face was rather long and pale, his eyes looked tired.

'Hello Jack! Well, Jack!' exclaimed Malcolm and Joe. Fred Henry merely said 'Jack!'

'What's doing?' asked the newcomer, evidently addressing Fred Henry.

'Same. We've got to be out by Wednesday.—Got a cold?'

'I have—got it bad, too.'

'Why don't you stop in?'

'*Me* stop in? When I can't stand on my legs, perhaps I shall have a chance.' The young man spoke huskily. He had a slight Scotch accent.

'It's a knock-out, isn't it,' said Joe boisterously, 'if a doctor goes round croaking with a cold. Looks bad for the patients, doesn't it?'

The young doctor looked at him slowly.

'Anything the matter with *you*, then?' he asked, sarcastically.

'Not as I know of. Damn your eyes, I hope not. Why?'

'I thought you were very concerned about the patients, wondered if you might be one yourself.'

'Damn it, no, I've never been patient to no flaming doctor, and hope I never shall be,' returned Joe.

At this point Mabel rose from the table, and they all seemed to become aware of her existence. She began putting the dishes together. The young doctor looked at her, but did not address her. He had not greeted her. She went out of the room with the tray, her face impassive and unchanged.

'When are you off then, all of you?' asked the doctor.

'I'm catching the eleven-forty,' replied Malcolm. 'Are you goin' down wi' th' trap, Joe?'

'Yes, I've told you I'm going down wi' th' trap, haven't I?'

'We'd better be getting her in then.—So long, Jack, if I don't see you before I go,' said Malcolm, shaking hands.

He went out, followed by Joe, who seemed to have his tail between his legs.

'Well, this is the devil's own,' exclaimed the doctor, when he was left alone with Fred Henry. 'Going before Wednesday, are you?'

'That's the orders,' replied the other.

'Where, to Northampton?'

'That's it.'

'The devil!' exclaimed Fergusson, with quiet chagrin. And there was silence between the two.

'All settled up, are you?' asked Fergusson.

'About.'

There was another pause.

'Well, I shall miss yer, Freddy boy,' said the young doctor.

'And I shall miss thee, Jack,' returned the other.

'Miss you like hell,' mused the doctor.

Fred Henry turned aside. There was nothing to say. Mabel came in again, to finish clearing the table.

'What are *you* going to do then, Miss Pervin?' asked Fergusson. 'Going to your sister's, are you?'

Mabel looked at him with her steady, dangerous

eyes, that always made him uncomfortable, unsettling his superficial ease.

'No,' she said.

'Well, what in the name of fortune *are* you going to do? Say what you *mean* to do,' cried Fred Henry, with futile intensity.

But she only averted her head, and continued her work. She folded the white table-cloth, and put on the chenille cloth.

'The sulkiest bitch that ever trod!' muttered her brother.

But she finished her task with perfectly impassive face, the young doctor watching her interestedly all the while. Then she went out.

Fred Henry stared after her, clenching his lips, his blue eyes fixing in sharp antagonism, as he made a grimace of sour exasperation.

'You could bray her into bits, and that's all you'd get out of her,' he said, in a small, narrowed tone.

The doctor smiled faintly.

'What's she *going* to do then?' he asked.

'Strike me if *I* know!' returned the other.

There was a pause. Then the doctor stirred.

'I'll be seeing you to-night, shall I?' he said to his friend.

'Ay–where's it to be? Are we going over to Jessdale?'

'I don't know. I've got such a cold on me. I'll come round to the Moon and Stars, anyway.'

'Let Lizzie and May miss their night for once, eh?'

'That's it–if I feel as I do now.'

'All's one—'

The two young men went through the passage and down to the back door together. The house was large, but it was servantless now, and desolate. At the back was a small bricked house-yard, and beyond that a big square, gravelled fine and red, and having stables on two sides. Sloping, dank, winter-dark fields stretched away on the open sides.

But the stables were empty. Joseph Pervin, the father of the family, had been a man of no education, who had become a fairly large horse dealer. The stables had been full of horses, there was a great turmoil and come-and-go of horses and of dealers and grooms. Then the kitchen was full of servants. But of late things had declined. The old man had married a second time, to retrieve his fortunes. Now he was dead and everything was gone to the dogs, there was nothing but debt and threatening.

For months, Mabel had been servantless in the big house, keeping the home together in penury for her ineffectual brothers. She had kept house for ten years. But previously, it was with unstinted means. Then, however brutal and coarse everything was, the sense of money had kept her proud, confident. The men might be foul-mouthed, the women in the kitchen might have bad reputations, her brothers might have illegitimate children. But so long as there was money, the girl felt herself established, and brutally proud, reserved.

No company came to the house, save dealers and coarse men. Mabel had no associates of her own sex, after her sister went away. But she did not mind. She went regularly to church, she attended to her father. And she lived in the memory of her mother, who had died when she was fourteen, and whom she had loved. She had loved her father, too, in a different way, depending upon him, and feeling secure in him, until at the age of fifty-four he married again. And then she had set hard against him. Now he had died and left them all hopelessly in debt.

She had suffered badly during the period of poverty. Nothing, however, could shake the curious sullen, animal pride that dominated each member of the family. Now, for Mabel, the end had come. Still she would not cast about her. She would follow her own way just the same. She would always hold the keys of her own situation. Mindless and persistent, she endured from day to day.

Why should she think? Why should she answer anybody? It was enough that this was the end, and there was no way out. She need not pass any more darkly along the main street of the small town, avoiding every eye. She need not demean herself any more, going into the shops and buying the cheapest food. This was at an end. She thought of nobody, not even of herself. Mindless and persistent, she seemed in a sort of ecstasy to be coming nearer to her fulfilment, her own glorification, approaching her dead mother, who was glorified.

In the afternoon she took a little bag, with shears and sponge and a small scrubbing brush, and went out. It was a grey, wintry day, with saddened, dark-green fields and an atmosphere blackened by the smoke of foundries not far off. She went quickly, darkly along the causeway, heeding nobody, through the town to the churchyard.

There she always felt secure, as if no one could see her, although as a matter of fact she was exposed to the stare of everyone who passed along under the churchyard wall. Nevertheless, once under the shadow of the great looming church, among the graves, she felt immune from the world, reserved within the thick churchyard wall as in another country.

Carefully she clipped the grass from the grave, and arranged the pinky-white, small chrysanthemums in the tin cross. When this was done, she took an empty jar from a neighbouring grave, brought water, and carefully, most scrupulously sponged the marble headstone and the coping-stone.

It gave her sincere satisfaction to do this. She felt in immediate contact with the world of her mother. She took minute pains, went through the park in a state bordering on pure happiness, as if in performing this task she came into a subtle, intimate connection with her mother. For the life she followed here in the world was far less real than the world of death she inherited from her mother.

The doctor's house was just by the church. Fergusson, being a mere hired assistant, was slave to the countryside. As he hurried now to attend to the out-patients in the surgery, glancing across the graveyard with his quick eye, he saw the girl at her task at the grave. She seemed so intent and remote, it was like looking into another world. Some mystical element was touched in him. He slowed down as he walked, watching her as if spell-bound.

She lifted her eyes, feeling him looking. Their eyes met. And each looked again at once, each feeling, in some way, found out by the other. He lifted his cap and passed on down the road. There remained distinct in his consciousness, like a vision, the memory of her face, lifted from the tombstone in the churchyard, and looking at him with slow, large, portentous eyes. It *was* portentous, her face. It seemed to mesmerise him. There was a heavy power in her eyes which laid hold of his whole being, as if he had drunk some powerful drug. He had been feeling weak and done before. Now the life came back into him, he felt delivered from his own fretted, daily self.

He finished his duties at the surgery as quickly as might be, hastily filling up the bottles of the waiting people with cheap drugs. Then, in perpetual haste, he set off again to visit several cases in another part of his round, before teatime. At all times he preferred to walk, if he could, but particularly when he was not well. He fancied the motion restored him.

The afternoon was falling. It was grey, deadened, and wintry, with a slow, moist, heavy coldness sinking in and deadening all the faculties. But why should he think or notice? He hastily climbed the hill and turned across the dark-green fields, following the black cinder-track. In the distance, across a shallow dip in the country, the small town was clustered like smouldering ash, a tower, a spire, a heap of low, raw, extinct houses. And on the nearest fringe of the town, sloping into the dip, was Oldmeadow, the Pervins' house. He could see the stables and the outbuildings distinctly, as they lay towards him on the slope. Well, he would not go there many more times! Another resource would be lost to him, another place gone: the only company he cared for in the alien, ugly little town he was losing. Nothing but work, drudgery, constant hastening from dwelling to dwelling among the colliers and the iron-workers. It wore him out, but at the same time he had a craving for it. It was a stimulant to him to be in the homes of the working people, moving as it were through the innermost body of their life. His nerves were excited and gratified. He could come so near, into the very lives of the rough, inarticulate, powerfully emotional men and women. He grumbled, he said he hated the hellish hole. But as a matter of fact it excited him, the contact with the rough, strongly-feeling people was a stimulant applied direct to his nerves.

Below Oldmeadow, in the green, shallow, soddened hollow of fields, lay a square, deep pond. Roving across the landscape, the doctor's quick eye detected a figure in black passing through the gate of the field, down towards the pond. He looked again. It would be Mabel Pervin. His mind suddenly became alive and attentive.

Why was she going down there? He pulled up on the path on the slope above, and stood staring. He could just make sure of the small black figure moving in the hollow of the failing day. He seemed to see her in the midst of such obscurity, that he was like a clairvoyant, seeing rather with the mind's eye than with ordinary sight. Yet he could see her positively enough, whilst he kept his eye attentive. He felt, if he looked away from her, in the thick, ugly falling dusk, he would lose her altogether.

He followed her minutely as she moved, direct and intent, like something transmitted rather than stirring in voluntary activity, straight down the field towards the pond. There she stood on the bank for a moment. She never raised her head. Then she waded slowly into the water.

He stood motionless as the small black figure walked slowly and deliberately towards the centre of the pond, very slowly, gradually moving deeper into the motionless water, and still moving forward as the water got up to her breast. Then he could see her no more in the dusk of the dead afternoon.

'There!' he exclaimed. 'Would you believe it?'

And he hastened straight down, running over the wet, soddened fields, pushing through the hedges, down into the depression of callous wintry obscurity. It took him several minutes to come to the pond. He stood on the bank, breathing heavily. He could see nothing. His eyes seemed to penetrate the dead water. Yes, perhaps that was the dark shadow of her black clothing beneath the surface of the water.

He slowly ventured into the pond. The bottom was deep, soft clay, he sank in, and the water clasped dead cold round his legs. As he stirred he could smell the cold, rotten clay that fouled up into the water. It was objectionable in his lungs. Still, repelled and yet not heeding, he moved deeper into the pond. The cold water rose over his thighs, over his loins, upon his abdomen. The lower part of his body was all sunk in the hideous cold element. And the bottom was so deeply soft and uncertain, he was afraid of pitching with his mouth underneath. He could not swim, and was afraid.

He crouched a little, spreading his hands under the water and moving them round, trying to feel for her. The dead cold pond swayed upon his chest. He moved again, a little deeper, and again, with his hands underneath, he felt all around under the water. And he touched her clothing. But it evaded his fingers. He made a desperate effort to grasp it.

And so doing he lost his balance and went under, horribly suffocating in the foul earthy water, struggling madly for a few moments. At last, after what seemed an eternity, he got his footing, rose again into the air and looked around. He gasped, and knew he was in the world. Then he looked at the water. She had risen near him. He grasped her clothing, and drawing her nearer, turned to make his way to land again.

He went very slowly, carefully, absorbed in the slow progress. He rose higher, climbing out of the pond. The water was now only about his legs; he was thankful, full of relief to be out of the clutches of the pond. He lifted her and staggered on to the bank, out of the horror of wet, grey clay.

He laid her down on the bank. She was quite unconscious and running with water. He made the water come from her mouth, he worked to restore her. He did not have to work very long before he could feel the breathing begin again in her; she was breathing naturally. He worked a little longer. He could feel her live beneath his hands; she was coming back. He wiped her face, wrapped her in his overcoat, looked round into the dim, dark-grey world, then lifted her and staggered down the bank and across the fields.

It seemed an unthinkably long way, and his burden so heavy he felt he would never get to the house. But at last he was in the stable-yard, and then in the house-yard. He opened the door and went into the house. In the kitchen he laid her down on the hearthrug, and called. The house was empty. But the fire was burning in the grate.

Then again he kneeled to attend to her. She was breathing regularly, her eyes were wide open and as if conscious, but there seemed something missing in her look. She was conscious in herself, but unconscious of her surroundings.

He ran upstairs, took blankets from a bed, and put them before the fire to warm. Then he removed her saturated, earthy-smelling clothing, rubbed her dry with a towel, and wrapped her naked in the blankets. Then he went into the dining-room, to look for spirits. There was a little whiskey. He drank a gulp himself, and put some into her mouth.

The effect was instantaneous. She looked full into his face, as if she had been seeing him for some time, and yet had only just become conscious of him.

'Dr Fergusson?' she said.

'What?' he answered.

He was divesting himself of his coat, intending to find some dry clothing upstairs. He could not bear the smell of the dead, clayey water, and he was mortally afraid for his own health.

'What did I do?' she asked.

'Walked into the pond,' he replied. He had begun to shudder like one sick, and could hardly attend to her. Her eyes remained full on him, he seemed to be going dark in his mind, looking back at her helplessly. The shuddering became quieter in him, his life came back in him, dark and unknowing, but strong again.

'Was I out of my mind?' she asked, while her eyes were fixed on him all the time.

'Maybe, for the moment,' he replied. He felt quiet, because his strength had come back. The strange fretful strain had left him.

'Am I out of my mind now?' she asked.

'Are you?' he reflected a moment. 'No,' he answered truthfully, 'I don't see that you are.' He turned his face aside. He was afraid, now, because he felt dazed, and felt dimly that her power was stronger than his, in this issue. And she continued to look at him fixedly all the time. 'Can you tell me where I shall find some dry things to put on?' he asked.

'Did you dive into the pond for me?' she asked.

'No,' he answered. 'I walked in. But I went in overhead as well.'

There was silence for a moment. He hesitated. He very much wanted to go upstairs to get into dry clothing. But there was another desire in him. And she seemed to hold him. His will seemed to have gone to sleep, and left him, standing there slack before her. But he felt warm inside himself. He did not shudder at all, though his clothes were sodden on him.

'Why did you?' she asked.

'Because I didn't want you to do such a foolish thing,' he said.

'It wasn't foolish,' she said, still gazing at him as she lay on the floor, with a sofa cushion under her head. 'It was the right thing to do. *I* knew best, then.'

'I'll go and shift these wet things,' he said. But still he had not the power to move out of her presence, until she sent him. It was as if she had the life of his body in her hands, and he could not extricate himself. Or perhaps he did not want to.

Suddenly she sat up. Then she became aware of her own immediate condition. She felt the blankets about her, she knew her own limbs. For a moment it seemed as if her reason were going. She looked round, with wild eye, as if seeking something. He stood still with fear. She saw her clothing lying scattered.

'Who undressed me?' she asked, her eyes resting full and inevitable on his face.

'I did,' he replied, 'to bring you round.'

For some moments she sat and gazed at him awfully, her lips parted.

'Do you love me then?' she asked.

He only stood and stared at her, fascinated. His soul seemed to melt.

She shuffled forward on her knees, and put her arms round him, round his legs, as he stood there, pressing her breasts against his knees and thighs, clutching him with strange, convulsive certainty, pressing his thighs against her, drawing him to her face, her throat, as she looked up at him with flaring, humble eyes of transfiguration, triumphant in first possession.

'You love me,' she murmured, in strange transport, yearning and triumphant and confident. 'You love me. I know you love me, I know.'

And she was passionately kissing his knees, through the wet clothing, passionately and indiscriminately kissing his knees, his legs, as if unaware of everything.

He looked down at the tangled wet hair, the wild, bare, animal shoulders. He was amazed, bewildered, and afraid. He had never thought of loving her. He had never wanted to love her. When he rescued her and restored her, he was a doctor, and she was a patient. He had had no single personal thought of her. Nay, this introduction of the personal element was very distasteful to him, a violation of his professional honour. It was horrible to have her there embracing his knees. It was horrible. He revolted from it, violently. And yet—and yet—he had not the power to break away.

She looked at him again, with the same supplication of powerful love, and that same transcendent, frightening light of triumph. In view of the delicate flame which seemed to come from her face like a light, he was powerless. And yet he had never intended to love her. He had never intended. And something stubborn in him could not give way.

'You love me,' she repeated, in a murmur of deep, rhapsodic assurance. 'You love me.'

Her hands were drawing him, drawing him down to her. He was afraid, even a little horrified. For he had, really, no intention of loving her. Yet her hands were drawing him towards her. He put out his hand quickly to steady himself, and grasped her bare shoulder. A flame seemed to burn the hand that grasped her soft shoulder. He had no intention of loving her: his whole will was against his yielding. It was horrible— And yet wonderful was the touch of her shoulder, beautiful the shining of her face. Was she perhaps mad? He had a horror of yielding to her. Yet something in him ached also.

He had been staring away at the door, away from her. But his hand remained on her shoulder. She had gone suddenly very still. He looked down at her. Her eyes were now wide with fear, with doubt, the light was dying from her face, a shadow of terrible greyness was return-ing. He could not bear the touch of her eyes' question upon him, and the look of death behind the question.

With an inward groan he gave way, and let his heart yield towards her. A sudden gentle smile came on his face. And her eyes, which never left his face, slowly, slowly filled with tears. He watched the strange water rise in her eyes, like some slow fountain coming up. And his heart seemed to burn and melt away in his breast.

He could not bear to look at her any more. He dropped on his knees and caught her head with his arms and pressed her face against his throat. She was very still. His heart, which seemed to have broken, was burning with a kind of agony in his breast. And he felt her slow, hot tears wetting his throat. But he could not move.

He felt the hot tears wet his neck and the hollows of his neck, and he remained motionless, suspended through one of man's eternities. Only now it had become indispensable to him to have her face pressed close to him; he could never let her go again. He could never let her head go away from the close clutch of his arm. He wanted to remain like that for ever, with his heart hurting him in a pain that was also life to him. Without knowing, he was looking down on her damp, soft brown hair.

Then, as it were suddenly, he smelt the horrid stagnant smell of that water. And at the same moment she drew away from him and looked at him. Her eyes were wistful and unfathomable. He was afraid of them, and he fell to kissing her, not knowing what he was doing. He wanted her eyes not to have that terrible, wistful, unfathomable look.

When she turned her face to him again, a faint delicate flush was glowing, and there was again dawning that terrible shining of joy in her eyes, which really terrified him, and yet which he now wanted to see, because he feared the look of doubt still more.

'You love me?' she said, rather faltering.

'Yes.' The word cost him a painful effort. Not because it wasn't true. But because it was too newly true,

the *saying* seemed to tear open again his newly-torn heart.
And he hardly wanted it to be true, even now.

She lifted her face to him, and he bent forward and
kissed her on the mouth, gently, with the one kiss that is
an eternal pledge. And as he kissed her his heart strained
again in his breast. He never intended to love her. But
now it was over. He had crossed over the gulf to her, and
all that he had left behind had shrivelled and become
void.

After the kiss, her eyes again slowly filled with tears.
She sat still, away from him, with her face drooped aside,
and her hands folded in her lap. The tears fell very
slowly. There was complete silence. He too sat there
motionless and silent on the hearthrug. The strange pain
of his heart that was broken seemed to consume him.
That he should love her? That this was love! That he
should be ripped open in this way!—Him, a doctor!—How
they would all jeer if they knew!—It was agony to him to
think they might know.

In the curious naked pain of the thought he looked
again to her. She was sitting there drooped into a muse.
He saw a tear fall, and his heart flared hot. He saw for
the first time that one of her shoulders was quite
uncovered, one arm bare, he could see one of her small
breasts; dimly, because it had become almost dark in the
room.

'Why are you crying?' he asked, in an altered voice.

She looked up at him, and behind her tears the consciousness of her situation for the first time brought a
dark look of shame to her eyes.

'I'm not crying, really,' she said, watching him half
frightened.

He reached his hand, and softly closed it on her bare
arm.

'I love you! I love you!' he said in a soft, low, vibrating voice, unlike himself.

She shrank, and dropped her head. The soft,
penetrating grip of his hand on her arm distressed her.

She looked up at him.

'I want to go,' she said. 'I want to go and get you some dry things.'

'Why?' he said. 'I'm all right.'

'But I want to go,' she said. 'And I want you to change your things.'

He released her arm, and she wrapped herself in the blanket, looking at him rather frightened. And still she did not rise.

'Kiss me,' she said wistfully.

He kissed her, but briefly, half in anger.

Then, after a second, she rose nervously, all mixed up in the blanket. He watched her in her confusion, as she tried to extricate herself and wrap herself up so that she could walk. He watched her relentlessly, as she knew. And as she went, the blanket trailing, and as he saw a glimpse of her feet and her white leg, he tried to remember her as she was when he had wrapped her in the blanket. But then he didn't want to remember, because she had been nothing to him then, and his nature revolted from remembering her as she was when she was nothing to him.

A tumbling, muffled noise from within the dark house startled him. Then he heard her voice:–'There are clothes.' He rose and went to the foot of the stairs, and gathered up the garments she had thrown down. Then he came back to the fire, to rub himself down and dress. He grinned at his own appearance, when he had finished.

The fire was sinking, so he put on coal. The house was now quite dark, save for the light of a street-lamp that shone in faintly from beyond the holly trees. He lit the gas with matches he found on the mantel-piece. Then he emptied the pockets of his own clothes, and threw all his wet things in a heap into the scullery. After which he gathered up her sodden clothes, gently, and put them in a separate heap on the copper-top in the scullery.

It was six o'clock on the clock. His own watch had

stopped. He ought to go back to the surgery. He waited, and still she did not come down. So he went to the foot of the stairs and called:

'I shall have to go.'

Almost immediately he heard her coming down. She had on her best dress of black voile, and her hair was tidy, but still damp. She looked at him–and in spite of herself, smiled.

'I don't like you in those clothes,' she said.

'Do I look a sight?' he answered.

They were shy of one another.

'I'll make you some tea,' she said.

'No, I must go.'

'Must you?' And she looked at him again with the wide, strained, doubtful eyes. And again, from the pain of his breast, he knew how he loved her. He went and bent to kiss her, gently, passionately, with his heart's painful kiss.

'And my hair smells so horrible,' she murmured in distraction. 'And I'm so awful, I'm so awful! Oh, no, I'm too awful.' And she broke into bitter, heartbroken sobbing. 'You can't want to love me, I'm horrible.'

'Don't be silly, don't be silly,' he said, trying to comfort her, kissing her, holding her in his arms. 'I want you, I want to marry you, we're going to be married, quickly, quickly–to-morrow if I can.'

But she only sobbed terribly, and cried:

'I feel awful. I feel awful. I feel I'm horrible to you.'

'No, I want you, I want you,' was all he answered, blindly, with that terrible intonation which frightened her almost more than her horror lest he should *not* want her.

The Blind Man

Written November 1918 and published *English Review*, July 1920 and the collection *England, My England*.

Isabel Pervin was listening for two sounds–for the sound of wheels on the drive outside and for the noise of her husband's footsteps in the hall. Her dearest and oldest friend, a man who seemed almost indispensable to her living, would drive up in the rainy dusk of the closing November day. The trap had gone to fetch him from the station. And her husband, who had been blinded in Flanders, and who had a disfiguring mark on his brow, would be coming in from the out-houses.

He had been home for a year now. He was totally blind. Yet they had been very happy. The Grange was Maurice's own place. The back was a farmstead, and the Wernhams, who occupied the rear premises, acted as farmers. Isabel lived with her husband in the handsome rooms in front. She and he had been almost entirely alone together since he was wounded. They talked and sang and read together in a wonderful and unspeakable intimacy. Then she reviewed books for a Scottish newspaper, carrying on her old interest, and he occupied himself a good deal with the farm. Sightless, he could still discuss everything with Wernham, and he could also do a good deal of work about the place–menial work, it is true, but it gave him satisfaction. He milked the cows, carried in the pails, turned the separator, attended to the pigs and horses. Life was still very full and strangely serene for the blind man, peaceful with the almost incomprehensible peace of immediate contact in darkness. With his wife he had a whole world, rich and real and invisible.

They were newly and remotely happy. He did not even regret the loss of his sight in these times of dark, palpable joy. A certain exultance swelled his soul.

But as time wore on, sometimes the rich glamour would leave them. Sometimes, after months of this intensity, a sense of burden overcame Isabel, a weariness, a terrible *ennui,* in that silent house approached between a colonnade of tall-shafted pines. Then she felt she would go mad, for she could not bear it. And sometimes he had devastating fits of depression, which seemed to lay waste his whole being. It was worse than depression–a black misery, when his own life was a torture to him, and when his presence was unbearable to his wife. The dread went down to the roots of her soul as these black days recurred. In a kind of panic she tried to wrap herself up still further in her husband. She forced the old spontaneous cheerfulness and joy to continue. But the effort it cost her was almost too much. She knew she could not keep it up. She felt she would scream with the strain, and would give anything, anything, to escape. She longed to possess her husband utterly; it gave her inordinate joy to have him entirely to herself. And yet, when again he was gone in a black and massive misery, she could not bear him, she could not bear herself; she wished she could be snatched away off the earth altogether, anything rather than live at this cost.

Dazed, she schemed for a way out. She invited friends, she tried to give him some further connection with the outer world. But it was no good. After all their joy and suffering, after their dark, great year of blindness and solitude and unspeakable nearness, other people seemed to them both shallow, rattling, rather impertinent. Shallow prattle seemed presumptuous. He became impatient and irritated, she was wearied. And so they lapsed into their solitude again. For they preferred it.

But now, in a few weeks' time, her second baby would be born. The first had died, an infant, when her husband first went out to France. She looked with joy and relief to the coming of the second. It would be her salvation. But also she felt some anxiety. She was thirty years old, her husband was a year younger. They both wanted the child very much. Yet she could not help feeling afraid. She had her husband on her hands, a terrible joy to her, and a terrifying burden. The child would occupy her love and attention. And then, what of Maurice? What would he do? If only she could feel that he, too, would be at peace and happy when the child came! She did so want to luxuriate in a rich, physical satisfaction of maternity. But the man, what would he do? How could she provide for him, how avert those shattering black moods of his, which destroyed them both?

She sighed with fear. But at this time Bertie Reid wrote to Isabel. He was her old friend, a second or third cousin, a Scotchman, as she was a Scotchwoman. They had been brought up near to one another, and all her life he had been her friend, like a brother, but better than her own brothers. She loved him—though not in the marrying sense. There was a sort of kinship between them, an affinity. They understood one another instinctively. But Isabel would never have thought of marrying Bertie. It would have seemed like marrying in her own family.

Bertie was a barrister and a man of letters, a Scotchman of the intellectual type, quick, ironical, sentimental, and on his knees before the woman he adored but did not want to marry. Maurice Pervin was different. He came of a good old country family—the Grange was not a very great distance from Oxford. He was passionate, sensitive, perhaps over-sensitive, wincing—a big fellow with heavy limbs and a forehead that flushed painfully. For his mind was slow, as if drugged by the strong provincial blood that beat in his veins. He was very sensitive to his own mental slowness, his feelings being quick and acute. So that he was just the opposite to Bertie, whose mind was much quicker than his emotions, which were not so very fine.

From the first the two men did not like each other. Isabel felt that they *ought* to get on together. But they did not. She felt that if only each could have the clue to the other there would be such a rare understanding between them. It did not come off, however. Bertie adopted a slightly ironical attitude, very offensive to Maurice, who returned the Scotch irony with English resentment, a resentment which deepened sometimes into stupid hatred.

This was a little puzzling to Isabel. However, she accepted it in the course of things. Men were made freakish and unreasonable. Therefore, when Maurice was going out to France for the second time, she felt that, for her husband's sake, she must discontinue her friendship with Bertie. She wrote to the barrister to this effect. Bertram Reid simply replied that in this, as in all other matters, he must obey her wishes, if these were indeed her wishes.

For nearly two years nothing had passed between the two friends. Isabel rather gloried in the fact; she had no compunction. She had one great article of faith, which was, that husband and wife should be so important to one another, that the rest of the world simply did not count. She and Maurice were husband and wife. They loved one another. They would have children. Then let everybody and everything else fade into insignificance outside this connubial felicity. She professed herself quite happy and ready to receive Maurice's friends. She was happy and ready: the happy wife, the ready woman in possession. Without knowing why, the friends retired abashed, and came no more. Maurice, of course, took as much satisfaction in this connubial absorption as Isabel did.

He shared in Isabel's literary activities, she cultivated a real interest in agriculture and cattle-raising. For she, being at heart perhaps an emotional enthusiast, always cultivated the practical side of life, and prided herself on her mastery of practical affairs. Thus the husband and wife had spent the five years of their married life. The last had been one of blindness and un-speakable intimacy. And now Isabel felt a great indifference coming over her, a sort of lethargy. She wanted to be allowed to bear her child in peace, to nod by the fire and drift vaguely, physically, from day to day. Maurice was like an ominous thunder-cloud. She had to keep waking up to remember him.

When a little note came from Bertie, asking if he were to put up a tombstone to their dead friendship, and speaking of the real pain he felt on account of her husband's loss of sight, she felt a pang, a fluttering agita-tion of re-awakening. And she read the letter to Maurice.

'Ask him to come down,' he said.

'Ask Bertie to come here!' she re-echoed.

'Yes–if he wants to.'

Isabel paused for a few moments.

'I know he wants to–he'd only be too glad,' she replied. 'But what about you, Maurice? How would you like it?'

'I should like it.'

'Well–in that case— But I thought you didn't care for him—'

'Oh, I don't know. I might think differently of him now,' the blind man replied. It was rather abstruse to Isabel.

'Well, dear,' she said, 'if you're quite sure—'

'I'm sure enough. Let him come,' said Maurice.

So Bertie was coming, coming this evening, in the November rain and darkness. Isabel was agitated, racked with her old restlessness and indecision. She had always suffered from this pain of doubt, just an agonising sense of uncertainty. It had begun to pass off, in the lethargy of maternity. Now it returned, and she resented it. She struggled as usual to maintain her calm, composed, friendly bearing, a sort of mask she wore over all her body.

A woman had lighted a tall lamp beside the table, and spread the cloth. The long dining-room was dim, with its elegant but rather severe pieces of old furniture. Only the round table glowed softly under the light. It had a rich, beautiful effect. The white cloth glistened and dropped its heavy, pointed lace corners almost to the carpet, the china was old and handsome, creamy-yellow, with a blotched pattern of harsh red and deep blue, the cups large and bell-shaped, the teapot gallant. Isabel looked at it with superficial appreciation.

Her nerves were hurting her. She looked automatically again at the high, uncurtained windows. In the last dusk she could just perceive outside a huge fir-tree swaying its boughs: it was as if she thought it rather than saw it. The rain came flying on the window panes. Ah, why had she no peace? These two men, why did they tear at her? Why did they not come—why was there this suspense?

She sat in a lassitude that was really suspense and irritation. Maurice, at least, might come in—there was nothing to keep him out. She rose to her feet. Catching sight of her reflection in a mirror, she glanced at herself with a slight smile of recognition, as if she were an old friend to herself. Her face was oval and calm, her nose a little arched. Her neck made a beautiful line down to her shoulder. With hair knotted loosely behind, she had something of a warm, maternal look. Thinking this of herself, she arched her eyebrows and her rather heavy eyelids, with a little flicker of a smile, and for a moment her grey eyes looked amused and wicked, a little sardonic, out of her transfigured Madonna face.

Then, resuming her air of womanly patience—she

was really fatally self-determined—she went with a little jerk towards the door. Her eyes were slightly reddened.

She passed down the wide hall, and through a door at the end. Then she was in the farm premises. The scent of dairy, and of farm-kitchen, and of farm-yard and of leather almost overcame her: but particularly the scent of dairy. They had been scalding out the pans. The flagged passage in front of her was dark, puddled and wet. Light came out from the open kitchen door. She went forward and stood in the doorway. The farm-people were at tea, seated at a little distance from her, round a long, narrow table, in the centre of which stood a white lamp. Ruddy faces, ruddy hands holding food, red mouths working, heads bent over the tea-cups: men, land-girls, boys: it was tea-time, feeding-time. Some faces caught sight of her. Mrs Wernham, going round behind the chairs with a large black teapot, halting slightly in her walk, was not aware of her for a moment. Then she turned suddenly.

'Oh, is it Madam!' she exclaimed. 'Come in, then, come in! We're at tea.' And she dragged forward a chair.

'No, I won't come in,' said Isabel. 'I'm afraid I interrupt your meal.'

'No—no—not likely, Madam, not likely.'

'Hasn't Mr Pervin come in, do you know?'

'I'm sure I couldn't say! Missed him, have you, Madam?'

'No, I only wanted him to come in,' laughed Isabel, as if shyly.

'Wanted him, did ye? Get up, boy—get up, now—'

Mrs Wernham knocked one of the boys on the shoulder. He began to scrape to his feet, chewing largely.

'I believe he's in top stable,' said another face from the table.

'Ah! No, don't get up. I'm going myself,' said Isabel.

'Don't you go out of a dirty night like this. Let the lad go. Get along wi' ye, boy,' said Mrs Wernham.

'No, no,' said Isabel, with a decision that was always obeyed. 'Go on with your tea, Tom. I'd like to go across to the stable, Mrs Wernham.'

'Did ever you hear tell!' exclaimed the woman.

'Isn't the trap late?' asked Isabel.

'Why, no,' said Mrs Wernham, peering into the distance at the tall, dim clock. 'No, Madam—we can give it another quarter or twenty minutes yet, good—yes, every bit of a quarter.'

'Ah! It seems late when darkness falls so early,' said Isabel.

'It, do, that it do. Bother the days, that they draw in so,' answered Mrs Wernham. 'Proper miserable!'

'They are,' said Isabel, withdrawing.

She pulled on her overshoes, wrapped a large tartan shawl around her, put on a man's felt hat, and ventured out along the causeways of the first yard. It was very dark. The wind was roaring in the great elms behind the outhouses. When she came to the second yard the darkness seemed deeper. She was unsure of her footing. She wished she had brought a lantern. Rain blew against her. Half she liked it, half she felt unwilling to battle.

She reached at last the just visible door of the stable. There was no sign of a light anywhere. Opening the upper half, she looked in: into a simple well of darkness. The smell of horses, and ammonia, and of warmth was startling to her, in that full night. She listened with all her ears, but could hear nothing save the night, and the stirring of a horse.

'Maurice!' she called, softly and musically, though she was afraid. 'Maurice—are you there?'

Nothing came from the darkness. She knew the rain and wind blew in upon the horses, the hot animal life. Feeling it wrong, she entered the stable, and drew the lower half of the door shut, holding the upper part close. She did not stir, because she was aware of the presence of the dark hind-quarters of the horses, though she could not see them, and she was afraid. Something wild stirred in her heart.

She listened intensely. Then she heard a small noise

in the distance—far away, it seemed—the chink of a pan, and a man's voice speaking a brief word. It would be Maurice, in the other part of the stable. She stood motionless, waiting for him to come through the partition door. The horses were so terrifyingly near to her, in the invisible.

The loud jarring of the inner door-latch made her start; the door was opened. She could hear and feel her husband entering and invisibly passing among the horses near to her, darkness as they were, actively intermingled. The rather low sound of his voice as he spoke to the horses came velvety to her nerves. How near he was, and how invisible! The darkness seemed to be in a strange swirl of violent life, just upon her. She turned giddy.

Her presence of mind made her call, quietly and musically:

'Maurice! Maurice—dea-ar!'

'Yes,' he answered. 'Isabel?'

She saw nothing, and the sound of his voice seemed to touch her.

'Hello!' she answered cheerfully, straining her eyes to see him. He was still busy, attending to the horses near her, but she saw only darkness. It made her almost desperate.

'Won't you come in, dear?' she said.

'Yes, I'm coming. Just half a minute *Stand over—now!* Trap's not come, has it?'

'Not yet,' said Isabel.

His voice was pleasant and ordinary, but it had a slight suggestion of the stable to her. She wished he would come away. Whilst he was so utterly invisible, she was afraid of him.

'How's the time?' he asked.

'Not yet six,' she replied. She disliked to answer into the dark. Presently he came very near to her, and she retreated out of doors.

'The weather blows in here,' he said, coming steadily forward, feeling for the doors. She shrank away.

At last she could dimly see him.

'Bertie won't have much of a drive,' he said, as he closed the doors.

'He won't indeed!' said Isabel calmly, watching the dark shape at the door.

'Give me your arm, dear,' she said.

She pressed his arm close to her, as she went. But she longed to see him, to look at him. She was nervous. He walked erect, with face rather lifted, but with a curious tentative movement of his powerful, muscular legs. She could feel the clever, careful, strong contact of his feet with the earth, as she balanced against him. For a moment he was a tower of darkness to her, as if he rose out of the earth.

In the house-passage he wavered, and went cautiously, with a curious look of silence about him as he felt for the bench. Then he sat down heavily. He was a man with rather sloping shoulders, but with heavy limbs, powerful legs that seemed to know the earth. His head was small, usually carried high and light. As he bent down to unfasten his gaiters and boots he did not look blind. His hair was brown and crisp, his hands were large, reddish, intelligent, the veins stood out in the wrists; and his thighs and knees seemed massive. When he stood up his face and neck were surcharged with blood, the veins stood out on his temples. She did not look at his blindness.

Isabel was always glad when they had passed through the dividing door into their own regions of repose and beauty. She was a little afraid of him, out there in the animal grossness of the back. His bearing also changed, as he smelt the familiar indefinable odour that pervaded his wife's surroundings, a delicate, refined scent, very faintly spicy. Perhaps it came from the pot-pourri bowls.

He stood at the foot of the stairs, arrested, listening. She watched him, and her heart sickened. He seemed to be listening to fate.

'He's not here yet,' he said. 'I'll go up and change.'

'Maurice,' she said, 'you're not wishing he wouldn't come, are you?'

'I couldn't quite say,' he answered. 'I feel myself rather on the *qui vive*.'

'I can see you are,' she answered. And she reached up and kissed his cheek. She saw his mouth relax into a slow smile.

'What are you laughing at?' she said, roguishly.

'You consoling me,' he answered.

'Nay,' she answered. 'Why should I console you? You know we love each other—you know *how* married we are! What does anything else matter?'

'Nothing at all, my dear.'

He felt for her face, and touched it, smiling.

'*You're* all right, aren't you?' he asked, anxiously.

'I'm wonderfully all right, love,' she answered. 'It's you I am a little troubled about, at times.'

'Why me?' he said, touching her cheeks delicately with the tips of his fingers. The touch had an almost hypnotising effect on her.

He went away upstairs. She saw him mount into the darkness, unseeing and unchanging. He did not know that the lamps on the upper corridor were unlighted. He went on into the darkness with unchanging step. She heard him in the bath-room.

Pervin moved about almost unconsciously in his familiar surroundings, dark though everything was. He seemed to know the presence of objects before he touched them. It was a pleasure to him to rock thus through a world of things, carried on the flood in a sort of blood-prescience. He did not think much or trouble much. So long as he kept this sheer immediacy of blood-contact with the substantial world he was happy, he wanted no intervention of visual consciousness. In this state there was a certain rich positivity, bordering sometimes on rapture. Life seemed to move in him like a tide lapping, lapping, and advancing, enveloping all things darkly. It was a pleasure to stretch forth the hand and meet the unseen object, clasp it, and possess it in pure contact. He did not try to remember, to visualise. He did not want to. The new way of consciousness substituted itself in him.

The rich suffusion of this state generally kept him happy, reaching its culmination in the consuming passion for his wife. But at times the flow would seem to be checked and thrown back. Then it would beat inside him like a tangled sea, and he was tortured in the shattered chaos of his own blood. He grew to dread this arrest, this throw-back, this chaos inside himself, when he seemed merely at the mercy of his own powerful and conflicting elements. How to get some measure of control or surety, this was the question. And when the question rose maddening in him, he would clench his fists as if he would *compel* the whole universe to submit to him. But it was in vain. He could not even compel himself.

To-night, however, he was still serene, though little tremors of unreasonable exasperation ran through him. He had to handle the razor very carefully, as he shaved, for it was not at one with him, he was afraid of it. His hearing also was too much sharpened. He heard the woman lighting the lamps on the corridor, and attending to the fire in the visitors' room. And then, as he went to his room, he heard the trap arrive. Then came Isabel's voice, lifted and calling, like a bell ringing:

'Is it you, Bertie? Have you come?'

And a man's voice answered out of the wind:

'Hello, Isabel! There you are.'

'Have you had a miserable drive? I'm so sorry we couldn't send a closed carriage. I can't see you at all, you know.'

'I'm coming. No, I liked the drive–it was like Perthshire. Well, how are you? You're looking fit as ever, as far as I can see.'

'Oh, yes,' said Isabel. 'I'm wonderfully well. How are you? Rather thin, I think—'

'Worked to death–everybody's old cry. But I'm all

right, Ciss. How's Pervin?—isn't he here?'

'Oh, yes, he's upstairs changing. Yes, he's awfully well. Take off your wet things; I'll send them to be dried.'

'And how are you both, in spirits? He doesn't fret?'

'No—no, not at all. No, on the contrary, really. We've been wonderfully happy, incredibly. It's more than I can understand—so wonderful: the nearness, and the peace—'

'Ah! Well, that's awfully good news—'

They moved away. Pervin heard no more. But a childish sense of desolation had come over him, as he heard their brisk voices. He seemed shut out—like a child that is left out. He was aimless and excluded, he did not know what to do with himself. The helpless desolation came over him. He fumbled nervously as he dressed himself, in a state almost of childishness. He disliked the Scotch accent in Bertie's speech, and the slight response it found on Isabel's tongue. He disliked the slight purr of complacency in the Scottish speech. He disliked intensely the glib way in which Isabel spoke of their happiness and nearness. It made him recoil. He was fretful and beside himself like a child, he had almost a childish nostalgia to be included in the life circle. And at the same time he was a man, dark and powerful and infuriated by his own weakness. By some fatal flaw, he could not be by himself, he had to depend on the support of another. And this very dependence enraged him. He hated Bertie Reid, and at the same time he knew the hatred was nonsense, he knew it was the outcome of his own weakness.

He went downstairs. Isabel was alone in the dining-room. She watched him enter, head erect, his feet tentative. He looked so strong-blooded and healthy, and, at the same time, cancelled. Cancelled—that was the word that flew across her mind. Perhaps it was his scar suggested it.

'You heard Bertie come, Maurice?' she said.

Yes—isn't he here?'

'He's in his room. He looks very thin and worn.'

'I suppose he works himself to death.'

A woman came in with a tray—and after a few minutes Bertie came down. He was a little dark man, with a very big forehead, thin, wispy hair, and sad, large eyes. His expression was inordinately sad—almost funny. He had odd, short legs.

Isabel watched him hesitate under the door, and glance nervously at her husband. Pervin heard him and turned.

'Here you are, now,' said Isabel. 'Come, let us eat.'

Bertie went across to Maurice.

'How are you, Pervin?' he said, as he advanced.

The blind man stuck his hand out into space, and Bertie took it.

'Very fit. Glad you've come,' said Maurice.

Isabel glanced at them, and glanced away, as if she could not bear to see them.

'Come,' she said. 'Come to table. Aren't you both awfully hungry? I am, tremendously.'

'I'm afraid you waited for me,' said Bertie, as they sat down.

Maurice had a curious monolithic way of sitting in a chair, erect and distant. Isabel's heart always beat when she caught sight of him thus.

'No,' she replied to Bertie. 'We're having a sort of high tea, not dinner. Do you mind? It gives us such a nice long evening, uninterrupted.'

'I like it,' said Bertie.

Maurice was feeling, with curious little movements, almost like a cat kneading her bed, for his plate, his knife and fork, his napkin. He was getting the whole geography of his cover into his consciousness. He sat erect and inscrutable, remote-seeming. Bertie watched the static figure of the blind man, the delicate tactile discernment of the large, ruddy hands, and the curious mindless silence of the brow, above the scar. With difficulty he looked away, and without knowing what he did, picked up a little crystal bowl of violets from the table, and held them to his nose.

'They are sweet-scented,' he said. 'Where do they come from?'

'From the garden–under the windows,' said Isabel.

'So late in the year–and so fragrant! Do you remember the violets under Aunt Bell's south wall?'

The two friends looked at each other and exchanged a smile, Isabel's eyes lighting up.

'Don't I?' she replied. '*Wasn't* she queer!'

'A curious old girl,' laughed Bertie. 'There's a streak of freakishness in the family, Isabel.'

'Ah–but not in you and me, Bertie,' said Isabel. 'Give them to Maurice, will you?' she added, as Bertie was putting down the flowers. 'Have you smelled the violets, dear? Do!–they are so scented.'

Maurice held out his hand, and Bertie placed the tiny bowl against his large, warm-looking fingers. Maurice's hand closed over the thin white fingers of the barrister. Bertie carefully extricated himself. Then the two watched the blind man smelling the violets. He bent his head and seemed to be thinking. Isabel waited.

'Aren't they sweet, Maurice?' she said at last, anxiously.

'Very,' he said. And he held out the bowl. Bertie took it. Both he and Isabel were a little afraid, and deeply disturbed.

The meal continued. Isabel and Bertie chatted spasmodically. The blind man was silent. He touched his food repeatedly, with quick, delicate touches of his knife-point, then cut irregular bits. He could not bear to be helped. Both Isabel and Bertie suffered: Isabel wondered why. She did not suffer when she was alone with Maurice. Bertie made her conscious of a strangeness.

After the meal the three drew their chairs to the fire, and sat down to talk. The decanters were put on a table near at hand. Isabel knocked the logs on the fire, and clouds of brilliant sparks went up the chimney. Bertie noticed a slight weariness in her bearing.

'You will be glad when your child comes now, Isabel?' he said.

She looked up to him with a quick wan smile.

'Yes, I shall be glad,' she answered. 'It begins to seem long. Yes, I shall be very glad. So will you, Maurice, won't you?' she added.

'Yes, I shall,' replied her husband.

'We are both looking forward so much to having it,' she said.

'Yes, of course,' said Bertie.

He was a bachelor, three or four years older than Isabel. He lived in beautiful rooms overlooking the river, guarded by a faithful Scottish man-servant. And he had his friends among the fair sex—not lovers, friends. So long as he could avoid any danger of courtship or marriage, he adored a few good women with constant and unfailing homage, and he was chivalrously fond of quite a number. But if they seemed to encroach on him, he withdrew and detested them.

Isabel knew him very well, knew his beautiful constancy, and kindness, also his incurable weakness, which made him unable ever to enter into close contact of any sort. He was ashamed of himself, because he could not marry, could not approach women physically. He wanted to do so. But he could not. At the centre of him he was afraid, helplessly and even brutally afraid. He had given up hope, and ceased to expect any more that he could escape his own weakness. Hence he was a brilliant and successful barrister, also a *littérateur* of high repute, a rich man, and a great social success. At the centre he felt himself neuter, nothing.

Isabel knew him well. She despised him even while she admired him. She looked at his sad face, his little short legs, and felt contempt of him. She looked at his dark grey eyes, with their uncanny, almost childlike intuition, and she loved him. He understood amazingly—but she had no fear of his understanding. As a man she patronised him.

And she turned to the impassive, silent figure of her husband. He sat leaning back, with folded arms, and face a little uptilted. His knees were straight and massive. She sighed, picked up the poke, and again began to prod the fire, to rouse the clouds of soft brilliant sparks.

'Isabel tells me,' Bertie began suddenly, 'that you have not suffered unbearably from the loss of sight.'

Maurice straightened himself to attend, but kept his arms folded.

'No,' he said, 'not unbearably. Now and again one struggles against it, you know. But there are compensations.'

'They say it is much worse to be stone deaf,' said Isabel.

'I believe it is,' said Bertie. 'Are there compensations?' he added, to Maurice.

'Yes. You cease to bother about a great many things.' Again Maurice stretched his figure, stretched the strong muscles of his back, and leaned backwards, with uplifted face.

'And that is a relief,' said Bertie. 'But what is there in place of the bothering? What replaces the activity?'

There was a pause. At length the blind man replied, as out of a negligent, unattentive thinking:

'Oh, I don't know. There's a good deal when you're not active.'

'Is there?' said Bertie. 'What, exactly? It always seems to me that when there is no thought and no action, there is nothing.'

Again Maurice was slow in replying.

'There is something,' he replied. 'I couldn't tell you what it is.'

And the talk lapsed once more, Isabel and Bertie chatting gossip and reminiscence, the blind man silent.

At length Maurice rose restlessly, a big, obtrusive figure. He felt tight and hampered. He wanted to go away.

'Do you mind,' he said, 'if I go and speak to Wernham?'

'No—go along, dear,' said Isabel.

And he went out. A silence came over the two friends. At length Bertie said:

'Nevertheless, it is a great deprivation, Cissie.'

'It is, Bertie. I know it is.'

'Something lacking all the time,' said Bertie.

'Yes, I know. And yet—and yet—Maurice is right. There is something else, something *there,* which you never knew was there, and which you can't express.'

'What is there?' asked Bertie.

'I don't know—it's awfully hard to define it—but something strong and immediate. There's something strange in Maurice's presence—indefinable—but I couldn't do without it. I agree that it seems to put one's mind to sleep. But when we're alone I miss nothing; it seems awfully rich, almost splendid, you know.'

'I'm afraid I don't follow,' said Bertie.

They talked desultorily. The wind blew loudly outside, rain chattered on the window-panes, making a sharp drum-sound, because of the closed, mellow-golden shutters inside. The logs burned slowly, with hot, almost invisible small flames. Bertie seemed uneasy, there were dark circles round his eyes. Isabel, rich with her approaching maternity, leaned looking into the fire. Her hair curled in odd, loose strands, very pleasing to the man. But she had a curious feeling of old woe in her heart, old, timeless night-woe.

'I suppose we're all deficient somewhere,' said Bertie.

'I suppose so,' said Isabel wearily.

'Damned, sooner or later.'

'I don't know,' she said, rousing herself. 'I feel quite all right, you know. The child coming seems to make me indifferent to everything, just placid. I can't feel that there's anything to trouble about, you know.'

'A good thing, I should say,' he replied slowly.

'Well, there it is. I suppose it's just Nature. If only I felt I needn't trouble about Maurice, I should be perfectly content—'

'But you feel you must trouble about him?'

'Well–I don't know—' She even resented this much effort.

The night passed slowly. Isabel looked at the clock. 'I say,' she said. 'It's nearly ten o'clock. Where can Maurice be? I'm sure they're all in bed at the back. Excuse me a moment.'

She went out, returning almost immediately.

'It's all shut up and in darkness,' she said. 'I wonder where he is. He must have gone out to the farm—'

Bertie looked at her.

'I suppose he'll come in,' he said.

'I suppose so,' she said. 'But it's unusual for him to be out now.'

'Would you like me to go out and see?'

'Well–if you wouldn't mind. I'd go, but—' She did not want to make the physical effort.

Bertie put on an old overcoat and took a lantern. He went out from the side door. He shrank from the wet and roaring night. Such weather had a nervous effect on him: too much moisture everywhere made him feel almost imbecile. Unwilling, he went through it all. A dog barked violently at him. He peered in all the buildings. At last, as he opened the upper door of a sort of intermediate barn, he heard a grinding noise, and looking in, holding up his lantern, saw Maurice, in his shirt-sleeves, standing listening, holding the handle of a turnip-pulper. He had been pulping sweet roots, a pile of which lay dimly heaped in a corner behind him.

'That you, Wernham?' said Maurice, listening.

'No, it's me,' said Bertie.

A large, half-wild grey cat was rubbing at Maurice's leg. The blind man stooped to rub its sides. Bertie watched the scene, then unconsciously entered and shut the door behind him. He was in a high sort of barn-place,

from which, right and left, ran off the corridors in front of
the stalled cattle. He watched the slow, stooping motion
of the other man, as he caressed the great cat.

Maurice straightened himself.

'You came to look for me?' he said.

'Isabel was a little uneasy,' said Bertie.

'I'll come in. I like messing about doing these jobs.'

The cat had reared her sinister, feline length against
his leg, clawing at his thigh affectionately. He lifted her
claws out of his flesh.

'I hope I'm not in your way at all at the Grange
here,' said Bertie, rather shy and stiff.

'My way? No, not a bit. I'm glad Isabel has somebody to talk to. I'm afraid it's I who am in the way. I
know I'm not very lively company. Isabel's all right,
don't you think? She's not unhappy, is she?'

'I don't think so.'

'What does she say?'

'She says she's very content—only a little troubled
about you.'

'Why me?'

'Perhaps afraid that you might brood,' said Bertie,
cautiously.

'She needn't be afraid of that.' He continued to
caress the flattened grey head of the cat with his fingers.
'What I am a bit afraid of,' he resumed, 'is that she'll find
me a dead weight, always alone with me down here.'

'I don't think you need think that,' said Bertie,
though this was what he feared himself.

'I don't know,' said Maurice. 'Sometimes I feel it
isn't fair that she's saddled with me.' Then he dropped
his voice curiously. 'I say,' he asked, secretly struggling,
'is my face much disfigured? Do you mind telling me?'

'There is the scar,' said Bertie, wondering. 'Yes, it is
a disfigurement. But more pitiable than shocking.'

'A pretty bad scar, though,' said Maurice.

'Oh, yes.'

There was a pause.

'Sometimes I feel I am horrible,' said Maurice, in a low voice, talking as if to himself. And Bertie actually felt a quiver of horror.

'That's nonsense,' he said.

Maurice again straightened himself, leaving the cat.

'There's no telling,' he said. Then again, in an odd tone, he added: 'I don't really know you, do I?'

'Probably not,' said Bertie.

'Do you mind if I touch you?'

The lawyer shrank away instinctively. And yet, out of very philanthropy, he said, in a small voice: 'Not at all.'

But he suffered as the blind man stretched out a strong, naked hand to him. Maurice accidentally knocked off Bertie's hat.

'I thought you were taller,' he said, starting. Then he laid his hand on Bertie Reid's head, closing the dome of the skull in a soft, firm grasp, gathering it, as it were; then, shifting his grasp and softly closing again, with a fine, close pressure, till he had covered the skull and the face of the smaller man, tracing the brows, and touching the full, closed eyes, touching the small nose and the nostrils, the rough, short moustache, the mouth, the rather strong chin. The hand of the blind man grasped the shoulder, the arm, the hand of the other man. He seemed to take him, in the soft, travelling grasp.

'You seem young,' he said quietly, at last.

The lawyer stood almost annihilated, unable to answer.

'Your head seems tender, as if you were young,' Maurice repeated. 'So do your hands. Touch my eyes, will you?—touch my scar.'

Now Bertie quivered with revulsion. Yet he was under the power of the blind man, as if hypnotised. He lifted his hand, and laid the fingers on the scar, on the scarred eyes. Maurice suddenly covered them with his own hand, pressed the fingers of the other man upon his disfigured eye-sockets, trembling in every fibre, and rocking slightly, slowly, from side to side. He remained thus for a minute or more, whilst Bertie stood as if in a swoon, unconscious, imprisoned.

Then suddenly Maurice removed the hand of the other man from his brow, and stood holding it in his own.

'Oh, my God,' he said, 'we shall know each other now, shan't we? We shall know each other now.'

Bertie could not answer. He gazed mute and terror-struck, overcome by his own weakness. He knew he could not answer. He had an unreasonable fear, lest the other man should suddenly destroy him. Whereas Maurice was actually filled with hot, poignant love, the passion of friendship. Perhaps it was this very passion of friendship which Bertie shrank from most.

'We're all right together now, aren't we?' said Maurice. 'It's all right now, as long as we live, so far as we're concerned?'

'Yes,' said Bertie, trying by any means to escape.

Maurice stood with head lifted, as if listening. The new delicate fulfilment of mortal friendship had come as a revelation and surprise to him, something exquisite and unhoped-for. He seemed to be listening to hear if it were real.

Then he turned for his coat.

'Come,' he said, 'we'll go to Isabel.'

Bertie took the lantern and opened the door. The cat disappeared. The two men went in silence along the causeways. Isabel, as they came, thought their footsteps sounded strange. She looked up pathetically and anxiously for their entrance. There seemed a curious elation about Maurice. Bertie was haggard, with sunken eyes.

'What is it?' she asked.

'We've become friends,' said Maurice, standing with his feet apart, like a strange colossus.

'Friends!' re-echoed Isabel. And she looked again at Bertie. He met her eyes with a furtive, haggard look; his eyes were as if glazed with misery.

'I'm so glad,' she said, in sheer perplexity.

'Yes,' said Maurice.

He was indeed so glad. Isabel took his hand with both hers, and held it fast.

'You'll be happier now, dear,' she said.

But she was watching Bertie. She knew that he had one desire—to escape from this intimacy, this friendship, which had been thrust upon him. He could not bear it that he had been touched by the blind man, his insane reserve broken in. He was like a mollusc whose shell is broken.

Tickets, Please

Written November 1918 and published in *Strand*, April 1919 and *Metropolitan*, August 1919 before inclusion in the collection *England, My England*.

There is in the Midlands a single-line tramway system which boldly leaves the county town and plunges off into the black, industrial countryside, up hill and down dale, through the long, ugly villages of workmen's houses, over canals and railways, past churches perched high and nobly over the smoke and shadows, through stark, grimy, cold little market-places, tilting away in a rush past cinemas and shops down to the hollow where the collieries are, then up again, past a little rural church, under the ash trees, on in a rush to the terminus, the last little ugly place of industry, the cold little town that shivers on the edge of the wild, gloomy country beyond. There the green and creamy coloured tram-car seems to pause and purr with curious satisfaction. But in a few minutes—the clock on the turret of the Cooperative Wholesale Society's Shops gives the time—away it starts once more on the adventure. Again there are the reckless swoops downhill, bouncing the loops: again the chilly wait in the hill-top market-place: again the breathless slithering round the precipitous drop under the church: again the patient halts at the loops, waiting for the out-coming car: so on and on, for two long hours, till at last the city looms beyond the fat gas-works, the narrow factories draw near, we are in the sordid streets of the great town, once more we sidle to a standstill at our terminus, abashed by the great crimson and cream-coloured city cars, but still perky, jaunty, somewhat dare-devil, green as a jaunty sprig of parsley out of a black colliery garden.

To ride on these cars is always an adventure. Since we are in war-time, the drivers are men unfit for active service: cripples and hunchbacks. So they have the spirit of the devil in them. The ride becomes a steeple-chase. Hurray! we have leapt in a clear jump over the canal bridges—now for the four-lane corner. With a shriek and a trail of sparks we are clear again. To be sure, a tram often leaps the rails—but what matter! It sits in a ditch till other trams come to haul it out. It is quite common for a car, packed with one solid mass of living people, to come to a dead halt in the midst of unbroken blackness, the heart of nowhere on a dark night, and for the driver and the girl conductor to call, 'All get off—car's on fire!' Instead, however, of rushing out in a panic, the passengers stolidly reply: 'Get on—get on! We're not coming out. We're stopping where we are. Push on, George.' So till flames actually appear.

The reason for this reluctance to dismount is that the nights are howlingly cold, black, and windswept, and a car is a haven of refuge. From village to village the miners travel, for a change of cinema, of girl, of pub. The trams are desperately packed. Who is going to risk himself in the black gulf outside, to wait perhaps an hour for another tram, then to see the forlorn notice 'Depot Only', because there is something wrong! or to greet a unit of three bright cars all so tight with people that they sail past with a howl of derision. Trams that pass in the night.

This, the most dangerous tram-service in England, as the authorities themselves declare, with pride, is entirely conducted by girls, and driven by rash young men, a little crippled, or by delicate young men, who creep forward in terror. The girls are fearless young hussies. In their ugly blue uniform, skirts up to their knees, shapeless old peaked caps on their heads, they have all the *sang-froid* of an old non-commissioned officer. With a tram packed with howling colliers, roaring hymns downstairs and a sort of antiphony of obscenities upstairs, the lasses are perfectly at their ease. They pounce on the youths who try to evade their ticket-machine. They push off the men at the end of their distance. They are not going to be done in the eye–not they. They fear nobody–and everybody fears them.

'Hello, Annie!'

'Hello, Ted!'

'Oh, mind my corn, Miss Stone. It's my belief you've got a heart of stone, for you've trod on it again.'

'You should keep it in your pocket,' replies Miss Stone, and she goes sturdily upstairs in her high boots.

'Tickets, please.'

She is peremptory, suspicious, and ready to hit first. She can hold her own against ten thousand. The step of that tram-car is her Thermopylae.

Therefore, there is a certain wild romance aboard these cars–and in the sturdy bosom of Annie herself. The time for soft romance is in the morning, between ten o'clock and one, when things are rather slack: that is, except market-day and Saturday. Thus Annie has time to look about her. Then she often hops off her car and into a shop where she has spied something, while the driver chats in the main road. There is very good feeling between the girls and the drivers. Are they not companions in peril, shipments aboard this careering vessel of a tram-car, for ever rocking on the waves of a stormy land.

Then, also, during the easy hours, the inspectors are most in evidence. For some reason, everybody in this tram-service is young: there are no grey heads. It would not do. Therefore the inspectors are of the right age, and one, the chief, is also good-looking. See him stand on a wet, gloomy morning, in his long oil-skin, his peaked cap

well down over his eyes, waiting to board a car. His face
is ruddy; his small brown moustache is weathered, he
has a faint impudent smile. Fairly tall and agile, even in
his waterproof, he springs aboard a car and greets Annie.

'Hello, Annie! Keeping the wet out?'

'Trying to.'

There are only two people in the car. Inspecting is
soon over. Then for a long and impudent chat on the
foot-board, a good, easy, twelve-mile chat.

The inspector's name is John Thomas Raynor
—always called John Thomas, except sometimes, in
malice, Coddy. His face sets in fury when he is
addressed, from a distance, with this abbreviation. There
is considerable scandal about John Thomas in half a
dozen villages. He flirts with the girl conductors in the
morning, and walks out with them in the dark night,
when they leave their tram-car at the depot. Of course,
the girls quit the service frequently. Then he flirts and
walks out with the newcomer: always providing she is
sufficiently attractive, and that she will consent to walk.
It is remarkable, however, that most of the girls are quite
comely, they are all young, and this roving life aboard
the car gives them a sailor's dash and recklessness. What
matter how they behave when the ship is in port. To-
morrow they will be aboard again.

Annie, however, was something of a Tartar, and her
sharp tongue had kept John Thomas at arm's length for
many months. Perhaps, therefore, she liked him all the
more: for he always came up smiling, with impudence.
She watched him vanquish one girl, then another. She
could tell by the movement of his mouth and eyes, when
he flirted with her in the morning, that he had been
walking out with this lass, or the other, the night before.
A fine cock-of-the-walk he was. She could sum him up
pretty well.

In this subtle antagonism they knew each other like
old friends, they were as shrewd with one another almost

as man and wife. But Annie had always kept him sufficiently at arm's length. Besides, she had a boy of her
own.

The Statutes fair, however, came in November, at
Bestwood. It happened that Annie had the Monday
night off. It was a drizzling ugly night, yet she dressed
herself up and went to the fair ground. She was alone,
but she expected soon to find a pal of some sort.

The roundabouts were veering round and grinding
out their music, the side shows were making as much
commotion as possible. In the cocoanut shies there were
no cocoanuts, but artificial war-time substitutes, which
the lads declared were fastened into the irons. There was
a sad decline in brilliance and luxury. None the less, the
ground was muddy as ever, there was the same crush, the
press of faces lighted up by the flares and the electric
lights, the same smell of naphtha and a few fried
potatoes, and of electricity.

Who should be the first to greet Miss Annie, on the
show ground, but John Thomas. He had a black overcoat
buttoned up to his chin, and a tweed cap pulled down
over his brows, his face between was ruddy and smiling
and handy as ever. She knew so well the way his mouth
moved.

She was very glad to have a 'boy'. To be at the
Statutes without a fellow was no fun. Instantly, like the
gallant he was, he took her on the Dragons, grim-
toothed, round-about switchbacks. It was not nearly so
exciting as a tram-car actually. But, then, to be seated in
a shaking green dragon, uplifted above the sea of bubble
faces, careering in a rickety fashion in the lower heavens,
whilst John Thomas leaned over her, his cigarette in his
mouth, was after all the right style. She was a plump,
quick, alive little creature. So she was quite excited and
happy.

John Thomas made her stay on for the next round.
And therefore she could hardly for shame repulse him
when he put his arm round her and drew her a little
nearer to him, in a very warm and cuddly manner.

Besides, he was fairly discreet, he kept his movement as hidden as possible. She looked down, and saw that his red, clean hand was out of sight of the crowd. And they knew each other so well. So they warmed up to the fair.

After the dragons they went on the horses. John Thomas paid each time, so she could but be complaisant. He, of course, sat astride on the outer horse—named 'Black Bess'—and she sat sideways, towards him, on the inner horse—named 'Wildfire'. But of course John Thomas was not going to sit discreetly on 'Black Bess', holding the brass bar. Round they spun and heaved, in the light. And round he swung on his wooden steed, flinging one leg across her mount, and perilously tipping up and down, across the space, half lying back, laughing at her. He was perfectly happy; she was afraid her hat was on one side, but she was excited.

He threw quoits on a table, and won for her two large, pale-blue hat-pins. And then, hearing the noise of the cinemas, announcing another performance, they climbed the boards and went in.

Of course, during these performances pitch darkness falls from time to time, when the machine goes wrong. Then there is a wild whooping, and a loud smacking of simulated kisses. In these moments John Thomas drew Annie towards him. After all, he had a wonderfully warm, cosy way of holding a girl with his arm, he seemed to make such a nice fit. And after all, it was pleasant to be so held: so very comforting and cosy and nice. He leaned over her and she felt his breath on her hair; she knew he wanted to kiss her on the lips. And after all, he was so warm and she fitted in to him so softly. After all, she wanted him to touch her lips.

But the light sprang up; she also started electrically, and put her hat straight. He left his arm lying nonchalantly behind her. Well, it was fun, it was exciting to be at the Statutes with John Thomas.

When the cinema was over they went for a walk across the dark, damp fields. He had all the arts of love-making. He was especially good at holding a girl, when he sat with her on a stile in the black, drizzling darkness. He seemed to be holding her in space, against his own warmth and gratification. And his kisses were soft and slow and searching.

So Annie walked out with John Thomas, though she kept her own boy dangling in the distance. Some of the tram-girls chose to be huffy. But there, you must take things as you find them, in this life.

There was no mistake about it, Annie liked John Thomas a good deal. She felt so rich and warm in herself whenever he was near. And John Thomas really liked Annie, more than usual. The soft, melting way in which she could flow into a fellow, as if she melted into his very bones, was something rare and good. He fully appreciated this.

But with a developing acquaintance there began a developing intimacy. Annie wanted to consider him a person, a man; she wanted to take an intelligent interest in him, and to have an intelligent response. She did not want a mere nocturnal presence, which was what he was so far. And she prided herself that he could not leave her.

Here she made a mistake. John Thomas intended to remain a nocturnal presence; he had no idea of becoming an all-round individual to her. When she started to take an intelligent interest in him and his life and his character, he sheered off. He hated intelligent interest. And he knew that the only way to stop it was to avoid it. The possessive female was aroused in Annie. So he left her.

It is no use saying she was not surprised. She was at first startled, thrown out of her count. For she had been so *very* sure of holding him. For a while she was staggered, and everything became uncertain to her. Then she wept with fury, indignation, desolation, and misery. Then she had a spasm of despair. And then, when he came, still impudently, on to her car, still familiar, but letting her see by the movement of his head that he had gone away to somebody else for the time being, and was enjoying pastures new, then she determined to have her own back.

She had a very shrewd idea what girls John Thomas had taken out. She went to Nora Purdy. Nora was a tall, rather pale, but well-built girl, with beautiful yellow hair. She was rather secretive.

'Hey!' said Annie, accosting her; then softly, 'Who's John Thomas on with now?'

'I don't know,' said Nora.

'Why tha does,' said Annie, ironically lapsing into dialect. 'Tha knows as well as I do.'

'Well, I do, then,' said Nora. 'It isn't me, so don't bother.'

'It's Cissy Meakin, isn't it?'

'It is, for all I know.'

'Hasn't he got a face on him!' said Annie. 'I don't half like his cheek. I could knock him off the footboard when he comes round at me.'

'He'll get dropped-on one of these days,' said Nora.

'Ay, he will when somebody makes up their mind to drop it on him. I should like to see him taken down a peg or two, shouldn't you?'

'I shouldn't mind,' said Nora.

'You've got quite as much cause to as I have,' said Annie. 'But we'll drop on him one of these days, my girl. What? Don't you want to?'

'I don't mind,' said Nora.

But as a matter of fact, Nora was much more vindictive than Annie.

One by one Annie went the round of the old flames. It so happened that Cissy Meakin left the tramway service in quite a short time. Her mother made her leave. Then John Thomas was on the *qui-vive*. He cast his eyes over his old flock. And his eyes lighted on Annie. He thought she would be safe now. Besides, he liked her.

She arranged to walk home with him on Sunday night. It so happened that her car would be in the depot at half-past nine: the last car would come in at 10.15. So

John Thomas was to wait for her there.

At the depot the girls had a little waiting-room of their own. It was quite rough, but cosy, with a fire and an oven and a mirror, and table and wooden chairs. The half dozen girls who knew John Thomas only too well had arranged to take service this Sunday afternoon. So, as the cars began to come in, early, the girls dropped into the waiting-room. And instead of hurrying off home, they sat around the fire and had a cup of tea. Outside was the darkness and lawlessness of war-time.

John Thomas came on the car after Annie, at about a quarter to ten. He poked his head easily into the girls' waiting-room.

'Prayer-meeting?' he asked.

'Ay,' said Laura Sharp. 'Ladies only.'

'That's me!' said John Thomas. It was one of his favourite exclamations.

'Shut the door, boy,' said Muriel Baggaley.

'On which side of me?' said John Thomas.

'Which tha likes,' said Polly Birkin.

He had come in and closed the door behind him. The girls moved in their circle, to make a place for him near the fire. He took off his great-coat and pushed back his hat.

'Who handles the teapot?' he said.

Nora Purdy silently poured him out a cup of tea.

'Want a bit o' my bread and drippin'?' said Muriel Baggaley to him.

'Ay, give us a bit.'

And he began to eat his piece of bread.

'There's no place like home, girls,' he said.

They all looked at him as he uttered this piece of impudence. He seemed to be sunning himself in the presence of so many damsels.

'Especially if you're not afraid to go home in the dark,' said Laura Sharp.

'Me! By myself I am.'

They sat till they heard the last tram come in. In a

few minutes Emma Houselay entered.

'Come on, my old duck!' cried Polly Birkin.

'It *is* perishing,' said Emma, holding her fingers to the fire.

'But—I'm afraid to, go home in, the dark,' sang Laura Sharp, the tune having got into her mind.

Who're you going with to-night, John Thomas?' asked Muriel Baggaley, coolly.

'To-night?' said John Thomas. 'Oh, I'm going home by myself to-night—all on my lonely-O.'

'That's me!' said Nora Purdy, using his own ejaculation.

The girls laughed shrilly.

'Me as well, Nora,' said John Thomas.

'Don't know what you mean,' said Laura.

'Yes, I'm toddling,' said he, rising and reaching for his overcoat.

'Nay,' said Polly. 'We're all here waiting for you.'

'We've got to be up in good time in the morning,' he said, in the benevolent official manner.

They all laughed.

'Nay,' said Muriel. 'Don't leave us all lonely, John Thomas. Take one!'

'I'll take the lot, if you like,' he responded, gallantly.

'That you won't, either,' said Muriel. 'Two's company; seven's too much of a good thing.'

'Nay—take one,' said Laura. 'Fair and square, all above board, and say which.'

''Ay,' cried Annie, speaking for the first time. 'Pick, John Thomas; let's hear thee.'

'Nay,' he said, 'I'm going home quiet to-night. Feeling good, for once.'

'Whereabouts?' said Annie. 'Take a good un, then. But tha's got to take one of us!'

'Nay, how can I take one,' he said, laughing uneasily. 'I don't want to make enemies.'

'You'd only make *one*,' said Annie.

'The chosen *one*,' added Laura.

'Oh, my! Who said girls!' exclaimed John Thomas, again turning, as if to escape. 'Well–good-night.'

'Nay, you've got to make your pick,' said Muriel. 'Turn your face to the wall, and say which one touches you. Go on–we shall only just touch your back–one of us. Go on–turn your face to the wall, and don't look, and say which one touches you.'

He was uneasy, mistrusting them. Yet he had not the courage to break away. They pushed him to a wall and stood him there with his face to it. Behind his back they all grimaced, tittering. He looked so comical. He looked around uneasily.

'Go on!' he cried.

'You're looking–you're looking!' they shouted.

He turned his head away. And suddenly, with a movement like a swift cat, Annie went forward and fetched him a box on the side of the head that sent his cap flying, and himself staggering. He started round.

But at Annie's signal they all flew at him, slapping him, pinching him, pulling his hair, though more in fun than in spite or anger. He, however, saw red. His blue eyes flamed with strange fear as well as fury, and he butted through the girls to the door. It was locked. He wrenched at it. Roused, alert, the girls stood round and looked at him. He faced them, at bay. At that moment they were rather horrifying to him, as they stood in their short uniforms. He was distinctly afraid.

'Come on, John Thomas! Come on! Choose!' said Annie.

'What are you after? Open the door,' he said.

'We sha'n't–not till you've chosen!' said Muriel.

'Chosen what?' he said.

'Chosen the one you're going to marry,' she replied.

He hesitated a moment.

'Open the blasted door,' he said, 'and get back to your senses.' He spoke with official authority.

'You've got to choose!' cried the girls.

'Come on!' cried Annie, looking him in the eye.

'Come on! Come on!'

He went forward, rather vaguely. She had taken off
her belt, and swinging it, she fetched him a sharp blow
over the head with the buckle end. He sprang and seized
her. But immediately the other girls rushed upon him,
pulling and tearing and beating him. Their blood was
now thoroughly up. He was their sport now. They were
going to have their own back, out of him. Strange, wild
creatures, they hung on him and rushed at him to bear
him down. His tunic was torn right up the back, Nora
had hold at the back of his collar, and was actually
strangling him. Luckily the button burst. He struggled in
a wild frenzy of fury and terror, almost mad terror. His
tunic was simply torn off his back, his shirt-sleeves were
torn away, his arms were naked. The girls rushed at him,
clenched their hands on him and pulled at him: or they
rushed at him and pushed him, butted him with all their
might: or they struck him wild blows. He ducked and
cringed and struck sideways. They became more intense.

At last he was down. They rushed on him, kneeling
on him. He had neither breath nor strength to move. His
face was bleeding with a long scratch, his brow was
bruised.

Annie knelt on him, the other girls knelt and hung
on to him. Their faces were flushed, their hair wild, their
eyes were all glittering strangely. He lay at last quite still,
with face averted, as an animal lies when it is defeated
and at the mercy of the captor. Sometimes his eye
glanced back at the wild faces of the girls. His breast rose
heavily, his wrists were torn.

'Now, then, my fellow!' gasped Annie at length.
'Now then—now—'

At the sound of her terrifying, cold triumph, he
suddenly started to struggle as an animal might, but the
girls threw themselves upon him with unnatural strength
and power, forcing him down.

'Yes—now, then!' gasped Annie at length.

And there was a dead silence, in which the thud of

heart-beating was to be heard. It was a suspense of pure silence in every soul.

'Now you know where you are,' said Annie.

The sight of his white, bare arm maddened the girls. He lay in a kind of trance of fear and antagonism. They felt themselves filled with supernatural strength.

Suddenly Polly started to laugh—to giggle wildly—helplessly—and Emma and Muriel joined in. But Annie and Nora and Laura remained the same, tense, watchful, with gleaming eyes. He winced away from these eyes.

'Yes,' said Annie, in a curious low tone, secret and deadly. 'Yes! You've got it now! You know what you've done, don't you? You know what you've done.'

He made no sound nor sign, but lay with bright, averted eyes, and averted, bleeding face.

'You ought to be *killed*, that's what you ought,' said Annie, tensely. 'You ought to be *killed*.' And there was a terrifying lust in her voice.

Polly was ceasing to laugh, and giving long-drawn Oh-h-hs and sighs as she came to herself.

'He's got to choose,' she said vaguely.

'Oh, yes, he has,' said Laura, with vindictive decision.

'Do you hear—do you hear?' said Annie. And with a sharp movement, that made him wince, she turned his face to her.

'Do you hear?' she repeated, shaking him.

But he was quite dumb. She fetched him a sharp slap on the face. He started, and his eyes widened. Then his face darkened with defiance, after all.

'Do you hear?' she repeated.

He only looked at her with hostile eyes.

'Speak!' she said, putting her face devilishly near his.

'What?' he said, almost overcome.

'You've got to *choose*!' she cried, as if it were some terrible menace, and as if it hurt her that she could not exact more.

'What?' he said, in fear.

'Choose your girl, Coddy. You've got to choose her now. And you'll get your neck broken if you play any more of your tricks, my boy. You're settled now.'

There was a pause. Again he averted his face. He was cunning in his overthrow. He did not give in to them really—no, not if they tore him to bits.

'All right, then,' he said, 'I choose Annie.' His voice was strange and full of malice. Annie let go of him as if he had been a hot coal.

'He's chosen Annie!' said the girls in chorus.

'Me!' cried Annie. She was still kneeling, but away from him. He was still lying prostrate, with averted face. The girls grouped uneasily around.

'Me!' repeated Annie, with a terrible bitter accent.

Then she got up, drawing away from him with strange disgust and bitterness.

'I wouldn't touch him,' she said.

But her face quivered with a kind of agony, she seemed as if she would fall. The other girls turned aside. He remained lying on the floor, with his torn clothes and bleeding, averted face.

'Oh, if he's chosen—' said Polly.

'I don't want him—he can choose again,' said Annie, with the same rather bitter hopelessness.

'Get up,' said Polly, lifting his shoulder. 'Get up.'

He rose slowly, a strange, ragged, dazed creature. The girls eyed him from a distance, curiously, furtively, dangerously.

'Who wants him?' cried Laura, roughly.

'Nobody,' they answered, with contempt. Yet each one of them waited for him to look at her, hoped he would look at her. All except Annie, and something was broken in her.

He, however, kept his face closed and averted from them all. There was a silence of the end. He picked up the torn pieces of his tunic, without knowing what to do with them. The girls stood about uneasily, flushed, panting, tidying their hair and their dress unconsciously, and watching him. He looked at none of them. He espied his cap in a corner, and went and picked it up. He put it on his head, and one of the girls burst into a shrill, hysteric laugh at the sight he presented. He, however, took no heed, but went straight to where his overcoat hung on a peg. The girls moved away from contact with him as if he had been an electric wire. He put on his coat and buttoned it down. Then he rolled his tunic-rags into a bundle, and stood before the locked door, dumbly.

'Open the door, somebody,' said Laura.

'Annie's got the key,' said one.

Annie silently offered the key to the girls. Nora unlocked the door.

'Tit for tat, old man,' she said. 'Show yourself a man, and don't bear a grudge.'

But without a word or sign he had opened the door and gone, his face closed, his head dropped.

'That'll learn him,' said Laura.

'Coddy!' said Nora.

'Shut up, for God's sake!' cried Annie fiercely, as if in torture.

'Well, I'm about ready to go, Polly. Look sharp!' said Muriel.

The girls were all anxious to be off. They were tidying themselves hurriedly, with mute, stupefied faces.

You Touched Me

Written June 1919 as 'Hadrian'. Published in *Land and Water*, 29 April 1920 and the collection *England, My England*.

The Pottery House was a square, ugly, brick house girt in by the wall that enclosed the whole grounds of the pottery itself. To be sure, a privet hedge partly masked the house and its grounds from the pottery-yard and works: but only partly. Through the hedge could be seen the desolate yard, and the many-windowed, factory-like pottery, over the hedge could be seen the chimneys and the out-houses. But inside the hedge, a pleasant garden and lawn sloped down to a willow pool, which had once supplied the works.

The pottery itself was now closed, the great doors of the yard permanently shut. No more the great crates, with yellow straw showing through, stood in stacks by the packing shed. No more the drays drawn by great horses rolled down the hill with a high load. No more the pottery-lasses in their clay-coloured overalls, their faces and hair splashed with grey fine mud, shrieked and larked with the men. All that was over.

'We like it much better—oh, much better—quieter,' said Matilda Rockley.

'Oh, yes,' assented Emmie Rockley, her sister.

'I'm sure you do,' agreed the visitor.

But whether the two Rockley girls really liked it better, or whether they only imagined they did, is a ques-

213

tion. Certainly their lives were much more grey and dreary now that the grey clay had ceased to spatter its mud and silt its dust over the premises. They did not quite realise how they missed the shrieking, shouting lasses, whom they had known all their lives and disliked so much.

Matilda and Emmie were already old maids. In a thorough industrial district, it is not easy for the girls who have expectations above the common to find husbands. The ugly industrial town was full of men, young men who were ready to marry. But they were all colliers or pottery-hands, mere workmen. The Rockley girls would have about ten thousand pounds each when their father died: ten thousand pounds' worth of profitable house-property. It was not to be sneezed at: they felt so themselves, and refrained from sneezing away such a fortune on any mere member of the proletariat. Consequently, bank-clerks or nonconformist clergymen or even school-teachers having failed to come forward, Matilda had begun to give up all idea of ever leaving the Pottery House.

Matilda was a tall, thin, graceful fair girl, with a rather large nose. She was the Mary to Emmie's Martha: that is, Matilda loved painting and music, and read a good many novels, whilst Emmie looked after the housekeeping. Emmie was shorter, plumper than her sister, and she had no accomplishments. She looked up to Matilda, whose mind was naturally refined and sensible.

In their quiet, melancholy way, the two girls were happy. Their mother was dead. Their father was ill also. He was an intelligent man who had had some education, but preferred to remain as if he were one with the rest of the working people. He had a passion for music and played the violin pretty well. But now he was getting old, he was very ill, dying of a kidney disease. He had been rather a heavy whiskey-drinker.

This quiet household, with one servant-maid, lived on year after year in the Pottery House. Friends came in, the girls went out, the father drank himself more and more ill. Outside in the street there was a continual racket of the colliers and their dogs and children. But inside the pottery wall was a deserted quiet.

In all this ointment there was one little fly. Ted Rockley, the father of the girls, had had four daughters, and no son. As his girls grew, he felt angry at finding himself always in a household of women. He went off to London and adopted a boy out of a Charity Institution. Emmie was fourteen years old, and Matilda sixteen, when their father arrived home with his prodigy, the boy of six, Hadrian.

Hadrian was just an ordinary boy from a Charity Home, with ordinary brownish hair and ordinary bluish eyes and of ordinary rather cockney speech. The Rockley girls–there were three at home at the time of his arrival–had resented his being sprung on them. He, with his watchful, charity-institution instinct, knew this at once. Though he was only six years old, Hadrian had a subtle, jeering look on his face when he regarded the three young women. They insisted he should address them as Cousin: Cousin Flora, Cousin Matilda, Cousin Emmie. He complied, but there seemed a mockery in his tone.

The girls, however, were kind-hearted by nature. Flora married and left home. Hadrian did very much as he pleased with Matilda and Emmie, though they had certain strictnesses. He grew up in the Pottery House and about the Pottery premises, went to an elementary school, and was invariably called Hadrian Rockley. He regarded Cousin Matilda and Cousin Emmie with a certain laconic indifference, was quiet and reticent in his ways. The girls called him sly, but that was unjust. He was merely cautious, and without frankness. His Uncle, Ted Rockley, understood him tacitly, their natures were somewhat akin. Hadrian and the elderly man had a real but unemotional regard for one another.

When he was thirteen years old the boy was sent to

a High School in the County town. He did not like it. His
Cousin Matilda had longed to make a little gentleman of
him, but he refused to be made. He would give a little
contemptuous curve to his lip, and take on a shy, charity-
boy grin, when refinement was thrust upon him. He
played truant from the High School, sold his books, his
cap with its badge, even his very scarf and pocket-
handkerchief, to his school-fellows, and went raking off
heaven knows where with the money. So he spent two
very unsatisfactory years.

When he was fifteen he announced that he wanted
to leave England to go to the Colonies. He had kept
touch with the Home. The Rockleys knew that, when
Hadrian made a declaration, in his quiet, half-jeering
manner, it was worse than useless to oppose him. So at
last the boy departed, going to Canada under the protec-
tion of the Institution to which he had belonged. He said
good-bye to the Rockleys without a word of thanks, and
parted, it seemed without a pang. Matilda and Emmie
wept often to think of how he left them: even on their
father's face a queer look came. But Hadrian wrote fairly
regularly from Canada. He had entered some electricity
works near Montreal, and was doing well.

At last, however, the war came. In his turn, Hadrian
joined up and came to Europe. The Rockleys saw
nothing of him. They lived on, just the same, in the
Pottery House. Ted Rockley was dying of a sort of
dropsy, and in his heart he wanted to see the boy. When
the armistice was signed, Hadrian had a long leave, and
wrote that he was coming home to the Pottery House.

The girls were terribly fluttered. To tell the truth,
they were a little afraid of Hadrian. Matilda, tall and
thin, was frail in her health, both girls were worn with
nursing their father. To have Hadrian, a young man of
twenty-one, in the house with them, after he had left
them so coldly five years before, was a trying
circumstance.

They were in a flutter. Emmie persuaded her father

to have his bed made finally in the morning-room down-stairs, whilst his room upstairs was prepared for Hadrian. This was done, and preparations were going on for the arrival, when, at ten o'clock in the morning the young man suddenly turned up, quite unexpectedly. Cousin Emmie, with her hair bobbed up in absurd little bobs round her forehead, was busily polishing the stair-rods, while Cousin Matilda was in the kitchen washing the drawing-room ornaments in a lather, her sleeves rolled back on her thin arms, and her head tied up oddly and coquettishly in a duster.

Cousin Matilda blushed deep with mortification when the self-possessed young man walked in with his kit-bag, and put his cap on the sewing machine. He was little and self-confident, with a curious neatness about him that still suggested the Charity Institution. His face was brown, he had a small moustache, he was vigorous enough in his smallness.

'*Well*, is it Hadrian!' exclaimed Cousin Matilda, wringing the lather off her hand. 'We didn't expect you till to-morrow.'

'I got off Monday night,' said Hadrian, glancing round the room.

'Fancy!' said Cousin Matilda. Then, having dried her hands, she went forward, held out her hand, and said:

'How are you?'

'Quite well, thank you,' said Hadrian.

'You're quite a man,' said Cousin Matilda.

Hadrian glanced at her. She did not look her best: so thin, so large-nosed, with that pink-and-white checked duster tied round her head. She felt her disadvantage. But she had had a good deal of suffering and sorrow, she did not mind any more.

The servant entered—one that did not know Hadrian.

'Come and see my father,' said Cousin Matilda.

In the hall they roused Cousin Emmie like a

partridge from cover. She was on the stairs pushing the bright stair-rods into place. Instinctively her hand went to the little knobs, her front hair bobbed on her forehead.

'Why!' she exclaimed, crossly. 'What have you come today for?'

'I got off a day earlier,' said Hadrian, and his man's voice so deep and unexpected was like a blow to Cousin Emmie.

'Well, you've caught us in the midst of it,' she said, with resentment. Then all three went into the middle room.

Mr Rockley was dressed—that is, he had on his trousers and socks—but he was resting on the bed, propped up just under the window, from whence he could see his beloved and resplendent garden, where tulips and apple-trees were ablaze. He did not look as ill as he was, for the water puffed him up, and his face kept its colour. His stomach was much swollen. He glanced round swiftly, turning his eyes without turning his head. He was the wreck of a handsome, well-built man.

Seeing Hadrian, a queer, unwilling smile went over his face. The young man greeted him sheepishly.

'You wouldn't make a life-guardsman,' he said. 'Do you want something to eat?'

Hadrian looked round—as if for the meal.

'I don't mind,' he said.

'What shall you have—egg and bacon?' asked Emmie shortly.

'Yes, I don't mind,' said Hadrian.

The sisters went down to the kitchen, and sent the servant to finish the stairs.

'Isn't he *altered*?' said Matilda, *sotto voce*.

'Isn't he?' said Cousin Emmie. '*What* a little man!'

They both made a grimace, and laughed nervously.

'Get the frying-pan,' said Emmie to Matilda.

'But he's as cocky as ever,' said Matilda, narrowing her eyes and shaking her head knowingly, as she handed the frying-pan.

'Mannie!' said Emmie sarcastically. Hadrian's new-fledged, cock-sure manliness evidently found no favour in her eyes.

'Oh, he's not bad,' said Matilda. 'You don't want to be prejudiced against him.'

'I'm not prejudiced against him, I think he's all right for looks,' said Emmie, 'but there's too much of the little mannie about him.'

'Fancy catching us like this,' said Matilda.

'They've no thought for anything,' said Emmie with contempt. 'You go up and get dressed, our Matilda. I don't care about him. I can see to things, and you can talk to him. I shan't.'

'He'll talk to my father,' said Matilda, meaningful.

'*Sly*–!' exclaimed Emmie, with a grimace.

The sisters believed that Hadrian had come hoping to get something out of their father–hoping for a legacy. And they were not at all sure he would not get it.

Matilda went upstairs to change. She had thought it all out how she would receive Hadrian, and impress him. And he had caught her with her head tied up in a duster, and her thin arms in a basin of lather. But she did not care. She now dressed herself most scrupulously, carefully folded her long, beautiful, blonde hair, touched her pallor with a little rouge, and put her long string of exquisite crystal beads over her soft green dress. Now she looked elegant, like a heroine in a magazine illustration, and almost as unreal.

She found Hadrian and her father talking away. The young man was short of speech as a rule, but he could find his tongue with his 'uncle'. They were both sipping a glass of brandy, and smoking, and chatting like a pair of old cronies. Hadrian was telling about Canada. He was going back there when his leave was up.

'You wouldn't like to stop in England, then?' said Mr Rockley.

'No, I wouldn't stop in England,' said Hadrian.

'How's that? There's plenty of electricians here,'

said Mr Rockley.

'Yes. But there's too much difference between the men and the employers over here—too much of that for me,' said Hadrian.

The sick man looked at him narrowly, with oddly smiling eyes.

'That's it, is it?' he replied.

Matilda heard and understood. 'So that's your big idea, is it, my little man,' she said to herself. She had always said of Hadrian that he had no proper *respect* for anybody or anything, that he was sly and *common*. She went down to the kitchen for a *sotto voce* confab with Emmie.

'He thinks a rare lot of himself!' she whispered.

'He's somebody, he is!' said Emmie with contempt.

'He thinks there's too much difference between masters and men, over here,' said Matilda.

'Is it any different in Canada?' asked Emmie.

'Oh yes—democratic,' replied Matilda. 'He thinks they're all on a level over there.'

'Ay, well he's over here now,' said Emmie drily, 'so he can keep his place.'

As they talked they saw the young man sauntering down the garden, looking casually at the flowers. He had his hands in his pockets, and his soldier's cap neatly on his head. He looked quite at his ease, as if in possession. The two women, fluttered, watched him through the window.

'We know what he's come for,' said Emmie churlishly. Matilda looked a long time at the neat khaki figure. It had something of the charity-boy about it still; but now it was a man's figure, laconic, charged with plebeian energy. She thought of the derisive passion in his voice as he had declaimed against the propertied classes, to her father.

'You don't know, Emmie. Perhaps he's not come for that,' she rebuked her sister. They were both thinking of the money.

They were still watching the young soldier. He stood away at the bottom of the garden, with his back to them, his hands in his pockets, looking into the water of the willow pond. Matilda's dark-blue eyes had a strange, full look in them, the lids, with the faint blue veins showing, dropped rather low. She carried her head light and high, but she had a look of pain. The young man at the bottom of the garden turned and looked up the path. Perhaps he saw them through the window. Matilda moved into shadow.

That afternoon their father seemed weak and ill. He was easily exhausted. The doctor came, and told Matilda that the sick man might die suddenly at any moment—but then he might not. They must be prepared.

So the day passed, and the next. Hadrian made himself at home. He went about in the morning in his brownish jersey and his khaki trousers, collarless, his bare neck showing. He explored the pottery premises, as if he had some secret purpose in so doing, he talked with Mr Rockley, when the sick man had strength. The two girls were always angry when the two men sat talking together like cronies. Yet it was chiefly a kind of politics they talked.

On the second day after Hadrian's arrival, Matilda sat with her father in the evening. She was drawing a picture which she wanted to copy. It was very still, Hadrian was gone out somewhere, no one knew where, and Emmie was busy. Mr Rockley reclined on his bed, looking out in silence over his evening-sunny garden.

'If anything happens to me, Matilda,' he said, 'you won't sell this house—you'll stop here—'

Matilda's eyes took their slightly haggard look as she stared at her father.

'Well, we couldn't do anything else,' she said.

'You don't know what you might do,' he said. 'Everything is left to you and Emmie, equally. You do as you like with it—only don't sell this house, don't part with it.'

'No,' she said.

'And give Hadrian my watch and chain, and a hundred pounds out of what's in the bank—and help him if he ever wants helping. I haven't put his name in the will.'

'Your watch and chain, and a hundred pounds—yes. But you'll be here when he goes back to Canada, father.'

'You never know what'll happen,' said her father.

Matilda sat and watched him, with her full, haggard eyes, for a long time, as if tranced. She saw that he knew he must go soon—she saw like a clairvoyant.

Later on she told Emmie what her father had said about the watch and chain and the money.

'What right has *he*'—*he*—meaning Hadrian—'to my father's watch and chain—what has it to do with him? Let him have the money, and get off,' said Emmie. She loved her father.

That night Matilda sat late in her room. Her heart was anxious and breaking, her mind seemed entranced. She was too much entranced even to weep, and all the time she thought of her father, only her father. At last she felt she must go to him.

It was near midnight. She went along the passage and to his room. There was a faint light from the moon outside. She listened at his door. Then she softly opened and entered. The room was faintly dark. She heard a movement on the bed.

'Are you asleep?' she said softly, advancing to the side of the bed.

'Are you asleep?' she repeated gently, as she stood at the side of the bed. And she reached her hand in the darkness to touch his forehead. Delicately, her fingers met the nose and the eyebrows, she laid her fine, delicate hand on his brow. It seemed fresh and smooth—very fresh and smooth. A sort of surprise stirred her, in her entranced state. But it could not waken her. Gently, she leaned over the bed and stirred her fingers over the low-growing hair on his brow.

'Can't you sleep to-night?' she said.

There was a quick stirring in the bed. 'Yes, I can,' a voice answered. It was Hadrian's voice. She started away. Instantly, she was wakened from her late-at-night trance. She remembered that her father was downstairs, that Hadrian had his room. She stood in the darkness as if stung.

'Is it you, Hadrian?' she said. 'I thought it was my father.' She was so startled, so shocked, that she could not move. The young man gave an uncomfortable laugh, and turned in his bed.

At last she got out of the room. When she was back in her own room, in the light, and her door was closed, she stood holding up her hand that had touched him, as if it were hurt. She was almost too shocked, she could not endure.

'Well,' said her calm and weary mind, 'it was only a mistake, why take any notice of it.'

But she could not reason her feelings so easily. She suffered, feeling herself in a false position. Her right hand, which she had laid so gently on his face, on his fresh skin, ached now, as if it were really injured. She could not forgive Hadrian for the mistake: it made her dislike him deeply.

Hadrian too slept badly. He had been awakened by the opening of the door, and had not realised what the question meant. But the soft, straying tenderness of her hand on his face startled something out of his soul. He was a charity boy, aloof and more or less at bay. The fragile exquisiteness of her caress startled him most, revealed unknown things to him.

In the morning she could feel the consciousness in his eyes, when she came downstairs. She tried to bear herself as if nothing at all had happened, and she succeeded. She had the calm self-control, self-indifference, of one who has suffered and borne her suffering. She looked at him from her darkish, almost drugged blue eyes, she met the spark of consciousness in his eyes, and quenched it. And with her long, fine hand she put the sugar in his coffee.

But she could not control him as she thought she could. He had a keen memory stinging his mind, a new set of sensations working in his consciousness. Something new was alert in him. At the back of his reticent, guarded mind he kept his secret alive and vivid. She was at his mercy, for he was unscrupulous, his standard was not her standard.

He looked at her curiously. She was not beautiful, her nose was too large, her chin was too small, her neck was too thin. But her skin was clear and fine, she had a high-bred sensitiveness. This queer, brave, high-bred quality she shared with her father. The charity boy could see it in her tapering fingers, which were white and ringed. The same glamour that he knew in the elderly man he now saw in the woman. And he wanted to possess himself of it, he wanted to make himself master of it. As he went about through the old pottery-yard, his secretive mind schemed and worked. To be master of that strange soft delicacy such as he had felt in her hand upon his face,—this was what he set himself towards. He was secretly plotting.

He watched Matilda as she went about, and she became aware of his attention, as of some shadow following her. But her pride made her ignore it. When he sauntered near her, his hands in his pockets, she received him with that same commonplace kindliness which mastered him more than any contempt. Her superior breeding seemed to control him. She made herself feel towards him exactly as she had always felt: he was a young boy who lived in the house with them, but was a stranger. Only, she dared not remember his face under her hand. When she remembered that, she was bewildered. Her hand had offended her, she wanted to cut it off. And she wanted, fiercely, to cut off the memory in him. She assumed she had done so.

One day, when he sat talking with his 'uncle', he

looked straight into the eyes of the sick man, and said:

'But I shouldn't like to live and die here in Rawsley.'

'No—well—you needn't,' said the sick man.

'Do you think Cousin Matilda likes it?'

'I should think so.'

'I don't call it much of a life,' said the youth. 'How much older is she than me, Uncle?'

The sick man looked at the young soldier.

'A good bit,' he said.

'Over thirty?' said Hadrian.

'Well, not so much. She's thirty-two.'

Hadrian considered a while.

'She doesn't look it,' he said.

Again the sick father looked at him.

'Do you think she'd like to leave here?' said Hadrian.

'Nay, I don't know,' replied the father, restive.

Hadrian sat still, having his own thoughts. Then in a small, quiet voice, as if he were speaking from inside himself, he said:

'I'd marry her if you wanted me to.'

The sick man raised his eyes suddenly, and stared. He stared for a long time. The youth looked inscrutably out of the window.

'*You!*' said the sick man, mocking, with some contempt. Hadrian turned and met his eyes. The two men had an inexplicable understanding.

'If you wasn't against it,' said Hadrian.

'Nay,' said the father, turning aside, 'I don't think I'm against it. I've never thought of it. But— But Emmie's the youngest.'

He had flushed, and looked suddenly more alive. Secretly he loved the boy.

'You might ask her,' said Hadrian.

The elder man considered.

'Hadn't you better ask her yourself?' he said.

'She'd take more notice of you,' said Hadrian.

They were both silent. Then Emmie came in.

For two days Mr Rockley was excited and thoughtful. Hadrian went about quietly, secretly, unquestioning. At last the father and daughter were alone together. It was very early morning, the father had been in much pain. As the pain abated, he lay still, thinking.

'Matilda!' he said suddenly, looking at his daughter.

'Yes, I'm here,' she said.

'Ay! I want you to do something—'

She rose in anticipation.

'Nay, sit still—I want you to marry Hadrian—'

She thought he was raving. She rose, bewildered and frightened.

'Nay, sit you still, sit you still. You hear what I tell you.'

'But you don't know what you're saying, father.'

'Ay, I know well enough.—I want you to marry Hadrian, I tell you.'

She was dumbfounded. He was a man of few words.

'You'll do what I tell you,' he said.

She looked at him slowly.

'What put such an idea in your mind?' she said proudly.

'He did.'

Matilda almost looked her father down, her pride was so offended.

'Why, it's disgraceful,' she said.

'Why?'

She watched him slowly.

'What do you ask me for?' she said. 'It's disgusting.'

'The lad's sound enough,' he replied, testily.

'You'd better tell him to clear out,' she said coldly.

He turned and looked out of the window. She sat flushed and erect, for a long time. At length her father turned to her, looking really malevolent.

'If you won't,' he said, 'you're a fool, and I'll make you pay for your foolishness, do you see?'

Suddenly a cold fear gripped her. She could not

believe her senses. She was terrified and bewildered. She stared at her father, believing him to be delirious, or mad, or drunk. What could she do?

'I tell you,' he said. 'I'll send for Whittle to-morrow if you don't. You shall neither of you have anything of mine.'

Whittle was the solicitor. She understood her father well enough: he would send for his solicitor, and make a will leaving all his property to Hadrian: neither she nor Emmie should have anything. It was too much. She rose and went out of the room, up to her own room, where she locked herself in.

She did not come out for some hours. At last, late at night, she confided in Emmie.

'The sliving demon, he wants the money,' said Emmie. 'My father's out of his mind.'

The thought that Hadrian merely wanted the money was another blow to Matilda. She did not love the impossible youth—but she had not yet learned to think of him as a thing of evil. He now became hideous to her mind.

Emmie had a little scene with her father next day.

'You don't mean what you said to our Matilda yesterday, do you, father?' she asked aggressively.

'Yes,' he replied.

'What, that you'll alter your will?'

'Yes.'

'You won't,' said his angry daughter.

But he looked at her with a malevolent little smile.

'Annie!' he shouted. 'Annie?'

He had still power to make his voice carry. The servant maid came in from the kitchen.

'Put your things on, and go down to Whittle's office, and say I want to see Mr Whittle as soon as he can, and will he bring a will-form.'

The sick man lay back a little—he could not lie down. His daughter sat as if she had been struck. Then she left the room.

Hadrian was pottering about in the garden. She went straight down to him.

'Here,' she said. 'You'd better get off. You'd better take your things and go from here, quick.'

Hadrian looked slowly at the infuriated girl.

'Who says so?' he asked.

'*We* say so—get off, you've done enough mischief and damage.'

'Does Uncle say so?'

'Yes, he does.'

'I'll go and ask him.'

But like a fury Emmie barred his way.

'No, you needn't. You needn't ask him nothing at all. We don't want you, so you can go.'

'Uncle's boss here.'

'A man that's dying, and you crawling round and working on him for his money!—you're not fit to live.'

'Oh!' he said. 'Who says I'm working for his money?'

'I say. But my father told our Matilda, and *she* knows what you are. *She* knows what you're after. So you might as well clear out, for all you'll get—gutter-snipe!'

He turned his back on her, to think. It had not occurred to him that they would think he was after the money. He *did* want the money—badly. He badly wanted to be an employer himself, not one of the employed. But he knew, in his subtle, calculating way, that it was not for money he wanted Matilda. He wanted both the money and Matilda. But he told himself the two desires were separate, not one. He could not do with Matilda, *without* the money. But he did not want her *for* the money.

When he got this clear in his mind, he sought for an opportunity to tell it her, lurking and watching. But she avoided him. In the evening the lawyer came. Mr Rockley seemed to have a new access of strength—a will was drawn up, making the previous arrangements wholly conditional. The old will held good, if Matilda would consent to marry Hadrian. If she refused then at the end of six months the whole property passed to Hadrian.

Mr Rockley told this to the young man, with malevolent satisfaction. He seemed to have a strange desire, quite unreasonable, for revenge upon the women who had surrounded him for so long, and served him so carefully.

'Tell her in front of me,' said Hadrian.

So Mr Rockley sent for his daughters.

At last they came, pale, mute, stubborn. Matilda seemed to have retired far off, Emmie seemed like a fighter ready to fight to the death. The sick man reclined on the bed, his eyes bright, his puffed hand trembling. But his face had again some of its old, bright handsomeness. Hadrian sat quiet, a little aside: the indomitable, dangerous charity boy.

'There's the will,' said their father, pointing them to the paper.

The two women sat mute and immovable, they took no notice.

'Either you marry Hadrian, or he has everything,' said the father with satisfaction.

'Then let him have everything,' said Matilda coldly.

'He's not! He's not!' cried Emmie fiercely. 'He's not going to have it. The gutter-snipe!'

An amused look came on her father's face.

'You hear that, Hadrian,' he said.

'I didn't offer to marry Cousin Matilda for the money,' said Hadrian, flushing and moving on his seat.

Matilda looked at him slowly, with her dark-blue, drugged eyes. He seemed a strange little monster to her.

'Why, you liar, you know you did,' cried Emmie.

The sick man laughed. Matilda continued to gaze strangely at the young man.

'She knows I didn't,' said Hadrian.

He too had his courage, as a rat has indomitable courage in the end. Hadrian had some of the neatness, the reserve, the underground quality of the rat. But he had perhaps the ultimate courage, the most unquenchable courage of all.

Emmie looked at her sister.

'Oh, well,' she said. 'Matilda—don't you bother. Let him have everything, we can look after ourselves.'

'I know he'll take everything,' said Matilda abstractedly.

Hadrian did not answer. He knew in fact that if Matilda refused him he would take everything, and go off with it.

'A clever little mannie—!' said Emmie, with a jeering grimace.

The father laughed noiselessly to himself. But he was tired. . . .

'Go on then,' he said. 'Go on, let me be quiet.'

Emmie turned and looked at him.

'You deserve what you've got,' she said to her father bluntly.

'Go on,' he answered mildly. 'Go on.'

Another night passed—a night nurse sat up with Mr Rockley. Another day came. Hadrian was there as ever, in his woollen jersey and coarse khaki trousers and bare neck. Matilda went about, frail and distant, Emmie black-browed in spite of her blondness. They were all quiet, for they did not intend the mystified servant to learn everything.

Mr Rockley had very bad attacks of pain, he could not breathe. The end seemed near. They all went about quiet and stoical, all unyielding. Hadrian pondered within himself. If he did not marry Matilda he would go to Canada with twenty thousand pounds. This was itself a very satisfactory prospect. If Matilda consented he would have nothing—she would have her own money.

Emmie was the one to act. She went off in search of the solicitor and brought him home with her. There was an interview, and Whittle tried to frighten the youth into withdrawal—but without avail. Then clergyman and relatives were summoned—but Hadrian stared at them and took no notice. It made him angry, however.

He wanted to catch Matilda alone. Many days went by, and he was not successful: she avoided him. At last, lurking, he surprised her one day as she came to pick gooseberries, and he cut off her retreat. He came to the point at once.

'You don't want me then?' he said, in his subtle, insinuating voice.

'I don't want to speak to you,' she said, averting her face.

'You put your hand on me, though,' he said. 'You shouldn't have done that, and then I should never have thought of it. You shouldn't have touched me.'

'If you were anything decent, you'd know that was a mistake, and forget it,' she said.

'I know it was a mistake—but I shan't forget it. If you wake a man up, he can't go to sleep again because he's told to.'

'If you had any decent feeling in you, you'd have gone away,' she replied.

'I didn't want to,' he replied.

She looked away into the distance. At last she asked:

'What do you persecute me for, if it isn't for the money? I'm old enough to be your mother. In a way I've been your mother.'

'Doesn't matter,' he said. 'You've been no mother to me. Let us marry and go out to Canada—you might as well—you've touched me.'

She was white and trembling. Suddenly she flushed with anger.

'It's so *indecent*,' she said.

'How?' he retorted. 'You touched me.'

But she walked away from him. She felt as if he had trapped her. He was angry and depressed, he felt again despised.

That same evening, she went into her father's room.

'Yes,' she said suddenly. 'I'll marry him.'

Her father looked up at her. He was in pain, and very ill.

'You like him now, do you?' he said, with a faint smile.

She looked down into his face, and saw death not far off. She turned and went coldly out of the room.

The solicitor was sent for, preparations were hastily made. In all the interval Matilda did not speak to Hadrian, never answered him if he addressed her. He approached her in the morning.

'You've come round to it, then?' he said, giving her a pleasant look from his twinkling, almost kindly eyes. She looked down at him and turned aside. She looked down on him both literally and figuratively. Still he persisted, and triumphed.

Emmie raved and wept, the secret flew abroad. But Matilda was silent and unmoved, Hadrian was quiet and satisfied, and nipped with fear also. But he held out against his fear. Mr Rockley was very ill, but unchanged.

On the third day the marriage took place. Matilda and Hadrian drove straight home from the registrar, and went straight into the room of the dying man. His face lit up with a clear twinkling smile.

'Hadrian,–you've got her?' he said, a little hoarsely.

'Yes,' said Hadrian, who was pale round the gills.

'Ay, my lad, I'm glad you're mine,' replied the dying man. Then he turned his eyes closely on Matilda.

'Let's look at you, Matilda,' he said. Then his voice went strange and unrecognisable. 'Kiss me,' he said.

She stooped and kissed him. She had never kissed him before, not since she was a tiny child. But she was quiet, very still.

'Kiss him,' the dying man said.

Obediently, Matilda put forward her mouth and kissed the young husband.

'That's right! That's right!' murmured the dying man.

The Fox

Written November 1918. Revised July 1919 and published *Hutchinson's Story Magazine,* November 1920. Revised and extended November 1921 for publication in *Dial,* May – August 1922 and *The Ladybird* collection.

The two girls were usually known by their surnames, Banford and March. They had taken the farm together, intending to work it all by themselves: that is, they were going to rear chickens, make a living by poultry, and add to this by keeping a cow, and raising one or two young beasts. Unfortunately, things did not turn out well.

Banford was a small, thin, delicate thing with spectacles. She, however, was the principal investor, for March had little or no money. Banford's father, who was a tradesman in Islington, gave his daughter the start, for her health's sake, and because he loved her, and because it did not look as if she would marry. March was more robust. She had learned carpentry and joinery at the evening classes in Islington. She would be the man about the place. They had, moreover, Banford's old grandfather living with them at the start. He had been a farmer. But unfortunately the old man died after he had been at Bailey Farm for a year. Then the two girls were left alone.

They were neither of them young: that is, they were near thirty. But they certainly were not old. They set out quite gallantly with their enterprise. They had numbers of chickens, black Leghorns and white Leghorns, Plymouths and Wyandottes; also some ducks; also two heifers in the fields. One heifer, unfortunately, refused absolutely to stay in the Bailey Farm closes. No matter how March made up the fences, the heifer was out, wild in the woods, or trespassing on the neighbouring pasture, and March and Banford were away, flying after her, with more haste than success. So this heifer they sold in despair. Then, just before the other beast was expecting her first calf, the old man died, and the girls, afraid of the coming event, sold her in a panic, and limited their attentions to fowls and ducks.

In spite of a little chagrin, it was a relief to have no more cattle on hand. Life was not made merely to be slaved away. Both girls agreed in this. The fowls were quite enough trouble. March had set up her carpenter's bench at the end of the open shed. Here she worked, making coops and doors and other appurtenances. The fowls were housed in the bigger building, which had served as barn and cowshed in old days. They had a beautiful home, and should have been perfectly content. Indeed, they looked well enough. But the girls were disgusted at their tendency to strange illnesses, at their exacting way of life, and at their refusal, obstinate refusal to lay eggs.

March did most of the outdoor work. When she was out and about, in her puttees and breeches, her belted coat and her loose cap, she looked almost like some graceful, loose-balanced young man, for her shoulders were straight, and her movements easy and confident, even tinged with a little indifference, or irony. But her face was not a man's face, ever. The wisps of her crisp dark hair blew about her as she stooped, her eyes were big and wide and dark, when she looked up again, strange, startled, shy and sardonic at once. Her mouth, too, was almost pinched as if in pain and irony. There was something odd and unexplained about her. She would stand balanced on one hip, looking at the fowls pattering about in the obnoxious fine mud of the sloping yard, and calling to her favourite white hen, which came in answer to her name. But there was an almost satirical flicker in March's big, dark eyes as she looked at her three-toed flock pottering about under her gaze, and the same slight dangerous satire in her voice as she spoke to the favoured Patty, who pecked at March's boot by way of friendly demonstration.

Fowls did not flourish at Bailey Farm, in spite of all that March did for them. When she provided hot food for them in the morning, according to rule, she noticed that it made them heavy and dozy for hours. She expected to see them lean against the pillars of the shed in their languid processes of digestion. And she knew quite well that they ought to be busily scratching and foraging about, if they were to come to any good. So she decided to give them their hot food at night, and let them sleep on it. Which she did. But it made no difference.

War conditions, again, were very unfavourable to poultry keeping. Food was scarce and bad. And when the Daylight Saving Bill was passed, the fowls obstinately refused to go to bed as usual, about nine o'clock in the summer time. That was late enough, indeed, for there was no peace till they were shut up and asleep. Now they cheerfully walked around, without so much as glancing at the barn, until ten o'clock or later. Both Banford and March disbelieved in living for work alone. They wanted to read or take a cycle-ride in the evening, or perhaps March wished to paint curvilinear swans on porcelain, with green background, or else make a marvellous fire-screen by processes of elaborate cabinet work. For she was a creature of odd whims and unsatisfied tendencies. But from all these things she was prevented by the stupid fowls.

One evil there was greater than any other. Bailey Farm was a little homestead, with ancient wooden barn and low-gabled farm-house, lying just one field removed from the edge of the wood. Since the war the fox was a demon. He carried off the hens under the very noses of March and Banford. Banford would start and stare through her big spectacles with all her eyes, as another squawk and flutter took place at her heels. Too late! Another white Leghorn gone. It was disheartening.

They did what they could to remedy it. When it became permitted to shoot foxes, they stood sentinel with their guns, the two of them, at the favoured hours. But it was no good. The fox was too quick for them. So another year passed, and another, and they were living on their losses as Banford said. They let their farm-house one summer, and retired to live in a railway-carriage that was deposited as a sort of out-house in a corner of the field. This amused them, and helped their finances. None the less, things looked dark.

Although they were usually the best of friends, because Banford, though nervous and delicate, was a warm, generous soul, and March, though so odd and absent in herself, had a strange magnanimity, yet, in the long solitude, they were apt to become a little irritable with one another, tired of one another. March had four-fifths of the work to do, and though she did not mind, there seemed no relief, and it made her eyes flash curiously sometimes. Then Banford, feeling more nerve-worn than ever, would become despondent, and March would speak sharply to her. They seemed to be losing ground, somehow, losing hope as the months went by. There alone in the fields by the wood, with the wide country stretching hollow and dim to the round hills of the White Horse, in the far distance, they seemed to have to live too much off themselves. There was nothing to keep them up—and no hope.

The fox really exasperated them both. As soon as they had let the fowls out, in the early summer mornings, they had to take their guns and keep guard: and then again, as soon as evening began to mellow, they must go once more. And he was so sly. He slid along in the deep grass; he was difficult as a serpent to see. And he seemed to circumvent the girls deliberately. Once or twice March had caught sight of the white tip of his brush, or the ruddy shadow of him in the deep grass, and she had let fire at him. But he made no account of this.

One evening March was standing with her back to the sunset, her gun under her arm, her hair pushed under her cap. She was half watching, half musing. It was her constant state. Her eyes were keen and observant, but her inner mind took no notice of what she saw. She was always lapsing into this odd, rapt state, her mouth rather screwed up. It was a question whether she was there, actually conscious present, or not.

The trees on the wood-edge were a darkish, brownish green in the full light—for it was the end of August. Beyond, the naked, copper-like shafts and limbs of the pine-trees shone in the air. Nearer the rough grass, with its long brownish stalks all agleam, was full of light. The fowls were round about—the ducks were still swimming on the pond under the pine-trees. March looked at it all, saw it all, and did not see it. She heard Banford speaking to the fowls in the distance—and she did not hear. What was she thinking about? Heaven knows. Her consciousness was, as it were, held back.

She lowered her eyes, and suddenly saw the fox. He was looking up at her. His chin was pressed down, and his eyes were looking up. They met her eyes. And he knew her. She was spell-bound—she knew he knew her. So he looked into her eyes, and her soul failed her. He knew her, he was not daunted.

She struggled, confusedly she came to herself, and saw him making off, with slow leaps over some fallen boughs, slow, impudent jumps. Then he glanced over his shoulder, and ran smoothly away. She saw his brush held smooth like a feather, she saw his white buttocks twinkle. And he was gone, softly, soft as the wind.

She put her gun to her shoulder, but even then pursed her mouth, knowing it was nonsense to pretend to fire. So she began to walk slowly after him, in the direction he had gone, slowly, pertinaciously. She expected to find him. In her heart she was determined to find him.

What she would do when she saw him again she did not consider. But she was determined to find him. So she walked abstractedly about on the edge of the wood, with wide, vivid dark eyes, and a faint flush in her cheeks. She did not think. In strange mindlessness she walked hither and thither.

At last she became aware that Banford was calling her. She made an effort of attention, turned, and gave some sort of screaming call in answer. Then again she was striding off towards the homestead. The red sun was setting, the fowls were retiring towards their roost. She watched them, white creatures, black creatures, gathering to the barn. She watched them spell-bound, without seeing them. But her automatic intelligence told her when it was time to shut the door.

She went indoors to supper, which Banford had set on the table. Banford chatted easily. March seemed to listen, in her distant, manly way. She answered a brief word now and then. But all the time she was as if spell-bound. And as soon as supper was over, she rose again to go out, without saying why.

She took her gun again and went to look for the fox. For he had lifted his eyes upon her, and his knowing look seemed to have entered her brain. She did not so much think of him: she was possessed by him. She saw his dark, shrewd, unabashed eye looking into her, knowing her. She felt him invisibly master her spirit. She knew the way he lowered his chin as he looked up, she knew his muzzle, the golden brown, and the greyish white. And again, she saw him glance over his shoulder at her, half inviting, half contemptuous and cunning. So she went, with her great startled eyes glowing, her gun under her arm, along the wood edge. Meanwhile the night fell, and a great moon rose above the pine-trees. And again Banford was calling.

So she went indoors. She was silent and busy. She examined her gun, and cleaned it, musing abstractedly by the lamp-light. Then she went out again, under the great moon, to see if everything was right. When she saw the dark crests of the pine-trees against the blood-red sky, again her heart beat to the fox, the fox. She wanted to follow him, with her gun.

It was some days before she mentioned the affair to Banford. Then suddenly one evening she said:

'The fox was right at my feet on Saturday night.'

'Where?' said Banford, her eyes opening behind her spectacles.

'When I stood just above the pond.'

'Did you fire?' cried Banford.

'No, I didn't?'

'Why not?'

'Why, I was too much surprised, I suppose.'

It was the same old, slow, laconic way of speech March always had. Banford stared at her friend for a few moments.

'You saw him?' she cried.

'Oh yes! He was looking up at me, cool as anything.'

'I tell you,' cried Banford–'the cheek! They're not afraid of us, Nellie.'

'Oh no,' said March.

'Pity you didn't get a shot at him,' said Banford.

'Isn't it a pity! I've been looking for him ever since. But I don't suppose he'll come so near again.'

'I don't suppose he will,' said Banford.

And she proceeded to forget about it, except that she was more indignant than ever at the impudence of the beggar. March also was not conscious that she thought of the fox. But whenever she fell into her half-musing, when she was half rapt and half intelligently aware of what passed under her vision, then it was the fox which somehow dominated her unconsciousness, possessed the blank half of her musing. And so it was for weeks, and months. No matter whether she had been climbing the trees for the apples, or beating down the last of the damsons, or whether she had been digging out the ditch from the duck-pond, or clearing out the barn, when she had finished, or when she straightened herself, and pushed the wisps of hair away again from her forehead, and pursed up her mouth again in an odd, screwed fashion, much too old for her years, there was sure to come over her mind the old spell of the fox, as it came when he was looking at her. It was as if she could smell him at these times. And it always recurred, at unexpected moments, just as she was going to sleep at night, or just as she was pouring the water into the tea-pot to make tea—it was the fox, it came over her like a spell.

So the months passed. She still looked for him unconsciously when she went towards the wood. He had become a settled effect in her spirit, a state permanently established, not continuous, but always recurring. She did not know what she felt or thought: only the state came over her, as when he looked at her.

The months passed, the dark evenings came, heavy, dark November, when March went about in high boots, ankle deep in mud, when the night began to fall at four o'clock, and the day never properly dawned. Both girls dreaded these times. They dreaded the almost continuous darkness that enveloped them on their desolate little farm near the wood. Banford was physically afraid. She was afraid of tramps, afraid lest someone should come prowling round. March was not so much afraid as uncomfortable, and disturbed. She felt discomfort and gloom in all her physique.

Usually the two girls had tea in the sitting room. March lighted a fire at dusk, and put on the wood she had chopped and sawed during the day. Then the long evening was in front, dark, sodden, black outside, lonely and rather oppressive inside, a little dismal. March was content not to talk, but Banford could not keep still. Merely listening to the wind in the pines outside, or the drip of water, was too much for her.

One evening the girls had washed up the tea-things

in the kitchen, and March had put on her house-shoes, and taken up a roll of crochet-work, which she worked at slowly from time to time. So she lapsed into silence. Banford stared at the red fire, which, being of wood, needed constant attention. She was afraid to begin to read too early, because her eyes would not bear any strain. So she sat staring at the fire, listening to the distant sounds, sound of cattle lowing, of a dull, heavy moist wind, of the rattle of the evening train on the little railway not far off. She was almost fascinated by the red glow of the fire.

Suddenly both girls started, and lifted their heads. They heard a footstep—distinctly a footstep. Banford recoiled in fear. March stood listening. Then rapidly she approached the door that led into the kitchen. At the same time they heard the footsteps approach the back door. They waited a second. The back door opened softly. Banford gave a loud cry. A man's voice said softly:

'Hello!'

March recoiled, and took a gun from a corner.

'What do you want?' she cried, in a sharp voice.

Again the soft, softly-vibrating man's voice said:

'Hello! What's wrong?'

'I shall shoot!' cried March. 'What do you want?'

'Why, what's wrong? What's wrong?' came the soft, wondering, rather scared voice: and a young soldier, with his heavy kit on his back, advanced into the dim light.

'Why,' he said, 'who lives here then?'

'We live here,' said March. 'What do you want?'

'Oh!' came the long, melodious, wonder-note from the young soldier. 'Doesn't William Grenfel live here then?'

'No—you know he doesn't.'

'Do I? Do I? I don't you see. He *did* live here, because he was my grandfather, and I lived here myself five years ago. What's become of him then?'

The young man—or youth, for he would not be more than twenty—now advanced and stood in the inner doorway. March, already under the influence of his strange, soft, modulated voice, stared at him spellbound. He had a ruddy, roundish face, with fairish hair, rather long, flattened to his forehead with sweat. His eyes were blue, and very bright and sharp. On his cheeks, on the fresh ruddy skin were fine, fair hairs, like a down, but sharper. It gave him a slightly glistening look. Having his heavy sack on his shoulders, he stooped, thrusting his head forward. His hat was loose in one hand. He stared brightly, very keenly from girl to girl, particularly at March, who stood pale, with great dilated eyes, in her belted coat and puttees, her hair knotted in a big crisp knot behind. She still had the gun in her hand. Behind her, Banford, clinging to the sofa-arm, was shrinking away, with half-averted head.

'I thought my grandfather still lived here? I wonder if he's dead.'

'We've been here for three years,' said Banford, who was beginning to recover her wits, seeing something boyish in the round head with its rather long sweaty hair.

'Three years! You don't say so! And you don't know who was here before you?'

'I know it was an old man, who lived by himself.'

'Ay! Yes, that's him! And what became of him then?'

'He died. I know he died.'

'Ay! He's dead then!'

The youth stared at them without changing colour or expression. If he had any expression, besides a slight baffled look of wonder, it was one of sharp curiosity concerning the two girls; sharp, impersonal curiosity, the curiosity of that round young head.

But to March he was the fox. Whether it was the thrusting forward of his head, or the glisten of fine whitish hairs on the ruddy cheek-bones, or the bright, keen eyes, that can never be said: but the boy was to her the fox, and she could not see him otherwise.

'How is it you didn't know if your grandfather was alive or dead?' asked Banford, recovering her natural sharpness.

'Ay, that's it,' replied the softly-breathing youth. 'You see I joined up in Canada, and I hadn't heard for three or four years. I ran away to Canada.'

'And now have you just come from France?'

'Well–from Salonika really.'

There was a pause, nobody knowing quite what to say.

'So you've nowhere to go now?' said Banford rather lamely.

'Oh, I know some people in the village. Anyhow, I can go to the Swan.'

'You came on the train, I suppose. Would you like to sit down a bit?'

'Well–I don't mind.'

He gave an odd little groan as he swung off his kit. Banford looked at March.

'Put the gun down,' she said. 'We'll make a cup of tea.'

'Ay,' said the youth. 'We've seen enough of rifles.'

He sat down rather tired on the sofa, leaning forward.

March recovered her presence of mind, and went into the kitchen. There she heard the soft young voice musing:

'Well, to think I should come back and find it like this!' He did not seem sad, not at all–only rather interestedly surprised.

'And what a difference in the place, eh?' he continued, looking round the room.

'You see a difference, do you?' said Banford.

'Yes–don't I!'

His eyes were unnaturally clear and bright, though it was the brightness of abundant health.

March was busy in the kitchen preparing another

meal. It was about seven o'clock. All the time, while she was active, she was attending to the youth in the sitting-room, not so much listening to what he said as feeling the soft run of his voice. She primmed up her mouth tighter and tighter, puckering it as if it were sewed, in her effort to keep her will uppermost. Yet her large eyes dilated and glowed in spite of her; she lost herself. Rapidly and carelessly she prepared the meal, cutting large chunks of bread and margarine—for there was no butter. She racked her brain to think of something else to put on the tray—she had only bread, margarine, and jam, and the larder was bare. Unable to conjure anything up, she went into the sitting-room with her tray.

She did not want to be noticed. Above all, she did not want him to look at her. But when she came in, and was busy setting the table just behind him, he pulled himself up from his sprawling, and turned and looked over his shoulder. She became pale and wan.

The youth watched her as she bent over the table, looked at her slim, well-shapen legs, at the belted coat dropping around her thighs, at the knot of dark hair, and his curiosity, vivid and widely alert, was again arrested by her.

The lamp was shaded with a dark-green shade, so that the light was thrown downwards and the upper half of the room was dim. His face moved bright under the light, but March loomed shadowy in the distance.

She turned round, but kept her eyes sideways, dropping and lifting her dark lashes. Her mouth unpuckered as she said to Banford:

'Will you pour out?'

Then she went into the kitchen again.

'Have your tea where you are, will you?' said Banford to the youth—'unless you'd rather come to the table.'

'Well,' said he, 'I'm nice and comfortable, here, aren't I? I will have it here, if you don't mind.'

'There's nothing but bread and jam,' she said. And

she put his plate on a stool by him. She was very happy now, waiting on him. For she loved company. And now she was no more afraid of him than if he were her own younger brother. He was such a boy.

'Nellie,' she called. 'I've poured you a cup out.'

March appeared in the doorway, took her cup, and sat down in a corner, as far from the light as possible. She was very sensitive in her knees. Having no skirts to cover them, and being forced to sit with them boldly exposed, she suffered. She shrank and shrank, trying not to be seen. And the youth, sprawling low on the couch, glanced up at her, with long steady, penetrating looks, till she was almost ready to disappear. Yet she held her cup balanced, she drank her tea, screwed up her mouth and held her head averted. Her desire to be invisible was so strong that it quite baffled the youth. He felt he could not see her distinctly. She seemed like a shadow within the shadow. And ever his eyes came back to her, searching, unremitting, with unconscious fixed attention.

Meanwhile he was talking softly and smoothly to Banford, who loved nothing so much as gossip, and who was full of perky interest, like a bird. Also he ate largely and quickly and voraciously, so that March had to cut more chunks of bread and margarine, for the roughness of which Banford apologised.

'Oh well,' said March, suddenly speaking, 'if there's no butter to put on it, it's no good trying to make dainty pieces.'

Again the youth watched her, and he laughed, with a sudden, quick laugh, showing his teeth and wrinkling his nose.

'It isn't, is it,' he answered, in his soft, near voice.

It appeared he was Cornish by birth and upbringing. When he was twelve years old he had come to Bailey Farm with his grandfather, with whom he had never agreed very well. So he had run away to Canada, and worked far away in the West. Now he was here—and that was the end of it.

He was very curious about the girls, to find out exactly what they were doing. His questions were those of a farm youth; acute, practical, a little mocking. He was very much amused by their attitude to their losses: for they were amusing on the score of heifers and fowls.

'Oh well,' broke in March, 'we don't believe in living for nothing but work.'

'Don't you?' he answered. And again the quick young laugh came over his face. He kept his eyes steadily on the obscure woman in the corner.

'But what will you do when you've used up all your capital?' he said.

'Oh, I don't know,' answered March laconically. 'Hire ourselves out for land-workers, I suppose.'

'Yes, but there won't be any demand for women land-workers now the war's over,' said the youth.

'Oh, we'll see. We shall hold on a bit longer yet,' said March, with a plangent, half-sad, half-ironical indifference.

'There wants a man about the place,' said the youth softly.

Banford burst out laughing.

'Take care what you say,' she interrupted. 'We consider ourselves quite efficient.'

'Oh,' came March's slow plangent voice, 'it isn't a case of efficiency, I'm afraid. If you're going to do farming you must be at it from morning till night, and you might as well be a beast yourself.'

'Yes, that's it,' said the youth. 'You aren't willing to put yourselves into it.'

'We aren't,' said March, 'and we know it.'

'We want some of our time for ourselves,' said Banford.

The youth threw himself back on the sofa, his face tight with laughter, and laughed silently but thoroughly. The calm scorn of the girls tickled him tremendously.

'Yes,' he said, 'but why did you begin then?'

'Oh,' said March, 'we had a better opinion of the

nature of fowls then than we have now.'

'Of Nature altogether, I'm afraid,' said Banford. 'Don't talk to me about Nature.'

Again the face of the youth tightened with delighted laughter.

'You haven't a very high opinion of fowls and cattle, haven't you?' he said.

'Oh no—quite a low one,' said March.

He laughed out.

'Neither fowls nor heifers,' said Banford, 'nor goats nor the weather.'

The youth broke into a sharp yap of laughter, delighted. The girls began to laugh too, March turning aside her face and wrinkling her mouth in amusement.

'Oh, well,' said Banford, 'we don't mind, do we, Nellie?'

'No,' said March, 'we don't mind.'

The youth was very pleased. He had eaten and drunk his fill. Banford began to question him. His name was Henry Grenfel—no, he was not called Harry, always Henry. He continued to answer with courteous simplicity, grave and charming. March, who was not included, cast long, slow glances at him from her recess, as he sat there on the sofa, his hands clasping his knees, his face under the lamp bright and alert, turned to Banford. She became almost peaceful at last. He was identified with the fox—and he was here in full presence. She need not go after him any more. There in the shadow of her corner she gave herself up to a warm, relaxed peace, almost like sleep, accepting the spell that was on her. But she wished to remain hidden. She was only fully at peace whilst he forgot her, talking to Banford. Hidden in the shadow of the corner, she need not any more be divided in herself, trying to keep up two planes of consciousness. She could at last lapse into the odour of the fox.

For the youth, sitting before the fire in his uniform, sent a faint but distinct odour into the room, indefinable, but something like a wild creature. March no longer tried to reserve herself from it. She was still and soft in her corner like a passive creature in its cave.

At last the talk dwindled. The youth relaxed his clasp of his knees, pulled himself together a little, and looked round. Again he became aware of the silent, half-invisible woman in the corner.

'Well,' he said, unwillingly, 'I suppose I'd better be going, or they'll be in bed at the Swan.'

'I'm afraid they're in bed anyhow,' said Banford. 'They've all got this influenza.'

'Have they!' he exclaimed. And he pondered. 'Well,' he continued, 'I shall find a place somewhere.'

'I'd say you could stay here, only—' Banford began.

He turned and watched her, holding his head forward.

'What?' he asked.

'Oh, well,' she said, 'propriety, I suppose.' She was rather confused.

'It wouldn't be improper, would it?' he said, gently surprised.

'Not as far as we're concerned,' said Banford.

'And not as far as *I'm* concerned,' he said, with grave naiveté. 'After all, it's my own home, in a way.'

Banford smiled at this.

'It's what the village will have to say,' she said.

There was a moment's blank pause.

'What do you say, Nellie?' asked Banford.

'I don't mind,' said March, in her distinct tone. 'The village doesn't matter to me, anyhow.'

'No,' said the youth, quick and soft. 'Why should it? I mean, what should they say?'

'Oh, well,' came March's plangent, laconic voice, 'they'll easily find something to say. But it makes no difference what they say. We can look after ourselves.'

'Of course you can,' said the youth.

'Well then, stop if you like,' said Banford. 'The spare room is quite ready.'

His face shone with pleasure.

'If you're quite sure it isn't troubling you too much,' he said, with that soft courtesy which distinguished him.

'Oh, it's no trouble,' they both said.

He looked, smiling with delight, from one to another.

'It's awfully nice not to have to turn out again, isn't it?' he said gratefully.

'I suppose it is,' said Banford.

March disappeared to attend to the room. Banford was as pleased and thoughtful as if she had her own young brother home from France. It gave her just the same kind of gratification to attend on him, to get out the bath for him, and everything. Her natural warmth and kindliness had now an outlet. And the youth luxuriated in her sisterly attention. But it puzzled him slightly to know that March was silently working for him too. She was so curiously silent and obliterated. It seemed to him he had not really seen her. He felt he should not know her if he met her in the road.

That night March dreamed vividly. She dreamed she heard a singing outside which she could not understand, a singing that roamed round the house, in the fields, and in the darkness. It moved her so that she felt she must weep. She went out, and suddenly she knew it was the fox singing. He was very yellow and bright, like corn. She went nearer to him, but he ran away and ceased singing. He seemed near, and she wanted to touch him. She stretched out her hand, but suddenly he bit her wrist, and at the same instant, as she drew back, the fox, turning round to bound away, whisked his brush across her face, and it seemed his brush was on fire, for it seared and burned her mouth with a great pain. She awoke with the pain of it, and lay trembling as if she were really seared.

In the morning, however, she only remembered it as a distant memory. She arose and was busy preparing the house and attending to the fowls. Banford flew into the village on her bicycle to try and buy food. She was a hospitable soul. But alas in the year 1918 there was not much food to buy. The youth came downstairs in his shirt-sleeves. He was young and fresh, but he walked with his head thrust forward, so that his shoulders seemed raised and rounded, as if he had a slight curvature of the spine. It must have been only a manner of bearing himself, for he was young and vigorous. He washed himself and went outside, whilst the women were preparing breakfast.

He saw everything, and examined everything. His curiosity was quick and insatiable. He compared the state of things with that which he remembered before, and cast over in his mind the effect of the changes. He watched the fowls and the ducks, to see their condition; he noticed the flight of wood-pigeons overhead: they were very numerous; he saw the few apples high up, which March had not been able to reach; he remarked that they had borrowed a draw-pump, presumably to empty the big soft-water cistern which was on the north side of the house.

'It's a funny, dilapidated old place,' he said to the girls, as he sat at breakfast.

His eyes were wise and childish, with thinking about things. He did not say much, but ate largely. March kept her face averted. She, too, in the early morning could not be aware of him, though something about the glint of his khaki reminded her of the brilliance of her dream-fox.

During the day the girls went about their business. In the morning he attended to the guns, shot a rabbit and a wild duck that was flying high towards the wood. That was a great addition to the empty larder. The girls felt that already he had earned his keep. He said nothing about leaving, however. In the afternoon he went to the village. He came back at tea-time. He had the same alert, forward-reaching look on his roundish face. He hung his hat on a peg with a little swinging gesture. He was thinking about something.

'Well,' he said to the girls, as he sat at table. 'What am I going to do?'

'How do you mean–what are you going to do?' said Banford.

'Where am I going to find a place in the village to stay?' he said.

'I don't know,' said Banford. 'Where do you think of staying?'

'Well'–he hesitated–'at the Swan they've got this flu, and at the Plough and Harrow they've got the soldiers who are collecting the hay for the army: besides, in the private houses, there's ten men and a corporal altogether billeted in the village, they tell me. I'm not sure where I could get a bed.'

He left the matter to them. He was rather calm about it. March sat with her elbows on the table, her two hands supporting her chin, looking at him unconsciously. Suddenly he lifted his clouded blue eyes, and unthinking looked straight into March's eyes. He was startled as well as she. He, too, recoiled a little. March felt the same sly, taunting, knowing spark leap out of his eyes, as he turned his head aside, and fall into her soul, as it had fallen from the dark eyes of the fox. She pursed her mouth as if in pain, as if asleep too.

'Well, I don't know,' Banford was saying. She seemed reluctant, as if she were afraid of being imposed upon. She looked at March. But, with her weak, troubled sight, she only saw the usual semi-abstraction on her friend's face. 'Why don't you speak, Nellie?' she said.

But March was wide-eyed and silent, and the youth, as if fascinated, was watching her without moving his eyes.

'Go on–answer something,' said Banford. And March turned her head slightly aside, as if coming to consciousness, or trying to come to consciousness.

'What do you expect me to say?' she asked automatically.

'Say what you think,' said Banford.

'It's all the same to me,' said March.

And again there was silence. A pointed light seemed to be on the boy's eyes, penetrating like a needle.

'So it is to me,' said Banford. 'You can stop on here if you like.'

A smile like a cunning little flame came over his face, suddenly and involuntarily. He dropped his head quickly to hide it, and remained with his head dropped, his face hidden.

'You can stop on here if you like. You can please yourself, Henry,' Banford concluded.

Still he did not reply, but remained with his head dropped. Then he lifted his face. It was bright with a curious light, as if exultant, and his eyes were strangely clear as he watched March. She turned her face aside, her mouth suffering as if wounded, and her consciousness dim.

Banford became a little puzzled. She watched the steady, pellucid gaze of the youth's eyes as he looked at March, with the invisible smile gleaming on his face. She did not know how he was smiling, for no feature moved. It seemed only in the gleam, almost the glitter of the fine hairs on his cheeks. Then he looked with quite a changed look at Banford.

'I'm sure,' he said in his soft, courteous voice, 'you're awfully good. You're too good. You don't want to be bothered with me, I'm sure.'

'Cut a bit of bread, Nellie,' said Banford uneasily, adding : 'It's no bother, if you like to stay. It's like having my own brother here for a few days. He's a boy like you are.'

'That's awfully kind of you,' the lad repeated. 'I should like to stay ever so much, if you're sure I'm not a trouble to you.'

'No, of course you're no trouble. I tell you, it's a pleasure to have somebody in the house besides ourselves,' said warm-hearted Banford.

'But Miss March?' he said in his soft voice, looking

at her.

'Oh, it's quite all right as far as I'm concerned,' said March vaguely.

His face beamed, and he almost rubbed his hands with pleasure.

'Well then,' he said, 'I should love it, if you'd let me pay my board and help with the work.'

'You've no need to talk about board,' said Banford.

One or two days went by, and the youth stayed on at the farm. Banford was quite charmed by him. He was so soft and courteous in speech, not wanting to say much himself, preferring to hear what she had to say, and to laugh in his quick, half-mocking way. He helped readily with the work—but not too much. He loved to be out alone with the gun in his hands, to watch, to see. For his sharp-eyed, impersonal curiosity was insatiable, and he was most free when he was quite alone, half-hidden, watching.

Particularly he watched March. She was a strange character to him. Her figure, like a graceful young man's, piqued him. Her dark eyes made something rise in his soul, with a curious elate excitement, when he looked into them, an excitement he was afraid to let be seen, it was so keen and secret. And then her odd, shrewd speech made him laugh outright. He felt he must go further, he was inevitably impelled. But he put away the thought of her and went off towards the wood's edge with the gun.

The dusk was falling as he came home, and with the dusk, a fine, late November rain. He saw the fire-light leaping in the window of the sitting-room, a leaping light in the little cluster of the dark buildings. And he thought to himself it would be a good thing to have this place for his own. And then the thought entered him shrewdly: why not marry March? He stood still in the middle of the field for some moments, the dead rabbit hanging still in his hand, arrested by this thought. His mind waited in amazement—it seemed to calculate—and then he smiled curiously to himself in acquiescence. Why not? Why not indeed? It was a good idea. What if it was rather ridiculous? What did it matter? What if she was older than he? It didn't matter? When he thought of her dark, startled, vulnerable eyes he smiled subtly to himself. He was older than she, really. He was master of her.

He scarcely admitted his intention even to himself. He kept it as a secret even from himself. It was all too uncertain as yet. He would have to see how things went. If he wasn't careful, she would just simply mock at the idea. He knew, sly and subtle as he was, that if he went to her plainly and said: 'Miss March, I love you and want you to marry me,' her inevitable answer would be: 'Get out. I don't want any of that tomfoolery.' This was her attitude to men and their 'tomfoolery'. If he was not careful, she would turn round on him with her savage, sardonic ridicule, and dismiss him from the farm and from her own mind for ever. He would have to go gently. He would have to catch her as you catch a deer or a woodcock when you go out shooting. It's no good walking out into the forest and saying to the deer: 'Please fall to my gun.' No, it is a slow, subtle battle. When you really go out to get a deer, you gather yourself together, you coil yourself inside yourself, and you advance secretly, before dawn, into the mountains. It is not so much what you do, when you go out hunting, as how you feel. You have to be subtle and cunning and absolutely fatally ready. It becomes like a fate. Your own fate over-takes and determines the fate of the deer you are hunting. First of all, even before you come in sight of your quarry, there is a strange battle, like mesmerism. Your own soul, as a hunter, has gone out to fasten on the soul of the deer, even before you see any deer. And the soul of the deer fights to escape. Even before the deer has any wind of you, it is so. It is a subtle, profound battle of wills which takes place in the invisible. And it is a battle never finished till your bullet goes home. When you are *really* worked up to the true pitch, and you come at last into range, you don't then aim as you do when you are firing at a bottle. It is your own *will* which carries the bullet into the heart of your quarry. The bullet's flight home is a sheer projection of your own fate into the fate of the deer. It happens like a supreme wish, a supreme act of volition, not as a dodge of cleverness.

He was a huntsman in spirit, not a farmer, and not a soldier stuck in a regiment. And it was as a young hunter that he wanted to bring down March as his quarry, to make her his wife. So he gathered himself subtly together, seemed to withdraw into a kind of invisibility. He was not quite sure how he would go on. And March was suspicious as a hare. So he remained in appearance just the nice, odd stranger-youth, staying for a fortnight on the place.

He had been sawing logs for the fire in the afternoon. Darkness came very early. It was still a cold, raw mist. It was getting almost too dark to see. A pile of short sawed logs lay beside the trestle. March came to carry them indoors, or into the shed, as he was busy sawing the last log. He was working in his shirt-sleeves, and did not notice her approach; she came unwillingly, as if shy. He saw her stooping to the bright-ended logs, and he stopped sawing. A fire like lightning flew down his legs in the nerves.

'March?' he said, in his quiet, young voice.

She looked up from the logs she was piling.

'Yes?' she said.

He looked down on her in the dusk. He could see her not too distinctly.

'I wanted to ask you something,' he said.

'Did you? What was it?' she said. Already the fright was in her voice. But she was too much mistress of herself.

'Why'—his voice seemed to draw out soft and subtle, it penetrated her nerves—'why, what do you think it is?'

She stood up, placed her hands on her hips, and stood looking at him transfixed, without answering. Again he burned with a sudden power.

'Well,' he said, and his voice was so soft it seemed
rather like a subtle touch, like the merest touch of a cat's
paw, a feeling rather than a sound. 'Well—I wanted to ask
you to marry me.'

March felt rather than heard him. She was trying in
vain to turn aside her face. A great relaxation seemed to
have come over her. She stood silent, her head slightly on
one side. He seemed to be bending towards her, invisibly
smiling. It seemed to her fine sparks came out of him.

Then very suddenly she said:

'Don't try any of your tomfoolery on me.'

A quiver went over his nerves. He had missed. He
waited a moment to collect himself again. Then he said,
putting all the strange softness into his voice, as if he
were imperceptibly stroking her:

'Why, it's not tomfoolery. It's not tomfoolery. I
mean it. I mean it. What makes you disbelieve me?'

He sounded hurt. And his voice had such a curious
power over her; making her feel loose and relaxed. She
struggled somewhere for her own power. She felt for a
moment that she was lost—lost—lost. The word seemed to
rock in her as if she were dying. Suddenly again she
spoke.

'You don't know what you are talking about,' she
said, in a brief and transient stroke of scorn. 'What nonsense! I'm old enough to be your mother.'

'Yes, I do know what I'm talking about. Yes I do,'
he persisted softly, as if he were producing his voice in
her blood. 'I know quite well what I'm talking about.
You're not old enough to be my mother. That isn't true.
And what does it matter even if it was. You can marry
me whatever age we are. What is age to me? And what is
age to you! Age is nothing.'

A swoon went over her as he concluded. He spoke
rapidly—in the rapid Cornish fashion—and his voice
seemed to sound in her somewhere where she was
helpless against it. 'Age is nothing!' The soft, heavy
insistence of it made her sway dimly out there in the

darkness. She could not answer.

A great exultance leaped like fire over his limbs. He felt he had won.

'I want to marry you, you see. Why shouldn't I?' he proceeded, soft and rapid. He waited for her to answer. In the dusk he saw her almost phosphorescent. Her eyelids were dropped, her face half-averted and unconscious. She seemed to be in his power. But he waited, watchful. He dared not yet touch her.

'Say then,' he said, 'say then you'll marry me. Say—say!' He was softly insistent.

'What?' she asked, faint, from a distance, like one in pain. His voice was now unthinkably near and soft. He drew very near to her.

'Say yes.'

'Oh, I can't,' she wailed helplessly, half-articulate, as if semi-conscious, and as if in pain, like one who dies. 'How can I?'

'You can,' he said softly, laying his hand gently on her shoulder as she stood with her head averted and dropped, dazed. 'You can. Yes, you can. What makes you say you can't? You can. You can.' And with awful softness he bent forward and just touched her neck with his mouth and his chin.

'Don't!' she cried, with a faint mad cry like hysteria, starting away and facing round on him. 'What do you mean?' But she had no breath to speak with. It was as if she was killed.

'I mean what I say,' he persisted softly and cruelly. 'I want you to marry me. I want you to marry me. You know that, now, don't you? You know that, now? Don't you? Don't you?'

'What?' she said.

'Know,' he replied.

'Yes,' she said. 'I know you say so.'

'And you know I mean it, don't you?'

'I know you say so.'

'You believe me?' he said.

She was silent for some time. Then she pursed her lips.

'I don't know what I believe,' she said.

'Are you out there?' came Banford's voice, calling from the house.

'Yes, we're bringing in the logs,' he answered.

'I thought you'd gone lost,' said Banford disconsolately. 'Hurry up, do, and come and let's have tea. The kettle's boiling.'

He stooped at once, to take an armful of little logs and carry them into the kitchen, where they were piled in a corner. March also helped, filling her arms and carrying the logs on her breast as if they were some heavy child. The night had fallen cold.

When the logs were all in, the two cleaned their boots noisily on the scraper outside, then rubbed them on the mat. March shut the door and took off her old felt hat—her farm-hat. Her thick, crisp black hair was loose, her face was pale and strained. She pushed back her hair vaguely, and washed her hands. Banford came hurrying into the dimly-lighted kitchen, to take from the oven the scones she was keeping hot.

'Whatever have you been doing all this time?' she asked fretfully. 'I thought you were never coming in. And it's ages since you stopped sawing. What were you doing out there?'

'Well,' said Henry, 'we had to stop that hole in the barn, to keep the rats out.'

'Why I could see you standing there in the shed. I could see your shirt-sleeves,' challenged Banford.

'Yes, I was just putting the saw away.'

They went in to tea. March was quite mute. Her face was pale and strained and vague. The youth, who always had the same ruddy, self-contained look on his face, as though he were keeping himself to himself, had come to tea in his shirt-sleeves as if he were at home. He bent over his plate as he ate his food.

'Aren't you cold?' said Banford spitefully. 'In your

shirt-sleeves.'

He looked up at her, with his chin near his plate, and his eyes very clear, pellucid, and unwavering as he watched her.

'No, I'm not cold,' he said with his usual soft courtesy. 'It's much warmer in here than it is outside, you see.'

'I hope it is,' said Banford, feeling nettled by him. He had a strange suave assurance, and a wide-eyed bright look that got on her nerves this evening.

'But perhaps,' he said softly and courteously, 'you don't like me coming to tea without my coat. I forgot that.'

'Oh, I don't mind,' said Banford: although she *did*.

'I'll go and get it, shall I?' he said.

March's dark eyes turned slowly down to him.

'No, don't you bother,' she said in her queer, twanging tone. 'If you feel all right as you are, stop as you are.' She spoke with a crude authority.

'Yes,' said he, 'I *feel* all right, if I'm not rude.'

'It's usually considered rude,' said Banford. 'But we don't mind.'

'Go along, "considered rude",' ejaculated March. 'Who considers it rude?'

'Why you do, Nellie, in anybody else,' said Banford, bridling a little behind her spectacles, and feeling her food stick in her throat.

But March had again gone vague and unheeding, chewing her food as if she did not know she was eating at all. And the youth looked from one to another, with bright, watchful eyes.

Banford was offended. For all his suave courtesy and soft voice, the youth seemed to her impudent. She did not like to look at him. She did not like to meet his clear, watchful eyes, she did not like to see the strange glow in his face, his cheeks with their delicate fine hair, and his ruddy skin that was quite dull and yet which seemed to burn with a curious heat of life. It made her feel a little ill to look at him : the quality of his physical presence was too penetrating, too hot.

After tea the evening was very quiet. The youth rarely went into the village. As a rule he read: he was a great reader, in his own hours. That is, when he did begin, he read absorbedly. But he was not very eager to begin. Often he walked about the fields and along the hedges alone in the dark at night, prowling with a queer instinct for the night, and listening to the wild sounds.

To-night, however, he took a Captain Mayne Reid book from Banford's shelf and sat down with knees wide apart and immersed himself in his story. His brownish fair hair was long, and lay on his head like a thick cap, combed sideways. He was still in his shirt sleeves, and bending forward under the lamp-light, with his knees stuck wide apart and the book in his hand and his whole figure absorbed in the rather strenuous business of reading, he gave Banford's sitting-room the look of a lumber-camp. She resented this. For on her sitting-room floor she had a red Turkey rug and dark stain round, the fire-place had fashionable green tiles, the piano stood open with the latest dance-music—she played quite well: and on the walls were March's hand-painted swans and water-lilies. Moreover, with the logs nicely, tremulously burning in the grate, the thick curtains drawn, the doors all shut, and the pine-trees hissing and shuddering in the wind outside, it was cosy, it was refined and nice. She resented the big, raw, long-legged youth sticking his khaki knees out and sitting there with his soldier's shirt-cuffs buttoned on his thick red wrists. From time to time he turned a page, and from time to time he gave a sharp look at the fire, settling the logs. Then he immersed himself again in the intense and isolated business of reading.

March, on the far side of the table, was spasmodically crocheting. Her mouth was pursed in an odd way, as when she had dreamed the fox's brush burned it, her beautiful, crisp black hair strayed in wisps.

But her whole figure was absorbed in its bearing, as if she herself was miles away. In a sort of semi-dream she seemed to be hearing the fox singing round the house in the wind, singing wildly and sweetly and like a madness. With red but well-shaped hands she slowly crochetted the white cotton, very slowly, awkwardly.

Banford was also trying to read, sitting in her low chair. But between those two she felt fidgety. She kept moving and looking round and listening to the wind, and glancing secretly from one to the other of her companions. March, seated on a straight chair, with her knees in their close breeches crossed, and slowly, laboriously crochetting, was also a trial.

'Oh dear!' said Banford. 'My eyes are bad to-night.' And she pressed her fingers on her eyes.

The youth looked up at her with his clear, bright look, but did not speak.

'Are they, Jill?' said March absently.

Then the youth began to read again, and Banford perforce returned to her book. But she could not keep still. After a while she looked up at March, and a queer, almost malignant little smile was on her thin face.

'A penny for them, Nell,' she said suddenly.

March looked round with big, startled black eyes, and went pale as if with terror. She had been listening to the fox singing so tenderly, so tenderly, as he wandered round the house.

'What?' she said vaguely.

'A penny for them,' said Banford sarcastically. 'Or twopence, if they're as deep as all that.'

The youth was watching with bright, clear eyes from beneath the lamp.

'Why,' came March's vague voice, 'what do you want to waste your money for?'

'I thought it would be well spent,' said Banford.

'I wasn't thinking of anything except the way the wind was blowing,' said March.

'Oh dear,' replied Banford, 'I could have had as

original thoughts as that myself. I'm afraid I *have* wasted my money this time.'

'Well, you needn't pay,' said March.

The youth suddenly laughed. Both women looked at him : March rather surprised-looking, as if she had hardly known he was there.

'Why, do you ever pay up on these occasions?' he asked.

'Oh yes,' said Banford. 'We always do. I've sometimes had to pass a shilling a week to Nellie, in the winter time. It costs much less in summer.'

'What, paying for each other's thoughts?' he laughed.

'Yes, when we've absolutely come to the end of everything else.'

He laughed quickly, wrinkling his nose sharply like a puppy and laughing with quick pleasure, his eyes shining.

'It's the first time I ever heard of that,' he said.

'I guess you'd hear of it often enough if you stayed a winter on Bailey Farm,' said Banford lamentably.

'Do you get so tired, then?' he asked.

'So bored,' said Banford.

'Oh!' he said gravely. 'But why should you be bored?'

'Who wouldn't be bored?' said Banford.

'I'm sorry to hear that,' he said gravely.

'You must be, if you were hoping to have a lively time here,' said Banford.

He looked at her long and gravely.

'Well,' he said, with his odd, young seriousness, 'it's quite lively enough for me.'

'I'm glad to hear it,' said Banford.

And she returned to her book. In her thin, frail hair were already many threads of grey, though she was not yet thirty. The boy did not look down, but turned his eyes to March, who was sitting with pursed mouth laboriously crochetting, her eyes wide and absent. She

had a warm, pale, fine skin, and a delicate nose. Her
pursed mouth looked shrewish. But the shrewish look
was contradicted by the curious lifted arch of her dark
brows, and the wideness of her eyes; a look of startled
wonder and vagueness. She was listening again for the
fox, who seemed to have wandered farther off into the
night.

From under the edge of the lamp-light the boy sat
with his face looking up, watching her silently, his eyes
round and very clear and intent. Banford, biting her
fingers irritably, was glancing at him under her hair. He
sat there perfectly still, his ruddy face tilted up from the
low level under the light, on the edge of the dimness, and
watching with perfect abstract intentness. March
suddenly lifted her great, dark eyes from her crochetting,
and saw him. She started, giving a little exclamation.

'There he is!' she cried, involuntarily, as if terribly
startled.

Banford looked around in amazement, sitting up
straight.

'Whatever has got you, Nellie?' she cried.

But March, her face flushed a delicate rose colour,
was looking away to the door.

'Nothing! Nothing!' she said crossly. 'Can't one
speak?'

'Yes, if you speak sensibly,' said Banford. 'Whatever
did you mean?'

'I don't know what I meant,' cried March testily.

'Oh Nellie, I hope you aren't going jumpy and
nervy. I feel I can't stand another *thing*! Whoever did you
mean? Did you mean Henry?' cried poor, frightened
Banford.

'Yes. I suppose so,' said March laconically. She
would never confess to the fox.

'Oh dear, my nerves are all gone for to-night,'
wailed Banford.

At nine o'clock March brought in a tray with bread
and cheese and tea—Henry had confessed that he liked a

cup of tea. Banford drank a glass of milk, and ate a little bread. And soon she said:

'I'm going to bed, Nellie. I'm all nerves to-night. Are you coming?'

'Yes, I'm coming the minute I've taken the tray away,' said March.

'Don't be long then,' said Banford fretfully. 'Good-night, Henry. You'll see the fire is safe, if you come up last, won't you?'

'Yes, Miss Banford, I'll see it's safe,' he replied in his reassuring way.

March was lighting the candle to go to the kitchen. Banford took her candle and went upstairs. When March came back to the fire, she said to him:

'I suppose we can trust you to put out the fire and everything?' She stood there with her hand on her hip, and one knee loose, her head averted shyly, as if she could not look at him. He had his face lifted, watching her.

'Come and sit down a minute,' he said softly.

'No, I'll be going. Jill will be waiting, and she'll get upset if I don't come.'

'What made you jump like that this evening?' he asked.

'When did I jump?' she retorted, looking at him.

'Why, just now you did,' he said. 'When you cried out.'

'Oh!' she said, 'Then!—Why, I thought you were the fox!' And her face screwed into a queer smile, half-ironic.

'The fox! Why the fox?' he asked softly.

'Why, one evening last summer when I was out with the gun I saw the fox in the grass nearly at my feet, looking straight up at me. I don't know—I suppose he made an impression on me.' She turned aside her head again, and let one foot stray loose, self-consciously.

'And did you shoot him?' asked the boy.

'No, he gave me such a start, staring straight at me as he did, and then stopping to look back at me over his shoulder with a laugh on his face.'

'A laugh on his face!' repeated Henry, also laughing. 'He frightened you, did he?'

'No, he didn't frighten me. He made an impression on me, that's all.'

'And you thought I was the fox, did you?' he laughed, with the same queer, quick little laugh, like a puppy wrinkling its nose.

'Yes I did, for the moment,' she said. 'Perhaps he'd been in my mind without my knowing.'

'Perhaps you think I've come to steal your chickens or something,' he said, with the same young laugh.

But she only looked at him with a wide, dark, vacant eye.

'It's the first time,' he said, 'that I've ever been taken for a fox. Won't you sit down for a minute?' His voice was very soft and cajoling.

'No,' she said. 'Jill will be waiting.' But still she did not go, but stood with one foot loose and her face turned aside, just outside the circle of light.

'But won't you answer my question?' he said, lowering his voice still more.

'I don't know what question you mean.'

'Yes, you do. Of course you do. I mean the question of you marrying me.'

'No, I shan't answer that question,' she said flatly.

'Won't you?' The queer, young laugh came on his nose again. 'Is it because I'm like the fox? Is that why?' And still he laughed.

She turned and looked at him with a long, slow look.

'I wouldn't let that put you against me,' he said. 'Let me turn the lamp low, and come and sit down a minute.'

He put his red hand under the glow of the lamp, and suddenly made the light very dim. March stood there in the dimness quite shadowy, but unmoving. He rose silently to his feet, on his long legs. And now his voice was extraordinarily soft and suggestive, hardly audible.

'You'll stay a moment,' he said. 'Just a moment.' And he put his hand on her shoulder. She turned her face from him. 'I'm sure you don't really think I'm like the fox,' he said, with the same softness and with a suggestion of laughter in his tone, a subtle mockery. 'Do you now?' And he drew her gently towards him and kissed her neck, softly. She winced and trembled and hung away. But his strong, young arm held her, and he kissed her softly again, still on the neck, for her face was averted.

'Won't you answer my question? Won't you now?' came his soft, lingering voice. He was trying to draw her near to kiss her face. And he kissed her cheek softly, near the ear.

At that moment Banford's voice was heard calling fretfully, crossly from upstairs.

'There's Jill!' cried March, starting and drawing erect.

And as she did so, quick as lightning he kissed her on the mouth, with a quick brushing kiss. It seemed to burn through her every fibre. She gave a queer little cry.

'You will, won't you? You will?' he insisted softly.

'Nellie! *Nellie!* Whatever are you so long for?' came Banford's faint cry from the outer darkness.

But he held her fast, and was murmuring with that intolerable softness and insistency:

'You will, won't you? Say yes! Say yes!'

March, who felt as if the fire had gone through her and scathed her, and as if she could do no more, murmured :

'Yes! Yes! I do!' Her voice suddenly rose into a shrill cry. 'All right, Jill, I'm coming.'

Startled, he let her go, and she went straight upstairs.

In the morning at breakfast, after he had looked round the place and attended to the stock and thought to himself that one could live easily enough here, he said to Banford :

'Do you know what, Miss Banford?'

'Well, what?' said the good-natured, nervy Banford. He looked at March, who was spreading jam on her bread.

'Shall I tell?' he said to her.

She looked up at him, and a deep pink colour flushed over her face.

'Yes, if you mean Jill,' she said. 'I hope you won't go talking all over the village, that's all.' And she swallowed her dry bread with difficulty.

'Whatever's coming?' said Banford, looking up with wide, tired, slightly reddened eyes. She was a thin, frail little thing, and her hair, which was delicate and thin, was bobbed, so it hung softly by her worn face in its faded brown and grey.

'Why, what do you think?' he said, smiling like one who has a secret.

'How do I know!' said Banford.

'Can't you guess?' he said, making bright eyes, and smiling, pleased with himself.

'I'm sure I can't. What's more, I'm not going to try.'

'Nellie and I are going to be married.'

Banford put down her knife out of her thin, delicate fingers, as if she would never take it up to eat any more. She stared with blank, reddened eyes.

'You what?' she exclaimed.

'We're going to get married. Aren't we, Nellie?' and he turned to March.

'You say so, anyway,' said March laconically. But again she flushed with an agonised flush. She, too, could swallow no more.

Banford looked at her like a bird that has been shot: a poor, little sick bird. She gazed at her with all her wounded soul in her face, at the deep-flushed March.

'Never!' she exclaimed, helpless.

'It's quite right,' said the bright and gloating youth.

Banford turned aside her face, as if the sight of the food on the table made her sick. She sat like this for some moments, as if she were sick. Then, with one hand on the edge of the table, she rose to her feet.

'I'll *never* believe it, Nellie,' she cried. 'It's absolutely impossible!'

Her plaintive, fretful voice had a thread of hot anger and despair.

'Why? Why shouldn't you believe it?' asked the youth, with all his soft, velvety impertinence in his voice.

Banford looked at him from her wide, vague eyes, as if he were some creature in a museum.

'Oh,' she said languidly, 'because she can never be such a fool. She can't lose her self-respect to such an extent.' Her voice was cold and plaintive, drifting.

'In what way will she lose her self-respect?' asked the boy.

Banford looked at him with vague fixity from behind her spectacles.

'If she hasn't lost it already,' she said.

He became very red, vermilion, under the slow, vague stare from behind the spectacles.

'I don't see it at all,' he said.

'Probably you don't. I shouldn't expect you would,' said Banford, with that straying mild tone of remoteness which made her words even more insulting.

He sat stiff in his chair, staring with hot, blue eyes from his scarlet face. An ugly look had come on his brow.

'My word, she doesn't know what she's letting herself in for,' said Banford, in her plaintive, drifting, insulting voice.

'What has it got to do with you, anyway?' said the youth, in a temper.

'More than it has to do with you, probably,' she replied, plaintive and venomous.

'Oh, has it! I don't see that at all,' he jerked out.

'No, you wouldn't,' she answered, drifting.

'Anyhow,' said March, pushing back her chair and rising uncouthly. 'It's no good arguing about it.' And she seized the bread and the tea-pot, and strode away to the kitchen.

Banford let her fingers stray across her brow and along her hair, like one bemused. Then she turned and went away upstairs.

Henry sat stiff and sulky in his chair, with his face and his eyes on fire. March came and went, clearing the table. But Henry sat on, stiff with temper. He took no notice of her. She had regained her composure and her soft, even creamy complexion. But her mouth was pursed up. She glanced at him each time as she came to take things from the table, glanced from her large, curious eyes, more in curiosity than anything. Such a long, red-faced, sulky boy! That was all he was. He seemed as remote from her as if his red face were a red chimney-pot on a cottage across the fields, and she looked at him just as objectively, as remotely.

At length he got up and stalked out into the fields with the gun. He came in only at dinner-time, with the devil still in his face, but his manners quite polite. Nobody said anything particular; they sat each one at the sharp corner of a triangle, in obstinate remoteness. In the afternoon he went out again at once with the gun. He came in at nightfall with a rabbit and a pigeon. He stayed in all the evening, but hardly opened his mouth. He was in the devil of a tèmper, feeling he had been insulted.

Banford's eyes were red, she had evidently been crying. But her manner was more remote and supercilious than ever; the way she turned her head if he spoke at all, as if he were some tramp or inferior intruder of that sort, made his blue eyes go almost black with rage. His face looked sulkier. But he never forgot his polite intonation, if he opened his mouth to speak.

March seemed to flourish in this atmosphere. She seemed to sit between the two antagonists with a little wicked smile on her face, enjoying herself. There was even a sort of complacency in the way she laboriously crochetted this evening.

When he was in bed, the youth could hear the two women talking and arguing in their room. He sat up in bed and strained his ears to hear what they said. But he could hear nothing, it was too far off. Yet he could hear the soft, plaintive drip of Banford's voice, and March's deeper note.

The night was quiet, frosty. Big stars were snapping outside, beyond the ridge-tops of the pine-trees. He listened and listened. In the distance he heard a fox yelping: and the dogs from the farms barking in answer. But it was not that he wanted to hear. It was what the two women were saying.

He got stealthily out of bed, and stood by his door. He could hear no more than before. Very, very carefully he began to lift the door latch. After quite a time he had his door open. Then he stepped stealthily out into the passage. The old oak planks were cold under his feet, and they creaked preposterously. He crept very, very gently up the one step, and along by the wall, till he stood outside their door. And there he held his breath and listened. Banford's voice:

'No, I simply couldn't stand it. I should be dead in a month. Which is just what he would be aiming at, of course. That would just be his game, to see me in the churchyard. No, Nellie, if you were to do such a thing as to marry him, you could never stop here. I couldn't, I couldn't live in the same house with him. Oh–h! I feel quite sick with the smell of his clothes. And his red face simply turns me over. I can't eat my food when he's at the table. What a fool I was ever to let him stop. One ought *never* to try to do a kind action. It always flies back in your face like a boomerang.'

'Well, he's only got two more days,' said March.

'Yes, thank heaven. And when he's gone he'll never come in this house again. I feel so bad while he's here. And I know, I know he's only counting what he can get out of you. I *know* that's all it is. He's just a good-for-nothing, who doesn't want to work, and who thinks he'll

live on us. But he won't live on me. If you're such a fool,
then it's your own look-out. Mrs Burgess knew him all the
time he was here. And the old man could never get him
to do any steady work. He was off with the gun on every
occasion, just as he is now. Nothing but the gun! Oh, I
do hate it. You don't know what you're doing, Nellie,
you don't. If you marry him he'll just make a fool of you.
He'll go off and leave you stranded. I know he will, if he
can't get Bailey Farm out of us–and he's not going to,
while I live. While I live he's never going to set foot here.
I know what it would be. He'd soon think he was master
of both of us, as he thinks he's master of you already.'

'But he isn't,' said Nellie.

'He thinks he is, anyway. And that's what he wants:
to come and be master here. Yes, imagine it! That's what
we've got the place together for, is it, to be bossed and
bullied by a hateful red-faced boy, a beastly labourer.
Oh, we *did* make a mistake when we let him stop. We
ought never to have lowered ourselves. And I've had such
a fight with all the people here, not to be pulled down to
their level. No, he's not coming here. And then you see–if
he can't have the place, he'll run off to Canada or somewhere again, as if he'd never known you. And here you'll
be, absolutely ruined and made a fool of. I know I shall
never have any peace of mind again.'

'We'll tell him he can't come here. We'll tell him
that,' said March.

'Oh, don't you bother; I'm going to tell him that,
and other things as well, before he goes. He's not going to
have all his own way while I've got the strength left to
speak. Oh, Nellie, he'll despise you, he'll despise you,
like the awful little beast he is, if you give way to him. I'd
no more trust him than I'd trust a cat not to steal. He's
deep, he's deep, and he's bossy, and he's selfish through
and through, as cold as ice. All he wants is to make use of
you. And when you're no more use to him, then I pity
you.'

'I don't think he's as bad as all that,' said March.

'No, because he's been playing up to you. But you'll find out, if you see much more of him. Oh, Nellie, I can't bear to think of it.'

'Well, it won't hurt you, Jill, darling.'

'Won't it! Won't it! I shall never know a moment's peace again while I live, nor a moment's happiness. No, Nellie—' and Banford began to weep bitterly.

The boy outside could hear the stifled sound of the woman's sobbing, and could hear March's soft, deep, tender voice comforting, with wonderful gentleness and tenderness, the weeping woman.

His eyes were so round and wide that he seemed to see the whole night, and his ears were almost jumping off his head. He was frozen stiff. He crept back to bed, but felt as if the top of his head were coming off. He could not sleep. He could not keep still. He rose, quietly dressed himself, and crept out on to the landing once more. The women were silent. He went softly downstairs and out to the kitchen.

Then he put on his boots and his overcoat, and took the gun. He did not think to go away from the farm. No, he only took the gun. As softly as possible he unfastened the door and went out into the frosty December night. The air was still, the stars bright, the pine-trees seemed to bristle audibly in the sky. He went stealthily away down a fence-side, looking for something to shoot. At the same time he remembered that he ought not to shoot and frighten the women.

So he prowled round the edge of the gorse cover, and through the grove of tall old hollies, to the woodside. There he skirted the fence, peering through the darkness with dilated eyes that seemed to be able to grow black and full of sight in the dark, like a cat's. An owl was slowly and mournfully whooing round a great oak-tree. He stepped stealthily with his gun, listening, listening, watching.

As he stood under the oaks of the wood-edge he heard the dogs from the neighbouring cottage up the hill yelling suddenly and startlingly, and the wakened dogs from the farms around barking answer. And suddenly, it seemed to him England was little and tight, he felt the landscape was constricted even in the dark, and that there were too many dogs in the night, making a noise like a fence of sound, like the network of English hedges netting the view. He felt the fox didn't have a chance. For it must be the fox that had started all this hullabaloo.

Why not watch for him, anyhow! He would, no doubt, be coming sniffing round. The lad walked downhill to where the farmstead with its few pine-trees crouched blackly. In the angle of the long shed, in the black dark, he crouched down. He knew the fox would be coming. It seemed to him it would be the last of the foxes in this loudly-barking, thick-voiced England, tight with innumerable little houses.

He sat a long time with his eyes fixed unchanging upon the open gateway, where a little light seemed to fall from the stars or from the horizon, who knows. He was sitting on a log in a dark corner with the gun across his knees. The pine-trees snapped. Once a chicken fell off its perch in the barn with a loud crawk and cackle and commotion that startled him, and he stood up, watching with all his eyes, thinking it might be a rat. But he *felt* it was nothing. So he sat down again with the gun on his knees and his hands tucked in to keep them warm, and his eyes fixed unblinking on the pale reach of the open gateway. He felt he could smell the hot, sickly, rich smell of live chickens on the cold air.

And then—a shadow. A sliding shadow in the gateway. He gathered all his vision into a concentrated spark, and saw the shadow of the fox, the fox creeping on his belly through the gate. There he went, on his belly like a snake. The boy smiled to himself and brought the gun to his shoulder. He knew quite well what would happen. He knew the fox would go to where the fowl-door was boarded up, and sniff there. He knew he would lie there for a minute, sniffing the fowls within. And then he would start again prowling under the edge of the old barn, waiting to get in.

The fowl-door was at the top of a slight incline. Soft, soft as a shadow the fox slid up this incline, and crouched with his nose to the boards. And at the same moment there was the awful crash of a gun reverberating between the old buildings, as if all the night had gone smash. But the boy watched keenly. He saw even the white belly of the fox as the beast beat his paws in death. So he went forward.

There was a commotion everywhere. The fowls were scuffling and crawking, the ducks were quark-quarking, the pony had stamped wildly to his feet. But the fox was on his side, struggling in his last tremors. The boy bent over him and smelt his foxy smell.

There was a sound of a window opening upstairs, then March's voice calling:

'Who is it?'

'It's me,' said Henry; 'I've shot the fox.'

'Oh, goodness! You nearly frightened us to death.'

'Did I? I'm awfully sorry.'

'Whatever made you get up?'

'I heard him about.'

'And have you shot him?'

'Yes, he's here,' and the boy stood in the yard holding up the warm, dead brute. 'You can't see, can you? Wait a minute.' And he took his flash-light from his pocket, and flashed it on to the dead animal. He was holding it by the brush. March saw, in the middle of the darkness, just the reddish fleece and the white belly and the white underneath of the pointed chin, and the queer, dangling paws. She did not know what to say.

'He's a beauty,' he said. 'He will make you a lovely fur.'

'You don't catch me wearing a fox fur,' she replied.

'Oh!' he said. And he switched off the light.

'Well, I should think you'll come in and go to bed again now,' she said.

'Probably I shall. What time is it?'

'What time is it, Jill?' called March's voice. It was a quarter to one.

That night March had another dream. She dreamed that Banford was dead, and that she, March, was sobbing her heart out. Then she had to put Banford into her coffin. And the coffin was the rough wood-box in which the bits of chopped wood were kept in the kitchen, by the fire. This was the coffin, and there was no other, and March was in agony and dazed bewilderment, looking for something to line the box with, something to make it soft with, something to cover up the poor, dead darling. Because she couldn't lay her in there just in her white, thin nightdress, in the horrible wood-box. So she hunted and hunted, and picked up thing after thing, and threw it aside in the agony of dream-frustration. And in her dream-despair all she could find that would do was a fox-skin. She knew that it wasn't right, that this was not what she should have. But it was all she could find. And so she folded the brush of the fox, and laid her darling Jill's head on this, and she brought round the skin of the fox and laid it on the top of the body, so that it seemed to make a whole ruddy, fiery coverlet, and she cried and cried, and woke to find the tears streaming down her face.

The first thing that both she and Banford did in the morning was to go out to see the fox. Henry had hung it up by the heels in the shed, with its poor brush falling backwards. It was a lovely dog-fox in its prime, with a handsome, thick, winter coat: a lovely golden-red colour, with grey as it passed to the belly, and belly all white, and a great full brush with a delicate black and grey and pure white tip.

'Poor brute!' said Banford. 'If it wasn't such a thieving wretch, you'd feel sorry for it.'

March said nothing, but stood with her foot trailing aside, one hip out; her face was pale and her eyes big and black, watching the dead animal that was suspended

upside down. White and soft as snow his belly: white
and soft as snow. She passed her hand softly down it.
And his wonderful black-glinted brush was full and
frictional, wonderful. She passed her hand down this
also, and quivered. Time after time she took the full fur of
that thick tail between her fingers, and passed her hand
slowly downwards. Wonderful, sharp, thick, splendour
of a tail. And he was dead! She pursed her lips, and her
eyes went black and vacant. Then she took the head in
her hand.

Henry was sauntering up, so Banford walked
rather pointedly away. March stood there bemused, with
the head of the fox in her hand. She was wondering,
wondering, wondering over his long fine muzzle. For
some reason it reminded her of a spoon or a spatula. She
felt she could not understand it. The beast was a strange
beast to her, incomprehensible, out of her range.
Wonderful silver whiskers he had, like ice-threads. And
pricked ears with hair inside. But that long, long, slender
spoon of a nose!—and the marvellous white teeth
beneath! It was to thrust forward and bite with, deep,
deep into the living prey, to bite and bite the blood.

'He's a beauty, isn't he?' said Henry, standing by.

'Oh yes, he's a fine big fox. I wonder how many
chickens he's responsible for,' she replied.

'A good many. Do you think he's the same one you
saw in the summer?'

'I should think very likely he is,' she replied.

He watched her, but he could make nothing of her.
Partly she was so shy and virgin, and partly she was so
grim, matter-of-fact, shrewish. What she said seemed to
him so different from the look of her big, queer, dark
eyes.

'Are you going to skin him?' she asked.

'Yes, when I've had breakfast, and got a board to
peg him on.'

'My word, what a strong smell he's got! Pooo! It'll
take some washing off one's hands. I don't know why I

was so silly as to handle him.' And she looked at her right hand, that had passed down his belly and along his tail, and had even got a tiny streak of blood from one dark place in his fur.

'Have you seen the chickens when they smell him, how frightened they are?' he said.

'Yes, aren't they!'

'You must mind you don't get some of his fleas.'

'Oh, fleas!' she replied, nonchalant.

Later in the day she saw the fox's skin nailed flat on a board, as if crucified. It gave her an uneasy feeling.

The boy was angry. He went about with his mouth shut, as if he had swallowed part of his chin. But in behaviour he was polite and affable. He did not say anything about his intention. And he left March alone.

That evening they sat in the dining-room. Banford wouldn't have him in her sitting-room any more. There was a very big log on the fire. And everybody was busy. Banford had letters to write, March was sewing a dress, and he was mending some little contrivance.

Banford stopped her letter-writing from time to time to look round and rest her eyes. The boy had his head down, his face hidden over his job.

'Let's see,' said Banford. 'What train do you go by, Henry?'

He looked up straight at her.

'The morning train. In the morning,' he said

'What, the eight-ten or the eleven-twenty?'

'The eleven-twenty, I suppose,' he said.

'That is the day after to-morrow?' said Banford.

'Yes, the day after to-morrow.'

'Mm!' murmured Banford, and she returned to her writing. But as she was licking her envelope, she asked:

'And what plans have you made for the future, if I may ask?'

'Plans?' he said, his face very bright and angry.

'I mean about you and Nellie, if you are going on with this business. When do you expect the wedding to come off?' She spoke in a jeering tone.

'Oh, the wedding!' he replied. 'I don't know.'

'Don't you know anything?' said Banford. 'Are you going to clear out on Friday and leave things no more settled than they are?'

'Well, why shouldn't I? We can always write letters.'

'Yes, of course you can. But I wanted to know because of this place. If Nellie is going to get married all of a sudden, I shall have to be looking round for a new partner.'

'Couldn't she stay on here if she were married?' he said. He knew quite well what was coming.

'Oh,' said Banford, 'this is no place for a married couple. There's not enough work to keep a man going, for one thing. And there's no money to be made. It's quite useless your thinking of staying on here if you marry. Absolutely!'

'Yes, but I wasn't thinking of staying on here,' he said.

'Well, that's what I want to know. And what about Nellie, then? How long is *she* going to be here with me, in that case.'

The two antagonists looked at one another.

'That I can't say,' he answered.

'Oh, go along,' she cried petulantly. 'You must have some idea what you are going to do, if you ask a woman to marry you. Unless it's all a hoax.'

'Why should it be a hoax? I am going back to Canada.'

'And taking her with you?'

'Yes, certainly.'

'You hear that, Nellie?' said Banford.

March, who had had her head bent over her sewing, now looked up with a sharp, pink blush on her face, and a queer, sardonic laugh in her eyes and on her twisted mouth.

'That's the first time I've heard that I was going to

Canada,' she said.

'Well, you have to hear it for the first time, haven't you?' said the boy.

'Yes, I suppose I have,' she said nonchalantly. And she went back to her sewing.

'You're quite ready, are you, to go to Canada? Are you, Nellie?' asked Banford.

March looked up again. She let her shoulders go slack, and let her hand that held the needle lie loose in her lap.

'It depends on *how* I'm going,' she said. 'I don't think I want to go jammed up in the steerage, as a soldier's wife. I'm afraid I'm not used to that way.'

The boy watched her with bright eyes.

'Would you rather stay over here while I go first?' he asked.

'I would, if that's the only alternative,' she replied.

'That's much the wisest. Don't make it any fixed engagement,' said Banford. 'Leave yourself free to go or not after he's got back and found you a place, Nellie. Anything else is madness, madness.'

'Don't you think,' said the youth, 'we ought to get married before I go—and then go together, or separate, according to how it happens?'

'I think it's a terrible idea,' cried Banford.

But the boy was watching March.

'What do you think?' he asked her.

She let her eyes stray vaguely into space.

'Well, I don't know,' she said. 'I shall have to think about it.'

'Why?' he asked, pertinently.

'Why?' She repeated his question in a mocking way, and looked at him laughing, though her face was pink again. 'I should think there's plenty of reasons why.'

He watched her in silence. She seemed to have escaped him. She had got into league with Banford against him. There was again the queer sardonic look about her; she would mock stoically at everything he said or which life offered.

'Of course,' he said, 'I don't want to press you to do anything you don't wish to do.'

'I should think not, indeed,' cried Banford indignantly.

At bedtime Banford said plaintively to March:

'You take my hot bottle up for me, Nellie, will you.'

'Yes, I'll do it,' said March, with the kind of willing unwillingness she so often showed towards her beloved but uncertain Jill.

The two women went upstairs. After a time March called from the top of the stairs: 'Good-night, Henry. I shan't be coming down. You'll see to the lamp and the fire, won't you?'

The next day Henry went about with the cloud on his brow and his young cub's face shut up tight. He was cogitating all the time. He had wanted March to marry him and go back to Canada with him. And he had been sure she would do it. Why he wanted her he didn't know. But he did want her. He had set his mind on her. And he was convulsed with a youth's fury at being thwarted. To be thwarted, to be thwarted! It made him so furious inside that he did not know what to do with himself. But he kept himself in hand. Because even now things might turn out differently. She might come over to him. Of course she might. It was her business to do so.

Things drew to a tension again towards evening. He and Banford had avoided each other all day. In fact, Banford went in to the little town by the 11.20 train. It was market day. She arrived back on the 4.25. Just as the night was falling Henry saw her little figure in a dark-blue coat and a dark-blue tam-o'-shanter hat crossing the first meadow from the station. He stood under one of the wild pear-trees, with the old dead leaves round his feet. And he watched the little blue figure advancing persistently over the rough winter-ragged meadow. She had her arms full of parcels, and advanced slowly, frail thing she was, but with that devilish little certainty which he so detested in her. He stood invisible under the pear-tree, watching her every step. And if looks could have affected her, she would have felt a log of iron on each of her ankles as she made her way forward. 'You're a nasty little thing, you are,' he was saying softly, across the distance. 'You're a nasty little thing. I hope you'll be paid back for all the harm you've done me for nothing. I hope you will—you nasty little thing. I hope you'll have to pay for it. You will, if wishes are anything. You nasty little creature that you are.'

She was toiling slowly up the slope. But if she had been slipping back at every step towards the Bottomless Pit, he would not have gone to help her with her parcels. Aha, there went March, striding with her long, land stride in her breeches and her short tunic! Striding down hill at a great pace, and even running a few steps now and then, in her great solicitude and desire to come to the rescue of the little Banford. The boy watched her with rage in his heart. See her leap a ditch, and run, run as if a house was on fire, just to get to that creeping, dark little object down there! So, the Banford just stood still and waited. And March strode up and took *all* the parcels except a bunch of yellow chrysanthemums. These the Banford still carried—yellow chrysanthemums!

'Yes, you look well, don't you,' he said softly into the dusk air. 'You look well, pottering up there with a bunch of flowers, you do. I'd make you eat them for your tea, if you hug them so tight. And I'd give them you for breakfast again, I would. I'd give you flowers. Nothing but flowers.'

He watched the progress of the two women. He could hear their voices: March always outspoken and rather scolding in her tenderness, Banford murmuring rather vaguely. They were evidently good friends. He could not hear what they said till they came to the fence of the home meadow, which they must climb. Then he saw March manfully climbing over the bars with all her packages in her arms, and on the still air he heard

Banford's fretful:

'Why don't you let me help you with the parcels?' She had a queer, plaintive hitch in her voice. Then came March's robust and reckless:

'Oh, I can manage. Don't you bother about me. You've all you can do to get yourself over.'

'Yes, that's all very well,' said Banford fretfully. 'You say, *Don't you bother about me,* and then all the while you feel injured because nobody thinks of you.'

'When do I feel injured?' said March.

'Always. You always feel injured. Now you're feeling injured because I won't have that boy to come and live on the farm.'

'I'm not feeling injured at all,' said March.

'I know you are. When he's gone you'll sulk over it. I know you will.'

'Shall I?' said March. 'We'll see.'

'Yes, we *shall* see, unfortunately. I can't think how you can make yourself so cheap. I can't *imagine* how you can lower yourself like it.'

'I haven't lowered myself,' said March.

'I don't know what you call it, then. Letting a boy like that come so cheeky and impudent and make a mug of you. I don't know what you think of yourself. How much respect do you think he's going to have for you afterwards? My word, I wouldn't be in your shoes, if you married him.'

'Of course you wouldn't. My boots are a good bit too big for you, and not half dainty enough,' said March, with rather a miss-fire sarcasm.

'I thought you had too much pride, really I did. A woman's got to hold herself high, especially with a youth like that. Why, he's impudent. Even the way he forced himself on us at the start.'

'We asked him to stay,' said March.

'Not till he'd almost forced us to. And then he's so cocky and self-assured. My word, he puts my back up. I simply can't imagine how you can let him treat you so cheaply.'

'I don't let him treat me cheaply,' said March. 'Don't you worry yourself, nobody's going to treat me cheaply. And even you aren't either.' She had a tender defiance, and a certain fire in her voice.

'Yes, it's sure to come back to me,' said Banford bitterly. 'That's always the end of it. I believe you only do it to spite me.'

They went now in silence up the steep, grassy slope and over the brow, through the gorse-bushes. On the other side of the hedge the boy followed in the dusk, at some little distance. Now and then, through the huge ancient hedge of hawthorn, risen into trees, he saw the two dark figures creeping up the hill. As he came to the top of the slope he saw the homestead dark in the twilight, with a huge old pear-tree leaning from the near gable, and a little yellow light twinkling in the small side windows of the kitchen. He heard the clink of the latch and saw the kitchen door open into light as the two women went indoors. So, they were at home.

And so!—this was what they thought of him. It was rather in his nature to be a listener, so he was not at all surprised whatever he heard. The things people said about him always missed him personally. He was only rather surprised at the women's way with one another. And he disliked the Banford with an acid dislike. And he felt drawn to the March again. He felt again irresistibly drawn to her. He felt there was a secret bond, a secret thread between him and her, something very exclusive, which shut out everybody else and made him and her possess each other in secret.

He hoped again that she would have him. He hoped with his blood suddenly firing up that she would agree to marry him quite quickly: at Christmas, very likely. Christmas was not far off. He wanted, whatever else happened, to snatch her into a hasty marriage and a consummation with him. Then for the future, they could arrange later. But he hoped it would happen as he

wanted it. He hoped that to-night she would stay a little
while with him, after Banford had gone upstairs. He
hoped he could touch her soft, creamy cheek, her
strange, frightened face. He hoped he could look into her
dilated, frightened dark eyes, quite near. He hoped he
might even put his hand on her bosom and feel her soft
breasts under her tunic. His heart beat deep and powerful as he thought of that. He wanted very much to do so.
He wanted to make sure of her soft woman's breasts
under her tunic. She always kept the brown-linen coat
buttoned so close up to her throat. It seemed to him like
some perilous secret, that her soft woman's breasts must
be buttoned up in that uniform. It seemed to him,
moreover, that they were so much softer, tenderer, more
lovely and lovable, shut up in that tunic, than were the
Banford's breasts, under her soft blouses and chiffon
dresses. The Banford would have little iron breasts, he
said to himself. For all her frailty and fretfulness and
delicacy, she would have tiny iron breasts. But March,
under her crude, fast, workman's tunic, would have soft,
white breasts, white and unseen. So he told himself, and
his blood burned.

When he went into tea, he had a surprise. He
appeared at the inner door, his face very ruddy and vivid
and his blue eyes shining, dropping his head forward as
he came in, in his usual way, and hesitating in the
doorway to watch the inside of the room, keenly and
cautiously, before he entered. He was wearing a long-
sleeved waistcoat. His face seemed extraordinarily like a
piece of the out-of-doors come indoors: as holly-berries
do. In his second of pause in the doorway he took in the
two women sitting at table, at opposite ends, saw them
sharply. And to his amazement March was dressed in a
dress of dull, green silk crape. His mouth came open in
surprise. If she had suddenly grown a moustache he
could not have been more surprised.

'Why,' he said, 'do you wear a dress, then?'

She looked up, flushing a deep rose colour, and

twisting her mouth with a smile, said:

'Of course I do. What else do you expect me to wear, but a dress?'

'A land girl's uniform, of course,' said he.

'Oh,' she cried, nonchalant, 'that's only for this dirty, mucky work about here.'

'Isn't it your proper dress, then?' he said.

'No, not indoors it isn't,' she said. But she was blushing all the time as she poured out his tea. He sat down in his chair at table, unable to take his eyes off her. Her dress was a perfectly simple slip of bluey-green crape, with a line of gold stitching round the top and round the sleeves, which came to the elbow. It was cut just plain and round at the top, and showed her white, soft throat. Her arms he knew, strong and firm muscled, for he had often seen her with her sleeves rolled up. But he looked her up and down, up and down.

Banford, at the other end of the table, said not a word, but piggled with the sardine on her plate. He had forgotten her existence. He just simply stared at March, while he ate his bread and margarine in huge mouthfuls, forgetting even his tea.

'Well, I never knew anything make such a difference!' he murmured, across his mouthfuls.

'Oh goodness!' cried March, blushing still more. 'I might be a pink monkey!'

And she rose quickly to her feet and took the tea-pot to the fire, to the kettle. And as she crouched on the hearth with her green slip about her, the boy stared more wide-eyed than ever. Through the crape her woman's form seemed soft and womanly. And when she stood up and walked he saw her legs move soft within her modernly short skirt. She had on black silk stockings, and small patent shoes with little gold buckles.

No, she was another being. She was something quite different. Seeing her always in the hard-cloth breeches, wide on the hips, buttoned on the knee, strong as armour, and in the brown puttees and thick boots, it had never occurred to him that she had a woman's legs and feet. Now it came upon him. She had a woman's soft, skirted legs, and she was accessible. He blushed to the roots of his hair, shoved his nose in his tea-cup and drank his tea with a little noise that made Banford simply squirm: and strangely, suddenly he felt a man, no longer a youth. He felt a man, with all a man's grave weight of responsibility. A curious quietness and gravity came over his soul. He felt a man, quiet, with a little of the heaviness of male destiny upon him.

She was soft and accessible in her dress. The thought went home in him like an everlasting responsibility.

'Oh, for goodness sake, say something somebody,' cried Banford fretfully. 'It might be a funeral.' The boy looked at her, and she could not bear his face.

'A funeral!' said March, with a twisted smile. 'Why, that breaks my dream.'

Suddenly she had thought of Banford in the wood-box for a coffin.

'What, have you been dreaming of a wedding?' said Banford sarcastically.

'Must have been,' said March.

'Whose wedding?' asked the boy.

'I can't remember,' said March.

She was shy and rather awkward that evening, in spite of the fact that, wearing a dress, her bearing was much more subdued than in her uniform. She felt unpeeled and rather exposed. She felt almost improper.

They talked desultorily about Henry's departure next morning, and made the trivial arrangement. But of the matter on their minds, none of them spoke. They were rather quiet and friendly this evening; Banford had practically nothing to say. But inside herself she seemed still, perhaps kindly.

At nine o'clock March brought in the tray with the everlasting tea and a little cold meat which Banford had managed to procure. It was the last supper, so Banford did not want to be disagreeable. She felt a bit sorry for the boy, and felt she must be as nice as she could.

He wanted her to go to bed. She was usually the first. But she sat on in her chair under the lamp, glancing at her book now and then, and staring into the fire. A deep silence had come into the room. It was broken by March asking, in a rather small tone:

'What time is it, Jill?'

'Five past ten,' said Banford, looking at her wrist.

And then not a sound. The boy had looked up from the book he was holding between his knees. His rather wide, cat-shaped face had its obstinate look, his eyes were watchful.

'What about bed?' said March at last.

'I'm ready when you are,' said Banford.

'Oh, very well,' said March. 'I'll fill your bottle.'

She was as good as her word. When the hot-water bottle was ready, she lit a candle and went upstairs with it. Banford remained in her chair, listening acutely. March came downstairs again.

'There you are, then,' she said. 'Are you going up?'

'Yes, in a minute,' said Banford. But the minute passed, and she sat on in her chair under the lamp.

Henry, whose eyes were shining like a cat's as he watched from under his brows, and whose face seemed wider, more chubbed and cat-like with unalterable obstinacy, now rose to his feet to try his throw.

'I think I'll go and look if I can see the she-fox,' he said. 'She may be creeping round. Won't you come as well for a minute, Nellie, and see if we see anything?'

'Me!' cried March, looking up with her startled, wondering face.

'Yes. Come on,' he said. It was wonderful how soft and warm and coaxing his voice could be, how near. The very sound of it made Banford's blood boil. 'Come on for a minute,' he said, looking down into her uplifted, unsure face.

And she rose to her feet as if drawn up by his young,

ruddy face that was looking down on her.

'I should think you're never going out at this time of night, Nellie!' cried Banford.

'Yes, just for a minute,' said the boy, looking round on her, and speaking with an odd, sharp yelp in his voice.

March looked from one to the other, as if confused, vague. Banford rose to her feet for battle.

'Why, it's ridiculous. It's bitter cold. You'll catch your death in that thin frock. And in those slippers. You're not going to do any such thing.'

There was a moment's pause. Banford turtled up like a little fighting cock, facing March and the boy.

'Oh, I don't think you need worry yourself,' he replied. 'A moment under the stars won't do anybody any damage. I'll get the rug off the sofa in the dining-room. You're coming, Nellie.'

His voice had so much anger and contempt and fury in it as he spoke to Banford: and so much tenderness and proud authority as he spoke to March, that the latter answered:

'Yes, I'm coming.'

And she turned with him to the door.

Banford, standing there in the middle of the room, suddenly burst into a long wail and a spasm of sobs. She covered her face with her poor, thin hands, and her thin shoulders shook in an agony of weeping. March looked back from the door.

'Jill!' she cried in a frantic tone, like someone just coming awake. And she seemed to start towards her darling.

But the boy had March's arm in his grip, and she could not move. She did not know why she could not move. It was as in a dream when the heart strains and the body cannot stir.

'Never mind,' said the boy softly. 'Let her cry. Let her cry. She will have to cry sooner or later. And the tears will relieve her feelings. They will do her good.'

So he drew March slowly through the doorway. But

her last look was back to the poor little figure which stood in the middle of the room with covered face and thin shoulders shaken with bitter weeping.

In the dining-room he picked up the rug and said:

'Wrap yourself up in this.'

She obeyed–and they reached the kitchen door, he holding her soft and firm by the arm, though she did not know it. When she saw the night outside she started back.

'I must go back to Jill,' she said. 'I *must*! Oh yes, I must.'

Her tone sounded final. The boy let go of her and she turned indoors. But he seized her again and arrested her.

'Wait a minute,' he said. 'Wait a minute. Even if you go, you're not going yet.'

'Leave go! Leave go!' she cried. 'My place is at Jill's side. Poor little thing, she's sobbing her heart out.'

'Yes,' said the boy bitterly. 'And your heart too, and mine as well.'

'Your heart?' said March. He still gripped her and detained her.

'Isn't it as good as her heart?' he said. 'Or do you think it's not?'

'Your heart?' she said again, incredulous.

'Yes, mine! Mine! Do you think I haven't *got* a heart?' And with his hot grasp he took her hand and pressed it under his left breast. 'There's my heart,' he said, 'if you don't believe in it.'

It was wonder which made her attend. And then she felt the deep, heavy, powerful stroke of his heart, terrible, like something from beyond. It was like something from beyond, something awful from outside, signalling to her. And the signal paralysed her. It beat upon her very soul, and made her helpless. She forgot Jill. She could not think of Jill any more. She could not think of her. That terrible signalling from outside!

The boy put his arm round her waist.

'Come with me,' he said gently. 'Come and let us say what we've got to say.'

And he drew her outside, closed the door. And she went with him darkly down the garden path. That he should have a beating heart! And that he should have his arm round her, outside the blanket! She was too confused to think who he was or what he was.

He took her to a dark corner of the shed, where there was a tool-box with a lid, long and low.

'We'll sit here a minute,' he said.

And obediently she sat down by his side.

'Give me your hand,' he said.

She gave him both her hands, and he held them between his own. He was young, and it made him tremble.

'You'll marry me. You'll marry me before I go back, won't you?' he pleaded.

'Why, aren't we both a pair of fools?' she said.

He had put her in the corner, so that she should not look out and see the lighted window of the house, across the dark yard and garden. He tried to keep her all there inside the shed with him.

'In what way a pair of fools?' he said. 'If you go back to Canada with me, I've got a job and a good wage waiting for me, and it's a nice place, near the mountains. Why shouldn't you marry me? Why shouldn't we marry? I should like to have you there with me. I should like to feel I'd got somebody there, at the back of me, all my life.'

'You'd easily find somebody else who'd suit you better,' she said.

'Yes, I might easily find another girl. I know I could. But not one I really wanted. I've never met one I really wanted, for good. You see, I'm thinking of all my life. If I marry, I want to feel it's for all my life. Other girls: well, they're just girls, nice enough to go a walk with now and then. Nice enough for a bit of play. But when I think of my life, then I should be very sorry to have to marry one of them, I should indeed.'

'You mean they wouldn't make you a good wife.'

'Yes, I mean that. But I don't mean they wouldn't do their duty by me. I mean–I don't know what I mean. Only when I think of my life, and of you, then the two things go together.'

'And what if they didn't?' she said, with her odd, sardonic touch.

'Well, I think they would.'

They sat for some time silent. He held her hands in his, but he did not make love to her. Since he had realised that she was a woman, and vulnerable, accessible, a certain heaviness had possessed his soul. He did not want to make love to her. He shrank from any such performance, almost with fear. She was a woman, and vulnerable, accessible to him finally, and he held back from that which was ahead, almost with dread. It was a kind of darkness he knew he would enter finally, but of which he did not want as yet even to think. She was the woman, and he was responsible for the strange vulnerability he had suddenly realised in her.

'No,' she said at last, 'I'm a fool. I know I'm a fool.'

'What for?' he asked.

'To go on with this business.'

'Do you mean me?' he asked.

'No, I mean myself. I'm making a fool of myself, and a big one.'

'Why, because you don't want to marry me, really?'

'Oh, I don't know whether I'm against it, as a matter of fact. That's just it. I don't know.'

He looked at her in the darkness, puzzled. He did not in the least know what she meant.

'And don't you know whether you like to sit here with me this minute, or not?' he asked.

'No, I don't really. I don't know whether I wish I was somewhere else, or whether I like being here. I don't know, really.'

'Do you wish you were with Miss Banford? Do you

wish you'd gone to bed with her?' he asked, as a challenge.

She waited a long time before she answered:

'No,' she said at last. 'I don't wish that.'

'And do you think you would spend all your life with her—when your hair goes white, and you are old?' he said.

'No,' she said, without much hesitation. 'I don't see Jill and me two old women together.'

'And don't you think, when I'm an old man and you're an old woman, we might be together still, as we are now?' he said.

'Well, not as we are now,' she replied. 'But I could imagine—no, I can't. I can't imagine you an old man. Besides, it's dreadful!'

'What, to be an old man?'

'Yes, of course.'

'Not when the time comes,' he said. 'But it hasn't come. Only it will. And when it does, I should like to think you'd be there as well.'

'Sort of old age pensioners,' she said drily.

Her kind of witless humour always startled him. He never knew what she meant. Probably she didn't quite know herself.

'No,' he said, hurt.

'I don't know why you harp on old age,' she said. 'I'm not ninety.'

'Did anybody ever say you were?' he asked, offended.

They were silent for some time, pulling different ways in the silence.

'I don't want you to make fun of me,' he said.

'Don't you?' she replied, enigmatic.

'No, because just this minute I'm serious. And when I'm serious, I believe in not making fun of it.'

'You mean nobody else must make fun of you,' she replied.

'Yes, I mean that. And I mean I don't believe in

making fun of it myself. When it comes over me so that I'm serious, then–there it is, I don't want it to be laughed at.'

She was silent for some time. Then she said, in a vague, almost pained voice:

'No, I'm not laughing at you.'

A hot wave rose in his heart.

'You believe me, do you?' he asked.

'Yes, I believe you,' she replied, with a twang of her old tired nonchalance, as if she gave in because she was tired. But he didn't care. His heart was hot and clamorous.

'So you agree to marry me before I go?–perhaps at Christmas?'

'Yes, I agree.'

'There!' he exclaimed. 'That's settled it.'

And he sat silent, unconscious, with all the blood burning in all his veins, like fire in all the branches and twigs of him. He only pressed her two hands to his chest, without knowing. When the curious passion began to die down, he seemed to come awake to the world.

'We'll go in, shall we?' he said: as if he realised it was cold.

She rose without answering.

'Kiss me before we go, now you've said it,' he said.

And he kissed her gently on the mouth, with a young, frightened kiss. It made her feel so young, too, and frightened, and wondering: and tired, tired, as if she were going to sleep.

They went indoors. And in the sitting-room, there, crouched by the fire like a queer little witch, was Banford. She looked round with reddened eyes as they entered, but did not rise. He thought she looked frightening, unnatural, crouching there and looking round at them. Evil he thought her look was, and he crossed his fingers.

Banford saw the ruddy, elate face of the youth: he seemed strangely tall and bright and looming. And

March had a delicate look on her face; she wanted to hide her face, to screen it, to let it not be seen.

'You've come at last,' said Banford uglily.

'Yes, we've come,' said he.

'You've been long enough for anything,' she said.

'Yes, we have. We've settled it. We shall marry as soon as possible,' he replied.

'Oh, you've settled it, have you! Well, I hope you won't live to repent it,' said Banford.

'I hope so too,' he replied.

'Are you going to bed *now*, Nellie?' said Banford.

'Yes, I'm going now.'

'Then for goodness sake come along.'

March looked at the boy. He was glancing with his very bright eyes at her and at Banford. March looked at him wistfully. She wished she could stay with him. She wished she had married him already, and it was all over. For oh, she felt suddenly so safe with him. She felt so strangely safe and peaceful in his presence. If only she could sleep in his shelter, and not with Jill. She felt afraid of Jill. In her dim, tender state, it was agony to have to go with Jill and sleep with her. She wanted the boy to save her. She looked again at him.

And he, watching with bright eyes, divined something of what she felt. It puzzled and distressed him that she must go with Jill.

'I shan't forget what you've promised,' he said, looking clear into her eyes, right into her eyes, so that he seemed to occupy all her self with his queer, bright look.

She smiled to him, faintly, gently. She felt safe again–safe with him.

But in spite of all the boy's precautions, he had a set-back. The morning he was leaving the farm he got March to accompany him to the market-town, about six miles away, where they went to the registrar and had their names stuck up as two people who were going to marry. He was to come at Christmas, and the wedding was to take place then. He hoped in the spring to be able to take March back to Canada with him, now the war was really over. Though he was so young, he had saved some money.

'You never have to be without *some* money at the back of you, if you can help it,' he said.

So she saw him off in the train that was going West: his camp was on Salisbury Plain. And with big, dark eyes she watched him go, and it seemed as if everything real in life was retreating as the train retreated with his queer, chubby, ruddy face, that seemed so broad across the cheeks, and which never seemed to change its expression, save when a cloud of sulky anger hung on the brow, or the bright eyes fixed themselves in their stare. This was what happened now. He leaned there out of the carriage window as the train drew off, saying good-bye and staring back at her, but his face quite unchanged. There was no emotion on his face. Only his eyes tightened and became fixed and intent in their watching like a cat's when suddenly she sees something and stares. So the boy's eyes stared fixedly as the train drew away, and she was left feeling intensely forlorn. Failing his physical presence, she seemed to have nothing of him. And she had nothing of anything. Only his face was fixed in her mind: the full, ruddy, unchanging cheeks, and the straight snout of a nose, and the two eyes staring above. All she could remember was how he suddenly wrinkled his nose when he laughed, as a puppy does when he is playfully growling. But him, himself, and what he was—she knew nothing, she had nothing of him when he left her.

On the ninth day after he had left her he received this letter.

'Dear Henry,

I have been over it all again in my mind, this business of me and you, and it seems to me impossible. When you aren't there I see what a fool I am. When you are there you seem to blind me to things as they actually are. You make me see things all unreal, and I don't know what. Then when I am alone again with Jill I seem to come to my own senses and realise what a fool I am making of myself, and how I am treating you unfairly. Because it must be unfair to you for me to go on with this affair when I can't feel in my heart that I really love you. I know people talk a lot of stuff and nonsense about love, and I don't want to do that. I want to keep to plain facts and act in a sensible way. And that seems to me what I'm not doing. I don't see on what grounds I am going to marry you. I know I am not head over heels in love with you, as I have fancied myself to be with fellows when I was a young fool of a girl. You are an absolute stranger to me, and it seems to me you will always be one. So on what grounds am I going to marry you? When I think of Jill, she is ten times more real to me. I know her and I'm awfully fond of her, and I hate myself for a beast if I ever hurt her little finger. We have a life together. And even if it can't last for ever, it is a life while it does last. And it might last as long as either of us lives. Who knows how long we've got to live? She is a delicate little thing, perhaps nobody but me knows how delicate. And as for me, I feel I might fall down the well any day. What I don't seem to see at all is you. When I think of what I've been and what I've done with you, I'm afraid I am a few screws loose. I should be sorry to think that softening of the brain is setting in so soon, but that is what it seems like. You are such an absolute stranger, and so different from what I'm used to, and we don't seem to have a thing in common. As for love, the very word seems impossible. I know what love means even in Jill's case, and I know that in this affair with you it's an absolute impossibility. And then going to Canada. I'm sure I must have been clean off my chump when I promised such a thing. It makes me feel fairly frightened of myself. I feel I might do something really silly, that I wasn't responsible for—and end my days in a lunatic asylum. You may think that's all I'm fit for after the way I've gone on, but it isn't a very nice thought for me. Thank goodness Jill is here, and her being here makes me feel sane again, else I don't know what I might do; I might have an accident with the gun one evening. I love Jill, and she makes me feel safe and sane, with her loving anger against me for being such a fool. Well, what I want to say is, won't you let us cry the whole thing off? I can't marry you, and really, I won't do such a thing if it seems to me wrong. It is all a great mistake. I've made a complete fool of myself, and all I can do is to apologise to you and ask you please to forget it, and please to take no further notice of me. Your fox skin is nearly ready, and seems all right. I will post it to you if you will let me know if this address is still right, and if you will accept my apology for the awful and lunatic way I have behaved with you, and then let the matter rest.

Jill sends her kindest regards. Her mother and father are staying with us over Christmas.

Yours very sincerely,
Ellen March.'

The boy read this letter in camp as he was cleaning his kit. He set his teeth, and for a moment went almost pale, yellow round the eyes with fury. He said nothing and saw nothing and felt nothing but a livid rage that was quite unreasoning. Balked! Balked again! Balked! He wanted the woman, he had fixed like doom upon having her. He felt that was his doom, his destiny, and his reward, to have this woman. She was his heaven and hell on earth, and he would have none elsewhere. Sightless with rage and thwarted madness he got through the morning. Save that in his mind he was lurking and scheming towards an issue, he would have committed some insane act. Deep in himself he felt like roaring and howling and gnashing his teeth and breaking things. But he was too intelligent. He knew society was on top of him, and he must scheme. So with his teeth bitten together, and his nose curiously slightly lifted, like some creature that is vicious, and his eyes fixed and staring, he went through the morning's affairs drunk with anger and suppression. In his mind was one thing–Banford. He took no heed of all March's outpouring: none. One thorn rankled, stuck in his mind. Banford. In his mind, in his soul, in his whole being, one thorn rankling to insanity. And he would have to get it out. He would have to get the thorn of Banford out of his life, if he died for it.

With this one fixed idea in his mind, he went to ask for twenty-four hours' leave of absence. He knew it was not due to him. His consciousness was supernaturally keen. He knew where he must go–he must go to the captain. But how could he get at the captain? In that great camp of wooden huts and tents he had no idea where his captain was.

But he went to the officers' canteen. There was his captain standing talking with three other officers. Henry stood in the doorway at attention.

'May I speak to Captain Berryman?' The captain was Cornish like himself.

'What do you want?' called the captain.

'May I speak to you, Captain?'

'What do you want?' replied the captain, not stirring from among his group of fellow officers.

Henry watched his superior for a minute without speaking.

'You won't refuse me, sir, will you?' he asked gravely.

'It depends what it is.'

'Can I have twenty-four hours' leave?'

'No, you've no business to ask.'

'I know I haven't. But I must ask you.'

'You've had your answer.'

'Don't send me away, Captain.'

There was something strange about the boy as he stood there so everlasting in the doorway. The Cornish captain felt the strangeness at once, and eyed him shrewdly.

'Why, what's afoot?' he said, curious.

'I'm in trouble about something. I must go to Blewbury,' said the boy.

'Blewbury, eh? After the girls?'

'Yes, it is a woman, Captain.' And the boy, as he stood there with his head reaching forward a little, went suddenly terribly pale, or yellow, and his lips seemed to give off pain. The captain saw and paled a little also. He turned aside.

'Go on, then,' he said. 'But for God's sake don't cause any trouble of any sort.'

'I won't Captain, thank you.'

He was gone. The captain, upset, took a gin and bitters. Henry managed to hire a bicycle. It was twelve o'clock when he left the camp. He had sixty miles of wet and muddy cross-roads to ride. But he was in the saddle and down the road without a thought of food.

At the farm, March was busy with a work she had had some time in hand. A bunch of Scotch fir-trees stood at the end of the open shed, on a little bank where ran the fence between two of the gorse-shaggy meadows. The furthest of these trees was dead—it had died in the summer, and stood with all its needles brown and sere in the air. It was not a very big tree. And it was absolutely dead. So March determined to have it, although they were not allowed to cut any of the timber. But it would make such splendid firing, in these days of scarce fuel.

She had been giving a few stealthy chops at the trunk for a week or more, every now and then hacking away for five minutes, low down, near the ground, so no one should notice. She had not tried the saw, it was such hard work, alone. Now the tree stood with a great yawning gap in his base, perched as it were on one sinew, and ready to fall. But he did not fall.

It was late in the damp December afternoon, with cold mists creeping out of the woods and up the hollows, and darkness waiting to sink in from above. There was a bit of yellowness where the sun was fading away beyond the low woods of the distance. March took her axe and went to the tree. The small thud-thud of her blows resounded rather ineffectual about the wintry homestead. Banford came out wearing her thick coat, but with no hat on her head, so that her thin, bobbed hair blew on the uneasy wind that sounded in the pines and in the wood.

'What I'm afraid of,' said Banford, 'is that it will fall on the shed and we sh'll have another job repairing that.'

'Oh, I don't think so,' said March, straightening herself and wiping her arm over her hot brow. She was flushed red, her eyes were very wide-open and queer, her upper lip lifted away from her two white, front teeth with a curious, almost rabbit-look.

A little stout man in a black overcoat and a bowler hat came pottering across the yard. He had a pink face and a white beard and smallish, pale-blue eyes. He was not very old, but nervy, and he walked with little short steps.

'What do you think, father?' said Banford. 'Don't you think it might hit the shed in falling?'

'Shed, no!' said the old man. 'Can't hit the shed. Might as well say the fence.'

'The fence doesn't matter,' said March, in her high voice.

'Wrong as usual, am I!' said Banford, wiping her straying hair from her eyes.

The tree stood as it were on one spelch of itself, leaning, and creaking in the wind. It grew on the bank of a little dry ditch between the two meadows. On the top of the bank straggled one fence, running to the bushes uphill. Several trees clustered there in the corner of the field near the shed and near the gate which led into the yard. Towards this gate, horizontal across the weary meadows, came the grassy, rutted approach from the high road. There trailed another ricketty fence, long split poles joining the short, thick, wide-apart uprights. The three people stood at the back of the tree, in the corner of the shed meadow, just above the yard gate. The house, with its two gables and its porch, stood tidy in a little grassed garden across the yard. A little, stout, rosy-faced woman in a little red woollen shoulder shawl had come and taken her stand in the porch.

'Isn't it down yet,' she cried, in a high little voice.

'Just thinking about it,' called her husband. His tone towards the two girls was always rather mocking and satirical. March did not want to go on with her hitting while he was there. As for him, he wouldn't lift a stick from the ground if he could help it, complaining, like his daughter, of rheumatics in his shoulder. So the three stood there a moment silent in the cold afternoon, in the bottom corner near the yard.

They heard the far-off taps of a gate, and craned to look. Away across, on the green horizontal approach, a figure was just swinging on to a bicycle again, and lurching up and down over the grass, approaching.

'Why, it's one of our boys–it's Jack,' said the old man.

'Can't be,' said Banford.

March craned her head to look. She alone recognised the khaki figure. She flushed, but said nothing.

'No, it isn't Jack, I don't think,' said the old man, staring with little round blue eyes under his white lashes.

In another moment the bicycle lurched into sight, and the rider dropped off at the gate. It was Henry, his face wet and red and spotted with mud. He was altogether a muddy sight.

'Oh!' cried Banford, as if afraid. 'Why, it's Henry!'

'What!' muttered the old man. He had a thick, rapid, muttering way of speaking, and was slightly deaf. 'What? What? Who is it? Who is it, do you say? That young fellow? That young fellow of Nellie's? Oh! Oh!' And the satiric smile came on his pink face and white eyelashes.

Henry, pushing the wet hair off his steaming brow, had caught sight of them and heard what the old man said. His hot, young face seemed to flame in the cold light.

'Oh, are you all there!' he said, giving his sudden, puppy's little laugh. He was so hot and dazed with cycling he hardly knew where he was. He leaned the bicycle against the fence and climbed over into the corner on to the bank, without going into the yard.

'Well, I must say, we weren't expecting *you*,' said Banford laconically.

'No, I suppose not,' said he, looking at March.

She stood aside, slack, with one knee drooped and the axe resting its head loosely on the ground. Her eyes were wide and vacant, and her upper lip lifted from her teeth in that helpless, fascinated rabbit-look. The moment she saw his glowing, red face it was all over with her. She was as helpless as if she had been bound. The moment she saw the way his head seemed to reach forward.

'Well, who is it? Who is it, anyway?' asked the smiling, satiric old man in his muttering voice.

'Why, Mr Grenfel, whom you've heard us tell about, father,' said Banford coldly.

'Heard you tell about, I should think so. Heard of nothing else practically,' muttered the elderly man, with his queer little jeering smile on his face. 'How do you do,' he added, suddenly reaching out his hand to Henry.

The boy shook hands just as startled. Then the two men fell apart.

'Cycled over from Salisbury Plain, have you?' asked the old man.

'Yes.'

'Hm! Longish ride. How long d'it take you, eh? Some time, eh? Several hours, I suppose.'

'About four.'

'Eh? Four! Yes, I should have thought so. When are you going back, then?'

'I've got till to-morrow evening.'

'Till to-morrow evening, eh? Yes. Hm! Girls weren't expecting you, were they?'

And the old man turned his pale-blue, round little eyes under their white lashes mockingly towards the girls. Henry also looked round. He had become a little awkward. He looked at March, who was still staring away into the distance as if to see where the cattle were. Her hand was on the pommel of the axe, whose head rested loosely on the ground.

'What were you doing there?' he asked in his soft, courteous voice. 'Cutting a tree down?'

March seemed not to hear, as if in a trance.

'Yes,' said Banford. 'We've been at it for over a week.'

'Oh! And have you done it all by yourselves then?'

'Nellie's done it all, I've done nothing,' said Banford.

'Really! You must have worked quite hard,' he said, addressing himself in a curious gentle tone direct to March. She did not answer, but remained half averted staring away towards the woods above as if in a trance.

'*Nellie!*' cried Banford sharply. 'Can't you answer?'

'What—me?' cried March, starting round, and looking from one to the other. 'Did anyone speak to me?'

'Dreaming!' muttered the old man, turning aside to smile. 'Must be in love, eh, dreaming in the day-time!'

'Did you say anything to me?' said March, looking at the boy as from a strange distance, her eyes wide and doubtful, her face delicately flushed.

'I said you must have worked hard at the tree,' he replied courteously.

'Oh that! Bit by bit. I thought it would have come down by now.'

'I'm thankful it hasn't come down in the night, to frighten us to death,' said Banford.

'Let me just finish it for you, shall I?' said the boy.

March slanted the axe-shaft in his direction.

'Would you like to?' she said.

'Yes, if you wish it,' he said.

'Oh, I'm thankful when the thing's down, that's all,'

she replied, nonchalant.

'Which way is it going to fall?' said Banford. 'Will it hit the shed?'

'No, it won't hit the shed,' he said. 'I should think it will fall there—quite clear. Though it might give a twist and catch the fence.'

'Catch the fence!' cried the old man. 'What, catch the fence! When it's leaning at that angle? Why, it's further off than the shed. It won't catch the fence.'

'No,' said Henry, 'I don't suppose it will. It has plenty of room to fall quite clear, and I suppose it will fall clear.'

'Won't tumble backwards on top of *us*, will it?' asked the old man, sarcastic.

'No, it won't do that,' said Henry, taking off his short overcoat and his tunic. 'Ducks! Ducks! Go back!'

A line of four brown-speckled ducks led by a brown-and-green drake were stemming away downhill from the upper meadow, coming like boats running on a ruffled sea, cockling their way top speed downwards towards the fence and towards the little group of people, and cackling as excitedly as if they brought news of the Spanish Armada.

'Silly things! Silly things!' cried Banford, going forward to turn them off. But they came eagerly towards her, opening their yellow-green beaks and quacking as if they were so excited to say something.

'There's no food. There's nothing here. You must wait a bit,' said Banford to them. 'Go away. Go away. Go round to the yard.'

They didn't go, so she climbed the fence to swerve them round under the gate and into the yard. So off they waggled in an excited string once more, wagging their rumps like the stems of little gondolas, ducking under the bar of the gate. Banford stood on the top of the bank, just over the fence, looking down on the other three.

Henry looked up at her, and met her queer, round-pupilled, weak eyes staring behind her spectacles. He was perfectly still. He looked away, up at the weak, leaning tree. And as he looked into the sky, like a huntsman who is watching a flying bird, he thought to himself: 'If the tree falls in just such a way, and spins just so much as it falls, then the branch there will strike her exactly as she stands on top of that bank.'

He looked at her again. She was wiping the hair from her brow again, with that perpetual gesture. In his heart he had decided her death. A terrible still force seemed in him, and a power that was just his. If he turned even a hair's breadth in the wrong direction, he would lose the power.

'Mind yourself, Miss Banford,' he said. And his heart held perfectly still, in the terrible pure will that she should not move.

'Who, me, mind myself?' she cried, her father's jeering tone in her voice. 'Why, do you think you might hit me with the axe?'

'No, it's just possible the tree might, though,' he answered soberly. But the tone of his voice seemed to her to imply that he was only being falsely solicitous, and trying to make her move because it was his will to move her.

'Absolutely impossible,' she said.

He heard her. But he held himself icy still, lest he should lose his power.

'No, it's just possible. You'd better come down this way.'

'Oh, all right. Let us see some crack Canadian tree felling,' she retorted.

'Ready, then,' he said, taking the axe, looking round to see he was clear.

There was a moment of pure, motionless suspense, when the world seemed to stand still. Then suddenly his form seemed to flash up enormously tall and fearful, he gave two swift, flashing blows, in immediate succession, the tree was severed, turning slowly, spinning strangely in the air and coming down like a sudden darkness on the earth. No one saw what was happening except himself. No one heard the strange little cry which the Banford gave as the dark end of the bough swooped down, down on her. No one saw her crouch a little and receive the blow on the back of the neck. No one saw her flung outwards and laid, a little twitching heap, at the foot of the fence. No one except the boy. And he watched with intense bright eyes, as he would watch a wild goose he had shot. Was it winged, or dead? Dead!

Immediately he gave a loud cry. Immediately March gave a wild shriek that went far, far down the afternoon. And the father started a strange bellowing sound.

The boy leapt the fence and ran to the figure. The back of the neck and head was a mass of blood, of horror. He turned it over. The body was quivering with little convulsions. But she was dead really. He knew it, that it was so. He knew it in his soul and his blood. The inner necessity of his life was fulfilling itself, it was he who was to live. The thorn was drawn out of his bowels. So he put her down gently. She was dead.

He stood up. March was standing there petrified and absolutely motionless. Her face was dead white, her eyes big black pools. The old man was scrambling horribly over the fence.

'I'm afraid it's killed her,' said the boy.

The old man was making curious, blubbering noises as he huddled over the fence. 'What!' cried March, starting electric.

'Yes, I'm afraid,' repeated the boy.

March was coming forward. The boy was over the fence before she reached it.

'What do you say, killed her?' she asked in a sharp voice.

'I'm afraid so,' he answered softly.

She went still whiter, fearful. The two stood facing one another. Her black eyes gazed on him with the last look of resistance. And then in a last agonised failure she began to grizzle, to cry in a shivery little fashion of a child that doesn't want to cry, but which is beaten from within, and gives that little first shudder of sobbing which is not yet weeping, dry and fearful.

He had won. She stood there absolutely helpless, shuddering her dry sobs and her mouth trembling rapidly. And then, as in a child, with a little crash came the tears and the blind agony of sightless weeping. She sank down on the grass, and sat there with her hands on her breast and her face lifted in sightless, convulsed weeping. He stood above her, looking down on her, mute, pale, and everlasting seeming. He never moved, but looked down on her. And among all the torture of the scene, the torture of his own heart and bowels, he was glad, he had won.

After a long time he stooped to her and took her hands.

'Don't cry,' he said softly. 'Don't cry.'

She looked up at him with tears running from her eyes, a senseless look of helplessness and submission. So she gazed on him as if sightless, yet looking up to him. She would never leave him again. He had won her. And he knew it and was glad, because he wanted her for his life. His life must have her. And now he had won her. It was what his life must have.

But if he had won her, he had not yet got her. They were married at Christmas as he had planned, and he got again ten days leave. They went to Cornwall, to his own village, on the sea. He realised that it was awful for her to be at the farm any more.

But though she belonged to him, though she lived in his shadow, as if she could not be away from him, she was not happy. She did not want to leave him: and yet she did not feel free with him. Everything around her seemed to watch her, seemed to press on her. He had won her, he had her with him, she was his wife. And she—she belonged to him, she knew it. But she was not glad. And he was still foiled. He realised that though he was married to her and possessed her in every possible way, apparently, and though she *wanted* him to possess her, she wanted it, she wanted nothing else, now, still he did not quite succeed.

Something was missing. Instead of her soul swaying with new life, it seemed to droop, to bleed, as if it were wounded. She would sit for a long time with her hand in his, looking away at the sea. And in her dark, vacant eyes was a sort of wound, and her face looked a little peaked. If he spoke to her, she would turn to him with a faint new smile, the strange, quivering little smile of a woman who has died in the old way of love, and can't quite rise to the new way. She still felt she ought to *do* something, to strain herself in some direction. And there was nothing to do, and no direction in which to strain herself. And she could not quite accept the submergence which his new love put upon her. If she was in love, she ought to *exert* herself, in some way, loving. She felt the weary need of our day to *exert* herself in love. But she knew that in fact she must no more exert herself in love. He would not have the love which exerted itself towards him. It made his brow go black. No, he wouldn't let her exert her love towards him. No, she had to be passive, to acquiesce, and to be submerged under the surface of love. She had to be like the seaweeds she saw as she peered down from the boat, swaying forever delicately under water, with all their delicate fibrils put tenderly out upon the flood, sensitive, utterly sensitive and receptive within the shadowy sea, and never, never rising and looking forth above water while they lived. Never. Never looking forth from the water until they died, only then washing, corpses, upon the surface. But while they lived, always submerged, always beneath the wave. Beneath the wave they might have powerful roots, stronger than iron; they might be tenacious and dangerous in their soft waving within the flood. Beneath the water they might be stronger, more indestructible than resistant oak trees are on land. But it was always under-water, always under-water. And she, being a woman, must be like that.

And she had been so used to the very opposite. She had had to take all the thought for love and for life, and all the responsibility. Day after day she had been responsible for the coming day, for the coming year: for her dear Jill's health and happiness and well-being. Verily, in her own small way, she had felt herself responsible for the well-being of the world. And this had been her great stimulant, this grand feeling that, in her own small sphere, she was responsible for the well-being of the world.

And she had failed. She knew that, even in her small way, she had failed. She had failed to satisfy her own feeling of responsibility. It was so difficult. It seemed so grand and easy at first. And the more you tried, the more difficult it became. It had seemed so easy to make one beloved creature happy. And the more you tried, the worse the failure. It was terrible. She had been all her life reaching, reaching, and what she reached for seemed so near, until she had stretched to her utmost limit. And then it was always beyond her.

Always beyond her, vaguely, unrealisably beyond her, and she was left with nothingness at last. The life she reached for, the happiness she reached for, the well-being she reached for all slipped back, became unreal, the further she stretched her hand. She wanted some goal, some finality—and there was none. Always this ghastly reaching, reaching, striving for something that might be just beyond. Even to make Jill happy. She was glad Jill was dead. For she had realised that she could never make her happy. Jill would always be fretting herself thinner and thinner, weaker and weaker. Her pains grew worse instead of less. It would be so for ever. She was glad she was dead.

And if Jill had married a man it would have been just the same. The woman striving, striving to make the man happy, striving within her own limits for the well-being of her world. And always achieving failure. Little, foolish successes in money or in ambition. But at the very point where she most wanted success, in the anguished effort to make some one beloved human being happy and perfect, there the failure was almost catastrophic. You wanted to make your beloved happy, and his happiness seemed always achievable. If only you did just this, that and the other. And you did this, that, and the other, in all good faith, and every time the failure became a little more ghastly. You could love yourself to ribbons, and strive and strain yourself to the bone, and things would go from bad to worse, bad to worse, as far as happiness went. The awful mistake of happiness.

Poor March, in her goodwill and her responsibility, she had strained herself till it seemed to her that the whole of life and everything was only a horrible abyss of nothingness. The more you reached after the fatal flower of happiness, which trembles so blue and lovely in a crevice just beyond your grasp, the more fearfully you become aware of the ghastly and awful gulf of the precipice below you, into which you will inevitably plunge, as into the bottomless pit, if you reach any further. You pluck flower after flower—it is never *the* flower. The flower itself—its calyx is a horrible gulf, it is the bottomless pit.

That is the whole history of the search for happiness, whether it be your own or somebody else's that you want to win. It ends, and it always ends, in the ghastly sense of the bottomless nothingness into which you will inevitably fall if you strain any further.

And women?—what goal can any woman conceive, except happiness? Just happiness, for herself and the whole world. That, and nothing else. And so, she assumes the responsibility, and sets off towards her goal. She can see it there, at the foot of the rainbow. Or she can see it a little way beyond, in the blue distance. Not far, not far.

But the end of the rainbow is a bottomless gulf down which you can fall forever without arriving, and the blue distance is a void pit which can swallow you and all your efforts into its emptiness, and still be no emptier. You and all your efforts. So, the illusion of attainable happiness!

Poor March, she had set off so wonderfully towards the blue goal. And the further and further she had gone, the more fearful had become the realisation of emptiness. An agony, an insanity at last.

She was glad it was over. She was glad to sit on the shore and look westwards over the sea, and know the great strain had ended. She would never strain for love and happiness any more. And Jill was safely dead. Poor Jill, poor Jill. It must be sweet to be dead.

For her own part, death was not her destiny. She would have to leave her destiny to the boy. But then, the boy. He wanted more than that. He wanted her to give herself without defences, to sink and become submerged in him. And she—she wanted to sit still, like a woman on the last milestone, and watch. She wanted to be alone: with him at her side.

And he! He did not want her to watch any more, to see any more, to understand any more. He wanted to veil her woman's spirit, as Orientals veil the woman's face. He wanted her to commit herself to him, and to put her independent spirit to sleep. He wanted to take away from her all her effort, all that seemed her very *raison d'être*. He wanted to make her submit, yield, blindly pass away out of all her strenuous consciousness. He wanted to take away her consciousness, and make her just his woman. Just his woman.

And she was so tired, so tired, like a child that wants to go to sleep, but which fights against sleep as if sleep were death. She seemed to stretch her eyes wider in the obstinate effort and tension of keeping awake. She *would* keep awake. She *would* know. She *would* consider and judge and decide. She *would* have the reins of her own life between her own hands. She *would* be an independent woman, to the last. But she was so tired, so tired of everything. And sleep seemed near. And there was such rest in the boy.

Yet there, sitting in a niche of the high, wild cliffs of West Cornwall, looking over the westward sea, she stretched her eyes wider and wider. Away to the West, Canada, America. She *would* know and she *would* see what was ahead. And the boy, sitting beside her, staring down at the gulls, had a cloud between his brows and the strain of discontent in his eyes. He wanted her asleep, at peace in him. He wanted her at peace, asleep in him. And *there* she was, dying with the strain of her own wakefulness. Yet she would not sleep: no, never. Sometimes he thought bitterly that he ought to have left her. He ought never to have killed Banford. He should have left Banford and March to kill one another.

But that was only impatience: and he knew it. He was waiting, waiting to go west. He was aching almost in torment to leave England, to go west, to take March away. To leave this shore! He believed that as they crossed the seas, as they left this England which he so hated, because in some way it seemed to have stung him with poison, she would go to sleep. She would close her eyes at last, and give in to him.

And then he would have her, and he would have his own life at last. He chafed, feeling he hadn't got his own life. He would never have it till she yielded and slept in him. Then he would have all his own life as a young man and a male, and she would have all her own life as a woman and a female. There would be no more of this awful straining. She would not be a man any more, an independent woman with a man's responsibility. Nay, even the responsibility for her own soul she would have to commit to him. He knew it was so, and obstinately held out against her, waiting for the surrender.

'You'll feel better when once we get over the seas to Canada over there,' he said to her as they sat among the rocks on the cliff.

She looked away to the sea's horizon, as if it were not real. Then she looked round at him, with the strained, strange look of a child that is struggling against sleep.

'Shall I?' she said.

'Yes,' he answered quietly.

And her eyelids dropped with the slow motion, sleep weighing them unconscious. But she pulled them open again to say:

'Yes, I may. I can't tell. I can't tell what it will be like over there.'

'If only we could go soon!' he said, with pain in his voice.

Jimmy and the Desperate Woman

Written January – March 1924 and published *Criterion*, October 1924 and the collection *The Woman Who Rode Away*. Included in *The Best British Short Stories of 1925*.

'He is very fine and strong somewhere, but he does need a level-headed woman to look after him.'

That was the *friendly* feminine verdict upon him. It flattered him, it pleased him, it galled him.

Having divorced a very charming and clever wife, who had held this opinion for ten years, and at last had got tired of the level-headed protective game, his gall was uppermost.

'I want to throw Jimmy out on the world, but I know the poor little man will go and fall on some woman's bosom. That's the worst of him. If he could only stand alone for ten minutes. But he can't. At the same time, there *is* something fine about him, something rare.'

This had been Clarissa's summing-up as she floated away in the arms of the rich young American. The rich young American got rather angry when Jimmy's name was mentioned. Clarissa was now *his* wife. But she did sometimes talk as if she were still married to Jimmy.

Not in Jimmy's estimation, however. That worm had turned. Gall was uppermost. Gall and wormwood. He knew exactly what Clarissa thought—and said—about him. And the 'something fine, something rare, something strong' which he was supposed to have 'about him' was

314

utterly outbalanced, in his feelings at least, by the 'poor little man' nestled upon 'some woman's bosom', which he was supposed to *be*.

'I am *not*', he said to himself, 'a poor little man nestled upon some woman's bosom. If I could only find the right sort of woman, she should nestle on mine.'

Jimmy was now thirty-five, and this point, to nestle or to be nestled, was the emotional crux and turning-point.

He imagined to himself some really *womanly* woman, to whom he should be *only* 'fine and strong', and not for one moment 'the poor little man'. Why not some simple uneducated girl, some Tess of the D'Urbervilles, some wistful Gretchen, some humble Ruth gleaning an after-math? Why not? Surely the world was full of such!

The trouble was he never met them. He only met sophisticated women. He really never had a chance of meeting 'real' people. So few of us ever do. Only the people we *don't* meet are the 'real' people, the simple, genuine, direct, spontaneous, unspoilt souls. Ah, the simple genuine unspoilt people we *don't* meet! What a tragedy it is!

Because, of course, they must be there! Somewhere! Only we never come across them.

Jimmy was terribly handicapped by his position. It brought him into contact with so many people. Only never the right sort. Never the 'real' people: the simple, genuine, unspoilt, etc., etc.

He was editor of a high-class, rather high-brow, rather successful magazine, and his rather personal, very candid editorials brought him shoals, swarms, hosts of admiring acquaintances. Realise that he was handsome, and could be extraordinarily 'nice', when he liked, and was really very clever, in his own critical way, and you see how many chances he had of being adored and protected.

In the first place his good looks: the fine, clean lines of his face, like the face of the laughing faun in one of the

faun's unlaughing, moody moments. The long, clean
lines of the cheeks, the strong chin and the slightly
arched, full nose, the beautiful dark-grey eyes with long
lashes, and the thick black brows. In his mocking
moments, when he seemed most himself, it was a pure
Pan face, with thick black eyebrows cocked up, and grey
eyes with a sardonic goaty gleam, and nose and mouth
curling with satire. A good-looking, smooth-skinned
satyr. That was Jimmy at his best. In the opinion of his
men friends.

In his own opinion, he was a sort of Martyred Saint
Sebastian, at whom the wicked world shot arrow after
arrow–Mater Dolorosa nothing to him–and he counted
the drops of blood as they fell: when he could keep count.
Sometimes–as for instance when Clarissa said she was
really departing with the rich young American, and
should she divorce Jimmy, or was Jimmy going to
divorce her?–then the arrows assailed him like a flight of
starlings flying straight at him, jabbing at him, and the
drops of martyred blood simply spattered down, he
couldn't keep count.

So, naturally, he divorced Clarissa.

In the opinion of his men friends, he was, or should
be, a consistently grinning faun, satyr, or Pan-person. In
his own opinion, he was a Martyred Saint Sebastian with
the mind of a Plato. In the opinion of his woman friends,
he was a fascinating little man with a profound
understanding of life and the capacity really to
understand a woman and to make a woman feel a queen;
which of course was to make a woman feel her *real*
self . . .

He might, naturally, have made rich and resounding marriages, especially after the divorce. He didn't.
The reason was, secretly, his resolve never to make any
woman feel a queen any more. It was the turn of the
women to make him feel a king.

Some unspoilt, unsophisticated, wild-blooded
woman, to whom he would be a sort of Solomon of

wisdom, beauty, and wealth. She would need to be in reduced circumstances to appreciate his wealth, which amounted to the noble sum of three thousand pounds and a little week-ending cottage in Hampshire. And to be unsophisticated she would have to be a woman of the people. Absolutely.

At the same time, not just the 'obscure vulgar simplican'.

He received many letters, many, many, many, enclosing poems, stories, articles, or more personal unbosomings. He read them all: like a solemn rook pecking and scratching among the litter.

And one—not one letter, but one correspondent—might be *the* one—Mrs Emilia Pinnegar, who wrote from a mining village in Yorkshire. She was, of course, unhappily married.

Now Jimmy had always had a mysterious feeling about these dark and rather dreadful mining villages in the north. He himself had scarcely set foot north of Oxford. He felt that these miners up there must be the real stuff. And Pinnegar was a name, surely! And Emilia!

She wrote a poem, with a brief little note, that, if the editor of the *Commentator* thought the verses of no value, would he simply destroy them. Jimmy, as editor of the *Commentator*, thought the verses quite good and admired the brevity of the note. But he wasn't sure about printing the poem. He wrote back, Had Mrs Pinnegar nothing else to submit?

Then followed a correspondence. And at length, upon request, this from Mrs Pinnegar:

'You ask me about myself, but what shall I say? I am a woman of thirty-one, with one child, a girl of eight, and I am married to a man who lives in the same house with me, but goes to another woman. I try to write poetry, if it is poetry, because I have no other way of expressing myself at all, and even if it doesn't matter to anybody besides myself, I feel I must and will express myself, if only to save myself from developing cancer or some disease that women have. I was a school-teacher before I was married, and I got my certificates at Rotherham College. If I could, I would teach again, and live alone. But married women teachers can't get jobs any more, they aren't allowed—"

The Coal-Miner
By His Wife

The donkey-engine's beating noise
And the rattle, rattle of the sorting screens
Come down on me like the beat of his heart,
And mean the same as his breathing means.

The burning big pit-hill with fumes
Fills the air like the presence of that fair-haired
   man.
And the burning fire burning deeper and
   deeper
Is his will insisting since time began.

As he breathes the chair goes up and down
In the pit-shaft; he lusts as the wheel-fans spin
The sucking air: he lives in the coal
Underground: and his soul is a strange engine.

That is the manner of man he is.
I married him and I should know.
The mother earth from bowels of coal
Brought him forth for the overhead woe.

This was the poem that the editor of the *Commentator* hesitated about. He reflected, also, that Mrs Pinnegar didn't sound like one of the nestling, unsophisticated rustic type. It was something else that still attracted him: something desperate in a woman, something tragic.

The Next Event

If at evening, when the twilight comes,
   You ask me what the day has been,
I shall not know. The distant drums
   Of some new-comer intervene

Between me and the day that's been.
   Some strange man leading long columns
Of unseen soldiers through the green
   Sad twilight of these smoky slums.

And as the darkness slowly numbs
   My senses, everything I've seen
Or heard the daylight through, becomes
   Rubbish behind an opaque screen.

Instead, the sound of muffled drums
   Inside myself: I have to lean
And listen as my strength succumbs,
   To hear what these oncomings mean.

Perhaps the Death-God striking his thumbs
   On the drums in a deadly rat-ta-ta-plan.
Or a strange man marching slow as he strums
   The tune of a new weird hope in Man.

What does it matter! The day that began
   In coal-dust is ending the same, in crumbs
Of darkness like coal. I live if I can;
   If I can't, then I welcome whatever comes.

This poem sounded so splendidly desperate, the editor of the *Commentator* decided to print it, and, moreover, to see the authoress. He wrote, Would she care to see him, if he happened to be in her neighbourhood? He was going to lecture in Sheffield. She replied, Certainly.

He gave his afternoon lecture, on *Men in Books and Men in Life*. Naturally, men in books came first. Then he caught a train to reach the mining village where the Pinnegars lived.

It was February, with gruesome patches of snow. It was dark when he arrived at Mill Valley, a sort of thick, turgid darkness full of menace, where men speaking in a weird accent went past like ghosts, dragging their heavy feet and emitting the weird scent of the coal-mine underworld. Weird and a bit gruesome it was.

He knew he had to walk uphill to the little market-place. As he went, he looked back and saw the black valleys with bunches of light, like camps of demons it seemed to him. And the demonish smell of sulphur and coal in the air, in the heavy, pregnant, clammy darkness.

They directed him to New London Lane, and down he went down another hill. His skin crept a little. The place felt uncanny and hostile, hard, as if iron and minerals breathed into the black air. Thank goodness he couldn't see much, or be seen. When he had to ask his way the people treated him in a 'heave-half-a-brick-at-him' fashion.

After much weary walking and asking, he entered a lane between trees, in the cold slushy mud of the unfrozen February. The mines, apparently, were on the outskirts of the town, in some mud-sunk country. He could see the red, sore fires of the burning pit-hill through the trees, and he smelt the sulphur. He felt like some modern Ulysses wandering in the realms of Hecate. How much more dismal and horrible, a modern Odyssey among mines and factories, than any Sirens, Scyllas or Charybdises.

So he mused to himself as he waded through icy black mud, in a black lane, under black trees that moaned an accompaniment to the sound of the coal-mine's occasional hissing and chuffing, under a black sky that quenched even the electric sparkle of the colliery. And the place seemed unhabitated like a cold black jungle.

At last he came in sight of a glimmer. Apparently, there were dwellings. Yes, a new little street, with one street-lamp, and the houses all apparently dark. He paused. Absolute desertion. Then three children.

They told him the house, and he stumbled up a dark passage. There was light on the little backyard. He knocked, in some trepidation. A rather tall woman, looking down at him with a 'Who are you?' look, from the step above.

'Mrs Pinnegar?'

'Oh, is it you, Mr Frith? Come in.'

He stumbled up the step into the glaring light of the kitchen. There stood Mrs Pinnegar, a tall woman with a face like a mask of passive anger, looking at him coldly. Immediately he felt his own shabbiness and smallness. In utter confusion, he stuck out his hand.

'I had an awful time getting here,' he said. 'I'm afraid I shall make a frightful mess of your house.' He looked down at his boots.

'That's all right,' she said. 'Have you had your tea?'

'No—but don't you bother about me.'

There was a little girl with fair hair in a fringe over her forehead, troubled blue eyes under the fringe, and two dolls. He felt easier.

'Is this your little girl?' he asked. 'She's awfully nice. What is her name?'

'Jane.'

'How are you, Jane?' he said. But the child only stared at him with the baffled, bewildered, pained eyes of a child who lives with hostile parents.

Mrs Pinnegar set his tea, bread and butter, jam, and buns. Then she sat opposite him. She was handsome, dark straight brows and grey eyes with yellow grains in them, and a way of looking straight at you as if she were used to holding her own. Her eyes were the nicest part of her. They had a certain kindliness, mingled, like the yellow grains among the grey, with a relentless, unyielding feminine will. Her nose and mouth were straight, like a Greek mask, and the expression was fixed. She gave him at once the impression of a woman who has made a mistake, who knows it, but who will not change: who cannot now change.

He felt very uneasy. Being a rather small, shambling man, she made him aware of his physical inconspicuousness. And she said not a word, only looked down on him, as he drank his tea, with that changeless look of a woman who is holding her own against Man and Fate. While, from the corner across the kitchen, the little girl with her fair hair and her dolls, watched him also in absolute silence, from her hot blue eyes.

'This seems a pretty awful place,' he said to her.

'It is. It's absolutely awful,' the woman said.

'You ought to get away from it,' he said.

But she received this in dead silence.

It was exceedingly difficult to make any headway. He asked about Mr Pinnegar. She glanced at the clock.

'He comes up at nine,' she said.

'Is he down the mine?'

'Yes. He's on the afternoon shift.'

There was never a sound from the little girl.

'Doesn't Jane ever talk?' he asked.

'Not much,' said the mother, glancing round.

He talked a little about his lectures, about Sheffield, about London. But she was not really interested. She sat there rather distant, very laconic, looking at him with those curious unyielding eyes. She looked to him like a woman who has had her revenge, and is left stranded on the reefs where she wrecked her opponent. Still unrelenting, unregretting, unyielding, she seemed rather undecided as to what her revenge had been, and what it had all been about.

'You ought to get away from here,' he said to her.

'Where to?' she asked.

'Oh'–he made a vague gesture–'anywhere, so long as it is *quite* away.'

She seemed to ponder this, under her portentous brow.

'I don't see what difference it would make,' she said. Then glancing round at her child: 'I don't see what difference anything would make, except getting out of the world altogether. But there's *her* to consider.' And she jerked her head in the direction of the child.

Jimmy felt definitely frightened. He wasn't used to this sort of grimness. At the same time he was excited. This handsome, laconic woman, with her soft brown hair and her unflinching eyes with their gold flecks, seemed to be challenging him to something. There was a touch of challenge in her remaining gold-flecked kindness. Somewhere, she had a heart. But what had happened to it? And why?

What had gone wrong with her? In some way, she must have gone against herself.

'Why don't you come and live with me?' he said, like the little gambler he was.

The queer, conflicting smile was on his face. He had taken up her challenge, like a gambler. The very sense of a gamble, in which he could not lose desperately, excited him. At the same time, he was scared of her, and determined to get beyond his scare.

She sat and watched him, with the faintest touch of a grim smile on her handsome mouth.

'How do you mean, live with you?' she said.

'Oh–I mean what it usually means,' he said, with a little puff of self-conscious laughter.

'You're evidently not happy here. You're evidently in the wrong circumstances altogether. You're obviously *not* just an ordinary woman. Well, then, break away. When I say, Come and live with me, I mean just what I say. Come to London and live with me, as my wife, if you like, and then if we want to marry, when you get a divorce, why, we can do it.'

Jimmy made this speech more to himself than to the woman. That was how he was. He worked out all his things inside himself, as if it were all merely an interior problem of his own. And while he did so, he had an odd way of squinting his left eye and wagging his head loosely, like a man talking absolutely to himself, and turning his eyes inwards.

The woman watched him in a sort of wonder. This was something she was *not* used to. His extraordinary manner, and his extraordinary bald proposition, roused her from her own tense apathy.

'Well!' she said. 'That's got to be thought about. What about *her*?'—and again she jerked her head towards the round-eyed child in the corner. Jane sat with a completely expressionless face, her little red mouth fallen a little open. She seemed in a sort of trance: as if she understood like a grown-up person, but, as a child, sat in a trance, unconscious.

The mother wheeled round in her chair and stared at her child. The little girl stared back at her mother, with hot, troubled, almost guilty blue eyes. And neither said a word. Yet they seemed to exchange worlds of meaning.

'Why, of course,' said Jimmy, twisting his head again; 'she'd come, too.'

The woman gave a last look at her child, then turned to him, and started watching *him* with that slow, straight stare.

'It's not'—he began, stuttering— 'it's not anything *sudden* and unconsidered on my part. I've been considering it for quite a long time—ever since I had the first poem, and your letter.'

He spoke still with his eyes turned inwards, talking to himself. And the woman watched him unflinchingly.

'Before you ever saw me?' she asked, with a queer irony.

'Oh, of course. Of course before I ever saw you. Or else I never *should* have seen you. From the very first, I had a definite feeling—'

He made odd, sharp gestures, like a drunken man, and he spoke like a drunken man, his eyes turned inward, talking to himself. The woman was no more than a ghost moving inside his own consciousness, and he was addressing her there.

The actual woman sat outside looking on in a sort of wonder. This was really something new to her.

'And now you see me, do you want me, really, to come to London?'

She spoke in a dull tone of incredulity. The thing was just a little preposterous to her. But why not? It would have to be something a little preposterous, to get her out of the tomb she was in.

'Of course I do!' he cried, with another scoop of his head and scoop of his hand. '*Now* I do *actually* want you, now I actually see you.' He never looked at her. His eyes were still turned in. He was still talking to himself, in a sort of drunkenness with himself.

To her, it was something extraordinary. But it roused her from apathy.

He became aware of the hot blue eyes of the hot-cheeked little girl fixed upon him from the distant corner. And he gave a queer little giggle.

'Why, it's more than I could ever have hoped for,' he said, 'to have you and Jane to live with me! Why, it will mean *life* to me.' He spoke in an odd, strained voice, slightly delirious. And for the first time he looked up at the woman and, apparently, *straight* at her. But, even as he seemed to look straight at her, the curious cast was in his eye, and he was only looking at himself, inside himself, at the shadows inside his own consciousness.

'And when would you like me to come?' she asked, rather coldly.

'Why, as soon as possible. Come back with me to-morrow, if you will. I've got a little house in St John's Wood, *waiting* for you. Come with me tomorrow. That's the simplest.'

She watched him for some time, as he sat with ducked head. He looked like a man who is drunk—drunk with himself. He was going bald at the crown, his rather curly black hair was thin.

'I couldn't come to-morrow, I should need a few days,' she said.

She wanted to see his face again. It was as if she could not remember what his face was like, this strange man who had appeared out of nowhere, with such a strange proposition.

He lifted his face, his eyes still cast in that inturned, blind look. He looked now like a Mephistopheles who has gone blind. With his black brows cocked up, Mephistopheles, Mephistopheles blind and begging in the street.

'Why, of course it's wonderful that it's happened like this for me,' he said, with odd pouting emphasis pushing out his lips. 'I was finished, absolutely finished. I was finished while Clarissa was with me. But after she'd gone, I was *absolutely* finished. And I thought there was no chance for me in the world again. It seems to me perfectly marvellous that this has happened—that I've come across you—' he lifted his face sightlessly—'and Jane—Jane—why she's *really* too good to be true.' He gave a slight hysterical laugh. 'She really is.'

The woman, and Jane, watched him with some embarrassment.

'I shall have to settle up here, with Mr Pinnegar,' she said, rather coldly musing. 'Do you want to see him?'

'Oh, I—' he said, with a deprecating gesture, 'I don't *care*. But if you think I'd better —why, certainly—'

'I do think you'd better,' she said.

'Very well, then, I *will*. I'll see him whenever you like.'

'He comes in soon after nine,' she said.

'All right, I'll see him then. Much better. But I suppose I'd better see about finding a place to sleep first. Better not leave it too late.'

'I'll come with you and ask for you.'

'Oh, you'd better not, really. If you tell me where to go—'

He had taken on a protective tone: he was protecting her against herself and against scandal. It was his manner, his rather Oxfordy manner, more than anything else, that went beyond her. She wasn't used to it.

Jimmy plunged out into the gulfing blackness of the Northern night, feeling how horrible it was, but pressing his hat on his brow in a sense of strong adventure. He was going through with it.

At the baker's shop, where she had suggested he should ask for a bed, they would have none of him. Absolutely they didn't like the looks of him. At the Pub, too, they shook their heads: didn't want to have anything to do with him. But, in a voice more expostulatingly Oxford than ever, he said:

'But look here—you can't ask a man to sleep under one of these hedges. Can't I see the landlady?'

He persuaded the landlady to promise to let him sleep on the big, soft settee in the parlour, where the fire was burning brightly. Then, saying he would be back about ten, he returned through mud and drizzle up New London Lane.

The child was in bed, a saucepan was boiling by the fire. Already the lines had softened a little in the woman's face.

She spread a cloth on the table. Jimmy sat in silence, feeling that she was hardly aware of his presence. She was absorbed, no doubt, in the coming of her husband. The stranger merely sat on the sofa, and waited. He felt himself wound up tight. And once he was really wound up, he could go through with anything.

They heard the nine-o'clock whistle at the mine. The woman then took the saucepan from the fire and went into the scullery. Jimmy could smell the smell of the potatoes being strained. He sat quite still. There was nothing for him to do or to say. He was wearing his big black-rimmed spectacles, and his face, blank and expressionless in the suspense of waiting, looked like the death-mask of some sceptical philosopher, who could wait through the ages, and who could hardly distinguish life from death at any time.

Came the heavy-shod tread up the house entry, and

the man entered, rather like a blast of wind. The fair moustache stuck out from the blackish, mottled face, and the fierce blue eyes rolled their whites in the coal-blackened sockets.

'This gentleman is Mr Frith,' said Emily Pinnegar.

Jimmy got up, with a bit of an Oxford wriggle, and held out his hand, saying: 'How do you do?'

His grey eyes, behind the spectacles, had an uncanny whitish gleam.

'My hand's not fit to shake hands,' said the miner. 'Take a seat.'

'Oh, nobody minds coal-dust,' said Jimmy, subsiding on to the sofa. 'It's clean dirt.'

'They say so,' said Pinnegar.

He was a man of medium height, thin, but energetic in build.

Mrs Pinnegar was running hot water into a pail from the bright brass tap of the stove, which had a boiler to balance the oven. Pinnegar dropped heavily into a wooden armchair, and stooped to pull off his ponderous grey pit-boots. He smelled of the strange, stale underground. In silence he pulled on his slippers, then rose, taking his boots into the scullery. His wife followed with the pail of hot water. She returned and spread a coarse roller-towel on the steel fender. The man could be heard washing in the scullery, in the semi-dark. Nobody said anything. Mrs Pinnegar attended to her husband's dinner.

After a while, Pinnegar came running in, naked to the waist, and squatted plumb in front of the big red fire, on his heels. His head and face and the front part of his body were all wet. His back was grey and unwashed. He seized the towel from the fender and began to rub his face and head with a sort of brutal vigour, while his wife brought a bowl, and with a soapy flannel silently washed his back, right down to the loins, where the trousers were rolled back. The man was entirely oblivious of the stranger—this washing was part of the collier's ritual, and nobody existed for the moment. The woman, washing her husband's back, stooping there as he knelt with knees wide apart, squatting on his heels on the rag hearthrug, had a peculiar look on her strong, handsome face, a look sinister and derisive. She was deriding something or somebody; but Jimmy could not make out whom or what.

It was a new experience for him to sit completely and brutally excluded, from a personal ritual. The collier vigorously rubbed his own fair short hair, till it all stood on end, then he stared into the red-hot fire, oblivious, while the red colour burned in his cheeks. Then again he rubbed his breast and his body with the rough towel, brutally, as if his body were some machine he was cleaning, while his wife, with a peculiar slow movement, dried his back with another towel.

She took away the towel and bowl. The man was dry. He still squatted with his hands on his knees, gazing abstractedly, blankly into the fire. That, too, seemed part of his daily ritual. The colour flushed in his cheeks, his fair moustache was rubbed on end. But his hot blue eyes stared hot and vague into the red coals, while the red glare of the coal fell on his breast and naked body.

He was a man of about thirty-five, in his prime, with a pure smooth skin and no fat on his body. His muscles were not large, but quick, alive with energy. And as he squatted bathing abstractedly in the glow of the fire, he seemed like some pure-moulded engine that sleeps between its motions, with incomprehensible eyes of dark iron-blue.

He looked round, always averting his face from the stranger on the sofa, shutting him out of consciousness. The wife took out a bundle from the dresser-cupboard, and handed it to the out-stretched, work-scarred hand of the man on the hearth. Curious, that big, horny, work-battered clean hand, at the end of the suave, thin naked arm.

Pinnegar unrolled his shirt and undervest in front of

the fire, warmed them for a moment in the glow, vaguely, sleepily, then pulled them over his head. And then at last he rose, with his shirt hanging over his trousers, and in the same abstract, sleepy way, shutting the world out of his consciousness, he went out again to the scullery, pausing at the same dresser-cupboard to take out his rolled-up day trousers.

Mrs Pinnegar took away the towels and set the dinner on the table—rich, oniony stew out of a hissing brown stew-jar, boiled potatoes, and a cup of tea. The man returned from the scullery, in his clean flannelette shirt and black trousers, his fair hair neatly brushed. He planked his wooden armchair beside the table, and sat heavily down, to eat.

Then he looked at Jimmy, as one wary, probably hostile man looks at another.

'You're a stranger in these parts, I gather?' he said. There was something slightly formal, even a bit pompous, in his speech.

'An absolute stranger,' replied Jimmy, with a slight aside grin.

The man dabbed some mustard on his plate, and glanced at his food to see if he would like it.

'Come from a distance, do you?' he asked, as he began to eat. As he ate, he seemed to become oblivious again of Jimmy, bent his head over his plate, and ate. But probably he was ruminating something all the time, with barbaric wariness.

'From London,' said Jimmy, warily.

'London!' said Pinnegar, without looking from his plate.

Mrs Pinnegar came and sat, in ritualistic silence, in her tall-backed rocking-chair under the light.

'What brings you this way, then?' asked Pinnegar, stirring his tea.

'Oh!' Jimmy writhed a little on the sofa. 'I came to see Mrs Pinnegar.'

The miner took a hasty gulp of tea.

'You're acquainted then, are you?' he said, still without looking round. He sat with his side-face to Jimmy.

'Yes, we are *now*,' explained Jimmy. 'I didn't know Mrs Pinnegar till this evening. As a matter of fact, she sent me some poems for the *Commentator*—I'm the editor—and I thought they were good, so I wrote and told her so. Then I felt I wanted to come and see her, and she was willing, so I came.'

The man reached out, cut himself a piece of bread, and swallowed a large mouthful.

'You thought her poetry was good?' he said, turning at last to Jimmy and looking straight at him, with a stare something like the child's, but aggressive. 'Are you going to put it in your magazine?'

'Yes, I think I am,' said Jimmy.

'I never read but one of her poems—something about a collier she knew all about, because she'd married him,' he said, in his peculiar harsh voice, that had a certain jeering clang in it, and a certain indomitableness.

Jimmy was silent. The other man's harsh fighting-voice made him shrink.

'I could never get on with the *Commentator* myself,' said Pinnegar, looking round for his pudding, pushing his meat-plate aside. 'Seems to me to go a long way round to get nowhere.'

'Well, probably it *does*,' said Jimmy, squirming a little. 'But so long as the *way* is interesting! I don't see that anything gets anywhere at present—certainly no periodical.'

'I don't know,' said Pinnegar. 'There's some facts in the *Liberator*—and there's some ideas in the *Janus*. I can't see the use myself, of all these feelings folk say they have. They get you nowhere.'

'But,' said Jimmy, with a slight pouf of laughter, 'where do you *want* to get? It's all very well talking about getting somewhere, but where, where in the world to-day do you *want* to get? In general, I mean. If you want a better job in the mine—all right, go ahead and get it. But when you begin to talk about getting somewhere, in *life*–why, you've got to know what you're talking about.'

'I'm a man, aren't I?' said the miner, going very still and hard.

'But what do you *mean*, when you say you're a man?' snarled Jimmy, really exasperated. 'What do you mean? Yes, you *are* a man. But what about it?'

'Haven't I the right to say I won't be made use of?' said the collier, slow, harsh, and heavy.

'You've got a right to *say* it,' retorted Jimmy, with a pouf of laughter. 'But it doesn't *mean* anything. We're all made use of, from King George downwards. We have to be. When you eat your pudding you're making use of hundreds of people–including your wife.'

'I know it. I know it. It makes no difference, though. I'm not going to be made use of.'

Jimmy shrugged his shoulders.

'Oh, all right!' he said. 'That's just a phrase, like any other.'

The miner sat very still in his chair, his face going hard and remote. He was evidently thinking over something that was stuck like a barb in his consciousness, something he was trying to harden over, as the skin sometimes hardens over a steel splinter in the flesh.

'I'm nothing but made use of,' he said, now talking hard and final, to himself, and staring out into space. 'Down the pit, I'm made use of, and they give me a wage, such as it is. At the house, I'm made use of, and my wife sets the dinner on the table as if I was a customer in a shop.'

'But what do you *expect*?' cried Jimmy, writhing in his chair.

'Me? What do I expect? I expect nothing. But I tell you what—' he turned, and looked straight and hard into Jimmy's eyes–'I'm not going to put up with anything, either.'

Jimmy saw the hard finality in the other man's eyes,

and squirmed away from it.

'If you *know* what you're not going to put up with—' he said.

'I don't want my wife writing poetry! And sending it to a parcel of men she's never seen. *I* don't want my wife sitting like Queen Boadicea, when I come home, and a face like a stone wall with holes in it. I don't know what's wrong with her. She doesn't know herself. But she does as she likes. Only, mark you, I do the same.'

'Of course!' cried Jimmy, though there was no of course about it.

'She's told you I've got another woman?'

'Yes.'

'And I'll tell you for why. If I give in to the coal face, and go down the mine every day to eight hours' slavery, more or less, somebody's got to give in to me.'

'Then,' said Jimmy, after a pause, 'if you mean you want your wife to submit to you—well, that's the problem. You have to marry the woman who *will* submit.'

It was amazing, this from Jimmy. He sat there and lectured the collier like a Puritan Father, completely forgetting the disintegrating flutter of Clarissa, in his own background.

'I want a wife who'll please me, who'll want to please me,' said the collier.

'Why should *you* be pleased, any more than anybody else?' asked the wife coldly.

'My child, my little girl wants to please me—if her mother would let her. But the women hang together. I tell you'—and here he turned to Jimmy, with a blaze in his dark blue eyes—'I want a woman to please me, a woman who's anxious to please me. And if I can't find her in my own home, I'll find her out of it.'

'I hope she pleases you,' said the wife, rocking slightly.

'Well,' said the man, 'she does.'

'Then why don't you go and live with her altogether?' she said.

He turned and looked at her.

'Why don't I?' he said. 'Because I've got my home. I've got my house, I've got my wife, let her be what she may, as a woman to live with. And I've got my child. Why should I break it all up?'

'And what about me?' she asked, coldly and fiercely.

'You? You've got a home. You've got a child. You've got a man who works for you. You've got what you want. You do as you like—'

'Do I?' she asked, with intolerable sarcasm.

'Yes. Apart from the bit of work in the house, you do as you like. If you want to go, you can go. But while you live in my house, you must respect it. You bring no men here, you see.'

'Do *you* respect your home?' she said.

'Yes! I do! If I get another woman—who pleases me—I deprive you of nothing. All I ask of you is to do your duty as a housewife.'

'Down to washing your back!' she said, heavily sarcastic; and, Jimmy thought, a trifle vulgar.

'Down to washing my back, since it's got to be washed,' he said.

'What about the other woman? Let her do it.'

'This is my home.'

The wife gave a strange movement, like a mad woman.

Jimmy sat rather pale and frightened. Behind the collier's quietness he felt the concentration of almost cold anger and an unchanging will. In the man's lean face he could see the bones, the fixity of the male bones, and it was as if the human soul, or spirit, had gone into the living skull and skeleton, almost invulnerable.

Jimmy, for some strange reason, felt a wild anger against this bony and logical man. It was the hard-driven coldness, fixity, that he could not bear.

'Look here!' he cried, in a resonant Oxford voice, his eyes glaring and casting inwards behind his spectacles. 'You say Mrs Pinnegar is *free*—free to do as she pleases. In that case, you have no objection if she comes with me right away from here.'

The collier looked at the pale, strange face of the editor in wonder. Jimmy kept his face slightly averted, and sightless, seeing nobody. There was a Mephistophelian tilt about the eyebrows, and a Martyred Sebastian straightness about the mouth.

'Does she *want* to?' asked Pinnegar, with devastating incredulity. The wife smiled faintly, grimly. She could see the vanity of her husband in his utter inability to believe that she could prefer the other man to him.

'That,' said Jimmy, 'you must ask her yourself. But it's what I came here for: to ask her to come and live with me, and bring the child.'

'You came without having seen her, to ask her that?' said the husband, in growing wonder.

'Yes,' said Jimmy, vehemently, nodding his head with drunken emphasis. 'Yes! Without ever having seen her!'

'You've caught a funny fish this time, with your poetry,' he said, turning with curious husband-familiarity to his wife. She hated this off-hand husband-familiarity.

'What sort of fish have *you* caught?' she retorted. 'And what did you catch *her* with?'

'Bird-lime!' he said, with a faint, quick grin.

Jimmy was sitting in suspense. They all three sat in suspense, for some time.

'And what are you saying to him?' said the collier at length.

Jimmy looked up, and the malevolent half-smile on his face made him look rather handsome again, a mixture of faun and Mephisto. He glanced curiously, invitingly, at the woman who was watching him from afar.

'I say yes!' she replied, in a cool voice.

The husband became very still, sitting erect in his wooden armchair and staring into space. It was as if he were fixedly watching something fly away from him, out of his own soul. But he was not going to yield at all, to any emotion.

He could not now believe that this woman should *want* to leave him. Yet she did.

'I'm sure it's all for the best,' said Jimmy, in his Puritan-Father voice. 'You don't mind, really'–he drawled uneasily–'if she brings the child. I give you my word I'll do my very best for it.'

The collier looked at him as if he were very far away. Jimmy quailed under the look. He could see that the other man was relentlessly killing the emotion in himself, stripping himself, as it were, of his own flesh, stripping himself to the hard unemotional bone of the human male.

'I give her a blank cheque,' said Pinnegar, with numb lips. 'She does as she pleases.'

'So much for fatherly love, compared with selfishness,' she said.

He turned and looked at her with that curious power of remote anger. And immediately she became still, quenched.

'I give you a blank cheque, as far as I'm concerned,' he repeated abstractedly.

'It *is* blank indeed!' she said, with her first touch of bitterness.

Jimmy looked at the clock. It was growing late: he might be shut out of the public-house. He rose to go, saying he would return in the morning. He was leaving the next day, at noon, for London.

He plunged into the darkness and mud of that black, night-ridden country. There was a curious elation in his spirits, mingled with fear. But then he always needed an element of fear, really, to elate him. He thought with terror of those two human beings left in that house together. The frightening state of tension! He himself could never bear an extreme tension. He always had to compromise, to become apologetic and pathetic.

He would be able to manage Mrs Pinnegar that way. Emily! He must get used to saying it. Emily! The Emilia was absurd. He had never known an Emily.

He felt really scared, and really elated. He was doing something big. It was not that he was in *love* with the woman. But, my God, he wanted to take her away from that man. And he wanted the adventure of her. Absolutely the adventure of her. He felt really elated, really himself, really manly.

But in the morning he returned rather sheepishly to the collier's house. It was another dark, drizzling day, with black trees, black road, black hedges, blackish brick houses, and the smell and the sound of collieries under a skyless day. Like living in some weird underground.

Unwillingly he went up that passage-entry again, and knocked at the back door, glancing at the miserable little back garden with its cabbage-stalks and its ugly sanitary arrangements.

The child opened the door to him: with her fair hair, flushed cheeks, and hot, dark-blue eyes.

'Hello, Jane!' he said.

The mother stood tall and square, by the table, watching him with portentous eyes, as he entered. She was handsome, but her skin was not very good: as if the battle had been too much for her health. Jimmy glanced up at her smiling his slow, ingratiating smile, that always brought a glow of success into a woman's spirit. And as he saw her gold-flecked eyes searching in his eyes, without a bit of kindliness, he thought to himself: 'My God, however am I going to sleep with that woman!' His will was ready, however, and he would manage it somehow.

And when he glanced at the motionless, bony head and lean figure of the collier seated in the wooden armchair by the fire, he was the more ready. He must triumph over that man.

'What train are you going by?' asked Mrs Pinnegar.

'By the twelve thirty.' He looked up at her as he

spoke, with the wide, shining, childlike, almost coy eyes
that were his peculiar asset. She looked down at him in a
sort of interested wonder. She seemed almost fascinated
by his childlike, shining, inviting dark-grey eyes, with
their long lashes: such an absolute change from that
resentful unyielding that looked out always from the
back of her husband's blue eyes. Her husband always
seemed like a menace to her, in his thinness, his concentration, his eternal unyielding. And this man looked
at one with the wide, shining, fascinating eyes of a young
Persian kitten, something at once bold and shy and coy
and strangely inviting. She fell at once under their spell.

'You'll have dinner before you go,' she said.

'No!' he cried in panic, unwilling indeed to eat
before that other man. 'No, I ate a fabulous breakfast. I
will get a sandwich when I change in Sheffield: *really*!'

She had to go out shopping. She said she would go
out to the station with him when she got back. It was just
after eleven.

'But look here,' he said, addressing also the thin
abstracted man who sat unnoticing, with a newspaper,
'we've got to get this thing settled. I *want* Mrs Pinnegar to
come and live with me, her and the child. And she's
coming! So don't you think, now, it would be better if she
came right along with me to-day! Just put a few things in
a bag and come along. Why drag the thing out?'

'I tell you,' replied the husband, 'she has a blank
cheque from me to do as she likes.'

'All right, then! Won't you do that? Won't you
come along with me now?' said Jimmy, looking up at her
exposedly, but casting his eyes a bit inwards. Throwing
himself with deliberate impulsiveness on her mercy.

'I can't!' she said decisively. 'I can't come to-day.'

'But why not—really? Why not, while I'm here? You
have that blank cheque, you can do as you please—'

'The blank cheque won't get me far,' she said
rudely; 'I can't come to-day, anyhow.'

'When can you come, then?' he said, with that

queer, petulant pleading. 'The sooner the better, surely.'

'I can come on Monday,' she said abruptly.

'Monday!' He gazed up at her in a kind of panic, through his spectacles. Then he set his teeth again, and nodded his head up and down. 'All right, then! To-day is Saturday. Then Monday!'

'If you'll excuse me,' she said, 'I've got to go out for a few things. I'll walk to the station with you when I get back.'

She bundled Jane into a little sky-blue coat and bonnet, put on a heavy black coat and black hat herself, and went out.

Jimmy sat very uneasily opposite the collier, who also wore spectacles to read. Pinnegar put down the newspaper and pulled the spectacles off his nose, saying something about a Labour Government.

'Yes,' said Jimmy. 'After all, best be logical. If you *are* democratic, the only logical thing is a Labour Government. Though, personally, one Government is as good as another, to me.'

'Maybe so!' said the collier. "But *something's* got to come to an end, sooner or later.'

'Oh, a great deal!' said Jimmy, and they lapsed into silence.

'Have you been married before?' asked Pinnegar, at length.

'Yes. My wife and I are divorced.'

'I suppose you want me to divorce *my* wife?' said the collier.

'Why—yes!—that would be best—'

'It's the same to me,' said Pinnegar; 'divorce or no divorce. I'll *live* with another woman, but I'll never *marry* another. Enough is as good as a feast. But if she wants a divorce, she can have it.'

'It would certainly be best,' said Jimmy.

There was a long pause. Jimmy wished the woman would come back.

'I look on you as an instrument,' said the miner.

'Something had to break. You are the instrument that breaks it.'

It was strange to sit in the room with this thin, remote, wilful man. Jimmy was a bit fascinated by him. But, at the same time, he hated him because he could not be in the same room with him without being under his spell. He felt himself dominated. And he hated it.

'My wife', said Pinnegar, looking up at Jimmy with a peculiar, almost humorous, teasing grin, 'expects to see me go to the dogs when she leaves me. It is her last hope.'

Jimmy ducked his head and was silent, not knowing what to say. The other man sat still in his chair, like a sort of infinitely patient prisoner, looking away out of the window and waiting.

'She thinks,' he said again, 'that she has some wonderful future awaiting her somewhere, and you're going to open the door.'

And again the same amused grin was in his eyes.

And again Jimmy was fascinated by the man. And again he hated the spell of this fascination. For Jimmy wanted to be, in his own mind, the strongest man among men, but particularly among women. And this thin, peculiar man could dominate him. He knew it. The very silent unconsciousness of Pinnegar dominated the room, wherever he was.

Jimmy hated this.

At last Mrs Pinnegar came back, and Jimmy set off with her. He shook hands with the collier.

'Good-bye!' he said.

'Good-bye!' said Pinnegar, looking down at him with those amused blue eyes, which Jimmy knew he would never be able to get beyond.

And the walk to the station was almost a walk of conspiracy against the man left behind, between the man in spectacles and the tall woman. They arranged the details for Monday. Emily was to come by the nine o'clock train: Jimmy would meet her at Marylebone, and instal her in his house in St John's Wood. Then, with the child, they would begin a new life. Pinnegar would divorce his wife, or she would divorce him: and then, another marriage.

Jimmy got a tremendous kick out of it all on the journey home. He felt he had really done something desperate and adventurous. But he was in too wild a flutter to analyse any results. Only, as he drew near London, a sinking feeling came over him. He was desperately tired after it all, almost too tired to keep up.

Nevertheless, he went after dinner and sprang it all on Severn.

'You damn fool!' said Severn, in consternation. 'What did you do it for?'

'Well,' said Jimmy, writhing. 'Because *I wanted* to.'

'Good God! The woman sounds like the head of Medusa. You're a hero of some stomach, I must say! Remember Clarissa?'

'Oh,' writhed Jimmy. 'But this is different.'

'Ay, her name's Emma, or something of that sort, isn't it?'

'Emily!' said Jimmy briefly.

'Well, you're a fool, anyway, so you may as well keep on acting in character. I've no doubt, by playing weeping-willow, you'll outlive all the female storms you ever prepare for yourself. I never yet did see a weeping-willow uprooted by a gale, so keep on hanging your harp on it, and you'll be all right. Here's luck! But for a man who was looking for a little Gretchen to adore him, you're a corker!'

Which was all that Severn had to say. But Jimmy went home with his knees shaking. On Sunday morning he wrote an anxious letter. He didn't know how to begin it: *Dear Mrs Pinnegar* and *Dear Emily* seemed either too late in the day or too early. So he just plunged in, without dear anything.

'I want you to have this before you come. Perhaps we have been precipitate. I only beg you to decide *finally*, for yourself, before you come. Don't come, please, unless you are absolutely sure of yourself. If you are *in the least* unsure, wait a while, wait till you are quite certain, one way or the other.

'For myself, if you don't come I shall understand. But please send me a telegram. If you do come, I shall welcome both you and the child. Yours ever–J.F.'

He paid a man his return fare, and three pounds extra, to go on the Sunday and deliver this letter.

The man came back in the evening. He had delivered the letter. There was no answer.

Awful Sunday night: tense Monday morning!

A telegram: '*Arrive Marylebone 12.50 with Jane. Yours ever. Emily.*'

Jimmy set his teeth and went to the station. But when he felt her looking at him, and so met her eyes: and after that saw her coming slowly down the platform, holding the child by the hand, her slow cat's eyes smouldering under her straight brows, smouldering at him: he almost swooned. A sickly grin came over him as he held out his hand. Nevertheless he said:

'I'm *awfully* glad you came.'

And as he sat in the taxi, a perverse but intense desire for her came over him, making him almost helpless. He could feel, so strongly, the presence of that other man about her, and this went to his head like neat spirits. That other man! In some subtle, inexplicable way, he was actually bodily present, the husband. The woman moved in his aura. She was hopelessly married to him.

And this went to Jimmy's head like neat whisky. Which of the two would fall before him with a greater fall–the woman, or the man, her husband?

The Woman Who Rode Away

Written June 1924 and published *Dial*, July – August 1925, and *Criterion* July 1925 and January 1926 before inclusion in the collection to which it is the title-story. Chosen for *The Best British Short Stories of 1926*.

I

She had thought that this marriage, of all marriages, would be an adventure. Not that the man himself was exactly magical to her. A little, wiry, twisted fellow, twenty years older than herself, with brown eyes and greying hair, who had come to America a scrap of a wastrel, from Holland, years ago, as a tiny boy, and from the gold-mines of the west had been kicked south into Mexico, and now was more or less rich, owning silver-mines in the wilds of the Sierra Madre: it was obvious that the adventure lay in his circumstances, rather than his person. But he was still a little dynamo of energy, in spite of accidents survived, and what he had accomplished he had accomplished alone. One of those human oddments there is no accounting for.

When she actually *saw* what he had accomplished, her heart quailed. Great green-covered, unbroken mountain-hills, and in the midst of the lifeless isolation, the sharp pinkish mounds of the dried mud from the silver-works. Under the nakedness of the works, the walled-in, one-storey adobe house, with its garden inside, and its deep inner verandah with tropical climbers on the sides. And when you looked up from this

343

shut-in flowered patio, you saw the huge pink cone of the silver-mud refuse, and the machinery of the extracting plant against heaven above. No more.

To be sure, the great wooden doors were often open. And then she could stand outside, in the vast open world. And see great, void, tree-clad hills piling behind one another, from nowhere into nowhere. They were green in autumn time. For the rest, pinkish, stark dry, and abstract.

And in his battered Ford car her husband would take her into the dead, thrice-dead little Spanish town forgotten among the mountains. The great, sundried dead church, the dead portales, the hopeless covered market-place, where, the first time she went, she saw a dead dog lying between the meat stalls and the vegetable array, stretched out as if for ever, nobody troubling to throw it away. Deadness within deadness.

Everybody feebly talking silver, and showing bits of ore. But silver was at a standstill. The great war came and went. Silver was a dead market. Her husband's mines were closed down. But she and he lived on in the adobe house under the works, among the flowers that were never very flowery to her.

She had two children, a boy and a girl. And her eldest, the boy, was nearly ten years old before she aroused from her stupor of subjected amazement. She was not thirty-three, a large, blue-eyed, dazed woman, beginning to grow stout. Her little, wiry, tough, twisted, brown-eyed husband was fifty-three, a man as tough as wire, tenacious as wire, still full of energy, but dimmed by the lapse of silver from the market, and by some curious inaccessibility on his wife's part.

He was a man of principles, and a good husband. In a way, he doted on her. He never quite got over his dazzled admiration of her. But essentially, he was still a bachelor. He had been thrown out on the world, a little bachelor, at the age of ten. When he married he was over forty, and had enough money to marry on. But his capital was all a bachelor's. He was boss of his own works, and marriage was the last and most intimate bit of his own works.

He admired his wife to extinction, he admired her body, all her points. And she was to him always the rather dazzling Californian girl from Berkeley, whom he had first known. Like any sheik, he kept her guarded among those mountains of Chihuahua. He was jealous of her as he was of his silver-mine: and that is saying a lot.

At thirty-three she really was still the girl from Berkeley, in all but physique. Her conscious development had stopped mysteriously with her marriage, completely arrested. Her husband had never become real to her, neither mentally nor physically. In spite of his late sort of passion for her, he never meant anything to her, physically. Only morally he swayed her, downed her, kept her in an invincible slavery.

So the years went by, in the adobe house strung round the sunny patio, with the silver-works overhead. Her husband was never still. When the silver went dead, he ran a ranch lower down, some twenty miles away, and raised pure-bred hogs, splendid creatures. At the same time, he hated pigs. He was a squeamish waif of an idealist, and really hated the physical side of life. He loved work, work, work, and making things. His marriage, his children, were something he was making, part of his business, but with a sentimental income this time.

Gradually her nerves began to go wrong: she must get out. She must get out. So he took her to El Paso for three months. And at least it was the United States.

But he kept his spell over her. The three months ended: back she was, just the same, in her adobe house among those eternal green or pinky-brown hills, void as only the undiscovered is void. She taught her children, she supervised the Mexican boys who were her servants. And sometimes her husband brought visitors, Spaniards or Mexicans or occasionally white men.

He really loved to have white men staying on the place. Yet he had not a moment's peace when they were there. It was as if his wife were some peculiar secret vein of ore in his mines, which no one must be aware of except himself. And she was fascinated by the young gentlemen, mining engineers, who were his guests at times. He, too, was fascinated by a real gentleman. But he was an old-timer miner with a wife, and if a gentleman looked at his wife, he felt as if his mine were being looted, the secrets of it pryed out.

It was one of these young gentlemen who put the idea into her mind. They were all standing outside the great wooden doors of the patio, looking at the outer world. The eternal, motionless hills were all green, it was September, after the rains. There was no sign of anything, save the deserted mine, the deserted works, and a bunch of half-deserted miners' dwellings.

'I wonder,' said the young man, 'what there is behind those great blank hills.'

'More hills,' said Lederman. 'If you go that way, Sonora and the coast. This way is the desert—you came from there—And the other way, hills and the mountains.'

'Yes, but what *lives* in the hills and the mountains? *Surely* there is something wonderful? It looks *so* like nowhere on earth: like being on the moon.'

'There's plenty of game, if you want to shoot. And Indians, if you call *them* wonderful.'

'Wild ones?'

'Wild enough.'

'But friendly?'

'It depends. Some of them are quite wild, and they don't let anybody near. They kill a missionary at sight. And where a missionary can't get, nobody can.'

'But what does the government say?'

'They're so far from everywhere, the government leaves 'em alone. And they're wily; if they think there'll be trouble, they send a delegation to Chihuahua and make a formal submission. The government is glad to leave it at that.'

'And do they live quite wild, with their own savage customs and religion?'

'Oh, yes. They use nothing but bows and arrows. I've seen them in town, in the Plaza, with funny sort of hats with flowers round them, and a bow in one hand, quite naked except for a sort of shirt, even in cold weather–striding round with their savage's bare legs.'

'But don't you suppose it's wonderful, up there in their secret villages?'

'No. What would there be wonderful about it? Savages are savages, and all savages behave more or less alike: rather low-down and dirty, unsanitary, with a few cunning tricks, and struggling to get enough to eat.'

'But surely they have old, old religions and mysteries–it *must* be wonderful, surely it must.'

'I don't know about mysteries–howling and heathen practices, more or less indecent. No, I see nothing wonderful in that kind of stuff. And I wonder that you should, when you have lived in London or Paris or New York—'

'Ah, *everybody* lives in London or Paris or New York'– said the young man, as if this were an argument.

And his peculiar vague enthusiasm for unknown Indians found a full echo in the woman's heart. She was overcome by a foolish romanticism more unreal than a girl's. She felt it was her destiny to wander into the secret haunts of these timeless, mysterious, marvellous Indians of the mountains.

She kept her secret. The young man was departing, her husband was going with him down to Torreon, on business:–would be away for some days. But before the departure, she made her husband talk about the Indians: about the wandering tribes, resembling the Navajo, who were still wandering free; and the Yaquis of Sonora; and the different groups in the different valleys of Chihuahua State.

There was supposed to be one tribe, the Chilchuis,

living in a high valley to the south, who were the sacred tribe of all the Indians. The descendants of Montezuma and of the old Aztec or Totonac kings still lived among them, and the old priests still kept up the ancient religion, and offered human sacrifices—so it was said. Some scientists had been to the Chilchui country, and had come back gaunt and exhausted with hunger and bitter privation, bringing various curious, barbaric objects of worship, but having seen nothing extraordinary in the hungry, stark village of savages.

Though Lederman talked in this off-hand way, it was obvious he felt some of the vulgar excitement at the idea of ancient and mysterious savages.

'How far away are they?' she asked.

'Oh—three days on horseback—past Cuchitee and a little lake there is up there.'

Her husband and the young man departed. The woman made her crazy plans. Of late, to break the monotony of her life, she had harassed her husband into letting her go riding with him, occasionally, on horseback. She was never allowed to go out alone. The country truly was not safe, lawless and crude.

But she had her own horse, and she dreamed of being free as she had been as a girl, among the hills of California.

Her daughter, nine years old, was now in a tiny convent in the little half-deserted Spanish mining-town five miles away.

'Manuel,' said the woman to her house-servant, 'I'm going to ride to the convent to see Margarita, and take her a few things. Perhaps I shall stay the night in the convent. You look after Freddy and see everything is all right till I come back.'

'Shall I ride with you on the master's horse, or shall Juan?' asked the servant.

'Neither of you. I shall go alone.'

The young man looked her in the eyes, in protest. Absolutely impossible that the woman should ride alone!

'I shall go alone,' repeated the large, placid-seeming, fair-complexioned woman, with peculiar over-bearing emphasis. And the man silently, unhappily yielded.

'Why are you going alone, mother?' asked her son, as she made up parcels of food.

'Am I *never* to be let alone? Not one moment of my life?' she cried, with sudden explosion of energy. And the child, like the servant, shrank into silence.

She set off without a qualm, riding astride on her strong roan horse, and wearing a riding suit of coarse linen, a riding skirt over her linen breeches, a scarlet neck-tie over her white blouse, and a black felt hat on her head. She had food in her saddle-bags, an army canteen with water, and a large, native blanket tied on behind the saddle. Peering into the distance, she set off from her home. Manuel and the little boy stood in the gateway to watch her go. She did not even turn to wave them farewell.

But when she had ridden about a mile, she left the wild road and took a small trail to the right, that led into another valley, over steep places and past great trees, and through another deserted mining-settlement. It was September, the water was running freely in the little stream that had fed the now-abandoned mine. She got down to drink, and let the horse drink too.

She saw natives coming through the trees, away up the slope. They had seen her, and were watching her closely. She watched in turn. The three people, two women and a youth, were making a wide detour, so as not to come too close to her. She did not care. Mounting, she trotted ahead up the silent valley, beyond the silver-works, beyond any trace of mining. There was still a rough trail, that led over rocks and loose stones into the valley beyond. This trail she had already ridden, with her husband. Beyond that she knew she must go south.

Curiously she was not afraid, although it was a frightening country, the silent, fatal-seeming mountain-slopes, the occasional distant, suspicious, elusive natives among the trees, the great carrion birds occasionally hovering, like great flies, in the distance, over some carrion or some ranch house or some group of huts.

As she climbed the trees shrank and the trail ran through a thorny scrub, that was trailed over with blue convolvulus and an occasional pink creeper. Then these flowers lapsed. She was nearing the pine-trees.

She was over the crest, and before her another silent, void, green-clad valley. It was past midday. Her horse turned to a little runlet of water, so she got down to eat her midday meal. She sat in silence looking at the motionless unliving valley, and at the sharp-peaked hills, rising higher to rock and pine-trees, southwards. She rested two hours in the heat of the day, while the horse cropped around her.

Curious that she was neither afraid nor lonely. Indeed, the loneliness was like a drink of cold water to one who is very thirsty. And a strange elation sustained her from within.

She travelled on, and camped at night in a valley beside a stream, deep among the bushes. She had seen cattle and had crossed several trails. There must be a ranch not far off. She heard the strange wailing shriek of a mountain-lion, and the answer of dogs. But she sat by her small camp fire in a secret hollow place and was not really afraid. She was buoyed up always by the curious, bubbling elation within her.

It was very cold before dawn. She lay wrapped in her blanket looking at the stars, listening to her horse shivering, and feeling like a woman who has died and passed beyond. She was not sure that she had not heard, during the night, a great crash at the centre of herself, which was the crash of her own death. Or else it was a crash at the centre of the earth, and meant something big and mysterious.

With the first peep of light she got up, numb with cold, and made a fire. She ate hastily, gave her horse some pieces of oil-seed cake, and set off again. She avoided any meeting—and since she met nobody, it was evident that she in turn was avoided. She came at last in sight of the village of Cuchitee, with its black houses with their reddish roofs, a sombre, dreary little cluster below another silent, long-abandoned mine. And beyond, a long, great mountain-side, rising up green and light to the darker, shaggier green of pine trees. And beyond the pine trees stretches of naked rock against the sky, rock slashed already and brindled with white stripes of snow. High up, the new snow had already begun to fall.

And now, as she neared, more or less, her destination, she began to go vague and disheartened. She had passed the little lake among yellowing aspen trees whose white trunks were round and suave like the white round arms of some woman. What a lovely place! In California she would have raved about it. But here she looked and saw that it was lovely, but she didn't care. She was weary and spent with her two nights in the open, and afraid of the coming night. She didn't know where she was going, or what she was going for. Her horse plodded dejectedly on, towards that immense and forbidding mountain-slope, following a stony little trail. And if she had had any will of her own left, she would have turned back, to the village, to be protected and sent home to her husband.

But she had no will of her own. Her horse splashed through a brook, and turned up a valley, under immense yellowing cotton-wood trees. She must have been near nine thousand feet above sea-level, and her head was light with the altitude and with weariness. Beyond the cotton-wood trees she could see, on each side, the steep sides of mountain-slopes hemming her in, sharp-plumaged with overlapping aspen, and, higher up, with sprouting, pointed spruce and pine tree. Her horse went on automatically. In this tight valley, on this slight trail, there was nowhere to go but ahead, climbing.

Suddenly her horse jumped, and three men in dark

blankets were on the trail before her.

'Adios!' came the greeting, in the full, restrained Indian voice.

'Adios!' she replied, in her assured, American woman's voice.

'Where are you going?' came the quiet question, in Spanish.

The men in the dark sarapes had come closer, and were looking up at her.

'On ahead,' she replied coolly, in her hard, Saxon Spanish.

These were just natives to her: dark-faced, strongly-built men in dark sarapes and straw hats. They would have been the same as the men who worked for her husband, except, strangely, for the long black hair that fell over their shoulders. She noted this long black hair with a certain distaste. These must be the wild Indians she had come to see.

'Where do you come from?' the same man asked. It was always the one man who spoke. He was young, with quick, large, bright black eyes that glanced sideways at her. He had a soft black moustache on his dark face, and a sparse tuft of beard, loose hairs on his chin. His long black hair, full of life, hung unrestrained on his shoulders. Dark as he was, he did not look as if he had washed lately.

His two companions were the same, but older men, powerful and silent. One had a thin black line of moustache, but was beardless. The other had the smooth cheeks and the sparse dark hairs marking the lines of his chin with the beard characteristic of the Indians.

'I come from far away,' she replied, with half-jocular evasion.

This was received in silence.

'But where do you live?' asked the young man, with the same quiet insistence.

'In the north,' she replied airily.

Again there was a moment's silence. The young

man conversed quietly, in Indian, with his two companions.

'Where do you want to go, up this way?' he asked suddenly, with challenge and authority, pointing briefly up the trail.

'To the Chilchui Indians,' answered the woman laconically.

The young man looked at her. His eyes were quick and black, and inhuman. He saw, in the full evening light, the faint, sub-smile of assurance on her rather large, calm, fresh-complexioned face; the weary, bluish lines under her large blue eyes; and in her eyes, as she looked down at him, a half-childish, half-arrogant confidence in her own female power. But in her eyes also, a curious look of trance.

'*Usted es Señora?* You are a lady?' the Indian asked her.

'Yes, I am a lady,' she replied complacently.

'With a family?'

'With a husband and two children, boy and girl,' she said.

The Indian turned to his companions and translated, in the low, gurgling speech, like hidden water running. They were evidently at a loss.

'Where is your husband?' asked the young man.

'Who knows?' she replied airily. 'He has gone away on business for a week.'

The black eyes watched her shrewdly. She, for all her weariness, smiled faintly in the pride of her own adventure and the assurance of her own womanhood, and the spell of the madness that was on her.

'And what do *you* want to do?' the Indian asked her.

'I want to visit the Chilchui Indians—to see their houses and to know their gods,' she replied.

The young man turned and translated quickly, and there was a silence almost of consternation. The grave elder men were glancing at her sideways, with strange looks, from under their decorated hats. And they said something to the young man, in deep chest voices.

The latter still hesitated. Then he turned to the woman.

'Good!' he said. 'Let us go. But we cannot arrive until to-morrow. We shall have to make a camp to-night.'

'Good!' she said. 'I can make a camp.'

Without more ado, they set off at a good speed up the stony trail. The young Indian ran alongside her horse's head, the other two ran behind. One of them had taken a thick stick, and occasionally he struck her horse a resounding blow on the haunch, to urge him forward. This made the horse jump, and threw her back in the saddle, which, tired as she was, made her angry.

'Don't do that!' she cried, looking round angrily at the fellow. She met his black, large, bright eyes, and for the first time her spirit really quailed. The man's eyes were not human to her, and they did not see her as a beautiful white woman. He looked at her with a black, bright inhuman look, and saw no woman in her at all. As if she were some strange, unaccountable *thing*, incomprehensible to him, but inimical. She sat in her saddle in wonder, feeling once more as if she had died. And again he struck her horse, and jerked her badly in the saddle.

All the passionate anger of the spoilt white woman rose in her. She pulled her horse to a standstill, and turned with blazing eyes to the man at her bridle.

'Tell that fellow not to touch my horse again,' she cried.

She met the eyes of the young man, and in their bright black inscrutability she saw a fine spark, as in a snake's eye, of derision. He spoke to his companion in the rear, in the low tones of the Indian. The man with the stick listened without looking. Then, giving a strange low cry to the horse, he struck it again on the rear, so that it leaped forward spasmodically up the stony trail, scatter-ing the stones, pitching the weary woman in her seat.

The anger flew like a madness into her eyes, she went white at the gills. Fiercely she reined in her horse. But before she could turn, the young Indian had caught the reins under the horse's throat, jerked them forward, and was trotting ahead rapidly, leading the horse.

The woman was powerless. And along with her supreme anger there came a slight thrill of exultation. She knew she was dead.

The sun was setting, a great yellow light flooded the last of the aspens, flared on the trunks of the pine-trees, the pine-needles bristled and stood out with dark lustre, the rocks glowed with unearthly glamour. And through this effulgence the Indian at her horse's head trotted unweariedly on, his dark blanket swinging, his bare legs glowing with a strange transfigured ruddiness in the powerful light, and his straw hat with its half-absurd decorations of flowers and feathers shining showily above his river of long black hair. At times he would utter a low call to the horse, and then the other Indian, behind, would fetch the beast a whack with the stick.

The wonder-light faded off the mountains, the world began to grow dark, a cold air breathed down. In the sky, half a moon was struggling against the glow in the west. Huge shadows came down from steep rocky slopes. Water was rushing. The woman was conscious only of her fatigue, her unspeakable fatigue, and the cold wind from the heights. She was not aware how moonlight replaced daylight. It happened while she travelled unconscious with weariness.

For some hours they travelled by moonlight. Then suddenly they came to a standstill. The men conversed in low tones for a moment.

'We camp here,' said the young man.

She waited for him to help her down. He merely stood holding the horse's bridle. She almost fell from the saddle, so fatigued.

They had chosen a place at the foot of rocks that still gave off a little warmth of the sun. One man cut pine-boughs, another erected little screens of pine-boughs against the rock for shelter, and put boughs of balsam pine for beds. The third made a small fire, to heat tortillas. They worked in silence.

The woman drank water. She did not want to eat—only to lie down.

'Where do I sleep?' she asked.

The young man pointed to one of the shelters. She crept in and lay inert. She did not care what happened to her, she was so weary, and so beyond everything. Through the twigs of spruce she could see the three men squatting round the fire on their hams, chewing the tortillas they picked from the ashes with their dark fingers, and drinking water from a gourd. They talked in low, muttering tones, with long intervals of silence. Her saddle and saddle-bags lay not far from the fire, unopened, untouched. The men were not interested in her nor her belongings. There they squatted with their hats on their heads, eating, eating mechanically, like animals, the dark sarape with its fringe falling to the ground before and behind, the powerful dark legs naked and squatting like an animal's, showing the dirty white shirt and the sort of loin-cloth which was the only other garment, underneath. And they showed no more sign of interest in her than if she had been a piece of venison they were bringing home from the hunt, and had hung inside the shelter.

After a while they carefully extinguished the fire, and went inside their own shelter. Watching through the screen of boughs, she had a moment's thrill of fear and anxiety, seeing the dark forms cross and pass silently in the moonlight. Would they attack her now?

But no! They were as if oblivious of her. Her horse was hobbled; she could hear it hopping wearily. All was silent, mountain-silent, cold, deathly. She slept and woke and slept in a semi-conscious numbness of cold and fatigue. A long, long night, icy and eternal, and she was aware that she had died.

II

Yet when there was a stirring, and a clink of flint and steel, and the form of a man crouching like a dog over a bone, at a red splutter of fire, and she knew it was morning coming, it seemed to her the night had passed too soon.

When the fire was going she came out of her shelter with one real desire left: for coffee. The men were warming more tortillas.

'Can we make coffee?' she asked.

The young man looked at her, and she imagined the same faint spark of derision in his eyes. He shook his head.

'We don't take it,' he said. 'There is no time.'

And the elder men, squatting on their haunches, looked up at her in the terrible paling dawn, and there was not even derision in their eyes. Only that intense, yet remote, inhuman glitter which was terrible to her. They were inaccessible. They could not see her as a woman at all. As if she *were* not a woman. As if, perhaps, her whiteness took away all her womanhood, and left her as some giant, female white ant. That was all they could see in her.

Before the sun was up, she was in the saddle again, and they were climbing steeply, in the icy air. The sun came, and soon she was very hot, exposed to the glare in the bare places. It seemed to her they were climbing to the roof of the world. Beyond against heaven were slashes of snow.

During the course of the morning, they came to a place where the horse could not go farther. They rested for a time with a great slant of living rock in front of them, like the glossy breast of some earth-beast. Across this rock, along a wavering crack, they had to go. It seemed to her that for hours she went in torment, on her hands and knees, from crack to crevice, along the slanting face of this pure rock-mountain. An Indian in front and an Indian behind walked slowly erect, shod with sandals of braided leather. But she in her riding-boots dared not stand erect.

Yet what she wondered, all the time, was why she persisted in clinging and crawling along these mile-long sheets of rock. Why she did not hurl herself down, and have done! The world was below her.

When they emerged at last on a stony slope, she looked back, and saw the third Indian coming carrying her saddle and saddle-bags on his back, the whole hung from a band across his forehead. And he had his hat in his hand, as he stepped slowly, with the slow, soft, heavy tread of the Indian, unwavering in the chinks of rock, as if along a scratch in the mountain's iron shield.

The stony slope led downwards. The Indians seemed to grow excited. One ran ahead at a slow trot, disappearing round the curve of stones. And the track curved round and down, till at last in the full blaze of the mid-morning sun, they could see a valley below them between walls of rock, as in a great wide chasm let in the mountains. A green valley, with a river, and trees, and clusters of low flat sparkling houses. It was all tiny and perfect, three thousand feet below. Even the flat bridge over the stream, and the square with the houses around it, the bigger buildings piled up at opposite ends of the square, the tall cotton-wood trees, the pastures and stretches of yellow-sere maize, the patches of brown sheep or goats in the distance, on the slopes, the railed enclosures by the stream-side. There it was, all small and perfect, looking magical, as any place will look magical, seen from the mountains above. The unusual thing was that the low houses glittered white, whitewashed, looking like crystals of salt, or silver. This frightened her.

They began the long, winding descent at the head of the barranca, following the stream that rushed and fell. At first it was all rocks: then the pine-trees began, and soon, the silver-limbed aspens. The flowers of autumn, big pink daisy-like flowers, and white ones, and many yellow flowers, were in profusion. But she had to sit down and rest, she was so weary. And she saw the bright flowers shadowily, as pale shadows hovering, as one who is dead must see them.

At length came grass and pasture-slopes between mingled aspen and pine-trees. A shepherd, naked in the sun save for his hat and his cotton loin-cloth, was driving his brown sheep away. In a grove of trees they sat and waited, she and the young Indian. The one with the saddle had also gone forward.

They heard a sound of someone coming. It was three men, in fine sarapes of red and orange and yellow and black, and with brilliant feather head-dresses. The oldest had his grey hair braided with fur, and his red and orange-yellow sarape was covered with curious black markings, like a leopard-skin. The other two were not grey-haired, but they were elders too. Their blankets were in stripes, and their head-dresses not so elaborate.

The young Indian addressed the elders in a few quiet words. They listened without answering or looking at him or at the woman, keeping their faces averted and their eyes turned to the ground, only listening. And at length they turned and looked at the woman.

The old chief, or medicine man, whatever he was, had a deeply wrinkled and lined face of dark bronze, with a few sparse grey hairs round the mouth. Two long braids of grey hair, braided with fur and coloured feathers, hung on his shoulders. And yet, it was only his eyes that mattered. They were black and of extra-ordinary piercing strength, without a qualm of misgiving in their demonish, dauntless power. He looked into the eyes of the white woman with a long, piercing look, seeking she knew not what. She summoned all her strength to meet his eyes and keep up her guard. But it was no good. He was not looking at her as one human being looks at another. He never even perceived her resistance or her challenge, but looked past them both, into she knew not what.

She could see it was hopeless to expect any human communication with this old being.

He turned and said a few words to the young Indian.

'He asks what do you seek here?' said the young man in Spanish.

'I? Nothing! I only came to see what it was like.'

This was again translated, and the old man turned his eyes on her once more. Then he spoke again, in his low muttering tone, to the young Indian.

'He says, why does she leave her house with the white men? Does she want to bring the white man's God to the Chilchui?'

'No,' she replied, foolhardy. 'I came away from the white man's God myself. I came to look for the God of the Chilchui.'

Profound silence followed, when this was translated. Then the old man spoke again, in a small voice almost of weariness.

'Does the white woman seek the gods of the Chilchui because she is weary of her own God?' came the question.

'Yes, she does. She is tired of the white man's God,' she replied, thinking that was what they wanted her to say. She would like to serve the gods of the Chilchui.

She was aware of an extraordinary thrill of triumph and exultance passing through the Indians, in the tense silence that followed when this was translated. Then they all looked at her with piercing black eyes, in which a steely covetous intent glittered incomprehensible. She was the more puzzled, as there was nothing sensual or sexual in the look. It had a terrible glittering purity that was beyond her. She was afraid, she would have been paralysed with fear, had not something died within her, leaving her with a cold, watchful wonder only.

The elders talked a little while, then the two went away, leaving her with the young man and the oldest chief. The old man now looked at her with a certain solicitude.

'He says are you tired?' asked the young man.

'Very tired,' she said.

'The men will bring you a carriage,' said the young Indian.

The carriage, when it came, proved to be a litter consisting of a sort of hammock of dark woollen frieze, slung on to a pole which was borne on the shoulders of two long-haired Indians. The woollen hammock was spread on the ground, she sat down on it, and the two men raised the pole to their shoulders. Swinging rather as if she were in a sack, she was carried out of the grove of trees, following the old chief, whose leopard-spotted blanket moved curiously in the sunlight.

They had emerged in the valley-head. Just in front were the maize fields, with ripe ears of maize. The corn was not very tall, in this high altitude. The well-worn path went between it, and all she could see was the erect form of the old chief, in the flame and black sarape, stepping soft and heavy and swift, his head forward, looking neither to right nor left. Her bearers followed, stepping rhythmically, the long blue-black hair glistening like a river down the naked shoulders of the man in front.

They passed the maize, and came to a big wall or earthwork made of earth and adobe bricks. The wooden doors were open. Passing on, they were in a network of small gardens, full of flowers and herbs and fruit trees, each garden watered by a tiny ditch of running water. Among each cluster of trees and flowers was a small, glittering white house, windowless, and with closed door. The place was a network of little paths, small streams, and little bridges among square, flowering gardens.

Following the broadest path—a soft narrow track between leaves and grass, a path worn smooth by centuries of human feet, no hoof of horse nor any wheel to disfigure it—they came to the little river of swift bright water, and crossed on a log bridge. Everything was silent—there was not a human being anywhere. The road went on under magnificent cotton-wood trees. It emerged suddenly outside the central plaza or square of the village.

This was a long oblong of low white houses with flat roofs, and two bigger buildings, having as it were little square huts piled on top of bigger long huts, stood at either end of the oblong, facing each other rather askew. Every little house was a dazzling white, save for the great round beam-ends which projected under the flat eaves, and for the flat roofs. Round each of the bigger buildings, on the outside of the square, was a stockyard fence, inside which was garden with trees and flowers, and various small houses.

Not a soul was in sight. They passed silently between the houses into the central square. This was quite bare and arid, the earth trodden smooth by endless generations of passing feet, passing across from door to door. All the doors of the windowless houses gave on to this blank square, but all the doors were closed. The firewood lay near the threshold, a clay oven was still smoking, but there was no sign of moving life.

The old man walked straight across the square to the big house at the end, where the two upper storeys, as in a house of toy bricks, stood each one smaller than the lower one. A stone staircase, outside, led up to the roof of the first storey.

At the foot of this staircase the litter-bearers stood still, and lowered the woman to the ground.

'You will come up,' said the young Indian who spoke Spanish.

She mounted the stone stairs to the earthen roof of the first house, which formed a platform round the wall of the second storey. She followed around this platform to the back of the big house. There they descended again, into the garden at the rear.

So far they had seen no one. But now two men appeared, bare-headed, with long braided hair, and wearing a sort of white shirt gathered into a loin-cloth. These went along with the three newcomers, across the garden where red flowers and yellow flowers were blooming, to a long, low white house. There they entered without knocking.

It was dark inside. There was a low murmur of men's voices. Several men were present, their white shirts showing in the gloom, their dark faces invisible. They were sitting on a great log of smooth old wood, that lay along the far wall. And save for this log, the room seemed empty. But no, in the dark at one end was a couch, a sort of bed, and someone lying there, covered with furs.

The old Indian in the spotted sarape, who had accompanied the woman, now took off his hat and his blanket and his sandals. Laying them aside, he approached the couch, and spoke in a low voice. For some moments there was no answer. Then an old man with the snow-white hair hanging round his darkly-visible face, roused himself like a vision, and leaned on one elbow, looking vaguely at the company, in tense silence.

The grey-haired Indian spoke again, and then the young Indian, taking the woman's hand, led her forward. In her linen riding habit, and black boots and hat, and her pathetic bit of a red tie, she stood there beside the fur-covered bed of the old, old man, who sat reared up, leaning on one elbow, remote as a ghost, his white hair streaming in disorder, his face almost black, yet with a far-off intentness, not of this world, leaning forward to look at her.

His face was so old, it was like dark glass, and the few curling hairs that sprang white from his lips and chin were quite incredible. The long white locks fell unbraided and disorderly on either side of the glassy dark face. And under a faint powder of white eyebrows, the black eyes of the old chief looked at her as if from the far, far dead, seeing something that was never to be seen.

At last he spoke a few deep, hollow words, as if to

the dark air.

'He says, do you bring your heart to the god of the Chilchui?' translated the young Indian.

'Tell him yes,' she said, automatically.

There was a pause. The old Indian spoke again, as if to the air. One of the men present went out. There was a silence as if of eternity, in the dim room that was lighted only through the open door.

The woman looked round. Four old men with grey hair sat on the log by the wall facing the door. Two other men, powerful and impassive, stood near the door. They all had long hair, and wore white shirts gathered into a loin-cloth. Their powerful legs were naked and dark. There was a silence like eternity.

At length the man returned, with white and dark clothing on his arm. The young Indian took them, and holding them in front of the woman, said:

'You must take off your clothes, and put these on.'

'If all you men will go out,' she said.

'No one will hurt you,' he said quietly.

'Not while you men are here,' she said.

He looked at the two men by the door. They came quickly forward, and suddenly gripped her arms as she stood, without hurting her, but with great power. Then two of the old men came, and with curious skill slit her boots down with keen knives, and drew them off, and slit her clothing so that it came away from her. In a few moments she stood there white and uncovered. The old man on the bed spoke, and they turned her round for him to see. He spoke again, and the young Indian deftly took the pins and comb from her fair hair, so that it fell over her shoulders in a bunchy tangle.

Then the old man spoke again. The Indian led her to the bedside. The white-haired, glassy-dark old man moistened his fingertips at his mouth, and most delicately touched her on the breasts and on the body, then on the back. And she winced strangely each time, as the fingertips drew along her skin, as if Death itself were touching her.

And she wondered, almost sadly, why she did not feel shamed in her nakedness. She only felt sad and lost. Because nobody felt ashamed. The elder men were all dark and tense with some other deep, gloomy, incomprehensible emotion, which suspended all her agitation, while the young Indian had a strange look of ecstasy on his face. And she, she was only utterly strange and beyond herself, as if her body were not her own.

They gave her the new clothing: a long white cotton shift, that came to her knees: then a tunic of thick blue woollen stuff, embroidered with scarlet and green flowers. It was fastened over one shoulder only, and belted with a braid sash of scarlet and black wool.

When she was thus dressed, they took her away, barefoot, to a little house in the stockaded garden. The young Indian told her she might have what she wanted. She asked for water to wash herself. He brought it in a jar, together with a long wooden bowl. Then he fastened the gate-door of her house, and left her a prisoner. She could see through the bars of the gate-door of her house, the red flowers of the garden, and a humming bird. Then from the roof of the big house she heard the long, heavy sound of a drum, unearthly to her in its summons, and an uplifted voice calling from the house-top in a strange language, with a far-away emotionless intonation, delivering some speech or message. And she listened as if from the dead.

But she was very tired. She lay down on a couch of skins, pulling over her the blanket of dark wool, and she slept, giving up everything.

When she woke it was late afternoon, and the young Indian was entering with a basket-tray containing food, tortillas and corn-mush with bits of meat, probably mutton, and a drink made of honey, and some fresh plums. He brought her also a long garland of red and yellow flowers with knots of blue buds at the end. He sprinkled the garland with water from a jar, then offered it to her, with a smile. He seemed very gentle and thoughtful, and on his face and in his dark eyes was a curious look of triumph and ecstasy, that frightened her a little. The glitter had gone from the black eyes, with their curving dark lashes, and he would look at her with this strange soft glow of ecstasy that was not quite human, and terribly impersonal, and which made her uneasy.

'Is there anything you want?' he said, in his low, slow, melodious voice, that always seemed withheld, as if he were speaking aside to somebody else, or as if he did not want to let the sound come out to her.

'Am I going to be kept a prisoner here?' she asked.

'No, you can walk in the garden to-morrow,' he said softly. Always this curious solicitude.

'Do you like that drink?' he said, offering her a little earthenware cup. 'It is very refreshing.'

She sipped the liquor curiously. It was made with herbs and sweetened with honey, and had a strange, lingering flavour. The young man watched her with gratification.

'It has a peculiar taste,' she said.

'It is very refreshing,' he replied, his black eyes resting on her always with that look of gratified ecstasy. Then he went away. And presently she began to be sick, and to vomit violently, as if she had not control over herself.

Afterwards she felt a great soothing languor steal over her, her limbs felt strong and loose and full of languor, and she lay on her couch listening to the sounds of the village, watching the yellowing sky, smelling the scent of burning cedar-wood, or pine-wood. So distinctly she heard the yapping of tiny dogs, the shuffle of far-off feet, the murmur of voices, so keenly she detected the smell of smoke, and flowers, and evening falling, so vividly she saw the one bright star infinitely remote, stirring above the sunset, that she felt as if all her senses were diffused on the air, and she could distinguish the sound of evening flowers unfolding, and the actual crystal sound of the heavens, as the vast belts of the world-atmosphere slid past one another, and as if the moisture ascending and the moisture descending in the air resounded like some harp in the cosmos.

She was a prisoner in her house and in the stockaded garden, but she scarcely minded. And it was days before she realised that she never saw another woman. Only the men, the elderly men of the big house, that she imagined must be some sort of temple, and the men priests of some sort. For they always had the same colours, red, orange, yellow, and black, and the same grave, abstracted demeanour.

Sometimes an old man would come and sit in her room with her, in absolute silence. None spoke any language but Indian, save the one younger man. The older men would smile at her, and sit with her for an hour at a time, sometimes smiling at her when she spoke in Spanish, but never answering save with this slow, benevolent-seeming smile. And they gave off a feeling of almost fatherly solicitude. Yet their dark eyes, brooding over her, had something away in their depths that was awesomely ferocious and relentless. They would cover it with a smile, at once, if they felt her looking. But she had seen it.

Always they treated her with this curious impersonal solicitude, this utterly impersonal gentleness, as an old man treats a child. But underneath it she felt there was something else, something terrible. When her old visitor had gone away, in his silent, insidious, fatherly fashion, a shock of fear would come over her; though of what she knew not.

The young Indian would sit and talk with her freely as if with great candour. But with him, too, she felt that everything real was unsaid. Perhaps it was unspeakable. His big dark eyes would rest on her almost cherishingly, touched with ecstasy, and his beautiful, slow, languorous voice would trail out its simple, ungrammatical Spanish. He told her he was the grandson of the old, old man, son of the man in the spotted sarape: and they were caciques, kings from the old, old days, before even the Spaniards came. But he himself had been in Mexico City, and also in the United States. He had worked as a labourer, building the roads in Los Angeles. He had travelled as far as Chicago.

'Don't you speak English, then?' she asked.

His eyes rested on her with a curious look of duplicity and conflict, and he mutely shook his head.

'What did you do with your long hair, when you were in the United States?' she asked. 'Did you cut it off?'

Again, with the look of torment in his eyes, he shook his head.

'No,' he said, in a low, subdued voice, 'I wore a hat, and a handkerchief tied round my head.'

And he relapsed into silence, as if of tormented memories.

'Are you the only man of your people who has been to the United States?' she asked him.

'Yes. I am the only one who has been away from here for a long time. The others come back soon, in one week. They don't stay away. The old men don't let them.'

'And why did you go?'

'The old men want me to go—because I shall be the Cacique—'

He talked always with the same naiveté, an almost childish candour. But she felt that this was perhaps just the effect of his Spanish. Or perhaps speech altogether was unreal to him. Anyhow, she felt that all the real things were kept back.

He came and sat with her a good deal—sometimes more than she wished—as if he wanted to be near her. She asked him if he was married. He said he was—with two children.

'I should like to see your children,' she said.

But he answered only with that smile, a sweet,

almost ecstatic smile, above which the dark eyes hardly changed from their enigmatic abstraction.

It was curious, he would sit with her by the hour, without ever making her self-conscious, or sex-conscious. He seemed to have no sex, as he sat there so still and gentle and apparently submissive, with his head bent a little forward, and the river of glistening black hair streaming maidenly over his shoulders.

Yet when she looked again, she saw his shoulders broad and powerful, his eyebrows black and level, the short, curved, obstinate black lashes over his lowered eyes, the small, fur-like line of moustache above his blackish, heavy lips, and the strong chin, and she knew that in some other mysterious way he was darkly and powerfully male. And he, feeling her watching him, would glance up at her swiftly with a dark, lurking look in his eyes, which immediately he veiled with that half-sad smile.

The days and the weeks went by, in a vague kind of contentment. She was uneasy sometimes, feeling she had lost the power over herself. She was not in her own power, she was under the spell of some other control. And at times she had moments of terror and horror. But then these Indians would come and sit with her, casting their insidious spell over her by their very silent presence, their silent, sexless, powerful physical presence. As they sat they seemed to take her will away, leaving her will-less and victim to her own indifference. And the young man would bring her sweetened drink, often the same emetic drink, but sometimes other kinds. And after drinking, the languor filled her heavy limbs, her senses seemed to float in the air, listening, hearing. They had brought her a little female dog, which she called Flora. And once, in the trance of her senses, she felt she *heard* the little dog conceive, in her tiny womb, and begin to be complex, with young. And another day she could hear the vast sound of the earth going round, like some immense arrow-string booming.

But as the days grew shorter and colder, when she was cold, she would get a sudden revival of her will, and a desire to go out, to go away. And she insisted to the young man, she wanted to go out.

So one day, they let her climb to the topmost roof of the big house where she was, and look down the square. It was the day of the big dance, but not everybody was dancing. Women with babies in their arms stood in their doorways, watching. Opposite, at the other end of the square, there was a throng before the other big house, and a small, brilliant group on the terrace-roof of the first storey, in front of wide open doors of the upper storey. Through these wide open doors she could see fire glinting in darkness and priests in headdresses of black and yellow and scarlet feathers, wearing robe-like blankets of black and red and yellow, with long green fringe, were moving about. A big drum was beating slowly and regularly, in the dense, Indian silence. The crowd below waited—

Then a drum started on a high beat, and there came the deep, powerful burst of men singing a heavy, savage music, like a wind roaring in some timeless forest, many mature men singing in one breath, like the wind; and long lines of dancers walked out from under the big house. Men with naked, golden-bronze bodies and streaming black hair, tufts of red and yellow feathers on their arms, and kilts of white frieze with a bar of heavy red and black and green embroidery round their waists, bending slightly forward and stamping the earth in their absorbed, monotonous stamp of the dance, a fox-fur, hung by the nose from their belt behind, swaying with the sumptuous swaying of a beautiful fox-fur, the tip of the tail writhing above the dancer's heels. And after each man, a woman with a strange elaborate headdress of feathers and seashells, and wearing a short black tunic, moving erect, holding up tufts of feathers in each hand, swaying her wrists rhythmically and subtly beating the earth with her bare feet.

So, the long line of the dance unfurling from the big house opposite. And from the big house beneath her, strange scent of incense, strange tense silence, then the answering burst of inhuman male singing, and the long line of the dance unfurling.

It went on all day, the insistence of the drum, the cavernous, roaring, storm-like sound of male singing, the incessant swinging of the fox-skins behind the powerful, gold-bronze, stamping legs of the men, the autumn sun from a perfect blue heaven pouring on the rivers of black hair, men's and women's, the valley all still, the walls of rock beyond, the awful huge bulking of the mountain against the pure sky, its snow seething with sheer whiteness.

For hours and hours she watched, spell-bound, and as if drugged. And in all the terrible persistence of the drumming and the primeval, rushing deep singing, and the endless stamping of the dance of fox-tailed men, the tread of heavy, bird-erect women in their black tunics, she seemed at last to feel her own death; her own obliteration. As if she were to be obliterated from the field of life again. In the strange towering symbols on the heads of the changeless, absorbed women she seemed to read once more the *Mene Mene Tekel Upharsin*. Her kind of womanhood, intensely personal and individual, was to be obliterated again, and the great primeval symbols were to tower once more over the fallen individual independence of woman. The sharpness and the quivering nervous consciousness of the highly-bred white woman was to be destroyed again, womanhood was to be cast once more into the great stream of impersonal sex and impersonal passion. Strangely, as if clairvoyant, she saw the immense sacrifice prepared. And she went back to her little house in a trance of agony.

After this, there was always a certain agony when she heard the drums at evening, and the strange uplifted savage sound of men singing round the drum, like wild creatures howling to the invisible gods of the moon and the vanished sun. Something of the chuckling, sobbing cry of the coyote, something of the exultant bark of the fox, the far-off wild melancholy exultance of the howling wolf, the torment of the puma's scream, and the insistence of the ancient fierce human male, with his lapses of tenderness and his abiding ferocity.

Sometimes she would climb the high roof after nightfall, and listen to the dim cluster of young men round the drum on the bridge just beyond the square, singing by the hour. Sometimes there would be a fire, and in the fire-glow, men in their white shirts or naked save for a loin-cloth, would be dancing and stamping like spectres, hour after hour in the dark cold air, within the fire-glow, forever dancing and stamping like turkeys, or dropping squatting by the fire to rest, throwing their blankets round them.

'Why do you all have the same colours?' she asked the young Indian. 'Why do you all have red and yellow and black, over your white shirts? And the women have black tunics?'

He looked into her eyes, curiously, and the faint, evasive smile came on to his face. Behind the smile lay a soft, strange malignancy.

'Because our men are the fire and the daytime, and our women are the spaces between the stars at night,' he said.

'Aren't the women even stars?' she said.

'No. We say they are the spaces between the stars, that keep the stars apart.'

He looked at her oddly, and again the touch of derision came into his eyes.

'White people,' he said, 'they know nothing. They are like children, always with toys. We know the sun, and we know the moon. And we say, when a white woman sacrifice herself to our gods, then our gods will begin to make the world again, and the white man's gods will fall to pieces.'

'How sacrifice herself?' she asked quickly.

And he, as quickly covered, covered himself with a subtle smile.

'She sacrifice her own gods and come to our gods, I mean that,' he said, soothingly.

But she was not reassured. An icy pang of fear and certainty was at her heart.

'The sun he is alive at one end of the sky,' he continued, 'and the moon lives at the other end. And the man all the time have to keep the sun happy in his side of the sky, and the woman have to keep the moon quiet at her side of the sky. All the time she have to work at this. And the sun can't ever go into the house of the moon, and the moon can't ever go into the house of the sun, in the sky. So the woman, she asks the moon to come into her cave, inside her. And the man, he draws the sun down till he has the power of the sun. All the time he do this. Then when the man gets a woman, the sun goes into the cave of the moon, and that is how everything in the world starts.'

She listened, watching him closely, as one enemy watches another who is speaking with double meaning.

'Then,' she said, 'why aren't you Indians masters of the white men?'

'Because,' he said, 'the Indian got weak, and lost his power with the sun, so the white men stole the sun. But they can't keep him—they don't know how. They got him, but they don't know what to do with him, like a boy who catch a big grizzly bear, and can't kill him, and can't run away from him. The grizzly bear eats the boy that catch him, when he want to run away from him. White men don't know what they are doing with the sun, and white women don't know what they do with the moon. The moon she got angry with white women, like a puma when someone kills her little ones. The moon, she bites white women—here inside,' and he pressed his side. 'The moon, she is angry in a white woman's cave. The Indian can see it—And soon,' he added, 'the Indian women get the moon back and keep her quiet in their house. And the Indian men get the sun, and the power over all the world.

White men don't know what the sun is. They never know.'

He subsided into a curious exultant silence.

'But,' she faltered, 'why do you hate us so? Why do you hate me?'

He looked up suddenly with a light on his face, and a startling flame of a smile.

'No, we don't hate,' he said softly, looking with a curious glitter into her face.

'You do,' she said, forlorn and hopeless.

And after a moment's silence, he rose and went away.

III

Winter had now come, in the high valley, with snow that melted in the day's sun, and nights that were bitter cold. She lived on, in a kind of daze, feeling her power ebbing more and more away from her, as if her will were leaving her. She felt always in the same relaxed, confused, victimised state, unless the sweetened herb drink would numb her mind altogether, and release her senses into a sort of heightened, mystic acuteness and a feeling as if she were diffusing out deliciously into the harmony of things. This at length became the only state of consciousness she really recognised: this exquisite sense of bleeding out into the higher beauty and harmony of things. Then she could actually hear the great stars in heaven, which she saw through her door, speaking from their motion and brightness, saying things perfectly to the cosmos, as they trod in perfect ripples, like bells on the floor of heaven, passing one another and grouping in the timeless dance, with the spaces of dark between. And she could hear the snow on a cold, cloudy day twittering and faintly whistling in the sky, like birds that flock and fly away in autumn, suddenly calling farewell to the invisible moon, and slipping out of the plains of the air, releasing peaceful warmth. She herself would call to the arrested snow to fall from the upper air. She would call to the unseen moon to cease to be angry, to make peace again with the unseen sun like a woman who ceases to be angry in her house. And she would smell the sweetness of the moon relaxing to the sun in the wintry heaven, when the snow fell in a faint, cold-perfumed relaxation, as the peace of the sun mingled again in a sort of unison with the peace of the moon.

She was aware too of the sort of shadow that was on the Indians of the valley, a deep, stoical disconsolation, almost religious in its depth.

'We have lost our power over the sun, and we are trying to get him back. But he is wild with us, and shy like a horse that has got away. We have to go through a lot.' So the young Indian said to her, looking into her eyes with a strained meaning. And she, as if bewitched, replied:

'I hope you will get him back.'

The smile of triumph flew over his face.

'Do you hope it?' he said.

'I do,' she answered fatally.

'Then all right,' he said, 'We shall get him.'

And he went away in exultance.

She felt she was drifting on some consummation, which she had no will to avoid, yet which seemed heavy and finally terrible to her.

It must have been almost December, for the days were short, when she was taken again before the aged man, and stripped of her clothing, and touched with the old finger-tips.

The aged cacique looked her in the eyes, with his eyes of lonely, far-off, black intentness, and murmured something to her.

'He wants you to make the sign of peace,' the young man translated, showing her the gesture. 'Peace and farewell to him.'

She was fascinated by the black, glass-like, intent eyes of the old cacique, that watched her without blink-

ing, like a basilisk's, overpowering her. In their depths
also she saw a certain fatherly compassion, and pleading.
She put her hand before her face, in the required
manner, making the sign of peace and farewell. He made
the sign of peace back again to her, then sank among his
furs. She thought he was going to die, and that he knew
it.

There followed a day of ceremonial, when she was
brought out before the people, in a blue blanket with
white fringe, and holding blue feathers in her hands.
Before an altar of one house, she was perfumed with
incense and sprinkled with ash. Before the altar of the
opposite house she was fumigated again with incense by
the gorgeous, terrifying priests in yellow and scarlet and
black, their faces painted with scarlet paint. And then
they threw water on her. Meanwhile she was faintly
aware of the fire on the altar, the heavy, heavy sound of a
drum, the heavy sound of men beginning powerfully,
deeply savagely to sing, the swaying of the crowd of faces
in the plaza below, and the formation for a sacred dance.

But at this time her commonplace consciousness
was numb, she was aware of her immediate surroundings
as shadows, almost immaterial. With refined and
heightened senses she could hear the sound of the earth
winging on its journey, like a shot arrow, the ripple-
rustling of the air, and the boom of the great arrow-
string. And it seemed to her there were two great
influences in the upper air, one golden towards the sun,
and one invisible silver; the first travelling like rain
ascending to the gold presence sunwards, the second like
rain silverily descending the ladders of space towards the
hovering, lurking clouds over the snowy mountain-top.
Then between them, another presence, waiting to shake
himself free of moisture, of heavy white snow that had
mysteriously collected about him. And in summer, like a
scorched eagle, he would wait to shake himself clear of
the weight of heavy sunbeams. And he was coloured like
fire. And he was always shaking himself clear, of snow or

of heavy heat, like an eagle rustling.

Then there was a still stranger presence, standing watching from the blue distance, always watching. Sometimes running in upon the wind, or shimmering in the heat-waves. The blue wind itself, rushing as it were out of the holes in the earth into the sky, rushing out of the sky down upon the earth. The blue wind, the go-between, the invisible ghost that belonged to two worlds, that played upon the ascending and the descending chords of the rains.

More and more her ordinary personal consciousness had left her, she had gone into that other state of passional cosmic consciousness, like one who is drugged. The Indians, with their heavily religious natures, had made her succumb to their vision.

Only one personal question she asked the young Indian:

'Why am I the only one that wears blue?'

'It is the colour of the wind. It is the colour of what goes away and is never coming back, but which is always here, waiting like death among us. It is the colour of the dead. And it is the colour that stands away off, looking at us from a distance, that cannot come near to us. When we go near, it goes farther. It can't be near. We are all brown and yellow and black hair, and white teeth and red blood. We are the ones that are here. You with blue eyes, you are the messenger from the far-away, you cannot stay, and now it is time for you to go back.'

'Where to?' she asked.

'To the way-off things like the sun and the blue mother of rain, and tell them that we are the people on the world again, and we can bring the sun to the moon again, like a red horse to a blue mare; we are the people. The white women have driven back the moon in the sky, won't let her come to the sun. So the sun is angry. And the Indian must give the moon to the sun.'

'How?' she said.

'The white woman got to die and go like a wind to

the sun, tell him the Indians will open the gate to the
moon. And the Indian women will open the gate to the
moon. The white women don't let the moon come down
out of the blue coral. The moon used to come down
among the Indian women, like a white goat among the
flowers. And the sun want to come down to the Indian
men, like an eagle to the pine-trees. The sun, he is shut
out behind the white man, and the moon she is shut out
behind the white woman, and they can't get away. They
are angry, everything in the world gets angrier. The
Indian says, he will give the white woman to the sun, so
the sun will leap over the white man and come to the
Indian again. And the moon will be surprised, and she
will see the gate open, and she not know which way to go.
But the Indian woman will call to the moon, *Come! Come!
Come back into my grasslands. The wicked white woman can't
harm you any more.* Then the sun will look over the heads of
the white men, and see the moon in the pastures of our
women, with the Red Men standing around like pine
trees. Then he will leap over the heads of the white men,
and come running past to the Indians through the spruce
trees. And we, who are red and black and yellow, we who
stay, we shall have the sun on our right hand and the
moon on our left. So we can bring the rain down out of
the blue meadows, and up out of the black; and we can
call the wind that tells the corn to grow, when we ask
him, and we shall make the clouds to break, and the
sheep to have twin lambs. And we shall be full of power,
like a spring day. But the white people will be a hard
winter, without snow—'

'But,' said the white woman, 'I don't shut out the
moon—how can I?'

'Yes,' he said, 'you shut the gate, and then laugh,
think you have it all your own way.'

She could never quite understand the way he looked
at her. He was always so curiously gentle, and his smile
was so soft. Yet there was such a glitter in his eyes, and
an unrelenting sort of hate came out of his words, a

strange, profound, impersonal hate. Personally he liked
her, she was sure. He was gentle with her, attracted by
her in some strange, soft, passionless way. But
impersonally he hated her with a mystic hatred. He
would smile at her, winningly. Yet if, the next moment,
she glanced round at him unawares, she would catch
that gleam of pure after-hate in his eyes.

'Have I got to die and be given to the sun?' she
asked.

'Sometime,' he said, laughing evasively. 'Sometime
we all die.'

They were gentle with her, and very considerate
with her. Strange men, the old priests and the young
cacique alike, they watched over her and cared for her
like women. In their soft, insidious understanding, there
was something womanly. Yet their eyes, with that
strange glitter, and their dark, shut mouths that would
open to the broad jaw, the small, strong, white teeth, had
something very primitively male and cruel.

One wintry day, when snow was falling, they took
her to a great dark chamber in the big house. The fire
was burning in a corner on a high raised dais under a
sort of hood or canopy of adobe-work. She saw in the fire-
glow, the glowing bodies of the almost naked priests, and
strange symbols on the roof and walls of the chamber.
There was no door or window in the chamber, they had
descended by a ladder from the roof. And the fire of
pinewood danced continually, showing walls painted
with strange devices, which she could not understand,
and a ceiling of poles making a curious pattern of black
and red and yellow, and alcoves or niches in which were
curious objects she could not discern.

The older priests were going through some
ceremony near the fire, in silence, intense Indian silence.
She was seated on a low projection of the wall, opposite
the fire, two men seated beside her. Presently they gave
her a drink from a cup, which she took gladly, because of
the semi-trance it would induce.

In the darkness and in the silence she was accurately
aware of everything that happened to her: how they took
off her clothes, and, standing her before a great, weird
device on the wall, coloured blue and white and black,
washed her all over with water and the amole infusion;
washed even her hair, softly, carefully, and dried it on
white cloths, till it was soft and glistening. Then they laid
her on a couch under another great indecipherable image
of red and black and yellow, and now rubbed all her
body with sweet-scented oil, and massaged all her limbs,
and her back, and her sides, with a long, strange, hyp-
notic massage. Their dark hands were incredibly powerful, yet soft with a watery softness she could not
understand. And the dark faces, leaning near her white
body, she saw were darkened with red pigment, with
lines of yellow round the cheeks. And the dark eyes
glittered absorbed, as the hands worked upon the soft
white body of the woman.

They were so impersonal, absorbed in something
that was beyond her. They never saw her as a personal
woman: she could tell that. She was some mystic object
to them, some vehicle of passions too remote for her to
grasp. Herself in a state of trance, she watched their faces
bending over her, dark, strangely glistening with the
transparent red paint, and lined with bars of yellow. And
in this weird, luminous-dark mask of living face, the eyes
were fixed with an unchanging steadfast gleam, and the
purplish-pigmented lips were closed in a full, sinister,
sad grimness. The immense fundamental sadness, the
grimness of ultimate decision, the fixity of revenge, and
the nascent exultance of those that are going to
triumph—these things she could read in their faces, as she
lay and was rubbed into a misty glow, by their uncanny
dark hands. Her limbs, her flesh, her very bones at last
seemed to be diffusing into a roseate sort of mist, in
which her consciousness hovered like some sun-gleam in
a flushed cloud.

She knew the gleam would fade, the cloud would go

grey. But at present she did not believe it. She knew she was a victim; that all this elaborate work upon her was the work of victimising her. But she did not mind. She wanted it.

Later, they put a short blue tunic on her and took her to the upper terrace, and presented her to the people. She saw the plaza below her full of dark faces and of glittering eyes. There was no pity: only the curious hard exultance. The people gave a subdued cry when they saw her, and she shuddered. But she hardly cared.

Next day was the last. She slept in a chamber of the big house. At dawn they put on her a big blue blanket with a fringe, and led her out into the plaza, among the throng of silent, dark-blanketed people. There was pure white snow on the ground, and the dark people in their dark-brown blankets looked like inhabitants of another world.

A large drum was slowly pounding, and an old priest was declaring from a housetop. But it was not till noon that a litter came forth, and the people gave that low, animal cry which was so moving. In the sack-like litter sat the old, old cacique, his white hair braided with black braid and large turquoise stones. His face was like a piece of obsidian. He lifted his hand in token, and the litter stopped in front of her. Fixing her with his old eyes, he spoke to her for a few moments, in his hollow voice. No one translated.

Another litter came, and she was placed in it. Four priests moved ahead, in their scarlet and yellow and black, with plumed head-dresses. Then came the litter of the old cacique. Then the light drums began, and two groups of singers burst simultaneously into song, male and wild. And the golden-red, almost naked men, adorned with ceremonial feathers and kilts, the rivers of black hair down their backs, formed into two files and began to tread the dance. So they threaded out of the snowy plaza, in two long, sumptuous lines of dark red-gold and black fur, swaying with a faint tinkle of bits of shell and flint, winding over the snow between the two bee-clusters of men who sang around the drum.

Slowly they moved out, and her litter, with its attendance of feathered, lurid, dancing priests, moved after. Everybody danced the tread of the dance-step, even, subtly, the litter-bearers. And out of the plaza they went, past smoking ovens, on the trail to the great cotton-wood trees, that stood like grey-silver lace against the blue sky, bare and exquisite above the snow. The river diminished, rushed among fangs of ice. The chequer-squares of gardens within fences were all snowy, and the white houses now looked yellowish.

The whole valley glittered intolerably with pure snow, away to the walls of the standing rock. And across the flat cradle of snow-bed wound the long thread of the dance, shaking slowly and sumptuously in its orange and black motion. The high drums thudded quickly, and on the crystalline frozen air the swell and roar of the chant of savages was like an obsession.

She sat looking out of her litter with big, transfixed blue eyes, under which were the wan markings of her drugged weariness. She knew she was going to die, among the glisten of this snow, at the hands of this savage, sumptuous people. And as she stared at the blaze of blue sky above the slashed and ponderous mountain, she thought: 'I am dead already. What difference does it make, the transition from the dead I am to the dead I shall be, very soon!' Yet her soul sickened and felt wan.

The strange procession trailed on, in perpetual dance, slowly across the plain of snow, and then entered the slopes between the pine-trees. She saw the copper-dark men dancing the dance-tread, onwards, between the copper-pale tree trunks. And at last she, too, in her swaying litter, entered the pine-trees.

They were travelling on and on, upwards, across the snow under the trees, past the superb shafts of pale, flaked copper, the rustle and shake and tread of the threading dance, penetrating into the forest, into the mountain. They were following a stream-bed: but the stream was dry, like summer, dried up by the frozenness of the head-waters. There were dark, red-bronze willow bushes with wattles like wild hair, and pallid aspen trees looking like cold flesh against the snow. Then jutting dark rocks.

At last she could tell that the dancers were moving forward no more. Nearer and nearer she came upon the drums, as to a lair of mysterious animals. Then through the bushes she emerged into a strange amphitheatre. Facing was a great wall of hollow rock, down the front of which hung a great, dripping, fang-like spoke of ice. The ice came pouring over the rock from the precipice above, and then stood arrested, dripping out of high heaven, almost down to the hollow stones where the stream-pool should be below. But the pool was dry.

On either side the dry pool, the lines of dancers had formed, and the dance was continuing without intermission, against a background of bushes.

But what she felt was that fanged inverted pinnacle of ice, hanging from the lip of the dark precipice above. And behind the great rope of ice, she saw the leopard-like figures of priests climbing the hollow cliff face, to the cave that like a dark socket, bored a cavity, an orifice, half way up the crag.

Before she could realise, her litter-bearers were staggering in the footholds, climbing the rock. She, too, was behind the ice. There it hung, like a curtain that is not spread, but hangs like a great fang. And near above her was the orifice of the cave sinking dark into the rock. She watched it as she swayed upwards.

On the platform of the cave stood the priests, waiting in all their gorgeousness of feathers and fringed robes, watching her ascent. Two of them stooped to help her litter-bearers. And at length she was on the platform of the cave, far in behind the shaft of ice, above the hollow amphitheatre among the bushes below, where men were dancing, and the whole populace of the village was clustered in silence.

The sun was sloping down the afternoon sky, on the left. She knew that this was the shortest day of the year, and the last day of her life. They stood her facing the iridescent column of ice, which fell down marvellously arrested, away in front of her.

Some signal was given, and the dance below stopped. There was now absolute silence. She was given a little to drink, then two priests took off her mantle and her tunic, and in her strange pallor she stood there, between the lurid robes of the priests, beyond the pillar of ice, beyond and above the dark-faced people. The throng below gave the low, wild cry. Then the priests turned her round, so she stood with her back to the open world, her long blond hair to the people below. And they cried again.

She was facing the cave, inwards. A fire was burning and flickering in the depths. Four priests had taken off their robes, and were almost as naked as she was. They were powerful men in the prime of life, and they kept their dark, painted faces lowered.

From the fire came the old, old priest, with an incense-pan. He was naked and in a state of barbaric ecstasy. He fumigated his victim, reciting at the same time in a hollow voice. Behind him came another robeless priest, with two flint knives.

When she was fumigated, they laid her on a large flat stone, the four powerful men holding her by the outstretched arms and legs. Behind stood the aged man, like a skeleton covered with dark glass, holding a knife and transfixedly watching the sun; and behind him again was another naked priest, with a knife.

She felt little sensation, though she knew all that was happening. Turning to the sky, she looked at the yellow sun. It was sinking. The shaft of ice was like a shadow between her and it. And she realised that the yellow rays were filling half the cave, though they had not reached the altar where the fire was, at the far end of the funnel-shaped cavity.

Yes, the rays were creeping round slowly. As they grew ruddier, they penetrated farther. When the red sun was about to sink, he would shine full through the shaft of ice deep into the hollow of the cave, to the innermost.

She understood now that this was what the men were waiting for. Even those that held her down were bent and twisted round, their black eyes watching the sun with a glittering eagerness, and awe, and craving. The black eyes of the aged cacique were fixed like black mirrors on the sun, as if sightless, yet containing some terrible answer to the reddening winter planet. And all the eyes of the priests were fixed and glittering on the sinking orb, in the reddening, icy silence of the winter afternoon.

They were anxious, terribly anxious, and fierce. Their ferocity wanted something, and they were waiting the moment. And their ferocity was ready to leap out into a mystic exultance, of triumph. But still they were anxious.

Only the eyes of that oldest man were not anxious. Black, and fixed, and as if sightless, they watched the sun, seeing beyond the sun. And in their black, empty concentration there was power, power intensely abstract and remote, but deep, deep to the heart of the earth, and the heart of the sun. In absolute motionlessness he watched till the red sun should send his ray through the column of ice. Then the old man would strike, and strike home, accomplish the sacrifice and achieve the power.

The mastery that man must hold, and that passes from race to race.

In Love

Written October 1926 as 'More Modern Love'. Published *Dial*, November 1927 and the collection *The Woman Who Rode Away*. The title in *Dial* is followed by a question mark, which was dropped in subsequent printings.

'Well, my dear!' said Henrietta. 'If I had such a worried look on my face, when I was going down to spend the week-end with the man I was engaged to–and going to be married to in a month–well! I should either try and change my face, or hide my feelings, or something.'

'You shut up!' said Hester curtly. 'Don't look at my face, if it doesn't please you.'

'Now, my dear Hester, don't go into one of your tempers! Just look in the mirror, and you'll see what I mean.'

'Who cares what you mean! You're not responsible for my face,' said Hester desperately, showing no intention of looking in the mirror, or of otherwise following her sister's kind advice.

Henrietta, being the younger sister, and mercifully unengaged, hummed a tune lightly. She was only twenty-one, and had not the faintest intention of jeopardising her peace of mind by accepting any sort of fatal ring. Nevertheless, it *was* nice to see Hester 'getting off', as they say; for Hester was nearly twenty-five, which is serious.

The worst of it was, lately Hester had had her famous 'worried' look on her face, when it was a question of the faithful Joe: dark shadows under the eyes, drawn lines down the cheeks. And when Hester looked like that, Henrietta couldn't help feeling the most horrid jangled echo of worry and apprehension in her own heart, and she hated it. She simply couldn't stand that sudden feeling of fear.

'What I mean to say,' she continued, '*is*–that it's jolly unfair to Joe, if you go down looking like that. Either put a better face on it, or–' But she checked herself. She was going to say 'don't go'. But really, she did hope that Hester would go through with this marriage. Such a weight off her, Henrietta's, mind.

'Oh hang!' cried Hester. 'Shut up!' And her dark eyes flashed a spark of fury and misgiving at the young Henrietta.

Henrietta sat down on the bed, lifted her chin, and composed her face like a meditating angel. She really was intensely fond of Hester, and the worried look was such a terribly bad sign.

'Look here, Hester!' she said. 'Shall I come down to Markbury with you? *I* don't mind, if you'd like me to.'

'My dear girl,' cried Hester in desperation, 'what earthly use do you think that would be?'

'Well, I thought it might take the edge off the intimacy, if that's what worries you.'

Hester re-echoed with a hollow, mocking laugh.

'Don't be such a *child*, Henrietta, really!' she said.

And Hester set off alone, down to Wiltshire, where her Joe had just started a little farm, to get married on. After being in the artillery, he had got sick and tired of business: besides, Hester would never have gone into a little suburban villa. Every woman sees her home through a wedding ring. Hester had only taken a squint through her engagement ring, so far. But Ye Gods! not Golders Green, not even Harrow!

So Joe had built a little brown wooden bungalow–largely with his own hands: and at the back was a small stream with two willows, old ones. At the sides were brown sheds, and chicken runs. There were pigs in a hog-proof wire fence, and two cows in a field, and a horse. Joe had thirty-odd acres, with only a youth to help him. But of course, there would be Hester.

It all looked very new and tidy. Joe was a worker. He too looked rather new and tidy, very healthy and pleased with himself. He didn't even see the 'worried look'. Or if he did, he only said:

'You're looking a bit fagged, Hester. Going up to the City takes it out of you more than you know. You'll be another girl down here.'

'Shan't I just!' cried Hester.

She did like it, too!—the lots of white and yellow hens, and the pigs so full of pep! And the yellow thin blades of willow leaves showering softly down at the back of her house, from the leaning old trees. She liked it awfully: especially the yellow leaves on the earth.

She told Joe she thought it was all lovely, topping, fine! And he was awfully pleased. Certainly *he* looked fit enough.

The mother of the helping youth gave them dinner at half-past twelve. The afternoon was all sunshine and little jobs to do, after she had dried the dishes for the mother of the youth.

'Not long now, Miss, before you'll be cooking at this range: and a good little range it is.'

'Not long now, no!' echoed Hester, in the hot little wooden kitchen, that was overheated from the range.

The woman departed. After tea, the youth also departed and Joe and Hester shut up the chickens and the pigs. It was nightfall. Hester went in and made the supper, feeling somehow a bit of a fool, and Joe made a fire in the living-room, he feeling rather important and luscious.

He and Hester would be alone in the bungalow, till the youth appeared next morning. Six months ago, Hester would have enjoyed it. They were so perfectly comfortable together, he and she. They had been friends, and his family and hers had been friends for years, donkey's years. He was a perfectly decent boy, and there would never have been anything messy to fear from him. Nor from herself. Ye Gods, no!

But now, alas, since she had promised to marry him, he had made the wretched mistake of falling 'in love' with her. He had never been that way before. And if she had known he would get this way now, she would have said decidedly: Let us remain friends, Joe, for this sort of thing is a come-down. Once he started cuddling and petting, she couldn't stand him. Yet she felt she ought to. She imagined she even ought to like it. Though where the *ought* came from, she could not see.

'I'm afraid, Hester,' he said sadly, 'you're not in love with me as I am with you.'

'Hang it all!' she cried. 'If I'm not, you ought to be jolly well thankful, that's all I've got to say.'

Which double-barrelled remark he heard, but did not register. He never liked looking anything in the very pin-point middle of the eye. He just left it, and left all her feelings comfortably in the dark. Comfortably for him, that is.

He was extremely competent at motor-cars and farming and all that sort of thing. And surely she, Hester, was as complicated as a motor-car! Surely she had as many subtle little valves and magnetos and accelerators and all the rest of it, to her make-up! If only he would try to handle *her* as carefully as he handled his car! She needed starting, as badly as ever any automobile did. Even if a car had a self-starter, the man had to give it the right twist. Hester felt she would need a lot of cranking up, if ever she was to start off on the matrimonial road with Joe. And he, the fool, just sat in a motionless car and pretended he was making heaven knows how many miles an hour.

This evening she felt really desperate. She had been quite all right doing things with him, during the afternoon, about the place. Then she liked being with him. But now that it was evening and they were alone, the stupid little room, the cosy fire, Joe, Joe's pipe, and Joe's smug sort of hypocritical face, all was just too much for her.

'Come and sit here, dear,' said Joe persuasively, patting the sofa at his side. And she, because she believed a *nice* girl would have been only too delighted to go and sit 'there', went and sat beside him. But she was boiling. What cheek! What cheek of him even to have a sofa! She loathed the vulgarity of sofas.

She endured his arm round her waist, and a certain pressure of his biceps which she presumed was cuddling. He had carefully knocked his pipe out. But she thought how smug and silly his face looked, all its natural frankness and straightforwardness had gone. How ridiculous of him to stroke the back of her neck! How idiotic he was, trying to be lovey-dovey! She wondered what sort of sweet nothings Lord Byron, for example, had murmured to his various ladies. Surely not so blithering, not so incompetent! And how monstrous of him, to kiss her like that.

'I'd infinitely rather you'd play to me, Joe,' she snapped.

'You don't want me to play to you to-night, do you, dear?' he said.

'Why not to-night? I'd love to hear some Tchaikowsky, something to stir me up a bit.'

He rose obediently, and went to the piano. He played quite well. She listened. And Tchaikowsky might have stirred her up all right. The music itself, that is. If she hadn't been so desperately aware that Joe's love-making, if you can call it such, became more absolutely impossible after the sound of the music.

'That was fine!' she said. 'Now do me my favourite nocturne.'

While he concentrated on the fingering, she slipped out of the house.

Oh! she gasped a sigh of relief to be in the cool

October air. The darkness was dim, in the west was a half moon freshly shining, and all the air was motionless, dimness lay like a haze on the earth.

Hester shook her hair, and strode away from the bungalow, which was a perfect little drum, re-echoing to her favourite nocturne. She simply rushed to get out of earshot.

Ah! the lovely night! She tossed her short hair again, and felt like Mazeppa's horse, about to dash away into the infinite. Though the infinite was only a field belonging to the next farm. But Hester felt herself seething in the soft moonlight. Oh! to rush away over the edge of the beyond! if the beyond, like Joe's breadknife, did have an edge to it. 'I know I'm an idiot,' she said to herself. But that didn't take away the wild surge of her limbs. Oh! If there were only some other solution, instead of Joe and his spooning. Yes, SPOONING! The word made her lose the last shred of her self-respect, but she said it aloud.

There was, however, a bunch of strange horses in this field, so she made her way cautiously back through Joe's fence. It was just like him, to have such a little place that you couldn't get away from the sound of his piano, without trespassing on somebody else's ground.

As she drew near the bungalow, however, the drumming of Joe's piano suddenly ceased. Oh Heaven! she looked wildly round. An old willow leaned over the stream. She stretched, crouching, and with the quickness of a long cat, climbed up into the net of cool-bladed foliage.

She had scarcely shuffled and settled into a tolerable position, when he came round the corner of the house and into the moonlight, looking for her. How dare he look for her! She kept as still as a bat among the leaves, watching him as he sauntered with erect, tiresomely manly figure and lifted head, staring around in the darkness. He looked for once very ineffectual, insig-

nificant and at a loss. Where was his supposed male
magic? Why was he so slow and unequal to the situation?

There! He was calling softly and self-consciously:
'Hester! Hester! Where have you put yourself?'

He was angry really. Hester kept still in her tree,
trying not to fidget. She had not the faintest intention of
answering him. He might as well have been on another
planet. He sauntered vaguely and unhappily out of sight.

Then she had a qualm. 'Really, my girl, it's a bit
thick, the way you treat him! Poor old Joe!'

Immediately something began to hum inside her: 'I
hear those tender voices calling Poor Old Joe!'

Nevertheless, she didn't want to go indoors to spend
the evening tête-a-tête–my word!–with him.

'Of course it's absurd to think I could possibly fall in
love like that. I would rather fall into one of his pig-
troughs. It's so frightfully common. As a matter of fact,
it's just a proof that he doesn't love me.'

This thought went through her like a bullet. 'The
very fact of his being in love with me proves that he
doesn't love me. No man that loved a woman could be in
love with her like that. It's so insulting to her.'

She immediately began to cry. And fumbling in her
sleeve for her hanky, she nearly fell out of the tree. Which
brought her to her senses.

In the obscure distance she saw him returning to the
house, and she felt bitter. 'Why did he start all this mess?
I never wanted to marry anybody, and I certainly never
bargained for anybody falling in love with me. Now I'm
miserable, and I feel abnormal. Because the majority of
girls must like this in-love business, or men wouldn't do
it. And the majority must be normal. So I'm abnormal,
and I'm up a tree. I loathe myself. As for Joe, he's spoilt
all there was between us, and he expects me to marry
him on the strength of it. It's perfectly sickening! What a
mess life is. How I loathe messes!'

She immediately shed a few more tears, in the
course of which she heard the door of the bungalow shut

with something of a bang. He had gone indoors, and he was going to be righteously offended. A new misgiving came over her.

The willow tree was uncomfortable. The air was cold and damp. If she caught another chill she'd probably snuffle all winter long. She saw the lamplight coming warm from the window of the bungalow, and she said 'Damn!' which meant, in her case, that she was feeling bad.

She slid down out of the tree, and scratched her arm and probably damaged one of her nicest pair of stockings. 'Oh hang!' she said with emphasis, preparing to go into the bungalow and have it out with poor old Joe. 'I will *not* call him Poor Old Joe!'

At that moment she heard a motor-car slow down in the lane, and there came a low, cautious toot from a hooter. Headlights shone at a standstill near Joe's new iron gate.

'The cheek of it! The unbearable cheek of it! There's that young Henrietta come down on me!'

She flew along Joe's cinder-drive like a maenad.

'Hello, Hester!' came Henrietta's young voice, coolly floating from the obscurity of the car. 'How's everything?'

'What cheek!' cried Hester. 'What amazing cheek!' She leaned on Joe's iron gate, and panted.

'How's everything?' repeated Henrietta's voice blandly.

'What do you mean by it?' demanded Hester, still panting.

'Now my girl, don't go off at a tangent! We weren't coming in unless you came out. You needn't think we want to put our noses in your affairs. We're going down to camp on Bonamy. Isn't the weather too divine!'

Bonamy was Joe's pal, also an old artillery man, who had set up a 'farm' about a mile further along the land. Joe was by no means a Robinson Crusoe in his bungalow.

'Who are you, anyway?' demanded Hester.

'Same old birds,' said Donald, from the driver's seat. Donald was Joe's brother. Henrietta was sitting in front, next to him.

'Same as ever,' said Teddy, poking his head out of the car. Teddy was a second cousin.

'Well,' said Hester, sort of climbing down. 'I suppose you may as well come in, now you *are* here. Have you eaten?'

'Eaten, yes,' said Donald, 'But we aren't coming in this trip, Hester; don't you fret.'

''Why not?' flashed Hester, up in arms.

''Fraid of brother Joe,' said Donald.

'Besides, Hester,' said Henrietta anxiously, 'you know you don't want us.'

'Henrietta, don't be a fool!' flashed Hester.

'*Well*, Hester–!' remonstrated the pained Henrietta.

'Come on in, and no more nonsense!' said Hester.

'Not this trip, Hester,' said Donny.

'No sir!' said Teddy.

'But what idiots you all are! Why not?' cried Hester.

''Fraid of our elder brother,' said Donald.

'All right,' said Hester. 'Then I'll come along with you.'

She hastily opened the gate.

'Shall I just have a peep? I'm pining to see the house,' said Henrietta, climbing with a long leg over the door of the car.

The night was now dark, the moon had sunk. The two girls crunched in silence along the cinder track to the house.

'You'd say, if you'd rather I didn't come in–or if Joe'd rather,' said Henrietta anxiously. She was very much disturbed in her young mind, and hoped for a clue. Hester walked on without answering. Henrietta laid her hand on her sister's arm. Hester shook it off, saying:

'My dear Henrietta, do be normal!'

And she rushed up the three steps to the door, which she flung open, displaying the lamplit living-room, Joe in an arm-chair by the low fire, his back to the door. He did not turn round.

'Here's Henrietta!' cried Hester, in a tone which meant: *'How's that?'*

He got up and faced round, his brown eyes in his stiff face very angry.

'How did *you* get here?' he asked rudely.

'Came in a car,' said young Henrietta, from her Age of Innocence.

'With Donald and Teddy–they're just outside the gate,' said Hester. 'The old gang!'

'Coming in?' asked Joe, with greater anger in his voice.

'I suppose you'll go out and invite them,' said Hester.

Joe said nothing, just stood like a block.

'I expect you'll think it's awful of me to come intruding,' said Henrietta meekly. 'We're just going on to Bonamy's.' She gazed innocently round the room. 'But it's an adorable little place, awfully good taste in a cottagey sort of way. I like it awfully. Can I warm my hands?'

Joe moved from in front of the fire. He was in his slippers. Henrietta dangled her long red hands, red from the night air, before the grate.

'I'll rush right away again,' she said.

'Oh-h' drawled Hester curiously. 'Don't do that!'

'Yes, I must. Donald and Teddy are waiting.'

The door stood wide open, the headlights of the car could be seen in the lane.

'Oh-h!' Again that curious drawl from Hester. 'I'll tell them you're staying the night with me. I can do with a bit of company.'

Joe looked at her.

'What's the game?' he said.

'No game at all! Only now Tatty's come, she may as well stay.'

'Tatty' was the rather infrequent abbreviation of

'Henrietta'.

'Oh but Hester!' said Henrietta. 'I'm going on to Bonamy's with Donald and Teddy.'

'Not if I want you to stay here!' said Hester.

Henrietta looked all suprised, resigned helplessness.

'What's the game?' repeated Joe. 'Had you fixed up to come down here to-night?'

'No Joe, really!' said Henrietta, with earnest innocence. 'I hadn't the faintest idea of such a thing, till Donald suggested it, at four o'clock this afternoon. Only the weather was too perfectly divine, we had to go out somewhere, so we thought we'd descend on Bonamy. I hope *he* won't be frightfully put out, as well.'

'And if we had arranged it, it wouldn't have been a crime,' struck in Hester. 'And anyway, now you're here you might as well all camp here.'

'Oh no, Hester! I know Donald will never come inside the gate. He was angry with me for making him stop, and it was I who tooted. It wasn't him, it was me. The curiosity of Eve, I suppose. Anyhow I've put my foot in it, as usual. So now I'd better clear out as fast as I can. Good-night!'

She gathered her coat round her with one arm and moved vaguely to the door. 'In that case, I'll come along with you,' said Hester.

'But Hester!' cried Henrietta. And she looked inquiringly at Joe.

'I know as little as you do,' he said, 'what's going on.'

His face was wooden and angry, Henrietta could make nothing of him.

'Hester!' cried Henrietta. 'Do be sensible! What's gone wrong! Why don't you at least *explain*, and give everybody a chance! Talk about being normal!—you're always flinging it at *me*!'

There was a dramatic silence.

'What's happened?' Henrietta insisted, her eyes

very bright and distressed, her manner showing that she was determined to be sensible.

'Nothing, of course!' mocked Hester.

'Do *you* know, Joe?' said Henrietta, like another Portia, turning very sympathetically to the man.

For a moment Joe thought how much nicer Henrietta was than her sister. '

'I only know she asked me to play the piano, and then she dodged out of the house. Since then, her steering gear's been out of order.'

'Ha-ha-ha!' laughed Hester falsely and melodramatically. 'I like that. I like my dodging out of the house! I went out for a breath of fresh air. I should like to know whose steering gear is out of order, talking about my dodging out of the house!'

'You dodged out of the house,' said Joe.

'Oh did I? And why should I, pray?'

'I suppose you have your own reasons.'

'I have too. And very good reasons.'

There was a moment of stupefied amazement . . . Joe and Hester had known each other so well, for such a long time. And now look at them!

'But why did you, Hester?' asked Henrietta, in her most breathless naïve fashion.

'Why did I what?'

There was a low toot from the motor-car in the lane.

'They're calling me! Good-bye!' cried Henrietta, wrapping her coat round her and turning decisively to the door.

'If you go, my girl, I'm coming with you,' said Hester.

'But why?' cried Henrietta in amazement. The horn tooted again. She opened the door, and called into the night:

'Half a minute!' Then she closed the door again, softly, and turned once more in her amazement to Hester.

'But why, Hester?'

Hester's eyes almost squinted with exasperation. She could hardly bear even to glance at the wooden and angry Joe.

'Why?'

'Why?' came the soft reiteration of Henrietta's question.

All the attention focussed on Hester, but Hester was a sealed book.

'Why?'

'She doesn't know herself,' said Joe, seeing a loophole.

Out rang Hester's crazy and melodramatic laugh.

'Oh doesn't she!' Her face flew into sudden strange fury. 'Well, if you want to know, I absolutely *can't stand* your making love to me, if that's what you call the business.'

Henrietta let go the door handle, and sank weakly into a chair.

The worst had come to the worst. Joe's face became purple, then slowly paled to yellow.

'Then,' said Henrietta in a hollow voice, 'you can't marry him.'

'I couldn't possibly marry him if he kept on being *in love* with me.' She spoke the two words with almost snarling emphasis.

'And you couldn't possibly marry him if he *wasn't*,' said the guardian angel, Henrietta.

'Why not,' cried Hester. 'I could stand him all right till he started being in love with me. Now, he's simply out of the question.'

There was a pause, out of which came Henrietta's:

'After all, Hester, a man's *supposed* to be in love with the woman he wants to marry.'

'Then he'd better keep it to himself, that's all I've got to say.'

There was a pause. Joe, silent as ever, looked more wooden and sheepishly angry.

'But Hester! Hasn't a man *got* to be in love with

you–?'

'Not with me! You've not had it to put up with, my girl.'

Henrietta sighed helplessly.

'Then you can't marry him, that's obvious. What an awful pity!'

A pause.

'Nothing can be so perfectly humiliating as a man making love to you,' said Hester. 'I *loathe* it.'

'Perhaps it's because it's the wrong man,' said Henrietta sadly, with a glance at the wooden and sheepish Joe.

'I don't believe I could stand that sort of thing, with *any* man. Henrietta, do you know what it is, being stroked and cuddled? It's too perfectly awful and ridiculous.'

'Yes!' said Henrietta, musing sadly. 'As if one were a perfectly priceless meat pie, and the dog licked it tenderly before he gobbled it up. It *is* rather sickening, I agree.'

'And what's so awful, a perfectly decent man will go and get that way. Nothing is so awful as a man who has fallen in love,' said Hester.

'I know what you mean, Hester. So doggy!' said Henrietta sadly.

The motor horn tooted exasperatedly. Henrietta rose like a Portia who has been a failure. She opened the door, and suddenly yelled fiercely into the night:

'Go on without me. I'll walk. Don't wait.'

'How long will you be?' came a voice.

'I don't know. If I want to come, I'll walk,' she yelled.

'Come back for you in an hour.'

'Right,' she shrieked, and slammed the door in their distant faces. Then she sat down dejectedly, in the silence. She was going to stand by Hester. That *fool*, Joe, standing there like a mutton-head!

They heard the car start, and retreat down the lane.

'Men are awful!' said Henrietta dejectedly.

'Anyhow, you're mistaken,' said Joe with sudden venom, to Hester. 'I'm not in love with you, Miss Clever.'

The two women looked at him as if he were Lazarus risen.

'And I never was in love with you, that way,' he added, his brown eyes burning with a strange fire of self-conscious shame and anger, and naked passion.

'Well, what a liar you must be then. That's all I can say!' replied Hester coldly.

'Do you mean,' said young Henrietta acidly, 'that you put it all on?'

'I thought she expected it of me,' he said, with a nasty little smile that simply paralysed the two young women. If he had turned into a boa-constrictor, they would not have been more amazed. That sneering little smile! Their good-natured Joe!

'I thought it was expected of me,' he repeated, jeering.

Hester was horrified.

'Oh, but how beastly of you to do it!' cried Henrietta to him.

'And what a lie!' cried Hester. 'He liked it.'

'Do you think he did, Hester?' said Henrietta.

'I liked it in a way,' he said impudently. 'But I shouldn't have liked it, if I thought she didn't.'

Hester flung out her arms.

'Henrietta,' she cried, 'why can't we kill him?'

'I wish we could,' said Henrietta.

'What are you to do, when you know a girl's rather strict, and you like her for it—and you're not going to be married for a month—and—and you—and you've got to get over the interval somehow—and what else does Rudolf Valentino do for you?—you like *him*—'

'He's dead, poor dear. But I loathed him, *really*,' said Hester.

'You didn't seem to,' said he.

'Well, anyhow, you aren't Rudolf Valentino, and I

loathe *you* in the rôle.'

'You won't get a chance again. I loathe you altogether.'

'And I'm extremely relieved to hear it, my boy.'

There was a lengthy pause, after which Henrietta said with decision:

'Well, that's that! Will you come along to Bonamy's with me, Hester, or shall I stay here with you?'

'*I* don't care, my girl,' said Hester with bravado.

'Neither do I care what you do,' said he. 'But I call it pretty rotten of you, not to tell me right out, at first.'

'I thought it was real with you then, and I didn't want to hurt you,' said Hester.

'You look as if you didn't want to hurt me,' he said.

'Oh, *now*,' she said, 'since it was all pretence, it doesn't matter.'

'I should say it doesn't,' he retorted.

There was a silence. The clock, which was intended to be their family clock, ticked rather hastily.

'Anyway,' he said, 'I consider you've let me down.'

'I like that!' she cried, 'considering what you've played off on me!'

He looked her straight in the eye. They knew each other so well.

Why had he tried that silly love-making game on her? It was a betrayal of their simple intimacy. He saw it plainly, and repented.

And she saw the honest, patient love for her in his eyes, and the queer, quiet, central desire. It was the first time she had seen it, that quiet, patient, central desire of a young man who has suffered during his youth, and seeks now almost with the slowness of age. A hot flush went over her heart. She felt herself responding to him.

'What have you decided, Hester?' said Henrietta.

'I'll stay with Joe, after all,' said Hester.

'Very well,' said Henrietta. 'And I'll go along to Bonamy's.'

She opened the door quietly, and was gone.

Joe and Hester looked at one another from a distance.

'I'm sorry, Hester,' said he.

'You know, Joe,' she said, 'I don't mind what you do, if you iove me *really*.'

The Escaped Cock

First part written April 1927. Story enlarged June 1928. Published 1929 by The Black Sun Press, with water colour decorations by Lawrence. All later editions published under the title *The Man Who Died*.

PART I

There was a peasant near Jerusalem who acquired a young game-cock which looked a shabby little thing, but which put on brave feathers as spring advanced, and was resplendent with arched and orange neck by the time the fig-trees were letting out leaves from their end-tips.

This peasant was poor, he lived in a cottage of mud-brick, and had only a dirty little inner courtyard with a tough fig-tree for all his territory. He worked hard among the vines and olives and wheat of his master, then came home to sleep in the mud-brick cottage by the path. But he was proud of his young rooster. In the shut-in yard were three shabby hens which laid small eggs, shed the few feathers they had, and made a disproportionate amount of dirt. There was also, in a corner under a straw roof, a dull donkey that often went out with the peasant to work, but sometimes stayed at home. And there was the peasant's wife, a black-browed youngish woman who did not work too hard. She threw a little grain, or the remains of the porridge mess, to the fowls, and she cut green fodder with a sickle, for the ass.

403

The young cock grew to a certain splendour. By some freak of destiny, he was a dandy rooster, in that dirty little yard with three patchy hens. He learned to crane his neck and give shrill answers to the crowing of other cocks, beyond the walls, in a world he knew nothing of. But there was a special fiery colour to his crow, and the distant calling of the other cocks roused him to unexpected outbursts

'How he sings,' said the peasant, as he got up and pulled his day-shirt over his head.

'He is good for twenty hens,' said the wife.

The peasant went out and looked with pride at his young rooster. A saucy, flamboyant bird, that had already made the final acquaintance of the three tattered hens. But the cockerel was tipping his head, listening to the challenge of far-off unseen cocks, in the unknown world. Ghost voices, crowing at him mysteriously out of limbo. He answered with a ringing defiance, never to be daunted.

'He will surely fly away one of these days,' said the peasant's wife.

So they lured him with grain, caught him, though he fought with all his wings and feet, and they tied a cord round his shank, fastening it against the spur; and they tied the other end of the cord to the post that held up the donkey's straw pent-roof.

The young cock, freed, marched with a prancing stride of indignation away from the humans, came to the end of his string, gave a tug and a hitch of the tied leg, fell over for a moment, scuffed frantically on the unclean earthen floor, to the horror of the shabby hens, then with a sickening lurch, regained his feet, and stood to think. The peasant and the peasant's wife laughed heartily, and the young cock heard them. And he knew, with a gloomy, foreboding kind of knowledge, that he was tied by the leg.

He no longer pranced and ruffled and forged his feathers. He walked within the limits of his tether sombrely. Still he gobbled up the best bits of food. Still, sometimes, he saved an extra-best bit for his favourite hen of the moment. Still he pranced with quivering, rocking fierceness upon such of his harem as came nonchalantly within range, and gave off the invisible lure. And still he crowed defiance to the cock-crows that showered up out of limbo, in the dawn.

But there was now a grim voracity in the way he gobbled his food, and a pinched triumph in the way he seized upon the shabby hens. His voice, above all, had lost the full gold of its clangour. He was tied by the leg and he knew it. Body, soul and spirit were tied by that string.

Underneath, however, the life in him was grimly unbroken. It was the cord that should break. So one morning, just before the light of dawn, rousing from his slumbers with a sudden wave of strength, he leaped forward on his wings, and the string snapped. He gave a wild strange squawk, rose in one lift to the top of the wall, and there he crowed a loud and splitting crow. So loud, it woke the peasant.

At the same time, at the same hour before dawn, on the same morning, a man awoke from a long sleep in which he was tied up. He woke numb and cold, inside a carved hole in the rock. Through all the long sleep his body had been full of hurt, and it was still full of hurt. He did not open his eyes. Yet he knew that he was awake, and numb, and cold, and rigid, and full of hurt, and tied up. His face was banded with cold bands, his legs were bandaged together. Only his hands were loose.

He could move if he wanted: he knew that. But he had no want. Who would want to come back from the dead? A deep, deep nausea stirred in him, at the premonition of movement. He resented already the fact of the strange, incalculable moving that had already taken place in him: the moving back into consciousness. He had not wished it. He had wanted to stay outside, in the place where even memory is stone dead.

But now, something had returned to him, like a returned letter, and in that return he lay overcome with a sense of nausea. Yet suddenly his hands moved. They lifted up, cold, heavy and sore. Yet they lifted up, to drag away the cloth from his face, and push at the shoulder bands. Then they fell again, cold, heavy, numb, and sick with having moved even so much, unspeakably unwilling to move further.

With his face cleared, and his shoulders free, he lapsed again, and lay dead, resting on the cold nullity of being dead. It was the most desirable. And almost, he had it complete: the utter cold nullity of being outside.

Yet when he was most nearly gone, suddenly, driven by an ache at the wrists, his hands rose and began pushing at the bandages of his knees, his feet began to stir, even while his breast lay cold and dead still.

And at last, the eyes opened. On to the dark. The same dark! yet perhaps there was a pale chink, of the all-disturbing night, prizing open the pure dark. He could not lift his head. The eyes closed. And again it was finished.

Then suddenly he leaned up, and the great world reeled. Bandages fell away. And narrow walls of rock closed upon him, and gave the new anguish of imprisonment. There were chinks of light. With a wave of strength that came from revulsion, he leaned forward, in that narrow well of rock, and leaned frail hands on the rock near the chinks of light.

Strength came from somewhere, from revulsion; there was a crash and a wave of light, and the dead man was crouching in his lair, facing the animal onrush of light. Yet it was hardly dawn, and the strange piercing keenness of daybreak's sharp breath was on him. It meant full awakening.

Slowly, slowly he crept down from the cell of rock, with the caution of the bitterly wounded. Bandages and linen and perfume fell away, and he crouched on the ground against the wall of rock, to recover oblivion. But he saw his hurt feet touching the earth again, with unspeakable pain, the earth they had meant to touch no more, and he saw his thin legs that had died, and pain unknowable, pain like utter bodily disillusion, filled him so full that he stood up, with one torn hand on the ledge of the tomb.

To be back! To be back again, after all that! He saw the linen swathing-bands fallen round his dead feet, and stooping, he picked them up, folded them, and laid them back in the rocky cavity from which he had emerged. Then he took the perfumed linen sheet, wrapped it round him as a mantle, and turned away, to the wanness of the chill dawn.

He was alone; and having died, was even beyond loneliness.

Filled still with the sickness of unspeakable disillusion, the man stepped with wincing feet down the rocky slope, past the sleeping soldiers, who lay wrapped in their woollen mantles under the wild laurels. Silent, on naked, scarred feet, wrapped in a white linen shroud, he glanced down for a moment on the inert, heap-like bodies of the soldiers. They were repulsive, a slow squalor of limbs, yet he felt a certain compassion. He passed on towards the road, lest they should wake.

Having nowhere to go, he turned from the city that stood on her hills. He slowly followed the road away from the town, past the olives, under which purple anemones were drooping in the chill of dawn, and rich-green herbage was pressing thick. The world, the same as ever, the natural world, thronging with greenness, a nightingale winsomely, wistfully, coaxingly calling from the bushes beside a runnel of water, in the world, the natural world of morning and evening, forever undying, from which he had died.

He went on, on scarred feet, neither of this world nor of the next. Neither here nor there, neither seeing nor yet sightless, he passed dimly on, away from the city and its precincts, wondering why he should be travelling, yet driven by a dim, deep nausea of disillusion, and a resolution of which he was not even aware.

Advancing in a kind of half-consciousness under the dry stone wall of the olive orchard, he was roused by the shrill wild crowing of a cock just near him, a sound which made him shiver as if electricity had touched him. He saw a black and orange cock on a bough above the road, then running through the olives of the upper level, a peasant in a grey woollen shirt-tunic. Leaping out of greenness, came the black and orange cock with the red comb, his tail-feathers streaming lustrous.

'O stop him, Master!' called the peasant. 'My escaped cock!'

The man addressed, with a sudden flicker of a smile, opened his great white wings of a shroud in front of the leaping bird. The cock fell back with a squawk and a flutter, the peasant jumped forward, there was a terrific beating of wings, and whirring of feathers, then the peasant had the escaped cock safely under his arm, its wings shut down, its face crazily craning forward, its round eyes goggling from its white chops.

'It's my escaped cock!' said the peasant, soothing the bird with his left hand, as he looked perspiringly up into the face of the man wrapped in white linen.

The peasant changed countenance, and stood transfixed, as he looked into the dead-white face of the man who had died. That dead-white face, so still, with the black beard growing on it as if in death; and those wide-open black sombre eyes, that had died, and those washed scars on the waxy forehead! The slow-blooded man of the field let his jaw drop, in childish inability to meet the situation.

'Don't be afraid,' said the man in the shroud. 'I am not dead. They took me down too soon. So I have risen up. Yet if they discover me, they will do it all over again. . . .'

He spoke in a voice of old disgust. Humanity! Especially humanity in authority! There was only one thing it could do. He looked with black, indifferent eyes into the quick, shifty eyes of the peasant. The peasant quailed, and was powerless under the look of deathly indifference, and strange cold resoluteness. He could only say the one thing he was afraid to say:

'Will you hide in my house, Master?'

'I will rest there. But if you tell any one, you know what will happen. You will have to go before a judge.'

'Me! I shan't speak. Let us be quick!'

The peasant looked round in fear, wondering sulkily why he had let himself in for this doom. The man with scarred feet climbed painfully up to the level of the olive garden, and followed the sullen, hurrying peasant across the green wheat among the olive trees. He felt the cool silkiness of the young wheat under his feet that had been dead, and the roughishness of its separate life was apparent to him. At the edges of rocks, he saw the silky, silvery-haired buds of the scarlet anemone bending downwards. And they too were in another world. In his own world he was alone, utterly alone. These things around him were in a world that had never died. But he himself had died, or had been killed from out of it, and all that remained now was the great void nausea of utter disillusion.

They came to a clay cottage, and the peasant waited dejectedly for the other man to pass.

'Pass!' he said. 'Pass! We have not been seen.'

The man in white linen entered the earthen room, taking with him the aroma of strange perfumes. The peasant closed the door, and passed through the inner doorway into the yard, where the ass stood within the high walls, safe from being stolen. There the peasant, in great disquietude, tied up the cock. The man with the waxen face sat down on a mat near the hearth, for he was spent and barely conscious. Yet he heard outside the whispering of the peasant to his wife, for the woman had been watching from the roof.

Presently they came in, and the woman hid her face.

She poured water, and put bread and dried figs on a wooden platter.

'Eat, Master!' said the peasant. 'Eat! No one has seen.'

But the stranger had no desire for food. Yet he moistened a little bread in the water, and ate it, since life must be. But desire was dead in him, even for food and drink. He had risen without desire, without even the desire to live, empty save for the all-overwhelming disillusion that lay like nausea where his life had been. Yet perhaps, deeper even than disillusion, was a desireless resoluteness, deeper even than consciousness.

The peasant and his wife stood near the door, watching. They saw with terror the livid wounds on the thin waxy hands and the thin feet of the stranger, and the small lacerations in the still dead forehead. They smelled with terror the scent of rich perfumes that came from him, from his body. And they looked at the fine, snowy, costly linen. Perhaps he really was a dead king, from the region of terrors. And he was still cold and remote in the region of death, with perfumes coming from his transparent body as if from some strange flower.

Having with difficulty swallowed some of the moistened bread, he lifted his eyes to them. He saw them as they were: limited, meagre in their life, without any splendour of gesture and of courage. But they were what they were, slow inevitable parts of the natural world. They had no nobility, but fear made them compassionate.

And the stranger had compassion on them again, for he knew that they would respond best to gentleness, giving back a clumsy gentleness again.

'Do not be afraid,' he said to them gently. 'Let me stay a little while with you. I shall not stay long. And then I shall go away forever. But do not be afraid. No harm will come to you through me.'

They believed him at once, yet the fear did not leave them. And they said:

'Stay, Master, while ever you will. Rest! Rest quietly!'

But they were afraid.

So he let them be, and the peasant went away with the ass. The sun had risen bright, and in the dark house with the door shut, the man was again as if in the tomb. So he said to the woman, 'I would lie in the yard.'

And she swept the yard for him, and laid him a mat, and he lay down under the wall in the morning sun. There he saw the first green leaves spurting like flames from the ends of the enclosed fig-tree, out of the bareness to the sky of spring above. But the man who had died could not look, he only lay quite still in the sun, which was not yet too hot, and had no desire in him, not even to move. But he lay with his thin legs in the sun, his black perfumed hair falling into the hollows of his neck, and his thin colourless arms utterly inert. As he lay there, the hens clucked and scratched, and the escaped cock, caught and tied by the leg again, cowered in a corner.

The peasant woman was frightened. She came peeping, and, seeing him never move, feared to have a dead man in the yard. But the sun had grown stronger, he opened his eyes and looked at her. And now she was frightened of the man who was alive, but spoke nothing.

He opened his eyes, and saw the world again bright as glass. It was life, in which he had no share any more. But it shone outside him, blue sky, and a bare fig-tree with little jets of green leaf. Bright as glass, and he was not of it, for desire had failed.

Yet he was there, and not extinguished. The day passed in a kind of coma, and at evening he went into the house. The peasant man came home, but he was frightened, and had nothing to say. The stranger too ate of the mess of beans, a little. Then he washed his hands and turned to the wall, and was silent. The peasants were silent too. They watched their guest sleep. Sleep was so near death he could still sleep.

Yet when the sun came up, he went again to lie in

the yard. The sun was the one thing that drew him and swayed him, and he still wanted to feel the cool air of the morning in his nostrils, see the pale sky overhead. He still hated to be shut up.

As he came out, the young cock crowed. It was a diminished, pinched cry, but there was that in the voice of the bird stronger that chagrin. It was the necessity to live, and even to cry out the triumph of life. The man who had died stood and watched the cock who had escaped and been caught, ruffling himself up, rising forward on his toes, throwing up his head, and parting his beak in another challenge from life to death. The brave sounds rang out, and though they were diminished by the cord round the bird's leg, they were not cut off. The man who had died looked nakedly on life, and saw a vast resoluteness everywhere flinging itself up in stormy or subtle wave-crests, foam-tips emerging out of the blue invisible, a black and orange cock or the green flame-tongues out of the extremes of the fig-tree. They came forth, these things and creatures of spring, glowing with desire and with assertion. They came like crests of foam, out of the blue flood of the invisible desire, out of the vast invisible sea of strength, and they came coloured and tangible, evanescent, yet deathless in their coming. The man who had died looked on the great swing into existence of things that had not died, but he saw no longer their tremulous desire to exist and to be. He heard instead their ringing, ringing, defiant challenge to all other things existing.

The man lay still, with eyes that had died now wide open and darkly still, seeing the everlasting resoluteness of life. And the cock, with the flat, brilliant glance, glanced back at him, with a bird's half-seeing look. And always the man who had died saw not the bird alone, but the short, sharp wave of life of which the bird was the crest. He watched the queer, beaky motion of the creature as it gobbled into itself the scraps of food; its glancing of the eye of life, ever alert and watchful, overweening and cautious, and the voice of its life, crowing triumph and assertion, yet strangled by a cord of circumstance. He seemed to hear the queer speech of very life, as the cock triumphantly imitated the clucking of the favourite hen, when she had laid an egg, a clucking which still had, in the male bird the hollow chagrin of the cord round his leg. And when the man threw a bit of bread to the cock, it called with an extraordinary cooing tenderness, tousling and saving the morsel for the hens. The hens ran up greedily, and carried the morsel away beyond the reach of the string.

Then, walking complacently after them, suddenly the male bird's leg would hitch at the end of his tether, and he would yield with a kind of collapse. His flag fell, he seemed to diminish, he would huddle in the shade. And he was young, his tail-feathers, glossy as they were, were not fully grown. It was not till evening again that the tide of life in him made him forget. Then when his favourite hen came strolling unconcernedly near him, emitting the lure, he pounced on her with all his feathers vibrating. And the man who had died watched the unsteady, rocking vibration of the bent bird, and it was not the bird he saw, but one wave-tip of life overlapping for a minute another, in the tide of the swaying ocean of life. And the destiny of life seemed more fierce and compulsive to him even than the destiny of death. The doom of death was a shadow compared to the raging destiny of life, the determined surge of life.

At twilight the peasant came home with the ass, and he said: 'Master! It is said that the body was stolen from the garden and the tomb is empty, and the soldiers are taken away, accursed Romans! And the women are there to weep.'

The man who had died looked at the man who had not died.

'It is well,' he said. 'Say nothing, and we are safe.'

And the peasant was relieved. He looked rather dirty and stupid, and even as much flaminess as that of the young cock, which he had tied by the leg, would never glow in him. He was without fire. But the man who had died thought to himself:

'Why, then, should he be lifted up? Clods of earth are turned over for refreshment, they are not to be lifted up. Let the earth remain earthy, and hold its own against the sky. I was wrong to seek to lift it up. I was wrong to try to interfere. The ploughshare of devastation will be set in the soil of Judea, and the life of this peasant will be overturned like the sods of the field. No man can save the earth from tillage. It is tillage, not salvation. . . .'

So he saw the man, the peasant, with compassion; but the man who had died no longer wished to interfere in the soul of the man who had not died, and who could never die, save to return to earth. Let him return to earth in his own good hour, and let no one try to interfere when the earth claims her own.

So the man with scars let the peasant go from him, for the peasant had no birth in him. Yet the man who had died said to himself: 'He is my host.'

And at dawn, when he was better, the man who had died rose up, and on slow, sore feet retraced his way to the garden. For he had been betrayed in a garden, and buried in a garden. And as he turned round the screen of laurels, near the rock-face, he saw a woman hovering by the tomb, a woman in blue and yellow. She peeped again into the mouth of the hole, that was like a deep cupboard. But still there was nothing. And she wrung her hands and wept. And as she turned away, she saw the man in white, standing by the laurels, and she gave a cry, thinking it might be a spy, and she said:

'They have taken him away!'

So he said to her:

'Madeleine!'

Then she reeled as if she would fall, for she knew him. And he said to her:

'Madeleine! Do not be afraid. I am alive. They took me down too soon, so I came back to life. Then I was sheltered in a house.'

She did not know what to say, but fell at his feet to kiss them.

'Don't touch me, Madeleine,' he said. 'Not yet! I am not yet healed and in touch with men.'

So she wept because she did not know what to do. And he said:

'Let us go aside, among the bushes, where we can speak unseen.'

So in her blue mantle and her yellow robe, she followed him among the trees, and he sat down under a myrtle bush. And he said:

'I am not yet quite come to. Madeleine, what is to be done next?'

'Master!' she said. 'Oh, we have wept for you! And will you come back to us?'

'What is finished is finished, and for me the end is passed,' he said. 'The stream will run till no more rains fill it, then it will dry up. For me, that life is over.'

'And will you give up your triumph?' she said sadly.

'My triumph,' he said, 'is that I am not dead. I have outlived my mission, and know no more of it. It is my triumph. I have survived the day and the death of my interference, and am still a man. I am still young, Madeleine, not even come to middle age. I am glad all that is over. It had to be. But now I am glad it is over, and the day of my interference is done. The teacher and the saviour are dead in me; now I can go about my business, into my own single life.'

She heard him, and did not fully understand. But what he said made her feel disappointed.

'But you will come back to us?' she said, insisting.

'I don't know what I shall do,' he said. When I am healed, I shall know better. But my mission is over, and my teaching is finished, and death has saved me from my own salvation. Oh, Madeleine, I want to take my single way in life, which is my portion. My public life is over, the life of my self-importance. Now I can wait on life, and say nothing, and have no one betray me. I wanted to be greater than the limits of my hands and feet, so I brought betrayal on myself. And I know I wronged Judas, my poor Judas. For I have died, and now I know my own limits. Now I can live without striving to sway others any more. For my reach ends in my finger-tips, and my stride is no longer than the ends of my toes. Yet I would embrace multitudes, I who have never truly embraced even one. But Judas and the high priests saved me from my own salvation, and soon I can turn to my destiny like a bather in the sea at dawn, who has just come down to the shore alone.'

'Do you want to be alone henceforward?' she asked. 'And was your mission nothing? Was it all untrue?'

'Nay!' he said. 'Neither were your lovers in the past nothing. They were much to you, but you took more than you gave. Then you came to me for salvation from your own excess. And I, in my mission, I too ran to excess. I gave more than I took, and that also is woe and vanity. So Pilate and the high priests saved me from my own excessive salvation. Don't run to excess now in living, Madeleine. It only means another death.'

She pondered bitterly, for the need for excessive giving was in her, and she could not bear to be denied.

'And will you not come back to us?' she said. 'Have you risen for yourself alone?'

He heard the sarcasm in her voice, and looked at her beautiful face which still was dense with excessive need for salvation from the woman she had been, the female who had caught men at her will. The cloud of necessity was on her, to be saved from the old, wilful Eve, who had embraced many men and taken more than she gave. Now the other doom was on her. She wanted to give without taking. And that too, is hard, and cruel to the warm body.

'I have not risen from the dead in order to seek death again,' he said.

She glanced up at him, and saw the weariness

settling again on his waxy face, and the vast disillusion in his dark eyes, and the underlying indifference. He felt her glance, and said to himself.

'Now my own followers will want to do me to death again, for having risen up different from their expectation.'

'But you will come to us, to see us, us who love you?' she said.

He laughed a little and said:

'Ah, yes.' Then he added, 'Have you a little money? Will you give me a little money? I owe it.'

She had not much, but it pleased her to give it to him.

'Do you think,' he said to her, 'that I might come and live with you in your house?'

She looked up at him with large blue eyes, that gleamed strangely.

'Now?' she said with peculiar triumph.

And he, who shrank now from triumph of any sort, his own or another's, said:

'Not now! Later, when I am healed, and. . . and I am in touch with the flesh.'

The words faltered in him. And in his heart he knew he would never go to live in her house. For the flicker of triumph had gleamed in her eyes; the greed of giving. But she murmured in a humming rapture:

'Ah, you know I would give up everything to you.'

'Nay!' he said. 'I didn't ask that.'

A revulsion from all the life he had known came over him again, the great nausea of disillusion, and the spearthrust through his bowels. He crouched under the myrtle bushes, without strength. Yet his eyes were open. And she looked at him again, and she saw that it was not the Messiah. The Messiah had not risen. The enthusiasm and the burning purity were gone, and the rapt youth. His youth was dead. This man was middle-aged and disillusioned, with a certain terrible indifference, and a resoluteness which love would never conquer. This was

not the Master she had so adored, the young, flamy,
unphysical exalter of her soul. This was nearer to the
lovers she had known of old, but with a greater indifference to the personal issue, and a lesser susceptibility.

She was thrown out of balance of her rapturous,
anguished adoration. This risen man was the death of
her dream.

'You should go now,' he said to her. 'Do not touch
me, I am in death. I shall come again here, on the third
day. Come if you will, at dawn. And we will speak again.'

She went away, perturbed and shattered. Yet as she
went, her mind discarded the bitterness of the reality,
and she conjured up rapture and wonder, that the
Master was risen and was not dead. He was risen, the
Saviour, the exalter, the wonder-worker! He was risen,
but not as man; as pure God, who should not be touched
by flesh, and who should be rapt away into Heaven. It
was the most glorious and most ghostly of the miracles.

Meanwhile the man who had died gathered himself
together at last, and slowly made his way to the peasant's
house. He was glad to go back to them, and away from
Madeleine and his own associates. For the peasants had
the inertia of earth and would let him rest, and as yet,
would put no compulsion on him.

The woman was on the roof, looking for him. She
was afraid that he had gone away. His presence in the
house had become like gentle wine to her. She hastened
to the door, to him.

'Where have you been?' she said. 'Why did you go
away?'

'I have been to walk in a garden, and I have seen a
friend, who gave me a little money. It is for you.'

He held out his thin hand, with the small amount of
money, all that Madeleine could give him. The peasant's
wife's eyes glistened, for money was scarce, and she said:

'Oh, Master! And is it truly mine?'

'Take it!' he said. 'It buys bread, and bread brings
life.'

So he lay down in the yard again, sick with relief at being alone again. For with the peasants he could be alone, but his own friends would never let him be alone. And in the safety of the yard, the young cock was dear to him, as it shouted in the helpless zest of life, and finished in the helpless humiliation of being tied by the leg. This day the ass stood swishing her tail under the shed. The man who had died lay down and turned utterly away from life, in the sickness of death in life.

But the woman brought wine and water, and sweetened cakes, and roused him, so that he ate a little, to please her. The day was hot, and as she crouched to serve him, he saw her breasts sway from her humble body, under her smock. He knew she wished he would desire her, and she was youngish, and not unpleasant. And he, who had never known a woman, would have desired her if he could. But he could not want her, though he felt gently towards her soft, crouching, humble body. But it was her thoughts, her consciousness, he could not mingle with. She was pleased with the money, and now she wanted to take more from him. She wanted the embrace of his body. But her little soul was hard, and short-sighted, and grasping, her body had its little greed, and no gentle reverence of the return gift. So he spoke a quiet, pleasant word to her, and turned away. He could not touch the little, personal body, the little, personal life of this woman, nor in any other. He turned away from it without hesitation.

Risen from the dead, he had realized at last that the body, too, had its little life, and beyond that, the greater life. He was virgin, in recoil from the little, greedy life of the body. But now he knew that virginity is a form of greed; and that the body rises again to give and to take, to take and to give, ungreedily. Now he knew that he had risen for the woman, or women, who knew the greater life of the body, not greedy to give, not greedy to take, and with whom he could mingle his body. But having died, he was patient, knowing there was time, an eternity of time. And he was driven by no greedy desire, either to give himself to others, or to grasp anything for himself. For he had died.

The peasant came home from work, and said:

'Master, I thank you for the money. But we did not want it. And all I have is yours.'

But the man who had died was sad, because the peasant stood there in the little, personal body, and his eyes were cunning and sparkling with the hope of greater rewards in money, later on. True, the peasant had taken him in free, and had risked getting no reward. But the hope was cunning in him. Yet even this was as men are made. So when the peasant would have helped him to rise, for night had fallen, the man who had died said:

'Don't touch me, brother. I am not yet risen to the Father.'

The sun burned with greater splendour, and burnished the young cock brighter. But the peasant kept the string renewed, and the bird was a prisoner. Yet the flame of life burned up to a sharp point in the cock, so that it eyed askance and haughtily the man who had died. And the man smiled and held the bird dear, and he said to it:

'Surely thou art risen to the Father, among birds.'

And the young cock, answering, crowed.

When at dawn on the third morning the man went to the garden, he was absorbed, thinking of the greater life of the body, beyond the little, narrow, personal life. So he came through the thick screen of laurel and myrtle bushes, near the rock, suddenly, and he saw three women near the tomb. One was Madeleine, and one was the woman who had been his mother, and the third was a woman he knew, called Joan. He looked up, and saw them all, and they saw him, and they were all afraid.

He stood arrested in the distance, knowing they were there to claim him back, bodily. But he would in no wise return to them. Pallid, in the shadow of a grey morning that was blowing to rain, he saw them, and turned away. But Madeleine hastened towards him.

'I did not bring them,'' she said. 'They have come of themselves. See, I have brought you money! . . . Will you not speak to them?'

She offered him some gold pieces, and he took them, saying:

'May I have this money? I shall need it. I cannot speak to them, for I am not yet ascended to the Father. And I must leave you now.'

'Ah! Where will you go?' she cried.

He looked at her, and saw she was clutching for the man in him who had died and was dead, the man of his youth and his mission, of his chastity and his fear, of his little life, his giving without taking.

'I must go to my Father!' he said.

'And you will leave us? There is your mother!' she cried, turning round with the old anguish, which yet was sweet to her.

'But now I must ascend to my Father,' he said, and he drew back into the bushes, and so turned quickly, and went away, saying to himself:

'Now I belong to no one and have no connection, and mission or gospel is gone from me. Lo! I cannot make even my own life, and what have I to save? . . . I can learn to be alone.'

So he went back to the peasants' house, to the yard where the young cock was tied by the leg, with a string. And he wanted no one, for it was best to be alone; for the presence of people made him lonely. The sun and the subtle salve of spring healed his wounds, even the gaping wound of disillusion through his bowels was closing up. And his need of men and women, his fever to have them and to be saved by them, this too was healing in him. Whatever came of touch between himself and the race of men, henceforth, should come without trespass or compulsion. For he said to himself:

'I tried to compel them to live, so they compelled me to die. It is always so, with compulsion. The recoil kills the advance. Now is my time to be alone.'

Therefore he went no more to the garden, but lay still and saw the sun, or walked at dusk across the olive slopes, among the green wheat, that rose a palm-breadth higher every sunny day. And always he thought to himself:

'How good it is to have fulfilled my mission, and to be beyond it. Now I can be alone, and leave all things to themselves, and the fig-tree may be barren if it will, and the rich may be rich. My way is my own alone.'

So the green jets of leaves unspread on the fig-tree, with the bright, translucent, green blood of the tree. And the young cock grew brighter, more lustrous with the sun's burnishing; yet always tied by the leg with a string. And the sun went down more and more in pomp, out of the gold and red-flushed air. The man who had died was aware of it all, and he thought:

'The Word is but the midge that bites at evening. Man is tormented with words like midges, and they follow him right into the tomb. But beyond the tomb they cannot go. Now I have passed the place where words can bite no more and the air is clear, and there is nothing to say, and I am alone within my own skin, which is the walls of all my domain.'

So he healed of his wounds, and enjoyed his immortality of being alive without fret. For in the tomb he had slipped that noose which we call care. For in the tomb he had left his striving self, which cares and asserts itself. Now his uncaring self healed and became whole within his skin, and he smiled to himself with pure aloneness, which is one sort of immortality.

Then he said to himself: 'I will wander the earth, and say nothing. For nothing is so marvellous as to be alone in the phenomenal world, which is raging, and yet apart. And I have not seen it, I was too much blinded by my confusion within it. Now I will wander among the stirring of the phenomenal world, for it is the stirring of all things among themselves which leaves me purely alone.'

So he communed with himself, and decided to be a physician. Because the power was still in him to heal any man or child who touched his compassion. Therefore he cut his hair and his beard after the right fashion, and smiled to himself. And he bought himself shoes, and the right mantle, and put the right cloth over his head, hiding all the little scars. And the peasant said:

'Master, will you go forth from us?'

'Yes, for the time is come for me to return to men.'

So he gave the peasant a piece of money, and said to him:

'Give me the cock that escaped and is now tied by the leg. For he shall go forth with me.'

So for a piece of money the peasant gave the cock to the man who had died, and at dawn the man who had died set out into the phenomenal world, to be fulfilled in his own loneliness in the midst of it. For previously he had been too much mixed up in it. Then he had died. Now he must come back, to be alone in the midst. Yet even now he did not go quite alone, for under his arm, as he went, he carried the cock, whose tail fluttered gaily behind, and who craned his head, excitedly, for he too was adventuring out for the first time into the wider phenomenal world, which is the stirring of the body of cocks also. And the peasant woman shed a few tears, but then went indoors, being a peasant, to look again at the pieces of money. And it seemed to her, a gleam came out of the pieces of money, wonderful.

The man who had died wandered on, and it was a sunny day. He looked around as he went, and stood aside as the pack-train passed by, towards the city. And he said to himself:

'Strange is the phenomenal world, dirty and clean together! And I am the same. Yet I am apart! And life bubbles variously. Why should I have wanted it to bubble all alike? What a pity I preached to them! A sermon is so much more likely to cake into mud, and to close the fountains, than is a psalm or a song. I made a mistake. I understand that they executed me for preaching to them. Yet they could not finally execute me, for now I am risen in my own aloneness, and inherit the earth, since I lay no claim on it. And I will be alone in the seethe of all things; first and foremost, forever, I shall be alone. But I must toss this bird into the seethe of phenomena, for he must ride his wave. How hot he is with life! Soon, in some place, I shall leave him among the hens. And perhaps one evening, I shall meet a woman who can lure my risen body, yet leave me my aloneness. For the body of my desire has died, and I am not in touch anywhere. Yet how do I know! All at least is life. And this cock gleams with bright aloneness, though he answers the lure of hens. And I shall hasten on to that village on the hill ahead of me; already I am tired and weak, and want to close my eyes to everything.'

Hastening a little with the desire to have finished going, he overtook two men going slowly, and talking. And being soft-footed he heard they were speaking of himself. And he remembered them, for he had known them in his life, the life of his mission. So he greeted them, but did not disclose himself in the dusk, and they did not know him. He said to them:

'What then of him who would be king, and was put to death for it?'

They answered suspiciously: 'Why ask you of him?'

'I have known him, and thought much about him,' he said.

So they replied: 'He has risen.'

'Yea! And where is he, and how does he live?'

'We know not, for it is not revealed. Yet he is risen, and in a little while will ascend unto the Father.'

'Yea! And where then is his Father?'

'Know ye not? You are then of the Gentiles! The Father is in Heaven, above the cloud and the firmament.'

'Truly? Then how will he ascend?'

'As Elijah the Prophet, he shall go up in glory.'

'Even into the sky.'

'Into the sky.'

'Then he is not risen in the flesh?'

'He is risen in the flesh.'

'And will he take flesh up into the sky?'

'The Father in Heaven will take him up.'

The man who had died said no more, for his say was over, and words beget words, even as gnats. But the man asked him: 'Why do you carry a cock?'

'I am a healer,' he said, 'and the bird hath virtue.'

'You are not a believer?'

'Yea! I believe the bird is full of life and virtue.'

They walked on in silence after this, and he felt they disliked his answer. So he smiled to himself, for a dangerous phenomenon in the world is a man of narrow belief, who denies the right of his neighbour to be alone. And as they came to the outskirts of the village, the man who had died stood still in the gloaming and said in his old voice:

'Know ye me not?'

And they cried in fear: 'Master!'

'Yea!' he said, laughing softly. And he turned suddenly away, down a side lane, and was gone under the wall before they knew.

So he came to an inn where the asses stood in the yard. And he called for fritters, and they were made for him. So he slept under a shed. But in the morning he was wakened by a loud crowing, and his cock's voice ringing in his ears. So he saw the rooster of the inn walking forth to battle, with his hens, a goodly number, behind him. Then the cock of the man who had died sprang forth, and a battle began between the birds. The man of the inn ran to save his rooster, but the man who had died said:

'If my bird wins I will give him thee. And if he lose, thou shalt eat him.'

So the birds fought savagely, and the cock of the man who had died killed the common cock of the yard. Then the man who had died said to his young cock:

'Thou at least hast found thy kingdom, and the females to thy body. Thy aloneness can take on splendour, polished by the lure of thy hens.'

And he left his bird there, and went on deeper into the phenomenal world, which is a vast complexity of entanglements and allurements. And he asked himself a last question:

'From what, and to what, could this infinite whirl be saved?'

So he went his way, and was alone. But the way of the world was past belief, as he saw the strange entanglement of passions and circumstance and compulsion everywhere, but always the dread insomnia of compulsion. It was fear, the ultimate fear of death, that made men mad. So always he must move on, for if he stayed, his neighbours wound the strangling of their fear and bullying round him. There was nothing he could touch, for all, in a mad assertion of the ego, wanted to put a compulsion on him, and violate his intrinsic solitude. It was the mania of cities and societies and hosts, to lay a compulsion upon a man, upon all men. For men and women alike were mad with the egoistic fear of their own nothingness. And he thought of his own mission, how he had tried to lay the compulsion of love on all men. And the old nausea came back on him. For there was no contact without a subtle attempt to inflict a compulsion. And already he had been compelled even into death. The nausea of the old wound broke out afresh, and he looked again on the world with repulsion, dreading its mean contacts.

PART II

The wind came cold and strong from inland, from the invisible snows of Lebanon. But the temple, facing south and west, towards Egypt, faced the splendid sun of winter as he curved down towards the sea, the warmth and radiance flooded in between the pillars of painted wood. But the sea was invisible, because of the trees, though its dashing sounded among the hum of pines. The air was turning golden to afternoon. The woman who served Isis stood in her yellow robe, and looked up at the steep slopes coming down to the sea, where the olive-trees silvered under the wind like water splashing. She was alone save for the goddess. And in the winter afternoon the light stood erect and magnificent off the invisible sea, filling the hills of the coast. She went towards the sun, through the grove of Mediterranean pine-trees and ever-green oaks, in the midst of which the temple stood, on a little, tree-covered tongue of land between two bays.

It was only a very little way, and then she stood among the dry trunks of the outermost pines, on the rocks under which the sea smote and sucked, facing the open where the bright sun gloried in winter. The sea was dark, almost indigo, running away from the land, and crested with white. The hand of the wind brushed it strangely with shadow, as it brushed the olives of the slopes with silver. And there was no boat out. The three boats were drawn high upon the steep shingle of the little bay, by the small grey tower. Along the edge of the shingle ran a high wall, inside which was a garden occupying the brief flat of the bay, then rising in terraces up the steep slope of the coast. And there, some little way up, within another wall, stood the low white villa, white and alone as the coast, overlooking the sea. But higher, much higher up, where the olives had given way to pine-trees again, ran the coast road, keeping to the height to be above the gullies that came down to the bays.

Upon it all poured the royal sunshine of the January afternoon. Or rather, all was part of the great sun, glow and substance and immaculate loneliness of the sea, and pure brightness.

Crouching in the rocks above the dark water, which only swung up and down, two slaves, half naked, were dressing pigeons for the evening meal. They pierced the throat of a blue, live bird, and let the drops of blood fall into the heaving sea, with curious concentration. They were performing some sacrifice, or working some incantation. The woman of the temple, yellow and white and alone like a winter narcissus, stood between the pines of the small, humped peninsula where the temple secretly hid, and watched.

A black-and-white pigeon, vividly white, like a ghost escaped over the low dark sea, sped out, caught the wind, tilted, rode, soared, and swept over the pine-trees, and wheeled away, a speck, inland. It had escaped. The priestess heard the cry of the boy slave, a garden slave of about seventeen. He raised his arms to heaven in anger as the pigeon wheeled away, naked and angry and young he held out his arms. Then he turned and seized the girl in an access of rage, and beat her with his fist that was stained with pigeon's blood. And she lay down with her face hidden, passive and quivering. The woman who owned them watched. And as she watched, she saw another onlooker, a stranger, in a low, broad hat, and a cloak of grey homespun, a dark bearded man standing on the little causeway of a rock that was the neck of her temple peninsula. By the blowing of his dark-grey cloak she saw him. And he saw her, on the rocks like a white-and-yellow narcissus, because of the flutter of her white linen tunic, below the yellow mantle of wool. And both of them watched the two slaves.

The boy suddenly left off beating the girl. He crouched over her, touching her, trying to make her speak. But she lay quite inert, face down on the smoothed rock. And he put his arms round her and lifted her, but she slipped back to earth like one dead, yet far too quickly for anything dead. The boy, desperate, caught her by the hips and hugged her to him, turning her over there. There she seemed inert, all her fight was in her shoulders. He twisted her over, intent and unconscious, and pushed his hands between her thighs, to push them apart. And in an instant he was covering her in the blind, frightened frenzy of a boy's first passion. Quick and frenzied his young body quivered naked on hers, blind, for a minute. Then it lay quite still, as if dead.

And then, in terror, he peeped up. He peeped round, and drew slowly to his feet, adjusting his loin-rag. He saw the stranger, and then he saw, on the rocks beyond, the lady of Isis, his mistress. And as he saw her, his whole body shrank and cowed, and with a strange cringing motion he scuttled lamely towards the door in the wall.

The girl sat up and looked after him. When she had seen him disappear, she too looked round. And she saw the stranger and the priestess. Then with a sullen movement she turned away, as if she had seen nothing, to the four dead pigeons and the knife, which lay there on the rock. And she began to strip the small feathers, so that they rose on the wind like dust.

The priestess turned away. Slaves! Let the overseer watch them. She was not interested. She went slowly through the pines again, back to the temple, which stood in the sun in a small clearing at the centre of the tongue of land. It was a small temple of wood, painted all pink and white and blue, having at the front four wooden pillars rising like stems to the swollen lotus-bud of Egypt at the top, supporting the roof and open, spiky lotus-flowers of the outer frieze, which went round under the eaves. Two low steps of stone led up to the platform before the pillars, and the chamber behind the pillars was open. There a low stone altar stood, with a few embers in its hollow, and the dark stain of blood in its end groove.

She knew her temple so well, for she had built it at her own expense, and tended it for seven years. There it stood, pink and white, like a flower in the little clearing, backed by blackish ever-green oaks; and the shadow of afternoon was already washing over its pillar-bases.

She entered slowly, passing through to the dark inner chamber, lighted by a perfumed oil-flame. And once more she pushed shut the door, and once more she threw a few grains of incense on a brazier before the goddess, and once more she sat down before her goddess, in the almost-darkness, to muse, to go away into the dreams of the goddess.

It was Isis; but not Isis, Mother of Horus. It was Isis Bereaved, Isis in Search. The goddess, in painted marble, lifted her face and strode, one thigh forward through the frail fluting of her robe, in the anguish of bereavement and of search. She was looking for the fragments of the dead Osiris, dead and scattered asunder, dead, torn apart, and thrown in fragments over the wide world. And she must find his hands and his feet, his heart, his thighs, his head, his belly, she must gather him together and fold her arms round the reassembled body till it became warm again, and roused to life, and could embrace her, and could fecundate her womb. And the strange rapture and anguish of search went on through the years, as she lifted her throat and her hollowed eyes looked inward, in the tormented ecstasy of seeking, and the delicate navel of her bud-like belly showed through the frail, girdled robe with the eternal asking, asking, of her search. And through the years she found him bit by bit, heart and head and limbs and body. And yet she had not found the last reality, the final clue to him, that alone could bring him really back to her. For she was Isis of the subtle lotus, the womb which waits submerged and in bud, waits for the touch of that other inward sun that streams its rays from the loins of the male Osiris.

This was the mystery the woman had served alone for seven years, since she was twenty, till now she was twenty-seven. Before, when she was young, she had lived in the world, in Rome, in Ephesus, in Egypt. For her father had been one of Anthony's captains and comrades, had fought with Anthony and had stood with him when Caesar was murdered, and through to the days of shame. Then he had come again across to Asia, out of favour with Rome, and had been killed in the mountains beyond Lebanon. The widow, having no favour to hope for from Octavius, had retired to her small property on the coast under Lebanon, taking her daughter from the world, a girl of nineteen, beautiful but unmarried.

When she was young, the girl had known Caesar, and had shrunk from his eagle-like rapacity. The golden Anthony had sat with her many a half-hour, in the splendour of his great limbs and glowing manhood, and talked with her of the philosophies and the gods. For he was fascinated as a child by the gods, though he mocked at them, and forgot them in his own vanity. But he said to her:

'I have sacrificed two doves for you, to Venus, for I am afraid you make no offering to the sweet goddess. Beware you will offend her. Come, why is the flower of you so cool within? Does never a ray nor a glance find its way through? Ah, come, a maid should open to the sun, when the sun leans towards her to caress her.'

And the big, bright eyes of Anthony laughed down on her, bathing her in his glow. And she felt the lovely glow of his male beauty and his amorousness bathe all her limbs and her body. But it was as he said: the very flower of her womb was cool, was almost cold, like a bud in shadow of frost, for all the flooding of his sunshine. So Anthony, respecting her father, who loved her, had left her.

And it had always been the same. She saw many men, young and old. And on the whole, she liked the old ones best, for they talked to her still and sincere, and did not expect her to open like a flower to the sun of their maleness. Once she asked a philosopher: 'Are all women born to be given to men?' To which the old man answered slowly:

'Rare women wait for the re-born man. For the lotus, as you know, will not answer to all the bright heat of the sun. But she curves her dark, hidden head in the depths, and stirs not. Till, in the night, one of these rare, invisible suns that have been killed and shine no more, rises among the stars in unseen purple, and like the violet, sends it rare, purple rays out into the night. To these the lotus stirs as to a caress, and rises upwards through the flood, and lifts up her bent head, and opens with an expansion such as no other flower knows, and spreads her sharp rays of bliss, and offers her soft, gold depths such as no other flower possesses, to the penetration of the flooding, violet-dark sun that has died and risen and makes no show. But for the golden brief day-suns of show such as Anthony, and for the hard winter suns of power, such as Caesar, the lotus stirs not, nor will ever stir. Those will only tear open the bud. Ah, I tell you, wait for the re-born and wait for the bud to stir.'

So she had waited. For all the men were soldiers or politicians in the Roman spell, assertive, manly, splendid apparently, but of an inward meanness, an inadequacy. And Rome and Egypt alike, had left her alone, unroused. And she was a woman to herself, she would not give herself for a surface glow, nor marry for reasons. She would wait for the lotus to stir.

And then, in Egypt, she had found Isis, in whom she spelled her mystery. She had brought Isis to the shores of Sidon, and lived with her in the mystery of search; whilst her mother, who loved affairs, controlled the small estate and the slaves with a free hand.

When the woman had roused from her muse and risen to perform the last brief ritual to Isis, she replenished the lamp and left the sanctuary, locking the door. In the outer world, the sun had already set, and twilight was chill among the humming trees, which hummed still, though the wind was abating.

A stranger in a dark, broad hat rose from the corner of the temple steps, holding his hat in the wind. He was dark-faced, with a black pointed beard. 'O Madam, whose shelter may I implore?' he said to the woman, who stood in her yellow mantle on a step above him, beside a pink-and-white painted pillar. Her face was rather long and pale, her dusty blonde hair was held under a thin

gold net. She looked down on the vagabond with
indifference. It was the same she had seen watching the
slaves.

'Why come you down from the road?' she asked.

'I saw the temple like a pale flower on the coast, and
would rest among the trees of the precincts, if the lady of
the goddess permits.'

'It is Isis in Search,' she said, answering his first
question.

'The goddess is great,' he replied.

She looked at him still with mistrust. There was a
faint remote smile in the dark eyes lifted to her, though
the face was hollow with suffering. The vagabond divined
her hesitation, and was mocking her.

'Stay here upon the steps,' she said. 'A slave will
show you the shelter.'

'The lady of Egypt is gracious.'

She went down the rocky path of the humped
peninsula, in her gilded sandals. Beautiful were her ivory
feet, beneath the white tunic, and above the saffron
mantle her dusky-blonde head bent as with endless
musings. A woman entangled in her own dream. The
man smiled a little, half-bitterly, and sat again on the
step to wait, drawing his mantle round him, in the cold
twilight.

At length a slave appeared, also in hodden grey.

'Seek ye the shelter of our lady?' he said insolently.

'Even so.'

'Then come.'

With the brusque insolence of a slave waiting on a
vagabond, the young fellow led through the trees and
down into a little gully in the rock, where, almost in
darkness, was a small cave, with a litter of the tall heaths
that grew on the waste places of the coast, under the
stone-pines. The place was dark, but absolutely silent
from the wind. There was still a faint odour of goats.

'Here sleep!' said the slave. 'For the goats come no
more on this half-island. And there is water!' He pointed

to a little basin of rock where the maidenhair fern fringed a dripping mouthful of water.

Having scornfully bestowed his patronage, the slave departed. The man who had died climbed out to the tip of the peninsula, where the waves thrashed. It was rapidly getting dark, and the stars were coming out. The wind was abating for the night. Inland, the steep grooved upslope was dark to the long wavering outline of the crest against the translucent sky. Only now and then, a lantern flickered towards the villa.

The man who had died went back to the shelter. There he took bread from his leather pouch, dipped it in the water of the tiny spring, and slowly ate. Having eaten and washed his mouth, he looked once more at the bright stars in the pure windy sky, then settled the heath for his bed. Having laid his hat and his sandals aside, and put his pouch under his cheek for a pillow, he slept, for he was very tired. Yet during the night the cold woke him, pinching wearily through his weariness. Outside was brilliantly starry, and still windy. He sat and hugged himself in a sort of coma, and towards dawn went to sleep again.

In the morning the coast was still chill in shadow, though the sun was up behind the hills, when the woman came down from the villa towards the goddess. The sea was fair and pale blue, lovely in newness, and at last the wind was still. Yet the waves broke white in the many rocks, and tore in the shingle of the little bay. The woman came slowly, towards her dream. Yet she was aware of an interruption.

As she followed the little neck of rock on to her peninsula, and climbed the slope between the trees to the temple, a slave came down and stood, making his obeisance. There was a faint insolence in his humility. 'Speak!' she said.

'Lady, the man is there, he still sleeps. Lady, may I speak?'

'Speak!' she said, repelled by the fellow.

'Lady, the man is an escaped malefactor.'

The slave seemed to triumph in imparting the unpleasant news.

'By what sign?'

'Behold his hands and feet! Will the lady look on him?'

'Lead on!'

The slave led quickly over the mound of the hill down to the tiny ravine. There he stood aside, and the woman went into the crack towards the cave. Her heart beat a little. Above all she must preserve her temple inviolate.

The vagabond was asleep with his cheek on his scrip, his mantle wrapped round him, but his bare, soiled feet curling side by side, to keep each other warm, and his hand lying loosely clenched in sleep. And in the pale skin of his feet usually covered by sandal-straps, she saw the scars, and in the palm of the loose hand.

She had no interest in men, particularly in the servile class. Yet she looked at the sleeping face. It was worn, hollow, and rather ugly. But, a true priestess, she saw the other kind of beauty in it, the sheer stillness of the deeper life. There was even a sort of majesty in the dark brows, over the still, hollow cheeks. She saw that his black hair, left long, in contrast to the Roman fashion, was touched with gray at the temples, and the black pointed beard had threads of gray. But that must be suffering or misfortune, for the man was young. His dusky skin had the silvery glisten of youth still.

There was a beauty of much suffering, and the strange calm candour of finer life in the whole delicate ugliness of the face. For the first time she was touched on the quick at the sight of a man, as if the tip of a fine flame of living had touched her. It was the first time. Men had roused all kinds of feeling in her, but never had touched her with the flame-tip of life.

She went back under the rock to where the slave waited.

'Know!' she said. 'This is no malefactor, but a free citizen of the east. Do not disturb him. But when he comes forth, bring him to me; tell him I would speak with him.'

She spoke coldly, for she found slaves invariably repellent, a little repulsive. They were so embedded in the lesser life, and their appetites and their small consciousness were a little disgusting. So she wrapped her dream round her, and went to the temple, where a slave-girl brought winter roses and jasmine, for the altar. But to-day, even in her ministrations, she was disturbed.

The sun rose over the hill, sparkling, the light fell triumphantly on the little pine-covered peninsula of the coast, and on the pink temple, in the pristine newness. The man who had died woke up, and put on his sandals. He put on his hat too, slung his scrip under his mantle, and went out, to see the morning in all its blue and its new gold. He glanced at the little yellow-and-white narcissus sparkling gaily in the rocks. And he saw the slave waiting for him like a menace.

'Master!' said the slave. 'Our lady would speak with you at the house of Isis.'

'It is well,' said the wanderer.

He went slowly, staying to look at the pale blue sea like a flower in unruffled bloom, and the white fringes among the rocks, like white rock-flowers, the hollow slopes sheering up high from the shore, grey with olive-trees and green with bright young wheat, and set with the white small villa. All fair and pure in the January morning.

The sun fell on the corner of the temple, he sat down on the step in the sunshine, in the infinite patience of waiting. He had come back to life, but not the same life that he had left, the life of little people and the little day. Re-born, he was in the other life, the greater day of the human consciousness. And he was alone and apart from the little day, and out of contact with the daily people. Not yet had he accepted the irrevocable *noli me tangere* which separates the re-born from the vulgar. The separation was absolute, as yet here at the temple he felt peace, the hard, bright pagan peace with hostility of slaves beneath.

The woman came into the dark inner doorway of the temple, from the shrine, and stood there, hesitating. She could see the dark figure of the man, sitting in that terrible stillness that was portentous to her, had something almost menacing in its patience.

She advanced across the outer chamber of the temple, and the man, becoming aware of her, stood up. She addressed him in Greek, but he said:

'Madam, my Greek is limited. Allow me to speak vulgar Syrian.'

'Whence come you? Whither go you?' she asked, with a hurried preoccupation of a priestess.

'From the east beyond Damascus—and I go west as the road goes,' he replied slowly.

She glanced at him with sudden anxiety and shyness.

'But why do you have the marks of a malefactor?' she asked abruptly.

'Did the Lady of Isis spy upon me in my sleep?' he asked, with a gray weariness.

'The slave warned me—your hands and feet—' she said.

He looked at her. Then he said:

'Will the Lady of Isis allow me to bid her farewell, and go up to the road?'

The wind came in a sudden puff, lifting his mantle and his hat. He put up his hand to hold the brim, and she saw again the thin brown hand with its scar.

'See! The scar!' she said, pointing.

'Even so!' he said. 'But farewell, and to Isis my homage and my thanks for sleep.'

He was going. But she looked up at him with her wondering blue eyes.

'Will you not look at Isis?' she said, with sudden

impulse. And something stirred in him, like pain.

'Where then?' he said.

'Come!'

He followed her into the inner shrine, into the almost-darkness. When his eyes got used to the faint glow of the lamp, he saw the goddess striding like a ship, eager in the swirl of her gown, and he made his obeisance.

'Great is Isis!' he said. 'In her search she is greater than death. Wonderful is such walking in a woman, wonderful the goal. All men praise thee, Isis, thou greater than the mother unto man.'

The woman of Isis heard, and threw incense on the brazier. Then she looked at the man.

'Is it well with thee here?' she asked him. 'Has Isis brought thee home to herself?'

He looked at the priestess in wonder and trouble.

'I know not,' he said.

But the woman was pondering that this was the lost Osiris. She felt it in the quick of her soul. And her agitation was intense.

He would not stay in the close, dark, perfumed shrine. He went out again to the morning, to the cold air. He felt something approaching to touch him, and all his flesh was still woven with pain and the wild commandment: *Noli me tangere!* Touch me not! Oh, don't touch me!

The woman followed into the open with timid eagerness. He was moving away.

'O stranger, do not go! O stay awhile with Isis!'

He looked at her, at her face open like a flower, as if a sun had risen in her soul. And again his loins stirred.

'Would you detain me, girl of Isis?' he said.

'Stay! I am sure you are Osiris!' she said.

He laughed suddenly. 'Not yet!' he said. Then he looked at her wistful face. 'But I will sleep another night in the cave of the goats, if Isis wills it,' he added.

She put her hands together with a priestess's

childish happiness.

'Ah! Isis will be glad!' she said.

So he went down to the shore, in great trouble, saying to himself: 'Shall I give myself into this touch? Shall I give myself into this touch? Men have tortured me to death with their touch. Yet this girl of Isis is a tender flame of healing. I am a physician, yet I have no healing like the flame of this tender girl. The flame of this tender girl! Like the first pale crocus of the spring. How could I have been blind to the healing and the bliss in the crocus-like body of a tender woman! Ah, tenderness! More terrible and lovely than the death I died—'

He pried small shell-fish from the rocks, and ate them with relish and wonder for the simple taste of the sea. And inwardly, he was tremulous, thinking: 'Dare I come into touch? For this is further than death. I have dared to let them lay hands on me and put me to death. But dare I come into this tender touch of life? Oh, this is harder—'

But the woman went into the shrine again, and sat rapt in pure muse, through the long hours, watching the swirling stride of the yearning goddess, and the navel of the bud-like belly, like a seal on the virgin urge of the search. And she gave herself to the woman-flow and to the urge of Isis in Search.

Towards sundown she went on the peninsula to look for him. And she found him gone towards the sun, as she had gone the day before, and sitting on the pine-needles at the foot of the tree, where she had stood when first she saw him. Now she approached tremulously and slowly, afraid lest he did not want her. She stood near him unseen, till suddenly he glanced up at her from under his broad hat, and saw the westering sun in her netted hair. He was startled, yet he expected her.

'Is that your home?' he said, pointing to the white low villa on the slope of olives.

'It is my mother's house. She is a widow, and I am her only child.'

'And are these all her slaves?'

'Except those that are mine.'

Their eyes met for a moment.

'Will you too sit to see the sun go down?' he said.

He had not risen to speak to her. He had known too much pain. So she sat on the dry brown pine-needles, gathering her saffron mantle round her knees. A boat was coming in, out of the open glow into the shadow of the bay, and slaves were lifting small nets, their babble coming off the surface of the water.

'And this is home to you,' he said.

'But I serve Isis in Search,' she replied.

He looked at her. She was like a soft, musing cloud, somehow remote. His soul smote him with passion and compassion.

'Mayst thou find thy desire, maiden,' he said, with sudden earnestness.

'And art thou not Osiris?' she said.

He flushed suddenly.

'Yes, if thou wilt heal me!' he said. 'For the death aloofness is still upon me, and I cannot escape it.'

She looked at him for a moment in fear, from the soft blue sun of her eyes. Then she lowered her head, and they sat in silence in the warmth and glow of the western sun: the man who had died, and the woman of the pure search.

The sun was curving down to the sea, in grand winter splendour. It fell on the twinkling, naked bodies of the slaves, with their ruddy broad hams and their small black heads, as they ran spreading the nets on the pebble beach. The all-tolerant Pan watched over them. All-tolerant Pan should be their god for ever.

The woman rose as the sun's rim dipped, saying:

'If you will stay, I shall send down victual and covering.'

'The lady your mother, what will she say?'

The woman of Isis looked at him strangely, but with a tinge of misgiving.

'It is my own,' she said.

'It is good,' he said, smiling faintly, and foreseeing difficulties.

He watched her go, with her absorbed, strange motion of the self-dedicate. Her dun head was a little bent, the white linen swung about her ivory ankles. And he saw the naked slaves stand to look at her, with a certain wonder, and even a certain mischief. But she passed intent through the door in the wall, on the bay.

The man who had died sat on at the foot of the tree overlooking the strand, for on the little shore everything happened. At the small stream which ran in round the corner of the property wall, women slaves were still washing linen, and now and again came the hollow chock! chock! chock! as they beat it against the smooth stones, in the dark little hollow of the pool. There was a smell of olive-refuse on the air; and sometimes still the faint rumble of the grindstone that was milling the olives, inside the garden, and the sound of the slave calling to the ass at the mill. Then through the doorway a woman stepped, a gray-haired woman in a mantle of whitish wool, and there followed her a bare-headed man in a toga, a Roman: probably her steward or overseer. They stood on the high shingle above the sea, and cast round a rapid glance. The broad-hammed, ruddy-bodied slaves bent absorbed and abject over the nets, picking them clean, the women washing linen thrust their palms with energy down on the wash, the old slave bent absorbed at the water's edge, washing the fish and the polyps of the catch. And the woman and the overseer saw it all, in one glance. They also saw, seated at the foot of the tree on the rocks of the peninsula, the strange man silent and alone. And the man who had died saw that they spoke of him. Out of the little sacred world of the peninsula he looked on the common world, and saw it still hostile.

The sun was touching the sea, across the tiny bay stretched the shadow of the opposite humped headland. Over the shingle, now blue and cold in shadow, the elderly woman trod heavily, in shadow too, to look at the fish spread in the flat basket of the old man crouching at the water's edge: a naked old slave with fat hips and shoulders, on whose soft, fairish-orange body the last sun twinkled, then died. The old slave continued cleaning the fish absorbedly, not looking up: as if the lady were the shadow of twilight falling on him.

Then from the gateway stepped two slave-girls with flat baskets on their heads, and from one basket the terra-cotta wine-jar and the oil-jar poked up, leaning slightly. Over the massive shingle, under the wall, came the girls, and the woman of Isis in her saffron mantle stepped in twilight after them. Out at sea, the sun still shone. Here was shadow. The mother with gray head stood at the sea's edge and watched the daughter, all yellow and white, with dun blonde head, swinging unseeing and unheeding after the slave-girls, towards the neck of rock of the peninsula; the daughter, travelling in her absorbed other-world. And not moving from her place, the elderly mother watched the procession of three file up the rise of the headland, between the trees, and disappear, shut in by trees. No slave had lifted a head to look. The gray-haired woman still watched the trees where her daughter had disappeared. Then she glanced again at the foot of the tree, where the man who had died was still sitting, inconspicuous now, for the sun had left him; and only the far blade of the sea shone bright. It was evening. Patience! Let destiny move!

The mother plodded with a stamping stride up the shingle: not long and swinging and rapt, like the daughter, but short and determined. Then down the rocks opposite came two naked slaves trotting with huge bundles of dark green on their shoulders, so that their broad, naked legs twinkled underneath like insects' legs, and their heads were hidden. They came trotting across the shingle, heedless and intent on their way, when suddenly the man, the Roman-looking overseer, addressed them, and they stopped dead. They stood invisible under their loads, as if they might disappear altogether, now they were arrested. Then a hand came out and pointed to the peninsula. Then the two green-heaped slaves trotted on, towards the temple precincts. The gray-haired woman joined the man, and slowly the two passed through the door again, from the shingle of the sea to the property of the villa. Then the old, fat-shouldered slave rose, pallid in the shadow, with his tray of fish from the sea, and the woman rose from the pool, dusky and alive, piling the wet linen in a heap on to the flat baskets, and the slaves who had cleaned the net gathered its whitish folds together. And the old slave with the fish basket on his shoulder, and the women slaves with the heaped baskets of wet linen on their heads, and the two slaves with the folded net, and the slave with oars on his shoulders, and the boy with the folded sail on his arm, gathered in a naked group near the door, and the man who had died heard the low buzz of their chatter. Then as the wind wafted cold, they began to pass through the door.

It was the life of the little day, the life of little people. And the man who had died said to himself: 'Unless we encompass it in the greater day, and set the little life in the circle of the greater life, all is disaster.'

Even the tops of the hills were in shadow. Only the sky was still upwardly radiant. The sea was a vast milky shadow. The man who had died rose a little stiffly, and turned into the grove.

There was no one at the temple. He went on to his lair in the rock. There, the slave-men had carried out the old heath of the bedding, swept the rock floor, and were spreading with nice art the myrtle, then the rougher heath, then the soft, bushy heath-tips on top, for a bed. Over it all they put a well-tanned white ox-skin. The maids had laid folded woollen covers at the head of the cave, and the wine-jar, the oil-jar, a terra-cotta drinking-cup, and a basket containing bread, salt, cheese, dried figs and eggs, stood neatly arranged. There was also a little brazier of charcoal. The cave was suddenly full, and a dwelling-place.

The woman of Isis stood in the hollow by the tiny spring.

Only one slave at a time could pass. The girl-slaves waited at the entrance to the narrow place. When the man who had died appeared, the woman sent the girls away. The men-slaves still arranged the bed, making the job as long as possible. But the woman of Isis dismissed them too. And the man who had died came to look at his house.

'Is it well?' the woman asked him.

'It is very well,' the man replied. 'But the lady, your mother, and he who is no doubt the steward, watched while the slaves brought the goods. Will they not oppose you?'

'I have my own portion! Can I not give of my own? Who is going to oppose me and the gods?' she said, with a certain soft fury, touched with exasperation. So that he knew that her mother would oppose her, and that the spirit of the little life would fight against the spirit of the greater. And he thought: 'Why did the woman of Isis relinquish her portion in the daily world? She should have kept her goods fiercely!'

'Will you eat and drink?' she said. 'On the ashes are warm eggs. And I will go up to the meal at the villa. But in the second hour of the night I shall come down to the temple. O, then, will you come too to Isis?' She looked at him, and a queer glow dilated her eyes. This was her dream, and it was greater than herself. He could not bear to thwart her or hurt her in the least thing now. She was in the full glow of her woman's mystery.

'Shall I wait at the temple?' he said.

'O, wait at the second hour and I shall come.' He heard the humming supplication in her voice and his fibres quivered.

'But the lady, your mother?' he said gently.

The woman looked at him, startled.

'She will not thwart me!' she said.

So he knew that the mother would thwart the daughter, for the daughter had left her goods in the hands of her mother, who would hold fast to this power.

But she went, and the man who had died lay reclining on his couch, and ate the eggs from the ashes, and dipped his bread in oil, and ate it, for his flesh was dry: and he mixed wine and water, and drank. And so he lay still, and the lamp made a small bud of light.

He was absorbed and enmeshed in new sensations. The woman of Isis was lovely to him, not so much in form, as in the wonderful womanly glow of her. Suns beyond suns had dipped her in mysterious fire, the mysterious fire of a potent woman, and to touch her was like touching the sun. Best of all was her tender desire for him, like sunshine, soft and still.

'She is like sunshine upon me,' he said to himself, stretching his limbs. 'I have never before stretched my limbs in such sunshine, as her desire for me. The greatest of all gods granted me this.'

At the same time he was haunted by the fear of the outer world. 'If they can, they will kill us,' he said to himself. 'But there is a law of the sun which protects us.'

And again he said to himself: 'I have risen naked and branded. But if I am naked enough for this contact, I have not died in vain. Before I was clogged.'

He rose and went out. The night was chill and starry, and of a great wintry splendour. 'There are destinies of splendour,' he said to the night, 'after all our doom of littleness and meanness and pain.'

So he went up silently to the temple, and waited in darkness against the inner wall, looking out on a gray darkness, stars, and rims of trees. And he said again to himself: 'There are destinies of splendour, and there is a greater power.'

So at last he saw the light of her silk lanthorn swinging, coming intermittent between the trees, yet coming swiftly. She was alone, and near, the light softly swishing

on her mantle-hem. And he trembled with fear and with
joy, saying to himself: 'I am almost more afraid of this
touch than I was of death. For I am more nakedly
exposed to it.'

'I am here, Lady of Isis,' he said softly out of the
dark.

'Ah!' she cried, in fear also, yet in rapture. For she
was given to her dream.

She unlocked the door of the shrine, and he followed
after her. Then she latched the door shut again. The air
inside was warm and close and perfumed. The man who
had died stood by the closed door, and watched the
woman. She had come first to the goddess. And dim-lit,
the goddess-statue stood surging forward, a little
fearsome like a great woman-presence urging.

The priestess did not look at him. She took off her
saffron mantle and laid it on a low couch. In the dim
light she was bare armed, in her girdled white tunic. But
she was still hiding herself away from him. He stood back
in shadow, and watched her softly fan the brazier and
fling on incense. Faint clouds of sweet aroma arose on the
air. She turned to the statue in the ritual of approach,
softly swaying forward with a slight lurch, like a moored
boat, tipping towards the goddess.

He watched the strange rapt woman, and he said to
himself: 'I must leave her alone in her rapture, her female
mysteries.' So she tipped in her strange forward-swaying
rhythm before the goddess. Then she broke into a
murmur of Greek, which he could not understand. And,
as she murmured, her swaying softly subsided, like a
boat on a sea that grows still. And as he watched her, he
saw her soul in its aloneness, and its female difference.
He said to himself: How different she is from me, how
strangely different! She is afraid of me, and my male
difference. She is getting herself naked and clear of her
fear. How sensitive and softly alive she is, with a life so
different from mine! How beautiful with a soft strange
courage of life, so different from my courage of death!

What a beautiful thing, like the heart of a rose, like the core of a flame. She is making herself completely penetrable. Ah! how terrible to fail her, or to trespass on her!

She turned to him, her face glowing from the goddess.

'You are Osiris, aren't you?' she said naively.

'If you will,' he said.

'Will you let Isis discover you? Will you not take off your things?'

He looked at the woman, and lost his breath. And his wounds, and especially the death-wound through his belly, began to cry again.

'It has hurt so much!' he said. 'You must forgive if I am still held back.'

But he took off his cloak and his tunic, and went naked towards the idol, his breast panting with the sudden terror of overwhelming pain, memory of overwhelming pain, and grief too bitter.

'They did me to death!' he said in excuse of himself, turning his face to her for a moment.

And she saw the ghost of the death in him, as he stood there thin and stark before her, and suddenly she was terrified, and she felt robbed. She felt the shadow of the gray, grisly wing of death triumphant.

'Ah, Goddess,' he said to the idol, in the vernacular. 'I would be so glad to live, if you would give me my clue again.'

For here again he felt desperate, faced by the demand of life, and burdened still by his death.

'Let me anoint you!' the woman said to him softly. 'Let me anoint the scars! Show me, and let me anoint them!'

He forgot his nakedness in this re-evoked old pain. He sat on the edge of the couch, and she poured a little ointment into the palm of his hand. And as she chafed his hand, it all came back, the nails, the holes, the cruelty, the unjust cruelty against him who had offered only kindness. The agony of injustice and cruelty came over him again, as in his death-hour. But she chafed the palm, murmuring: 'What was torn becomes a new flesh, what was a wound is full of fresh life; the scar is the eye of the violet.'

And he could not help smiling at her, in her naive priestess's absorption. This was her dream, and he was only a dream-object to her. She would never know or understand what he was. Especially she would never know the death that was gone before in him. But what did it matter? She was different. She was woman: her life and her death were different from his. Only she was good to him.

When she chafed his feet with oil and tender, tender healing, he could not refrain from saying to her:

'Once a woman washed my feet with tears, and wiped them with her hair, and poured on precious ointment.'

The woman of Isis looked up at him from her earnest work, interrupted again.

'Were they hurt then?' she said. 'Your feet?'

'No, no! It was while they were whole.'

'And did you love her?'

'Love had passed in her. She only wanted to serve,' he replied. 'She had been a prostitute.'

'And did you let her serve you?' she asked.

'Yea.'

'Did you let her serve you with the corpse of her love?'

'Ay!'

Suddenly it dawned on him: I asked them all to serve me with the corpse of their love. And in the end I offered them only the corpse of my love. This is my body–take and eat–my corpse—

A vivid shame went through him. 'After all,' he thought, 'I wanted them to love with dead bodies. If I had kissed Judas with live love, perhaps he would never have kissed me with death. Perhaps he loved me in the flesh, and I willed that he should love me bodylessly, with the corpse of love—'

There dawned on him the reality of the soft warm love which is in touch, and which is full of delight. 'And I told them, blessed are they that mourn,' he said to himself. 'Alas, if I mourned even this woman here, now I am in death, I should have to remain dead, and I want so much to live. Life has brought me to this woman with warm hands. And her touch is more to me now than all my words. For I want to live—'

'Go then to the goddess!' she said softly, gently pushing him towards Isis. And as he stood there dazed and naked as an unborn thing, he heard the woman murmuring to the goddess, murmuring, murmuring with a plaintive appeal. She was stooping now, looking at the scar in the soft flesh of the socket of his side, a scar deep and like an eye sore with endless weeping, just in the soft socket above the hip. It was here that his blood had left him, and his essential seed. The woman was trembling softly and murmuring in Greek. And he in the recurring dismay of having died, and in the anguished perplexity of having tried to force life, felt his wounds crying aloud, and the deep places of the body howling again: 'I have been murdered, and I lent myself to murder. They murdered me, but I lent myself to murder—'

The woman, silent now, but quivering, laid oil in her hand and put her palm over the wound in his right side. He winced, and the wound absorbed his life again, as thousands of times before. And in the dark, wild pain and panic of his consciousness rang only one cry: 'Oh, how can she take this death out of me? How can she take from me this death? She can never know! She can never understand! She can never equal it! . . .'

In silence, she softly rhythmically chafed the scar with oil. Absorbed now in her priestess's task, softly, softly gathering power, while the vitals of the man howled in panic. But as she gradually gathered power, and passed in a girdle round him to the opposite scar, gradually warmth began to take the place of the cold terror, and he felt: 'I am going to be warm again, and I am going to be whole! I shall be warm like the morning. I shall be a man. It doesn't need understanding. It needs newness. She brings me newness—'

And he listened to the faint, ceaseless wail of distress of his wounds, sounding as if for ever under the horizons of his consciousness. But the wail was growing dim, more dim.

He thought of the woman toiling over him: 'She does not know! She does not realize the death in me. But she has another consciousness. She comes to me from the opposite end of the night.'

Having chafed all his lower body with oil, having worked with her slow intensity of a priestess, so that the sound of his wounds grew dimmer and dimmer, suddenly she put her breast against the wound in his left side, and her arms round him, folding over the wound in his right side, and she pressed him to her, in a power of living warmth, like the folds of a river. And the wailing died out altogether, and there was a stillness, and darkness in his soul, unbroken dark stillness, wholeness.

Then slowly, slowly, in the perfect darkness of his inner man, he felt the stir of something coming. A dawn, a new sun. A new sun was coming up in him, in the perfect inner darkness of himself. He waited for it breathless, quivering with a fearful hope. . . . 'Now I am not myself. I am something new. . . .'

And as it rose, he felt, with a cold breath of disappointment, the girdle of the living woman slip down from him, the warmth and the glow slipped from him, leaving him stark. She crouched, spent, at the feet of the goddess, hiding her face.

Stooping, he laid his hand softly on her warm, bright shoulder, and the shock of desire went through him, shock after shock, so that he wondered if it were another sort of death: but full of magnificence.

Now all his consciousness was there in the crouching, hidden woman. He stooped beside her and caressed her softly, blindly, murmuring inarticulate things. And his death and his passion of sacrifice were all as nothing to him now, he knew only the crouching fulness of the woman there, the soft white rock of life. . . 'On this rock I built my life.' The deep-folded, penetrable rock of the living woman! The woman, hiding her face. Himself bending over, powerful and new like dawn.

He crouched to her, and he felt the blaze of his manhood and his power rise up in his loins, magnificent.

'I am risen!'

Magnificent, blazing indomitable in the depths of his loins, his own sun dawned, and sent its fire running along his limbs, so that his face shone unconsciously.

He untied the string on the linen tunic, and slipped the garment down, till he saw the white glow of her white-gold breasts. And he touched them, and he felt his life go molten. 'Father!' he said, 'why did you hide this from me?' And he touched her with the poignancy of wonder, and the marvellous piercing transcendence of desire. 'Lo!' he said, 'this is beyond prayer.' It was the deep, interfolded warmth, warmth living and penetrable, the woman, the heart of the rose! My mansion is the intricate warm rose, my joy is this blossom!

She looked up at him suddenly, her face like a lifted light, wistful, tender, her eyes like many wet flowers. And he drew her to his breast with a passion of tenderness and consuming desire, and the last thought: 'My hour is upon me, I am taken unawares—'

So he knew her, and was one with her.

Afterwards, with a dim wonder, she touched the great scars in his sides with her finger-tips, and said:

'But they no longer hurt?'

'They are suns!' he said. 'They shine from your touch. They are my atonement with you.'

And when they left the temple, it was the coldness before dawn. As he closed the door, he looked again at the goddess, and he said: 'Lo, Isis is a kindly goddess; and full of tenderness. Great gods are warm-hearted, and have tender goddesses.'

The woman wrapped herself in her mantle and went home in silence, sightless, brooding like the lotus softly shutting again, with its gold core full of fresh life. She saw nothing, for her own petals were a sheath to her. Only she thought: 'I am full of Osiris. I am full of the risen Osiris! . . .'

But the man looked at the vivid stars before dawn, as they rained down to the sea, and the dogstar green towards the sea's rim. And he thought: 'How plastic it is, how full of curves and folds like an invisible rose of dark-petalled openness that shows where the dew touches its darkness! How full it is, and great beyond all gods. How it leans around me, and I am part of it, the great rose of Space. I am like a grain of its perfume, and the woman is a grain of its beauty. Now the world is one flower of many petalled darknesses, and I am in its perfume as in a touch.'

So, in the absolute stillness and fulness of touch, he slept in his cave while the dawn came. And after the dawn, the wind rose and brought a storm, with cold rain. So he stayed in his cave in the peace and the delight of being in touch, delighting to hear the sea, and the rain on the earth, and to see one white-and-gold narcissus bowing wet, and still wet. And he said: 'This is the great atonement, the being in touch. The gray sea and the rain, the wet narcissus and the woman I wait for, the invisible Isis and the unseen sun are all in touch, and at one.'

He waited at the temple for the woman, and she came in the rain. But she said to him:

'Let me sit awhile with Isis. And come to me, will you come to me, in the second hour of night?'

So he went back to the cave and lay in stillness and in the joy of being in touch, waiting for the woman who would come with the night, and consummate again the contact. Then when night came the woman came, and came gladly, for her great yearning too was upon her, to be in touch, to be in touch with him, nearer.

So the days came, and the nights came, and days came again, and the contact was perfected and fulfilled. And he said: 'I will ask her nothing, not even her name, for a name would set her apart.'

And she said to herself: 'He is Osiris. I wish to know no more.'

Plum-blossom blew from the trees, the time of the narcissus was past, anemones lit up the ground and were gone, the perfume of bean-field was in the air. All changed, the blossom of the universe changed its petals and swung round to look another way. The spring was fulfilled, a contact was established, the man and the woman were fulfilled of one another, and departure was in the air.

One day he met her under the trees, when the morning sun was hot, and the pines smelled sweet, and on the hills the last pear-bloom was scattering. She came slowly towards him, and in her gentle lingering, her tender hanging back from him, he knew a change in her.

'Hast thou conceived?' he asked her.

'Why?' she said.

'Thou art like a tree whose green leaves follow the blossom, full of sap. And there is a withdrawing about thee.'

'It is so,' she said. 'I am with young by thee. Is it good?'

'Yea!' he said. 'How should it not be good? So the nightingale calls no more from the valley-bed. But where wilt thou bear the child, for I am naked of all but life.'

'We will stay here,' she said.

'But the lady, your mother?'

A shadow crossed her brow. She did not answer.

'What when she knows?' he said.

'She begins to know.'

'And would she hurt you?'

'Ah, not me! What I have is all my own. And I shall be big with Osiris.... But thou, do you watch her slaves.'

She looked at him, and the peace of her maternity was troubled by anxiety.

'Let not your heart be troubled!' he said. 'I have died the death once.'

So he knew the time was come again for him to depart. He would go alone, with his destiny. Yet not alone, for the touch would be upon him, even as he left his touch on her. And invisible suns would go with him.

Yet he must go. For here on the bay the little life of jealousy and property was resuming sway again, as the suns of passionate fecundity relaxed their sway. In the name of property, the widow and her slaves would seek to be revenged on him for the bread he had eaten, and the living touch he had established, the woman he had delighted in. But he said: 'Not twice! They shall not now profane the touch in me. My wits against theirs.'

So he watched. And he knew they plotted. So he moved from the little cave, and found another shelter, a tiny cove of sand by the sea, dry and secret under the rocks.

He said to the woman:

'I must go now soon. Trouble is coming to me from the slaves. But I am a man, and the world is open. But what is between us is good, and is established. Be at peace. And when the nightingale calls again from your valley-bed, I shall come again, sure as Spring.'

She said: 'O don't go! Stay with me on half the island, and I will build a house for you and me under the pine-trees by the temple, where we can live apart.'

Yet she knew that he would go. And even she wanted the coolness of her own air around her, and the release from anxiety.

'If I stay,' he said, 'they will betray me to the Romans and to their justice. But I will never be betrayed again. So when I am gone, live in peace with the growing child. And I shall come again: all is good between us, near or apart. The suns come back in their seasons: and I shall come again.'

'Do not go yet,' she said. 'I have set a slave to watch at the neck of the peninsula. Do not go yet, till the harm shows.'

But as he lay in his little cove, on a calm, still night, he heard the soft knock of oars, and the bump of a boat against the rock. So he crept out to listen. And he heard the Roman overseer say:

'Lead softly to the goat's den. And Lysippus shall throw the net over the malefactor while he sleeps, and we will bring him before justice, and the Lady of Isis shall know nothing of it. . . .'

The man who had died caught a whiff of flesh from the oiled and naked slaves as they crept up, then the faint perfume of the Roman. He crept nearer to the sea. The slave who sat in the boat sat motionless, holding the oars, for the sea was quite still. And the man who had died knew him.

So out of the deep cleft of a rock he said, in a clear voice:

'Art thou not that slave who possessed the maiden under the eyes of Isis? Art thou not the youth? Speak!'

The youth stood up in the boat in terror. His movement sent the boat bumping against the rock. The slave sprang out in wild fear and fled up the rocks. The man who had died quickly seized the boat and stepped in, and pushed off. The oars were yet warm with the unpleasant warmth of the hands of the slaves. But the man pulled slowly out, to get into the current which set down the coast and would carry him in silence. The high coast was utterly dark against the starry night. There was no glimmer from the peninsula: the priestess came no more at night. The man who had died rowed slowly on, with the current, and laughed to himself: 'I have sowed the seed of my life and my resurrection, and put my touch forever upon the choice woman of this day, and I carry her perfume in my flesh like essence of roses. She is dear to me in the middle of my being. But the gold and flowing serpent is coiling up again, to sleep at the root of my tree.'

'So let the boat carry me. To-morrow is another day.'